MAGIC TREE HOUSE®

PIRATES PAST NOON

MARY POPE OSBORNE'S

✦ MAGIC ✦ TREE HOUSE ®

PIRATES PAST NOON

THE GRAPHIC NOVEL

ADAPTED BY

JENNY LAIRD

WITH ART BY

KELLY & NICHOLE MATTHEWS

A STEPPING STONE BOOK™
RANDOM HOUSE 🏠 NEW YORK

Text copyright © 2022 by Mary Pope Osborne
Art copyright © 2022 by Kelly Matthews & Nichole Matthews
Text adapted by Jenny Laird

All rights reserved. Published in the United States by Random House Children's Books, a division
of Penguin Random House LLC, New York. Adapted from *Pirates Past Noon*, published by
Random House Children's Books, a division of Penguin Random House LLC, New York, in 1994.

Random House and the colophon are registered trademarks and A Stepping Stone Book
and the colophon are trademarks of Penguin Random House LLC. RH Graphic with
the book design is a trademark of Penguin Random House LLC. Magic Tree House
is a registered trademark of Mary Pope Osborne; used under license.

Visit us on the Web!
rhcbooks.com
MagicTreeHouse.com

Educators and librarians, for a variety of teaching tools, visit us at RHTeachersLibrarians.com

Library of Congress Cataloging-in-Publication Data is available upon request.
ISBN 978-0-593-17483-8 (pb) — ISBN 978-0-593-17480-7 (hc) —
ISBN 978-0-593-17481-4 (lib. bdg.) — ISBN 978-0-593-17482-1 (ebook)

The artists used Clip Studio Paint to create the illustrations for this book.
The text of this book is set in 13-point Cartoonist Hand Regular.

MANUFACTURED IN CHINA
10 9 8 7 6 5 4 3 2 1
First Graphic Novel Edition

This book has been officially leveled by using the F&P Text Level Gradient™ Leveling System.

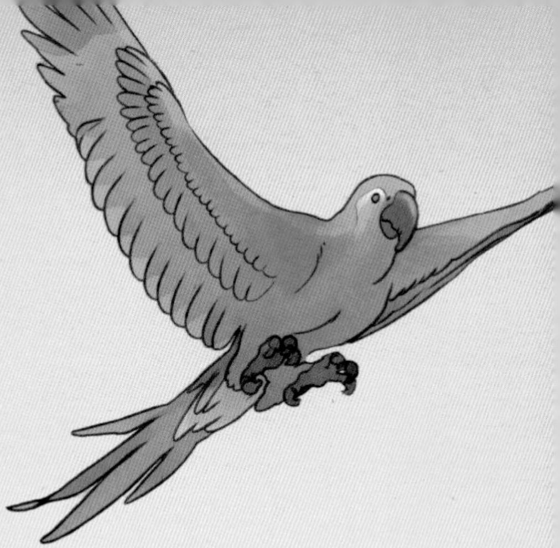

For Teddy and Clark Lettice
—M.P.O.

For June and Willie—beautiful,
beloved creatures of the sea
—J.L.

For Bones and Whitney—
thanks for believing in us!
—K.M. & N.M.

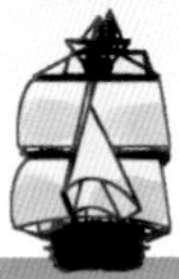

CHAPTER ONE
Too Late

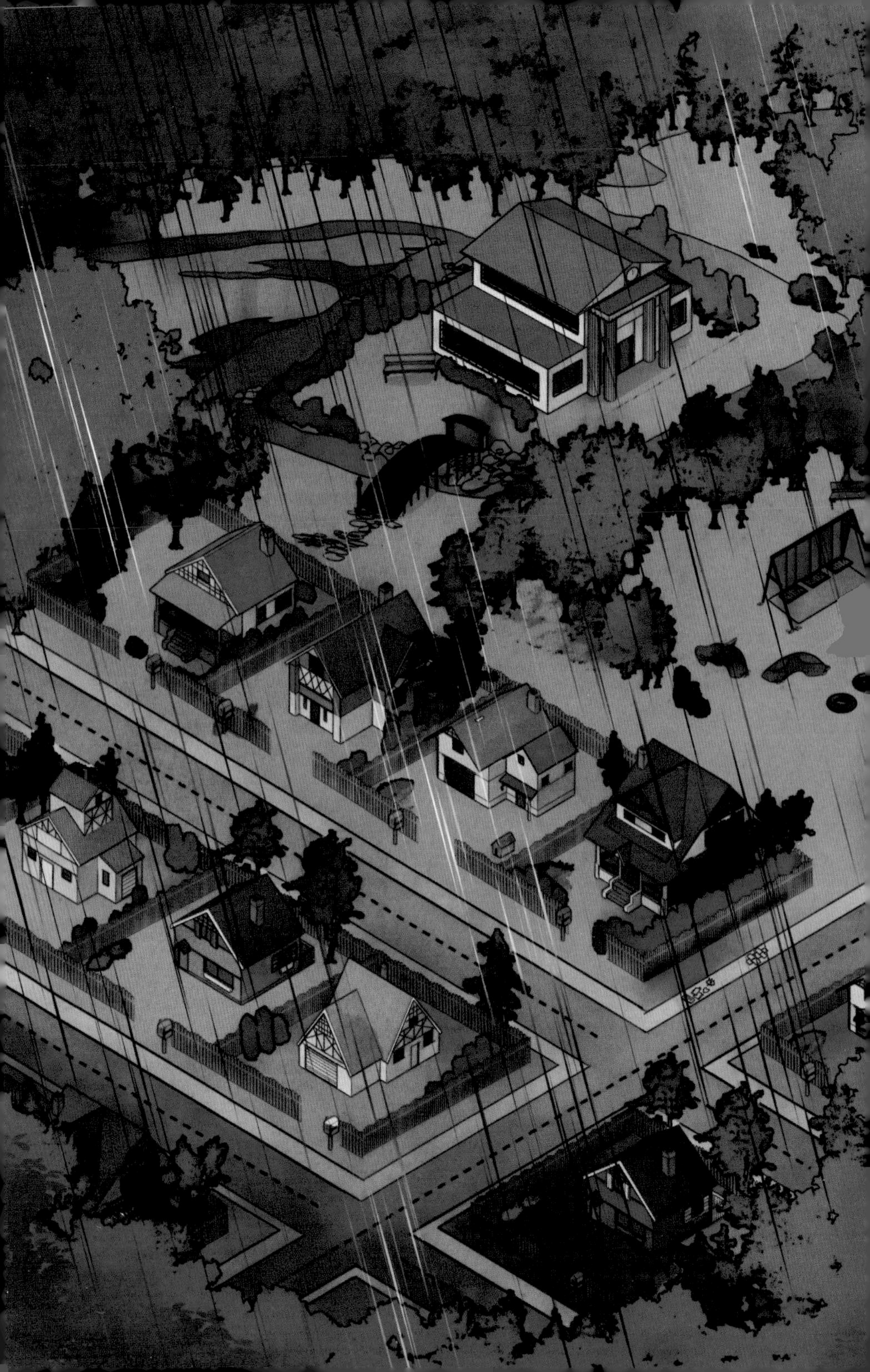

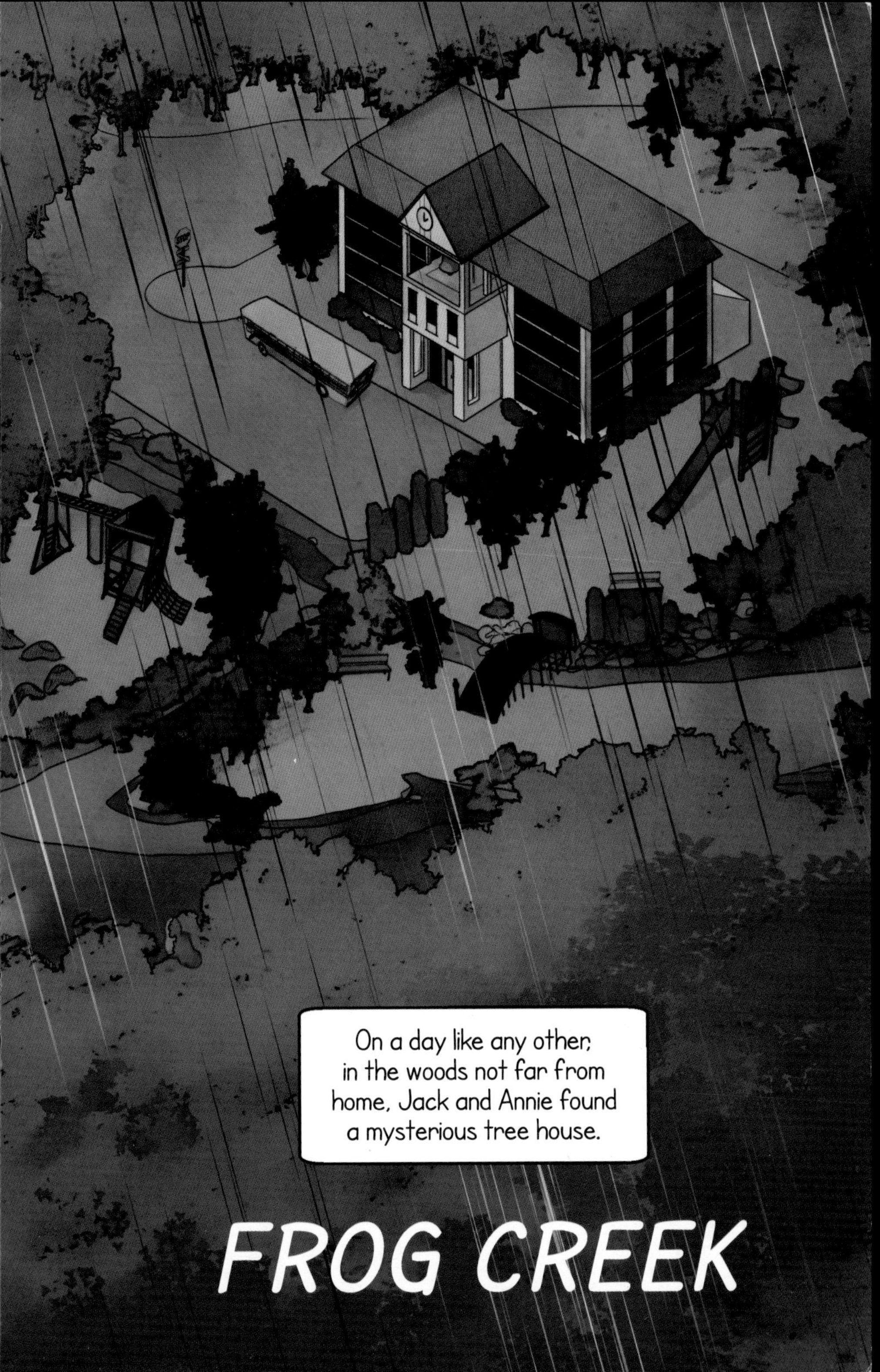
On a day like any other, in the woods not far from home, Jack and Annie found a mysterious tree house.
FROG CREEK

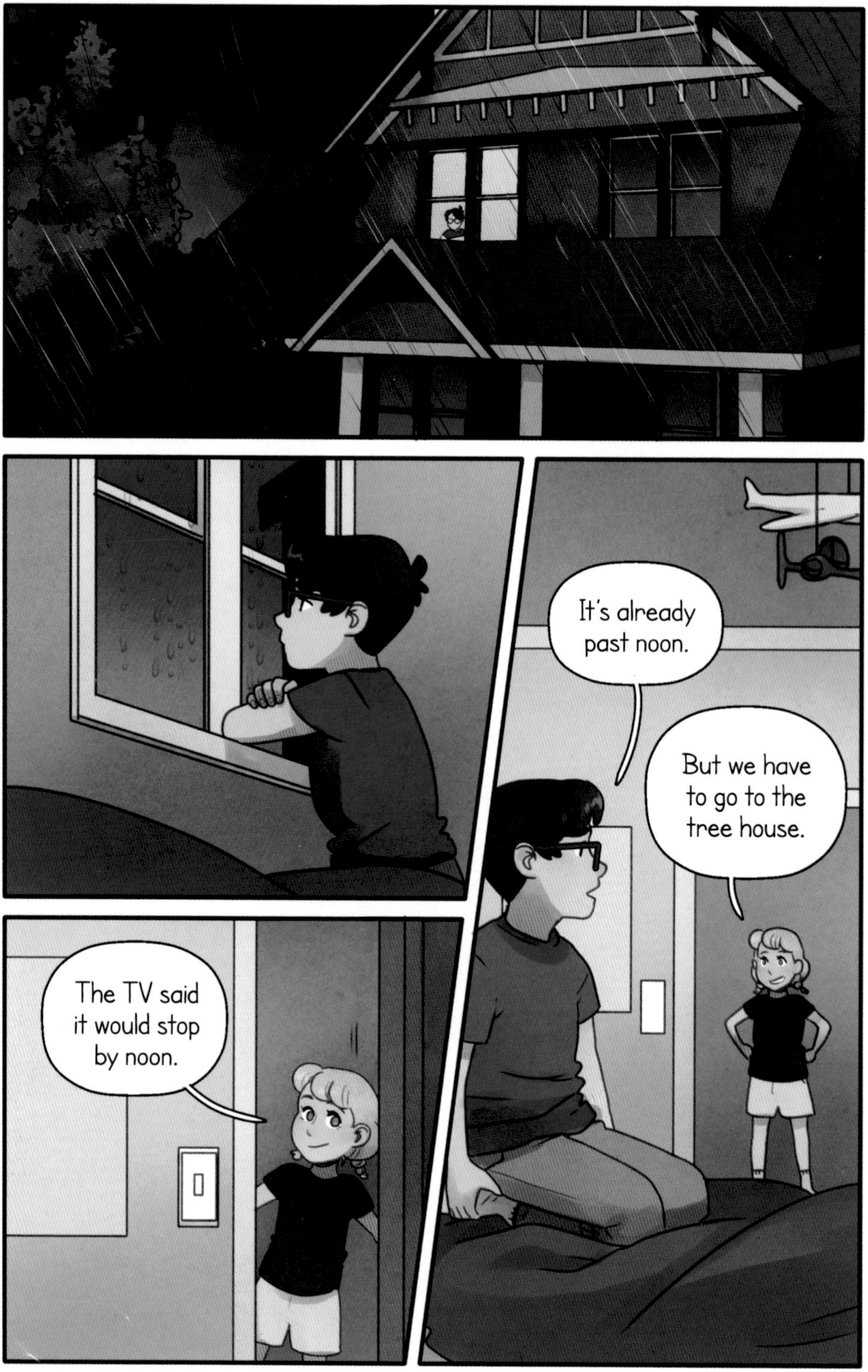
It's already past noon.
But we have to go to the tree house.
The TV said it would stop by noon.

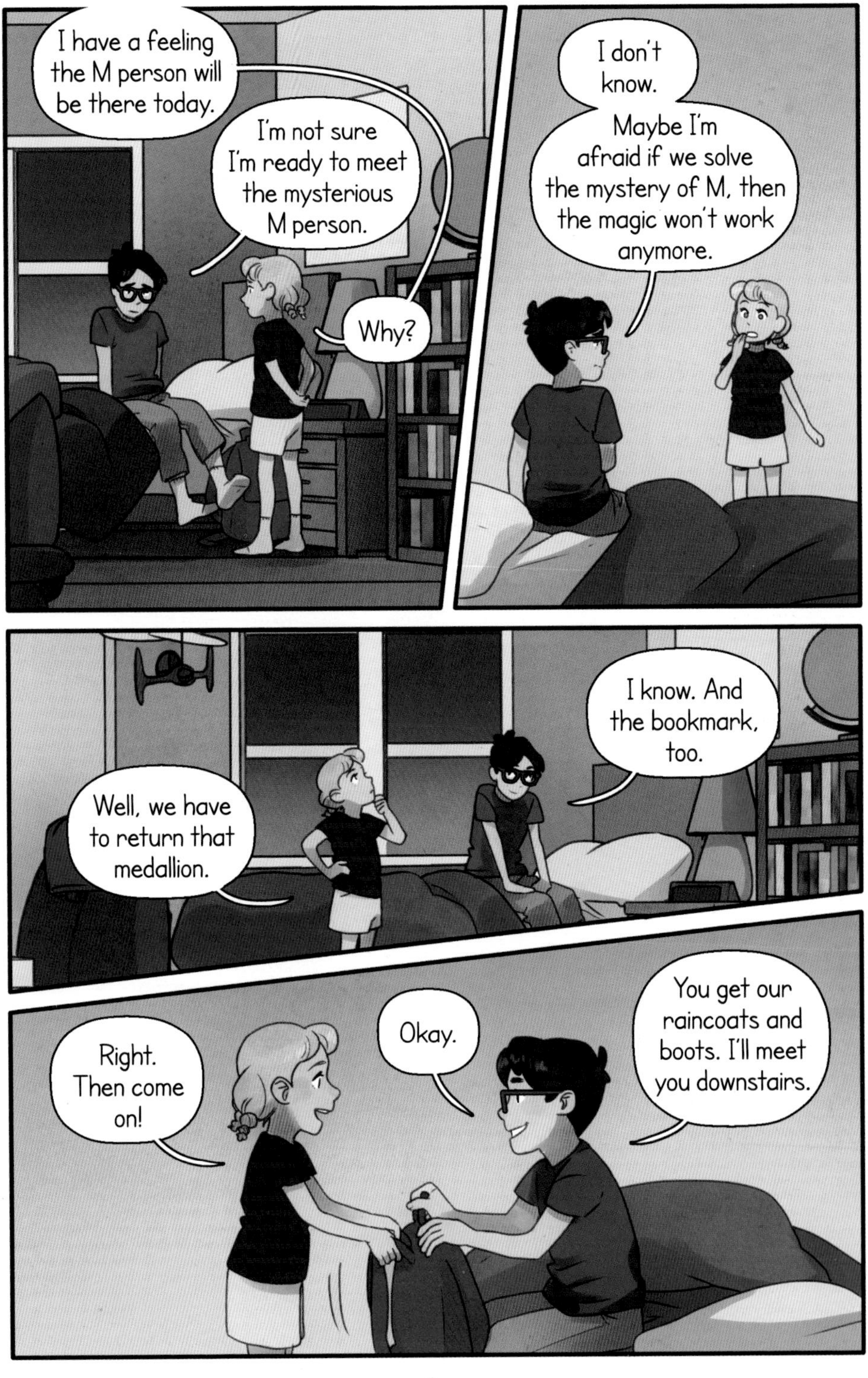
I have a feeling the M person will be there today.
I'm not sure I'm ready to meet the mysterious M person.
Why?
I don't know.
Maybe I'm afraid if we solve the mystery of M, then the magic won't work anymore.
Well, we have to return that medallion.
I know. And the bookmark, too.
Right. Then come on!
Okay.
You get our raincoats and boots. I'll meet you downstairs.

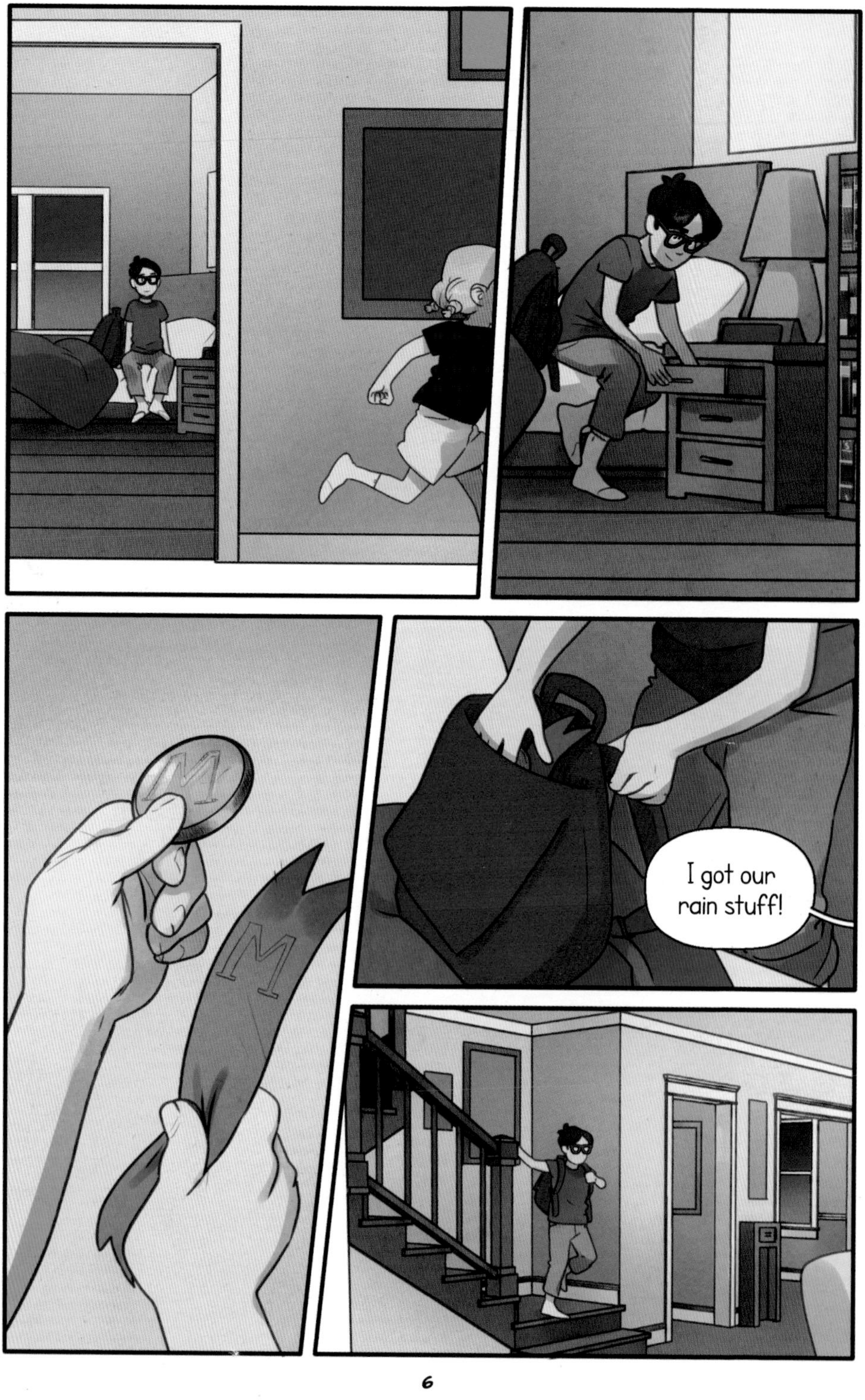
I got our
rain stuff!

Do you think the M person will send us another magical friend on this adventure?

I don't know. I don't even know for sure if M is magic.

But I thought you said the cat in Egypt was sent to help us—

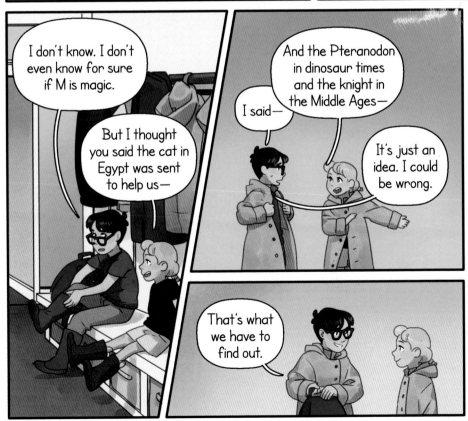
And the Pteranodon in dinosaur times and the knight in the Middle Ages—

I said—

It's just an idea. I could be wrong.

That's what we have to find out.

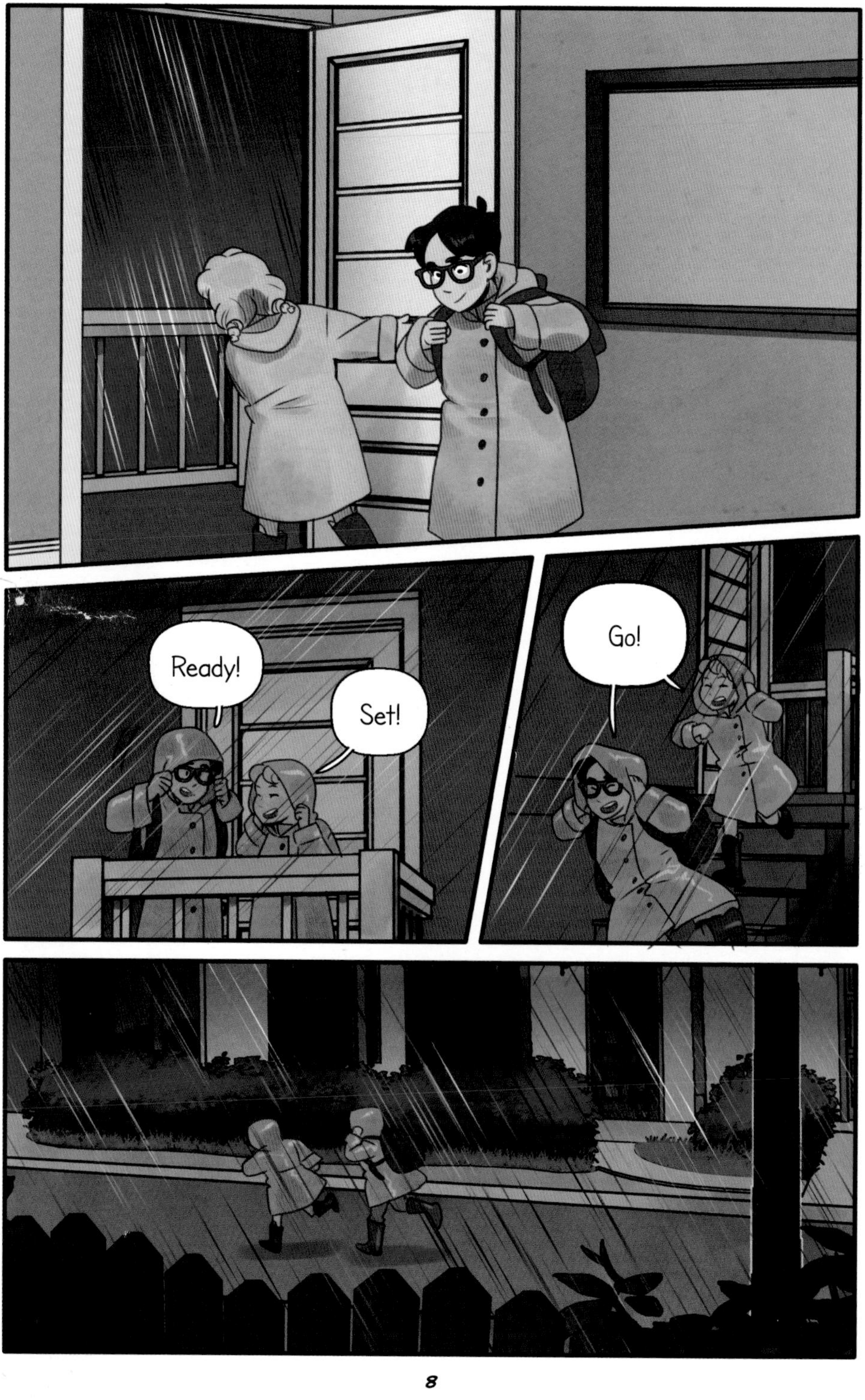
Ready!
Set!
Go!

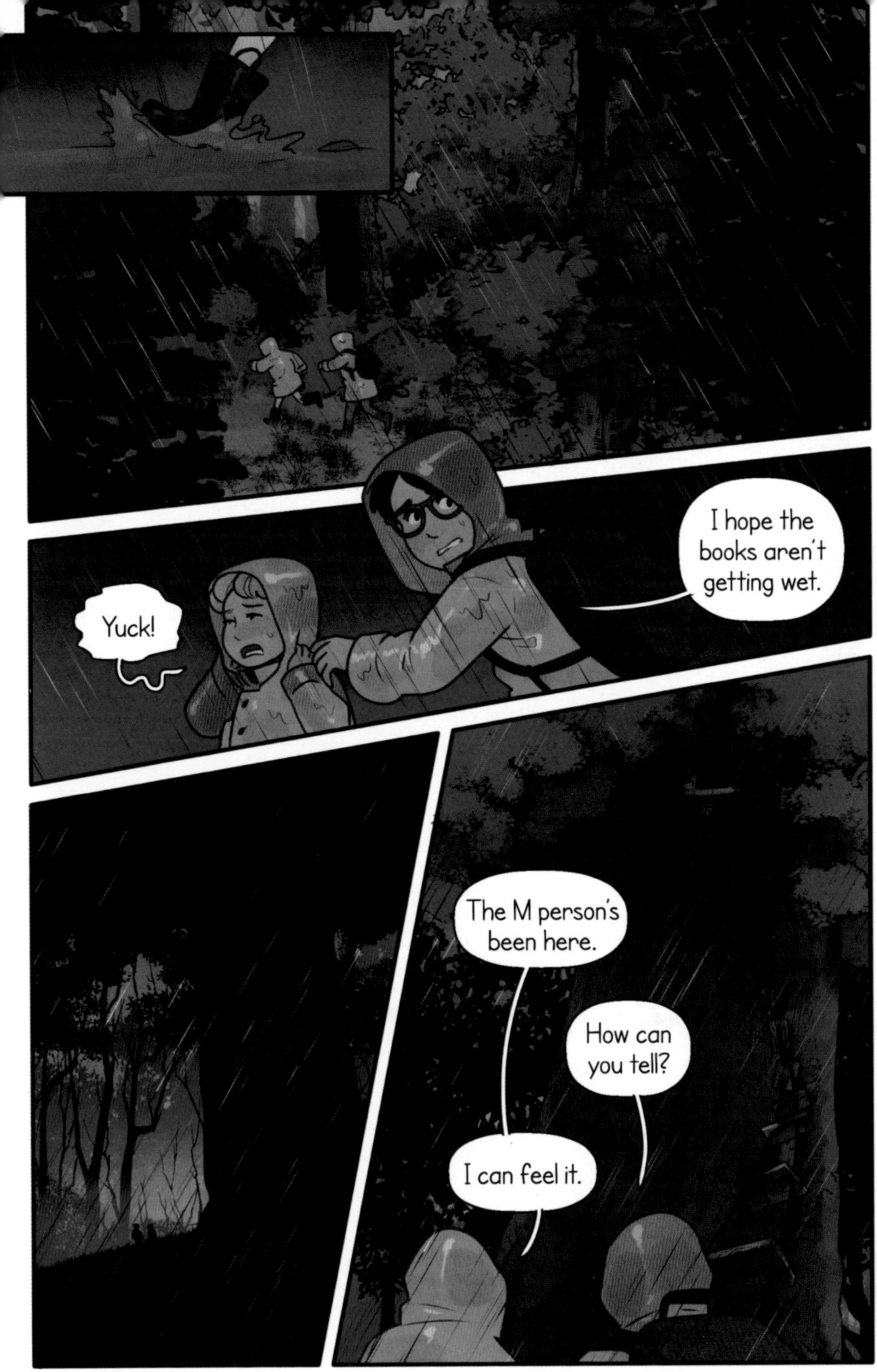
I hope the books aren't getting wet.
Yuck!
The M person's been here.
How can you tell?
I can feel it.

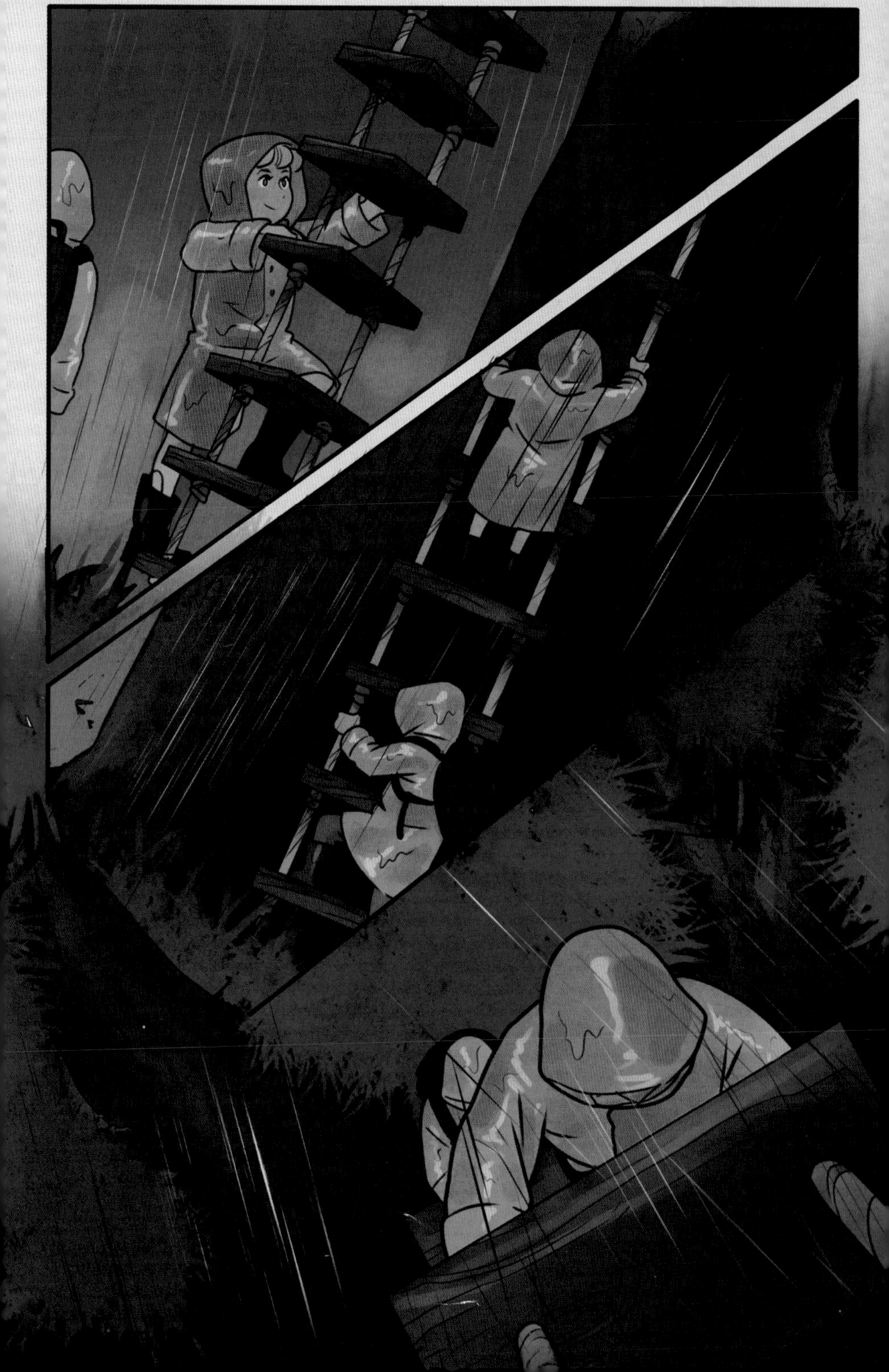

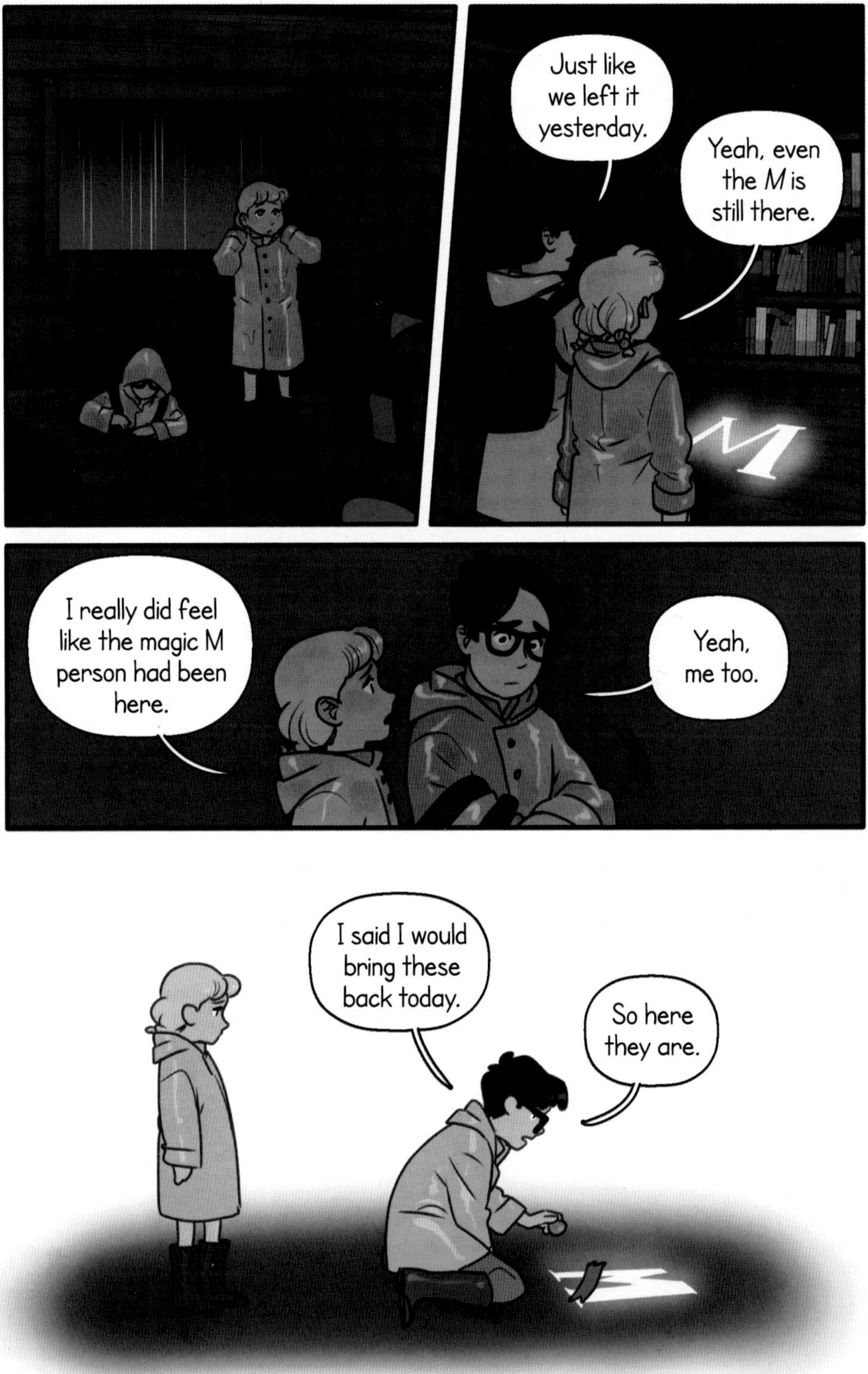
Just like we left it yesterday.
Yeah, even the *M* is still there.
I really did feel like the magic M person had been here.
Yeah, me too.
I said I would bring these back today.
So here they are.

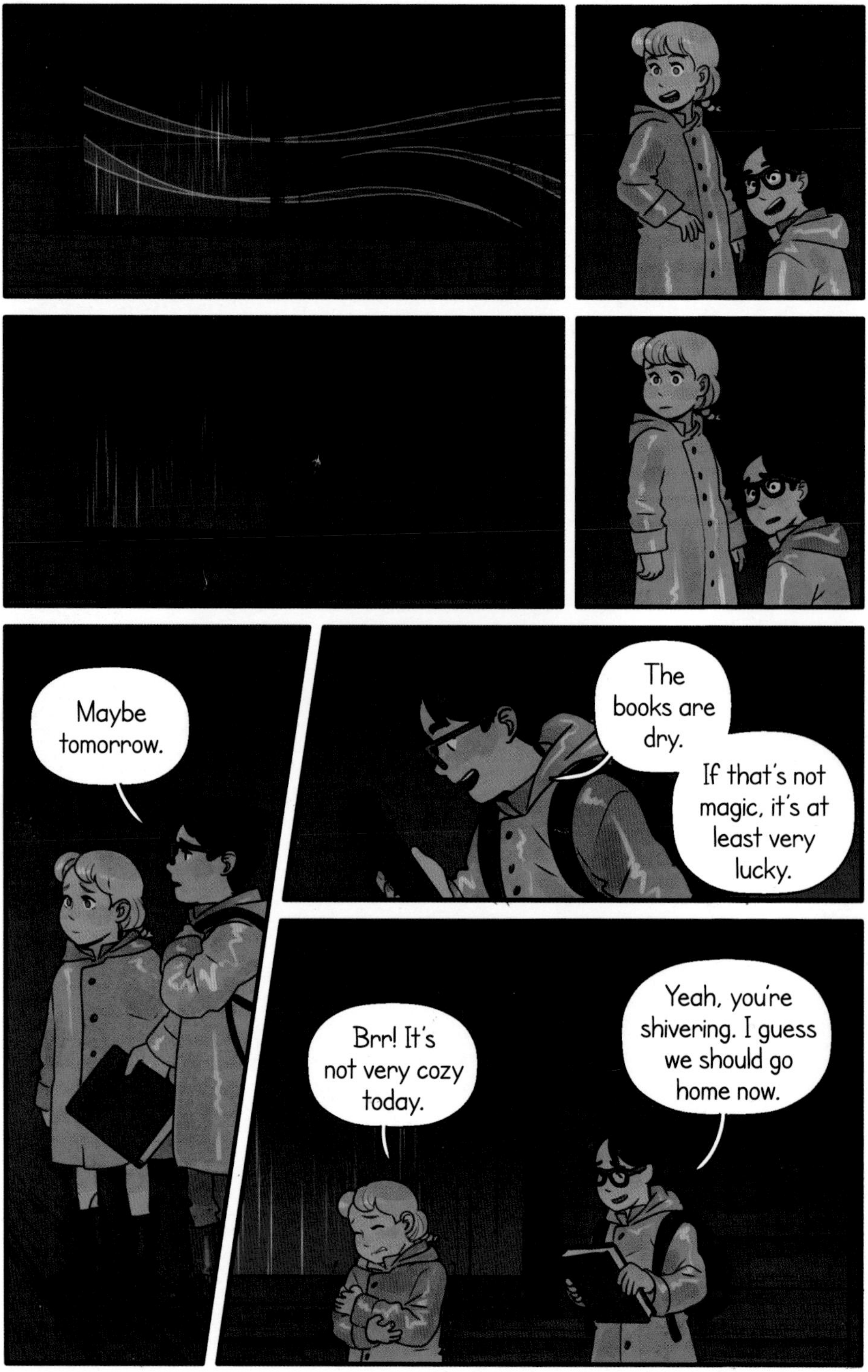
Maybe tomorrow.
The books are dry.
If that's not magic, it's at least very lucky.
Brr! It's not very cozy today.
Yeah, you're shivering. I guess we should go home now.

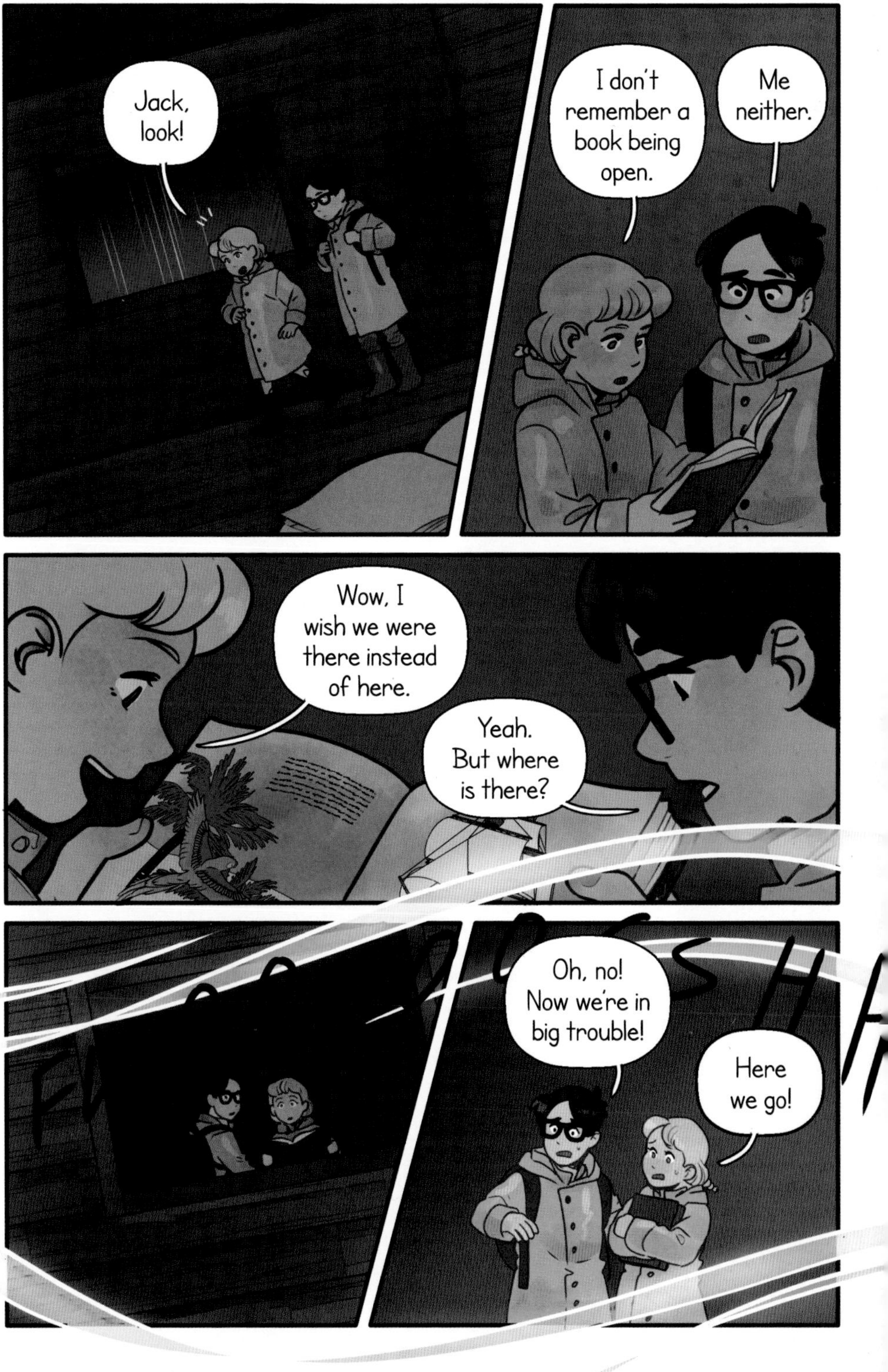
Jack, look!
I don't remember a book being open.
Me neither.
Wow, I wish we were there instead of here.
Yeah. But where is there?
Oh, no! Now we're in big trouble!
Here we go!

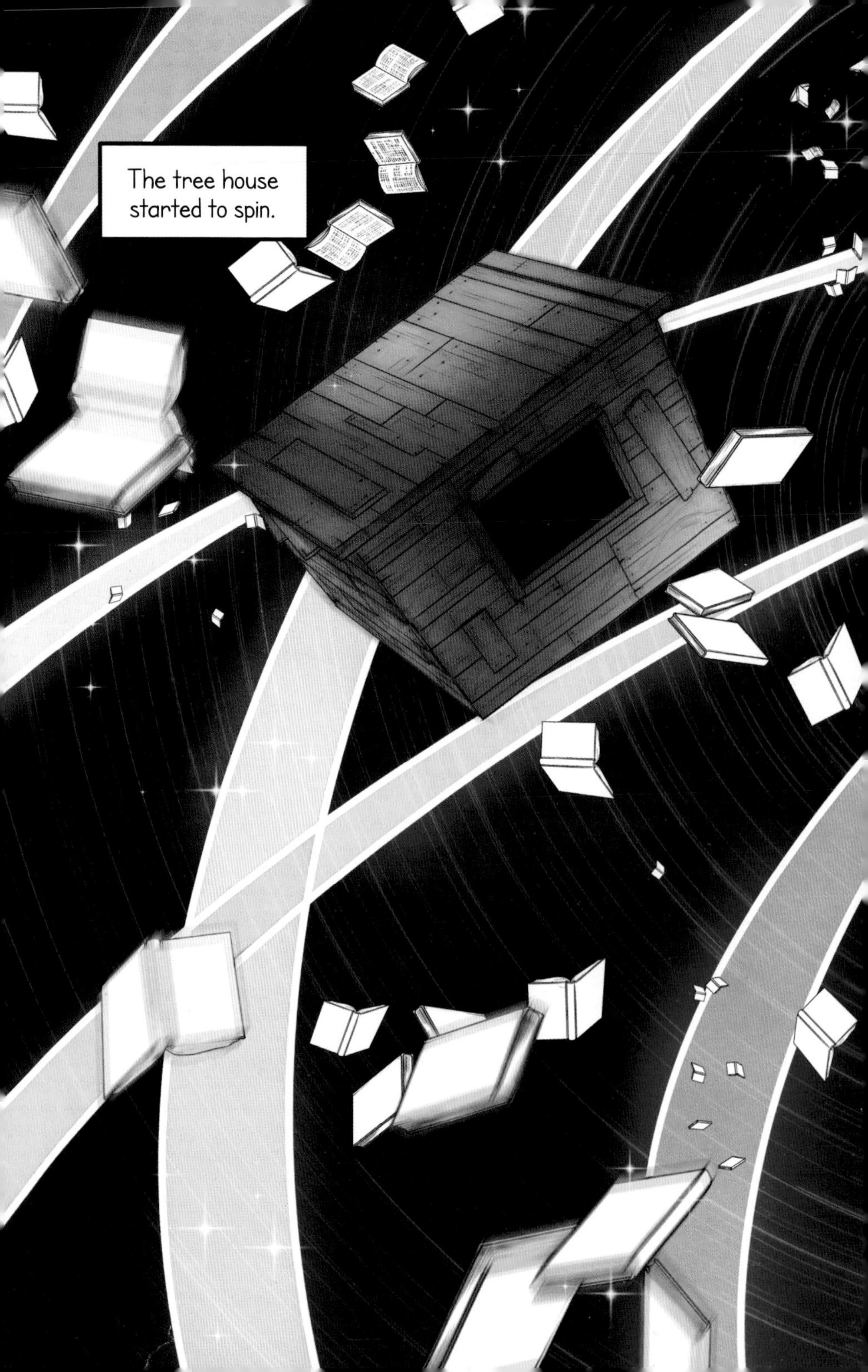
The tree house
started to spin.

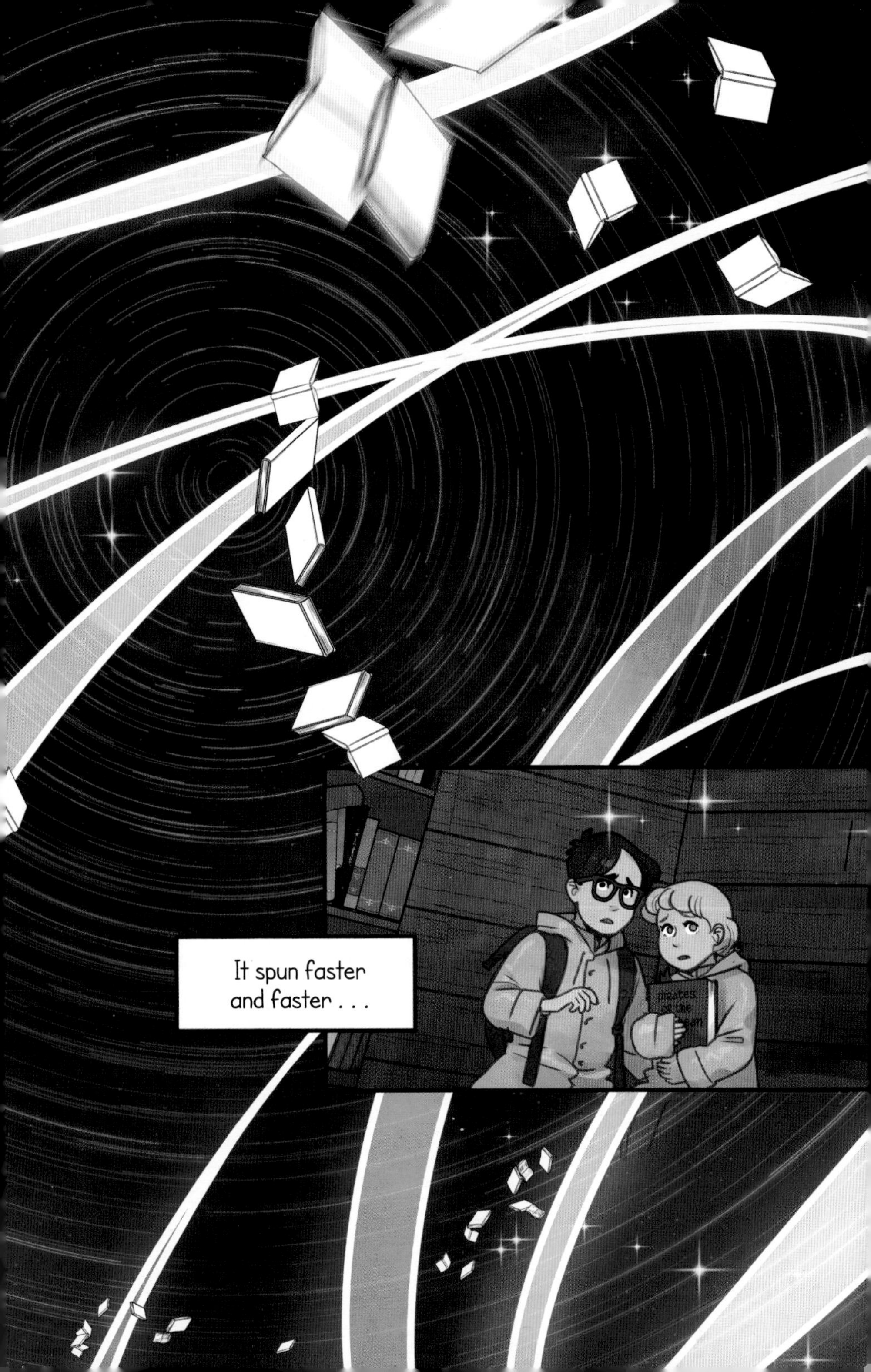
It spun faster
and faster . . .

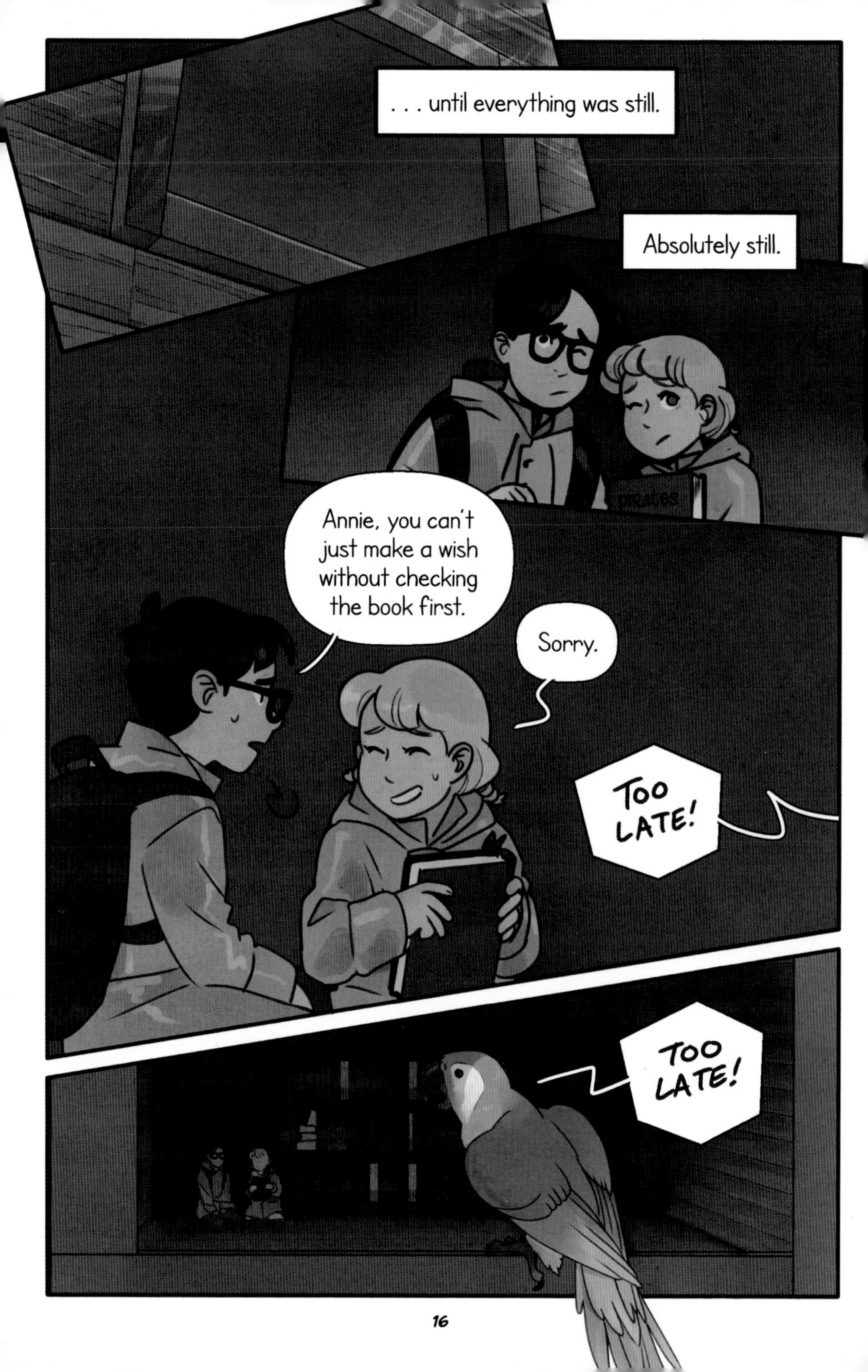
. . . until everything was still.
Absolutely still.
Annie, you can't just make a wish without checking the book first.
Sorry.
TOO LATE!
TOO LATE!

CHAPTER TWO
The Bright Blue Sea

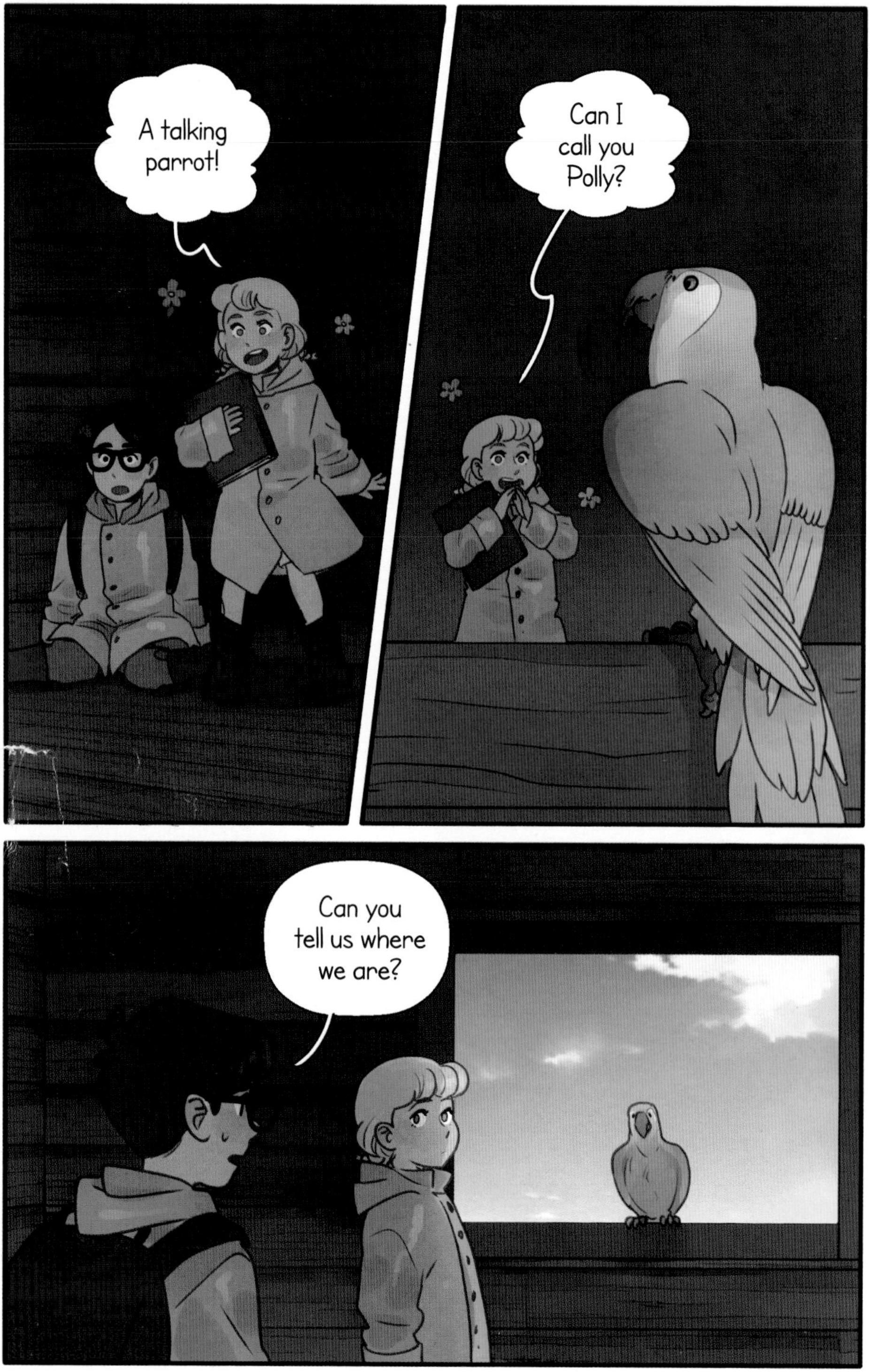
A talking parrot!
Can I call you Polly?
Can you tell us where we are?

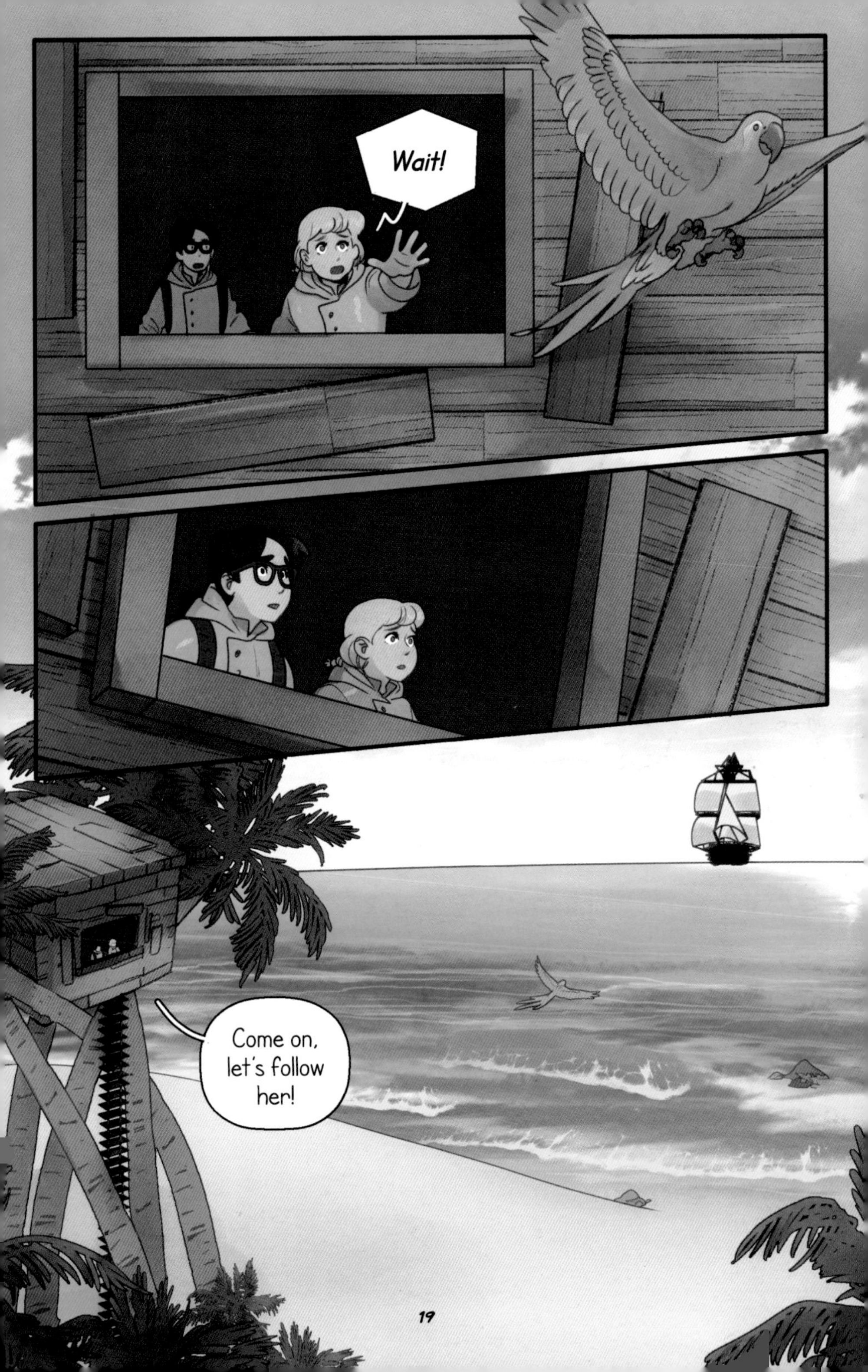
Wait!
Come on, let's follow her!

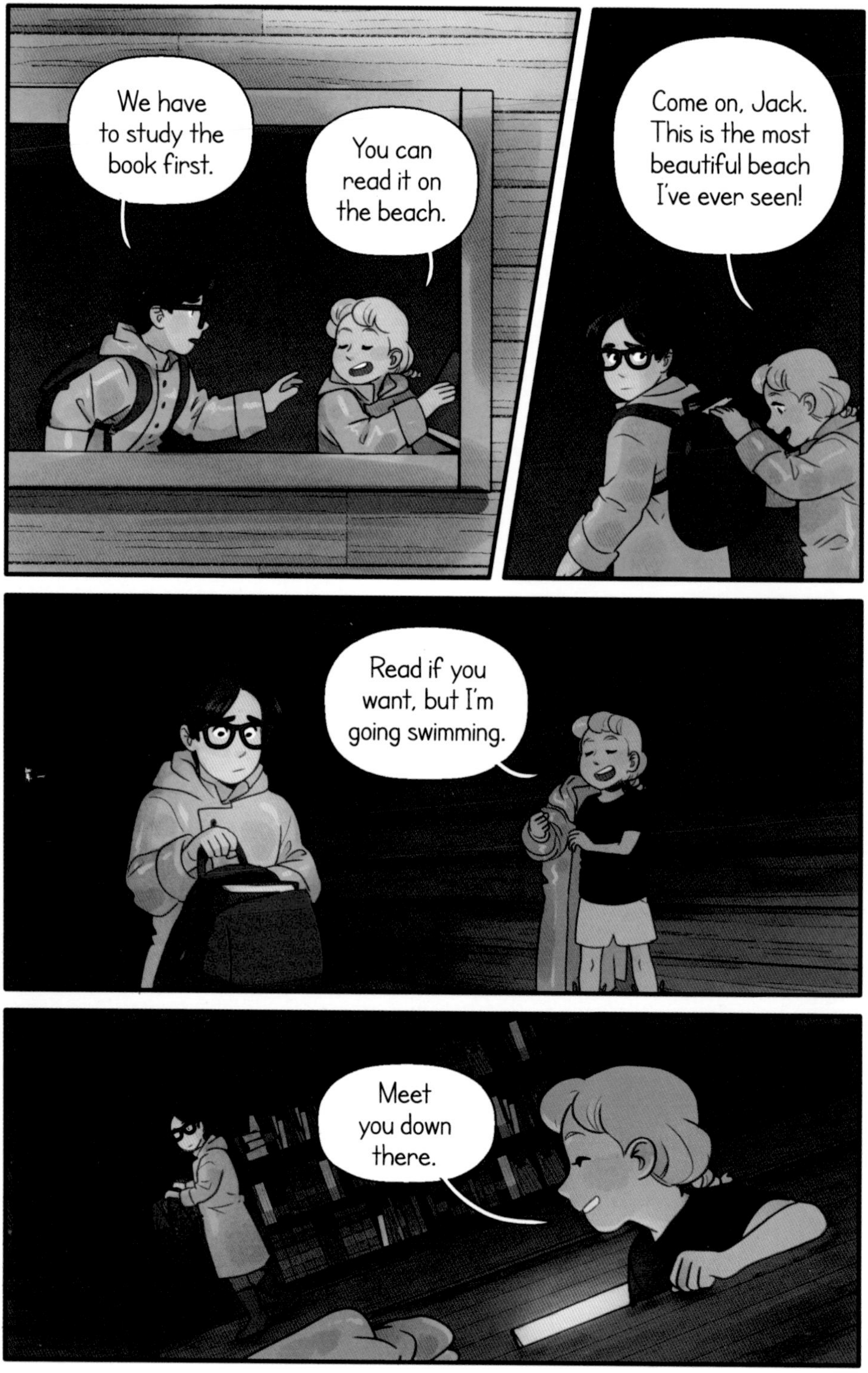
We have to study the book first.
You can read it on the beach.
Come on, Jack. This is the most beautiful beach I've ever seen!
Read if you want, but I'm going swimming.
Meet you down there.

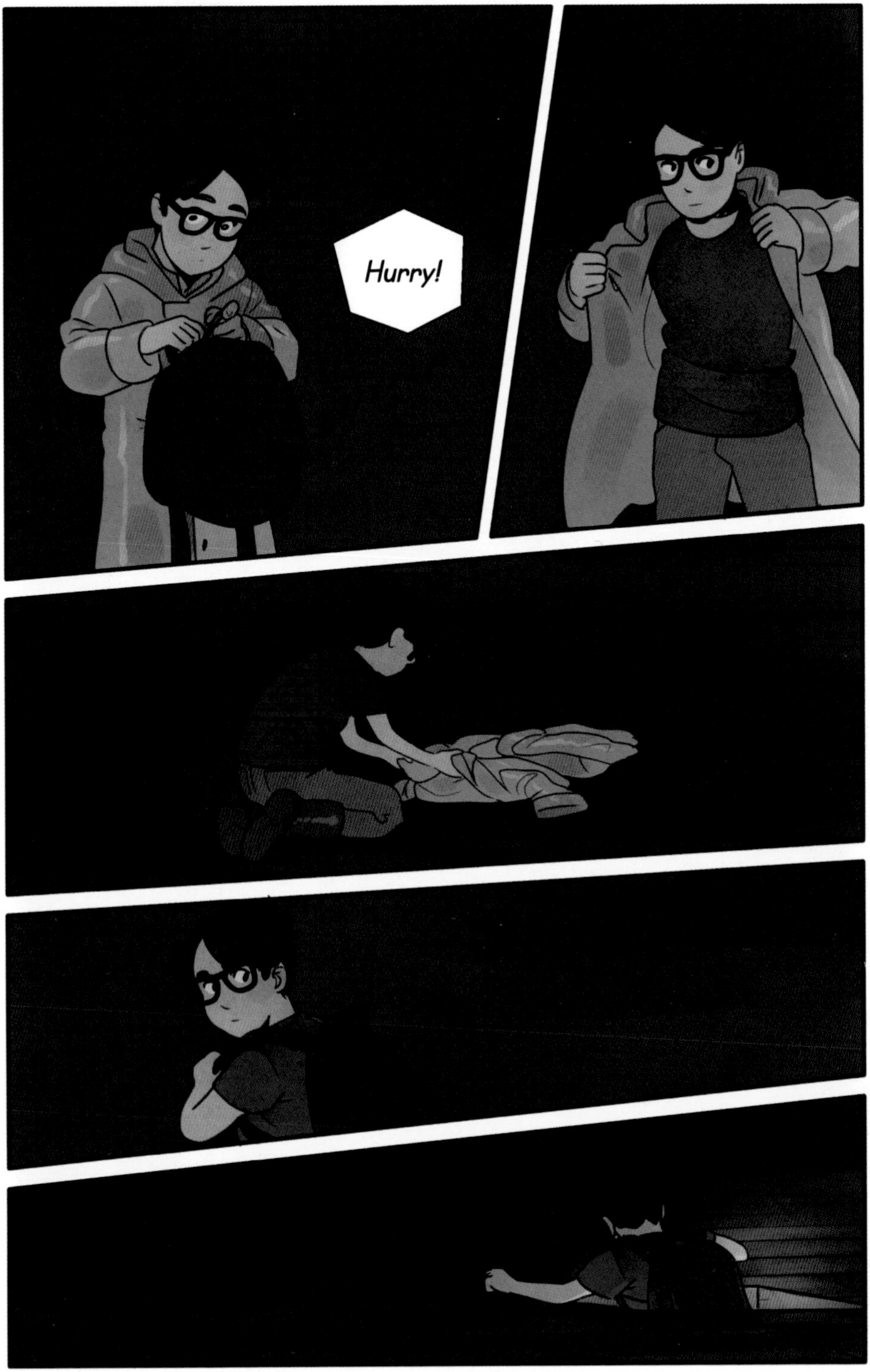
Hurry!

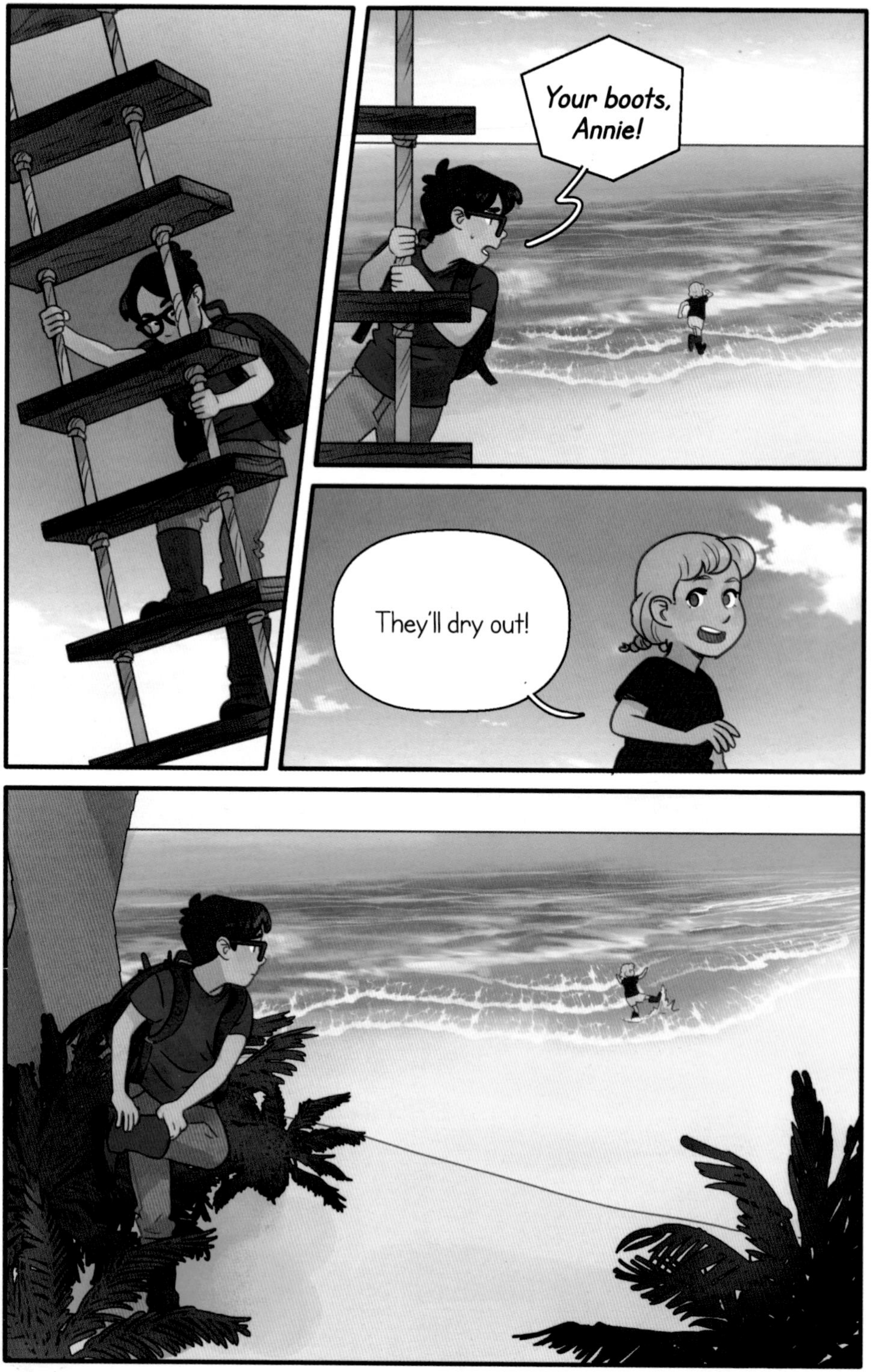
Your boots, Annie!
They'll dry out!

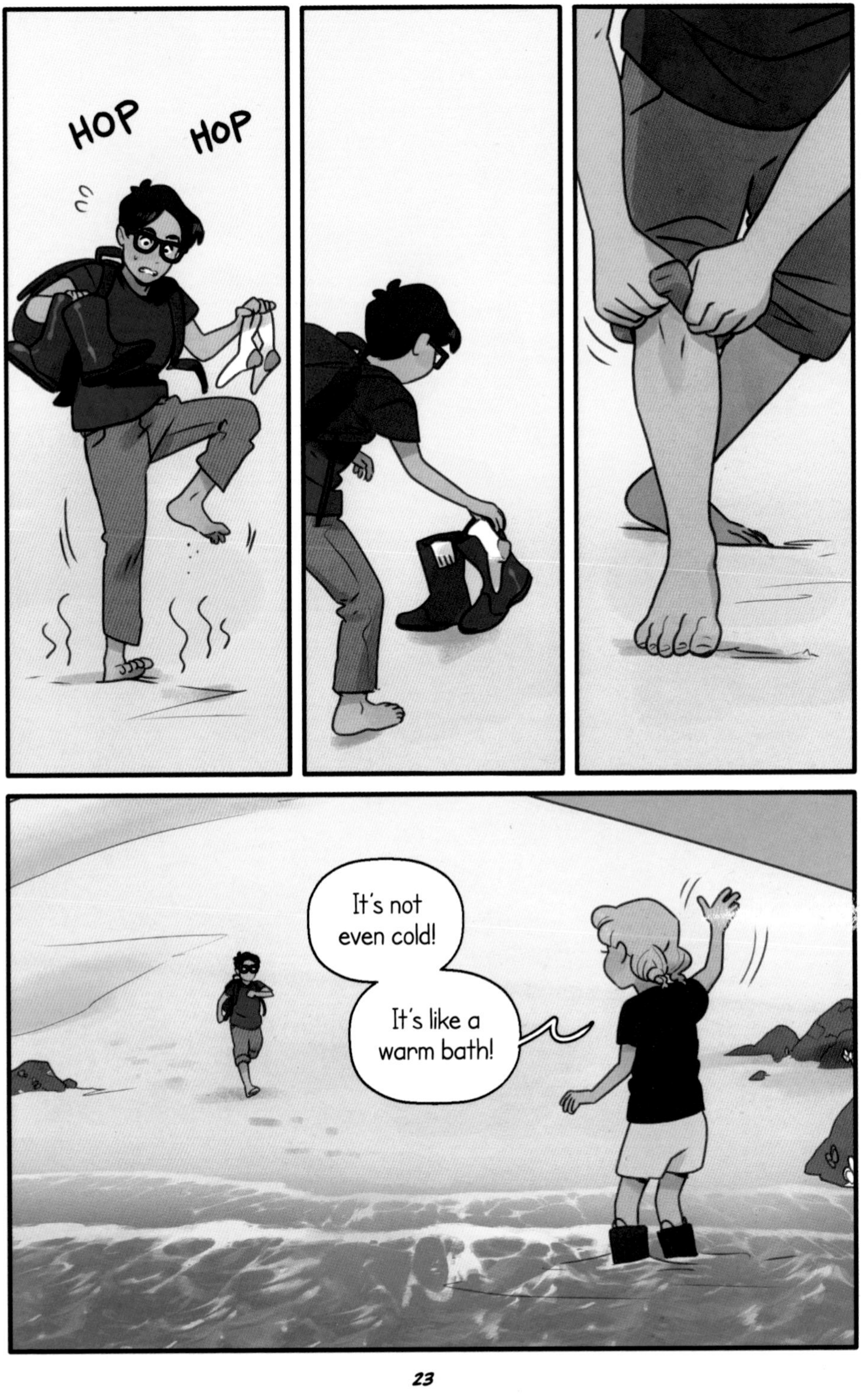
HOP
HOP
It's not even cold!
It's like a warm bath!

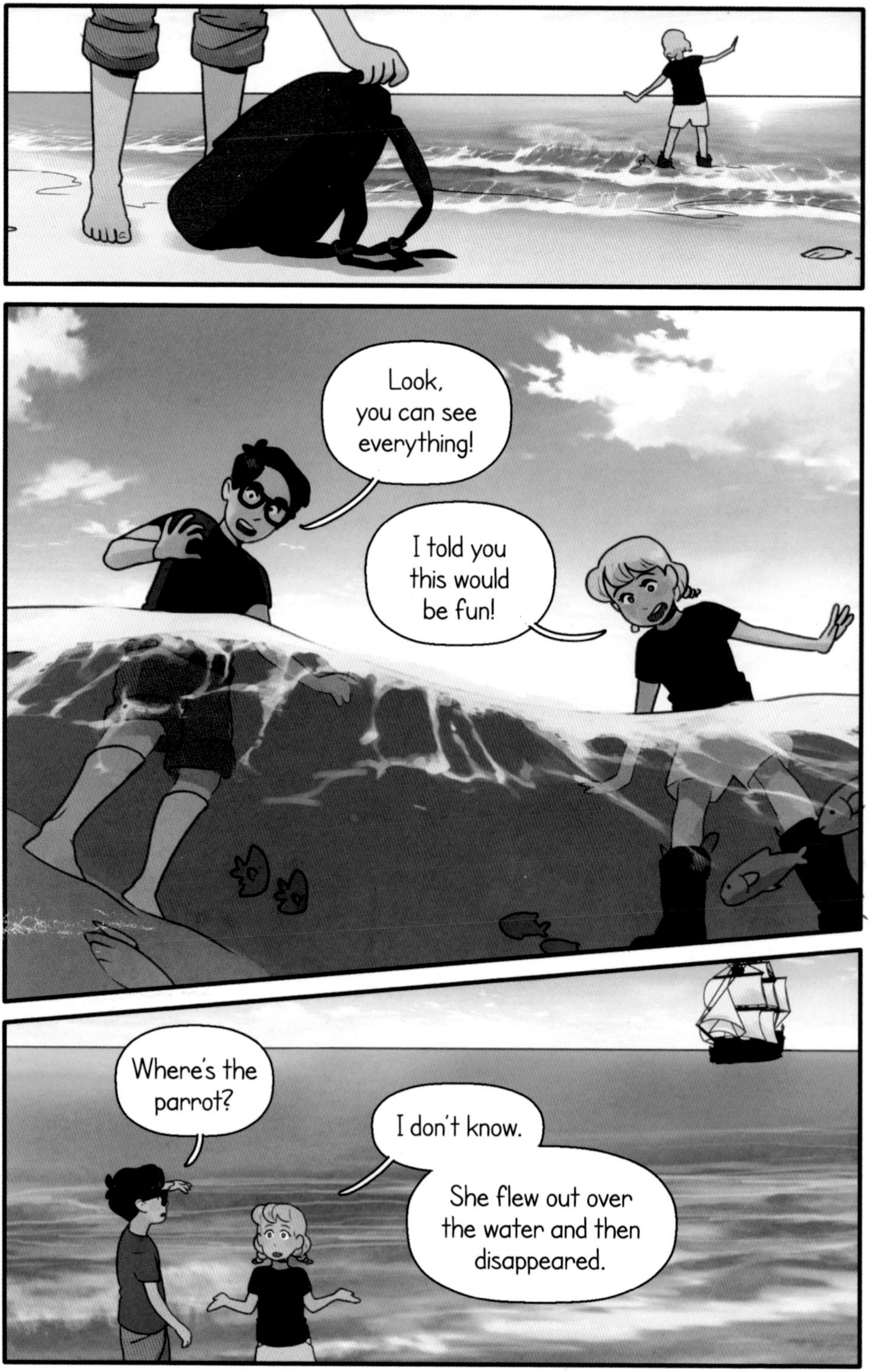
Look, you can see everything!
I told you this would be fun!
Where's the parrot?
I don't know.
She flew out over the water and then disappeared.

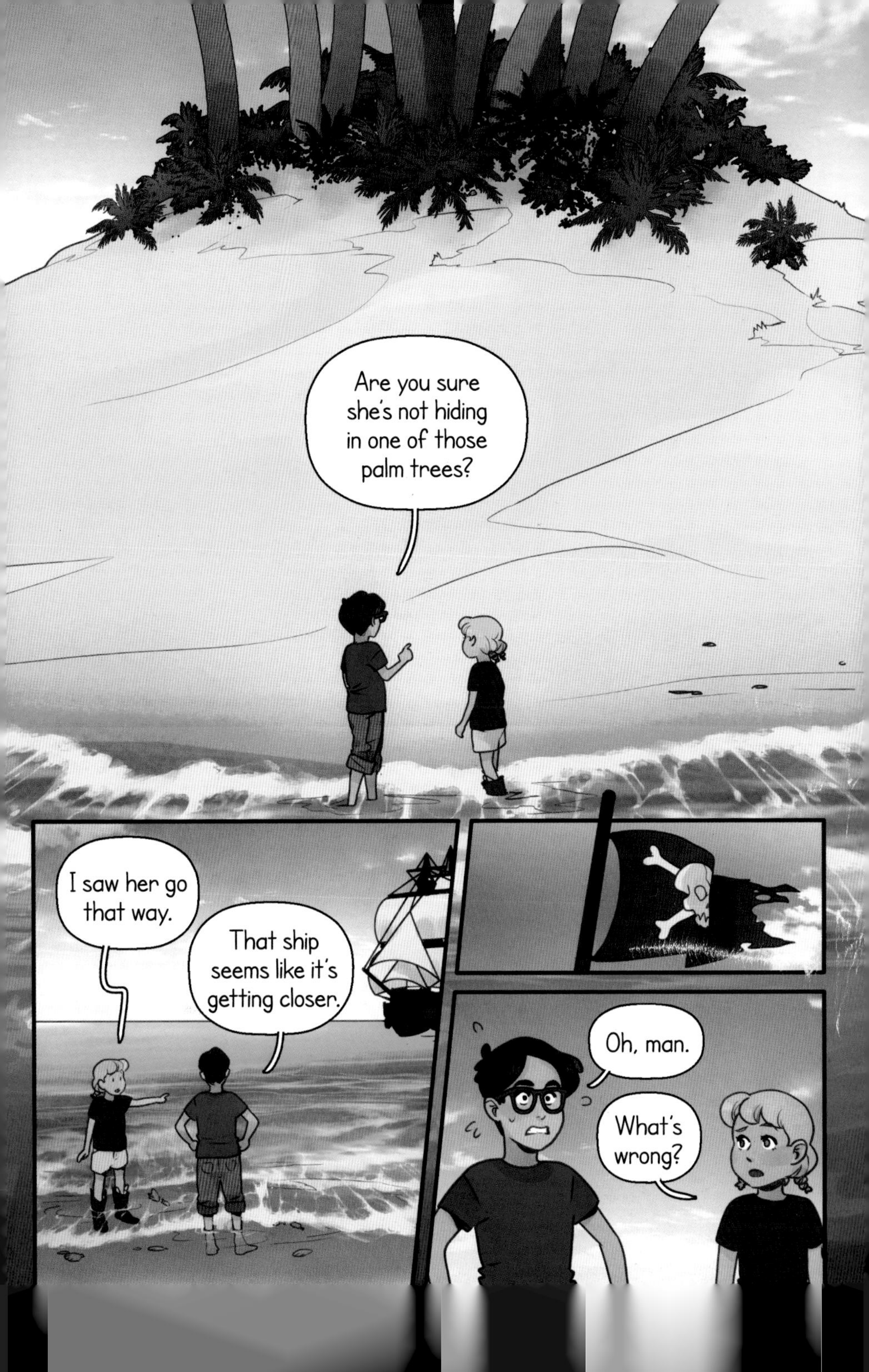

Are you sure she's not hiding in one of those palm trees?
I saw her go that way.
That ship seems like it's getting closer.
Oh, man.
What's wrong?

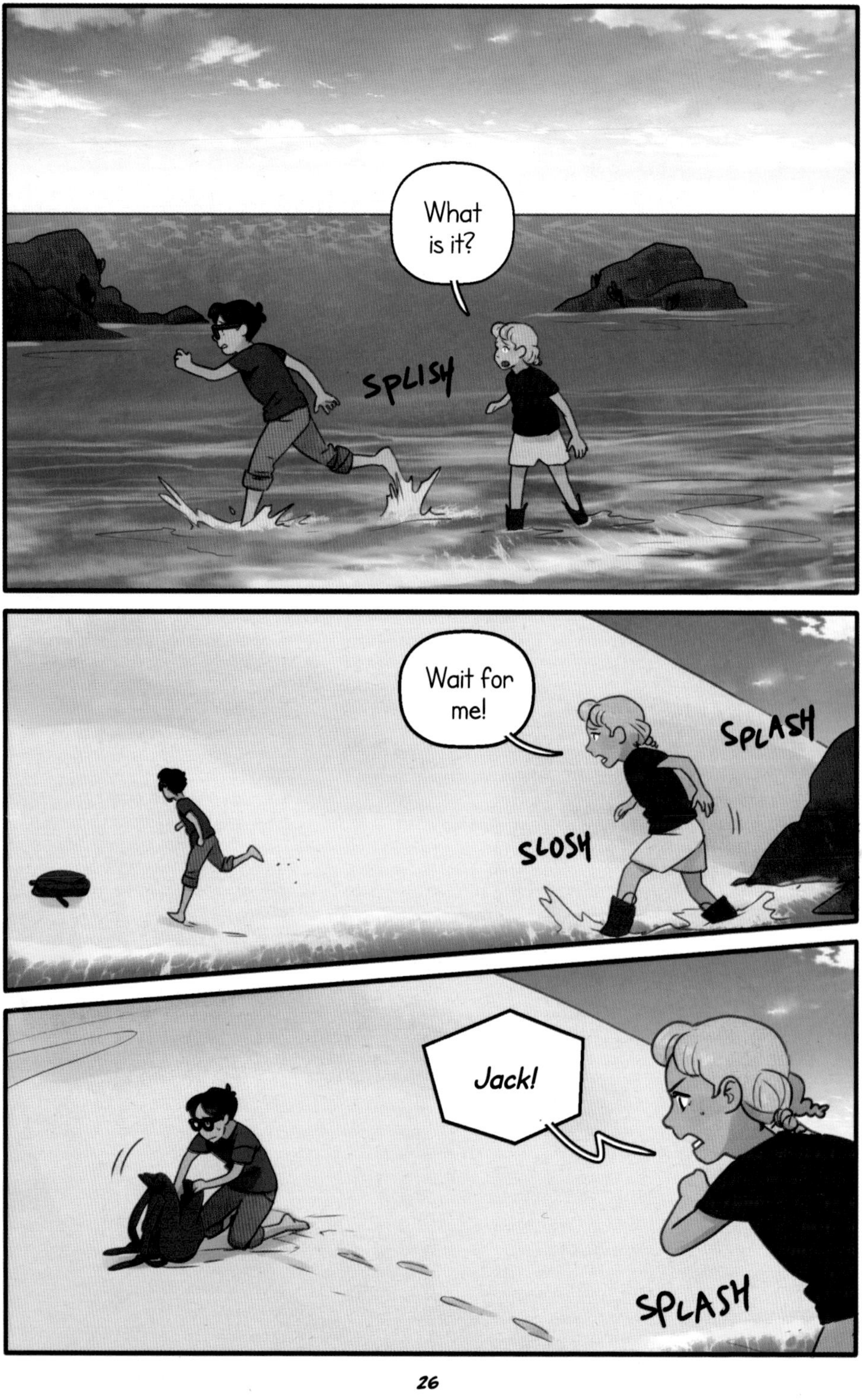
What is it?
SPLISH
Wait for me!
SPLASH
SLOSH
Jack!
SPLASH

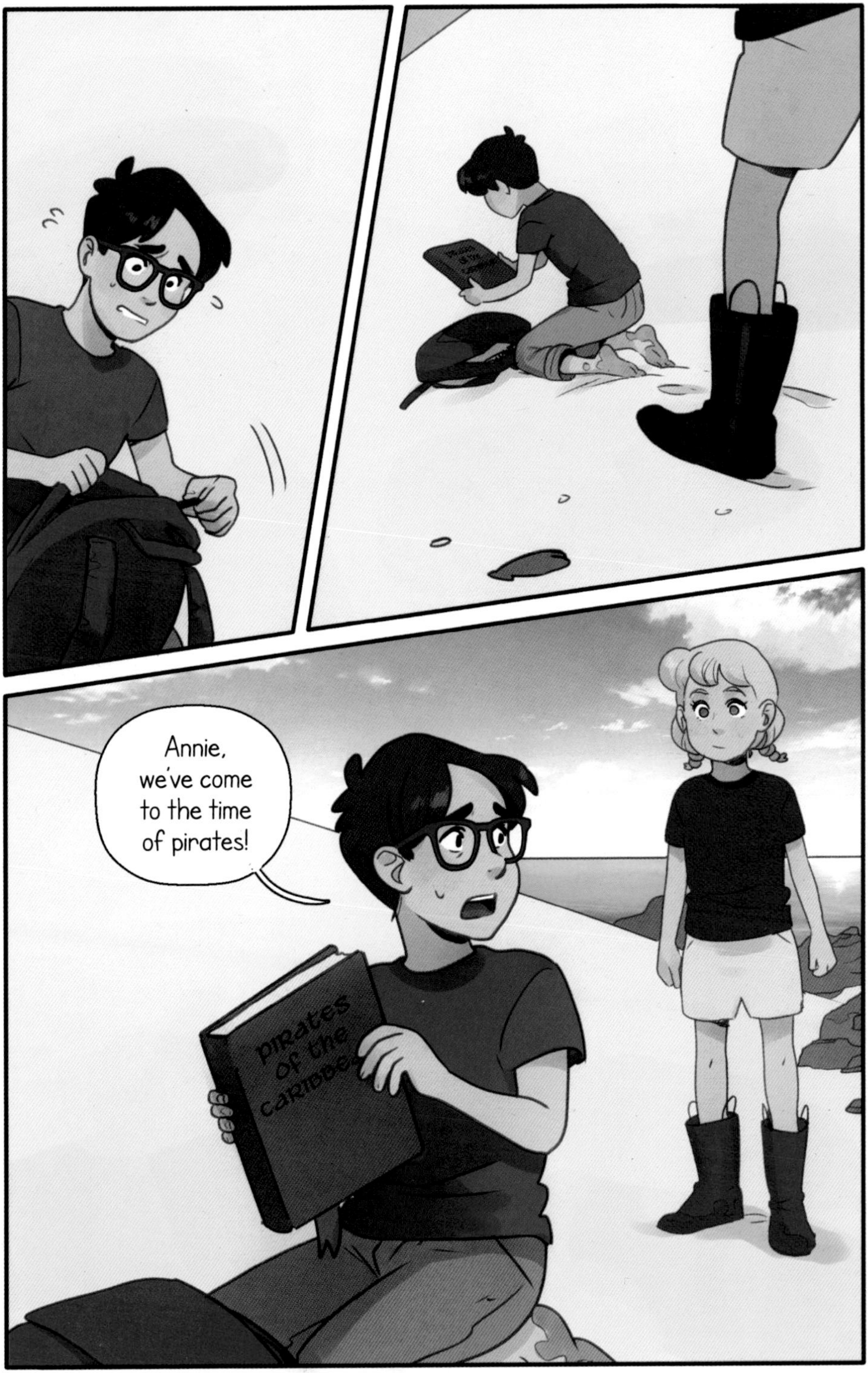
Annie, we've come to the time of pirates!

CHAPTER THREE
Three Men in a Boat

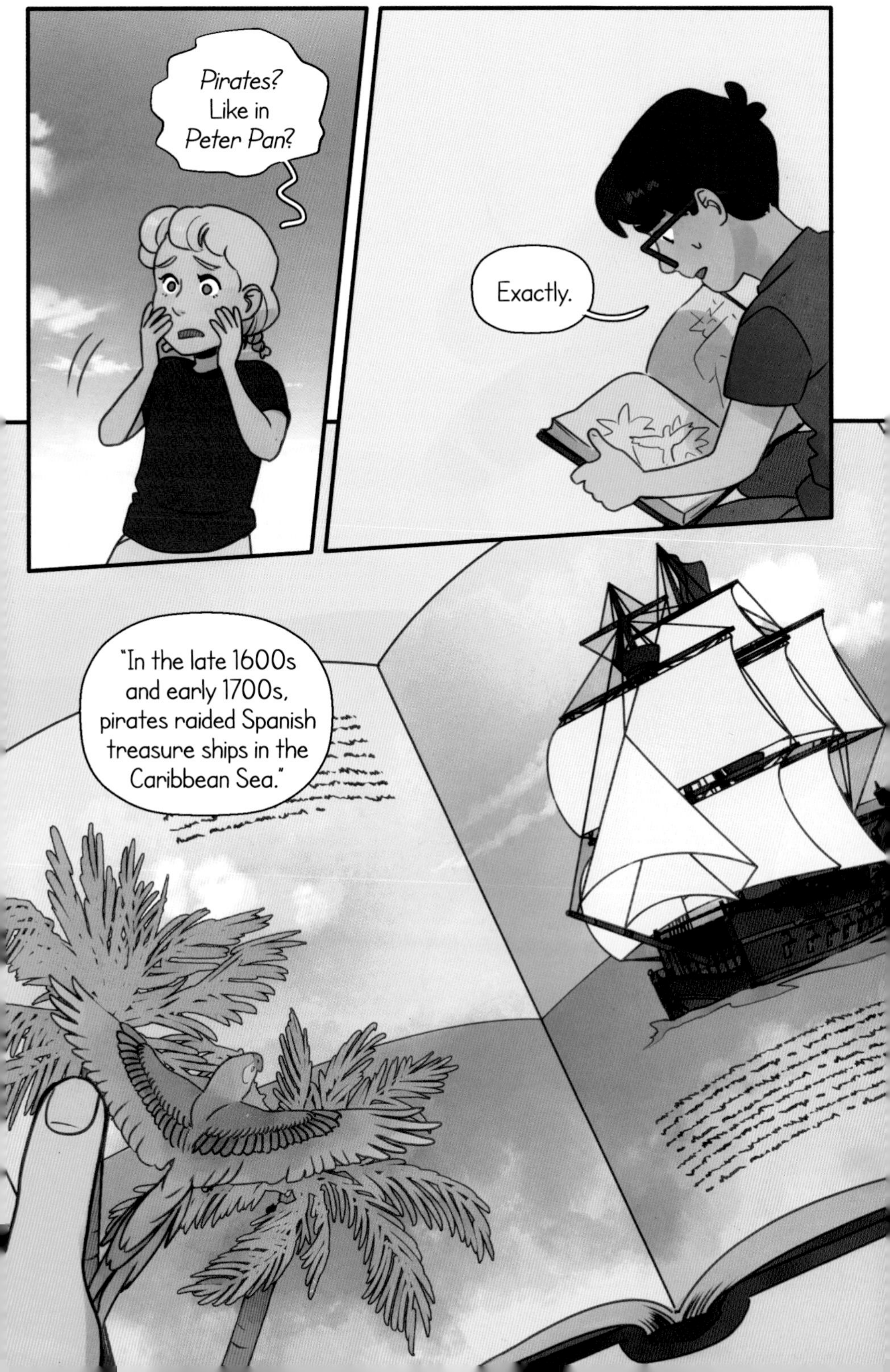
Pirates? Like in *Peter Pan?*
Exactly.
"In the late 1600s and early 1700s, pirates raided Spanish treasure ships in the Caribbean Sea."

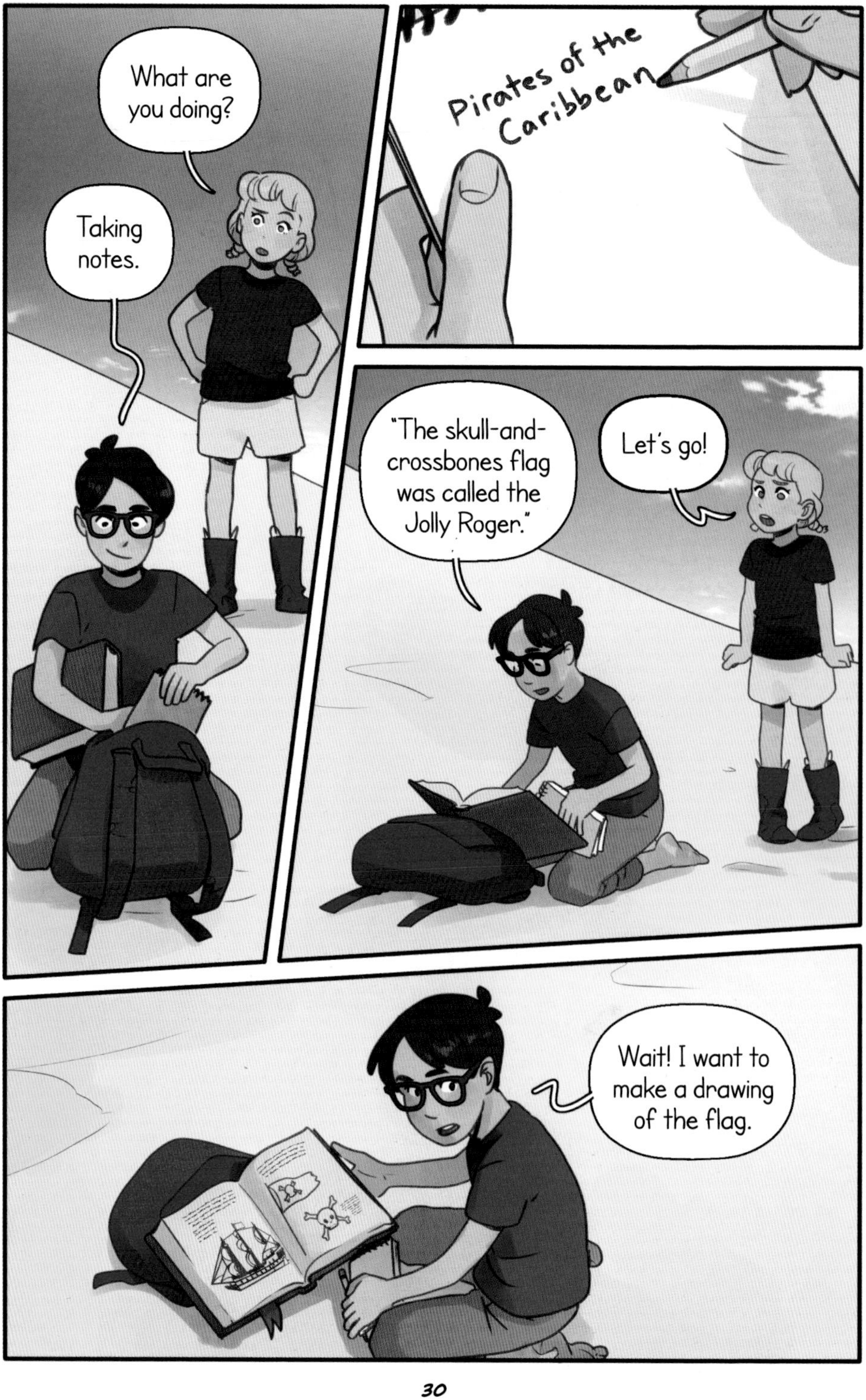
What are you doing?
Taking notes.
Pirates of the Caribbean
"The skull-and-crossbones flag was called the Jolly Roger."
Let's go!
Wait! I want to make a drawing of the flag.

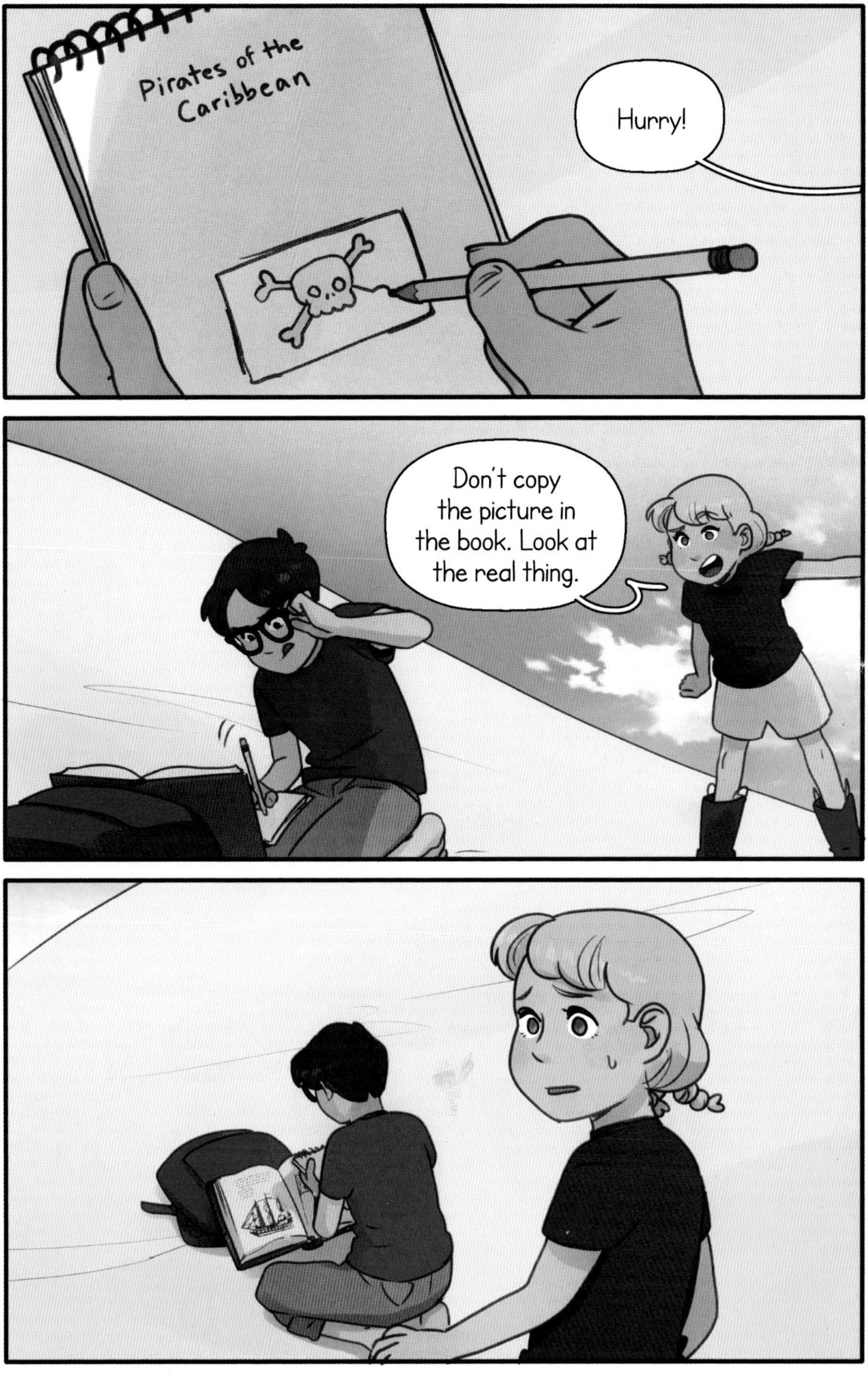
Pirates of the Caribbean
Hurry!
Don't copy the picture in the book. Look at the real thing.

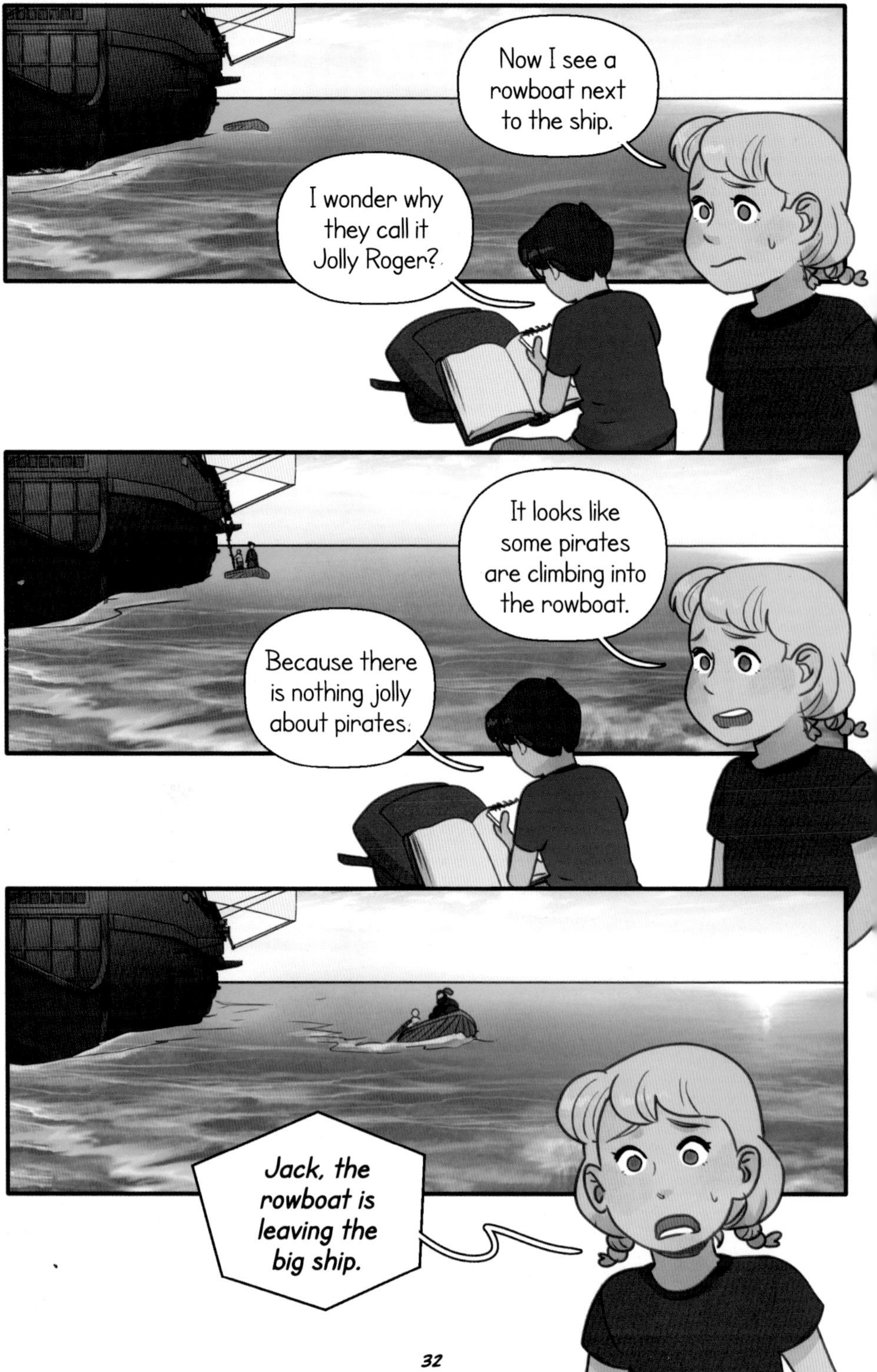
Now I see a rowboat next to the ship.
I wonder why they call it Jolly Roger?
It looks like some pirates are climbing into the rowboat.
Because there is nothing jolly about pirates.
Jack, the rowboat is leaving the big ship.

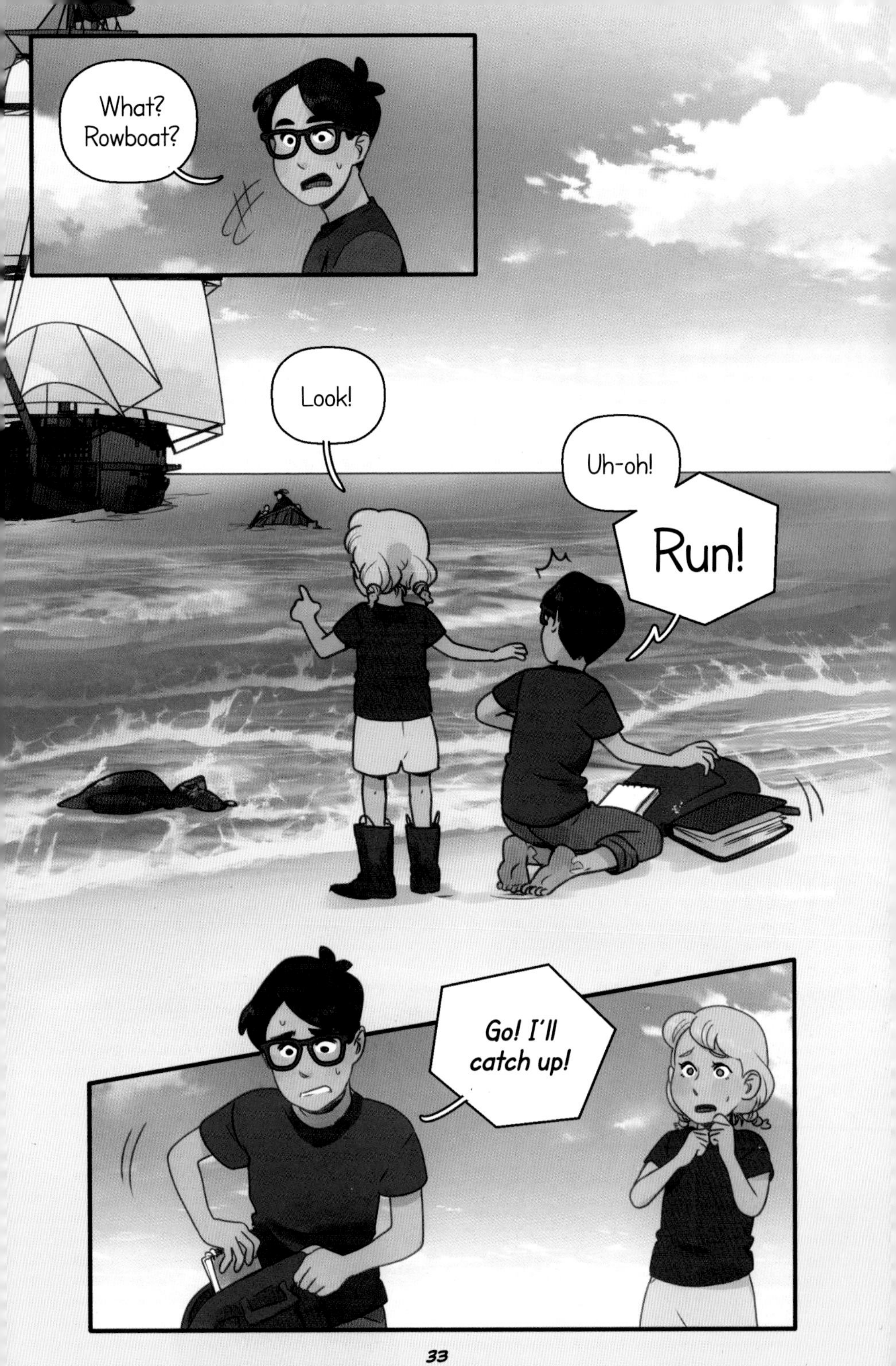
What? Rowboat?
Look!
Uh-oh!
Run!
Go! I'll catch up!

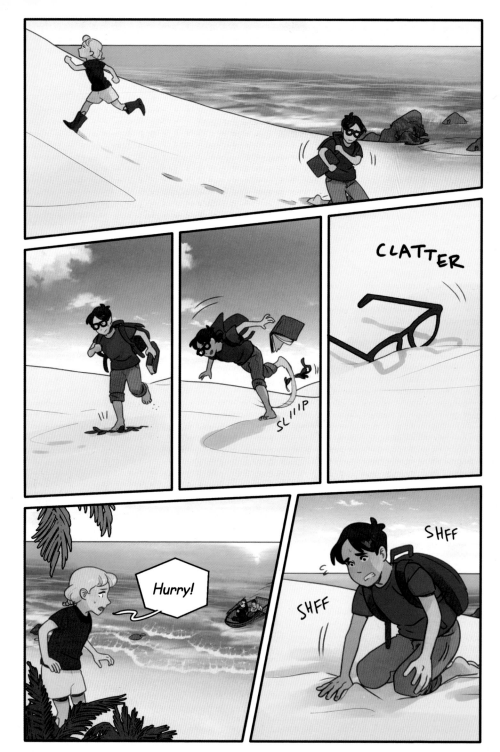

CLATTER

SLIIIP

Hurry!

SHFF

SHFF

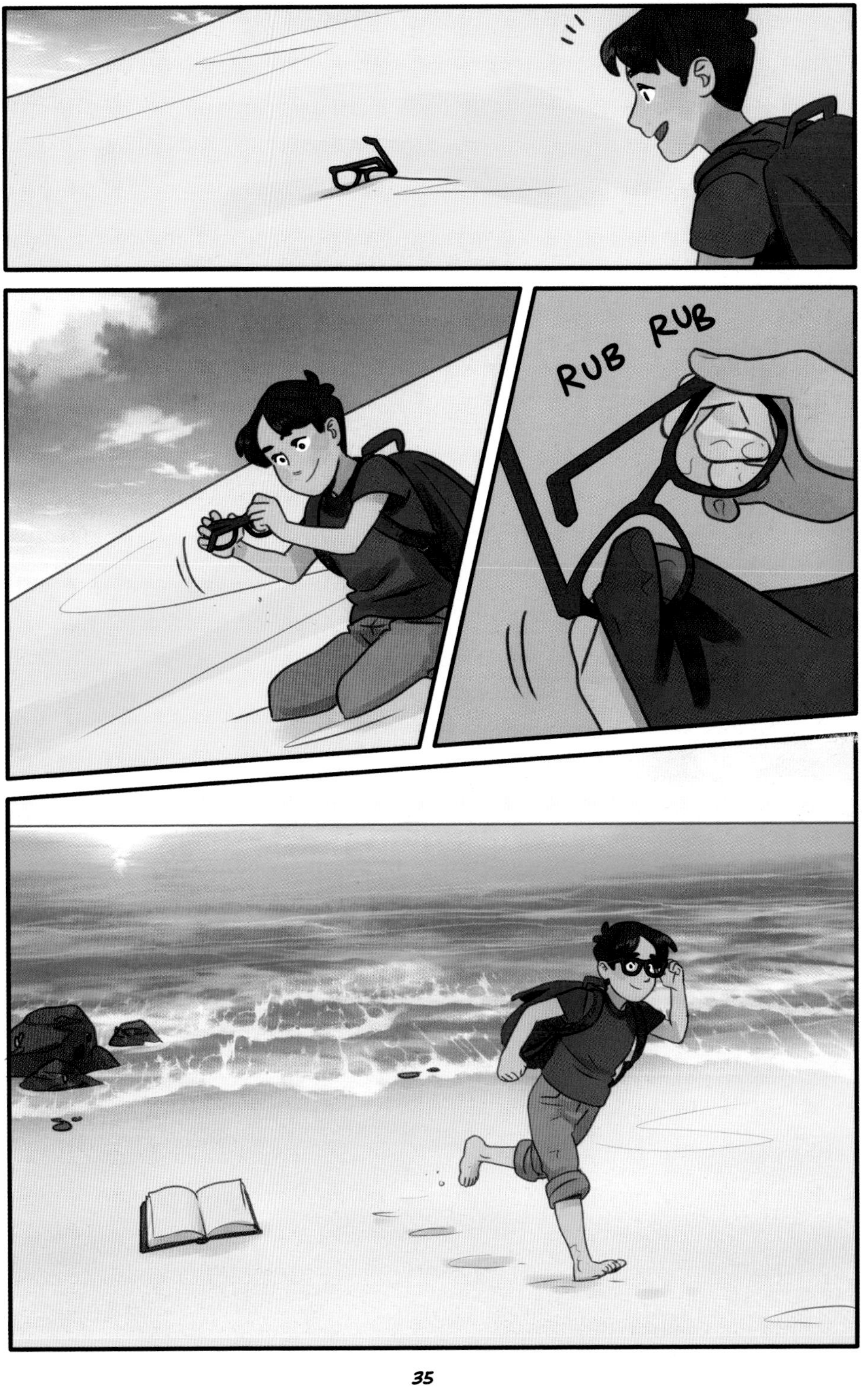
RUB RUB

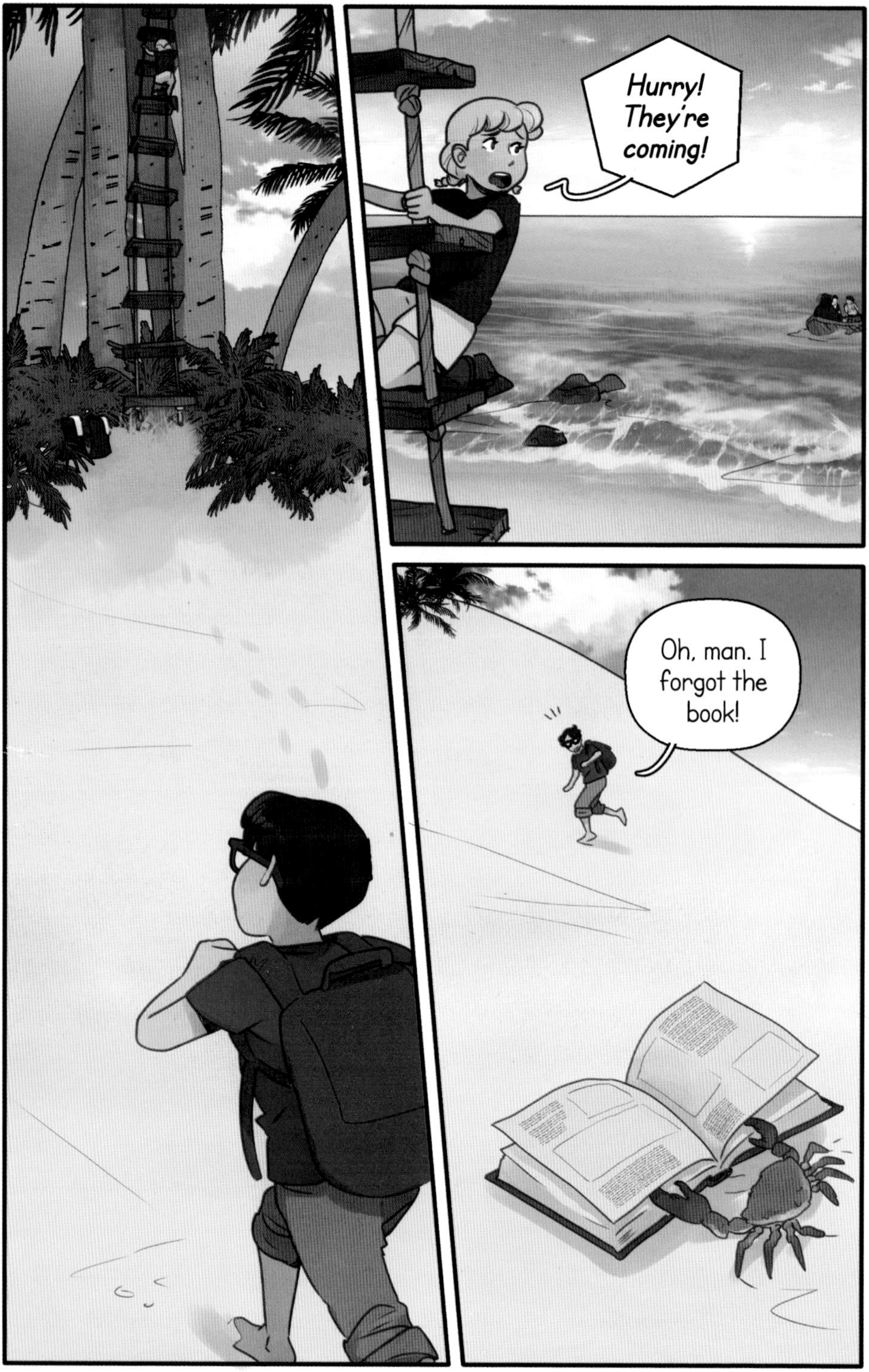
Hurry! They're coming!
Oh, man. I forgot the book!

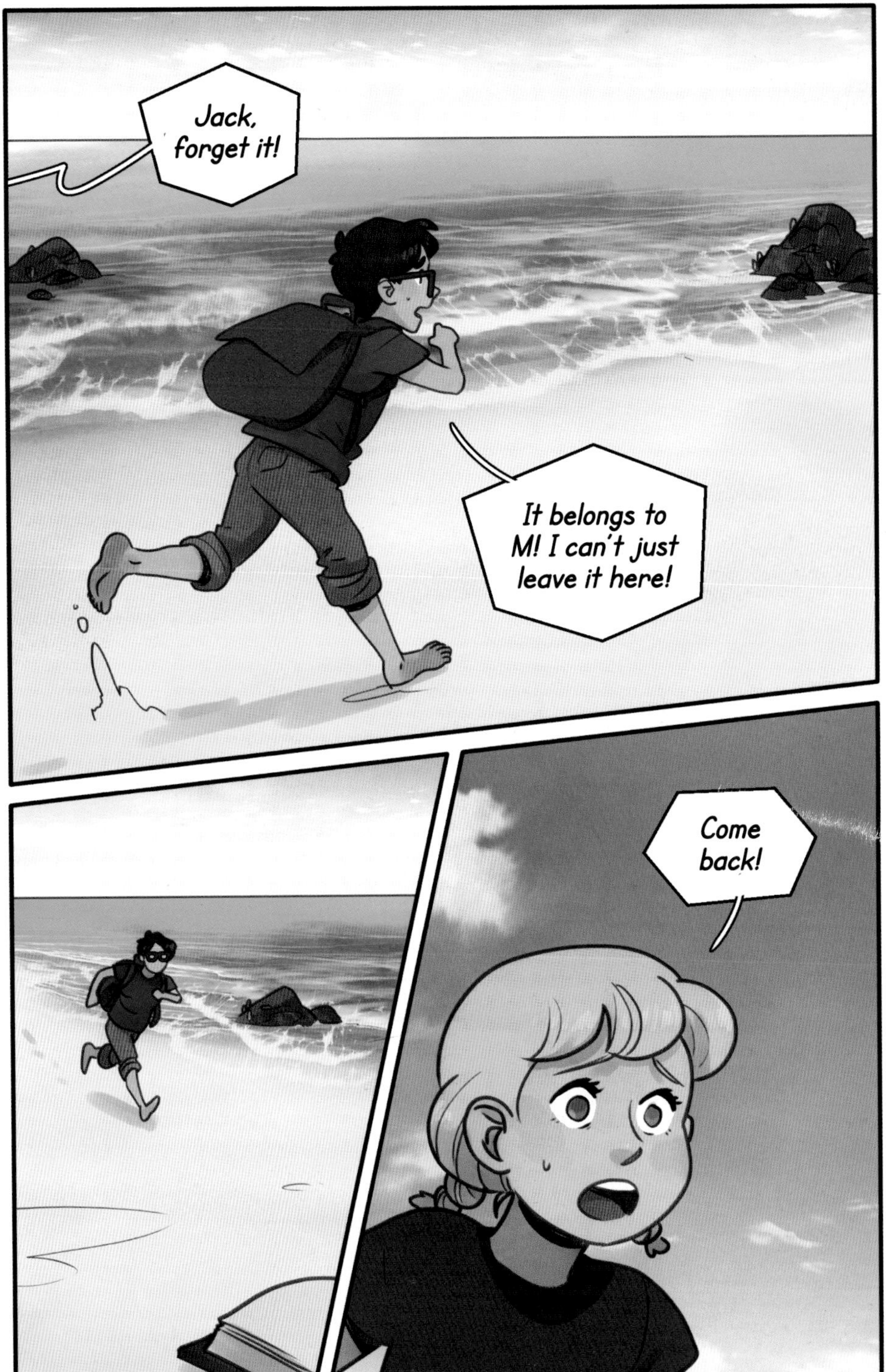
Jack, forget it!
It belongs to M! I can't just leave it here!
Come back!

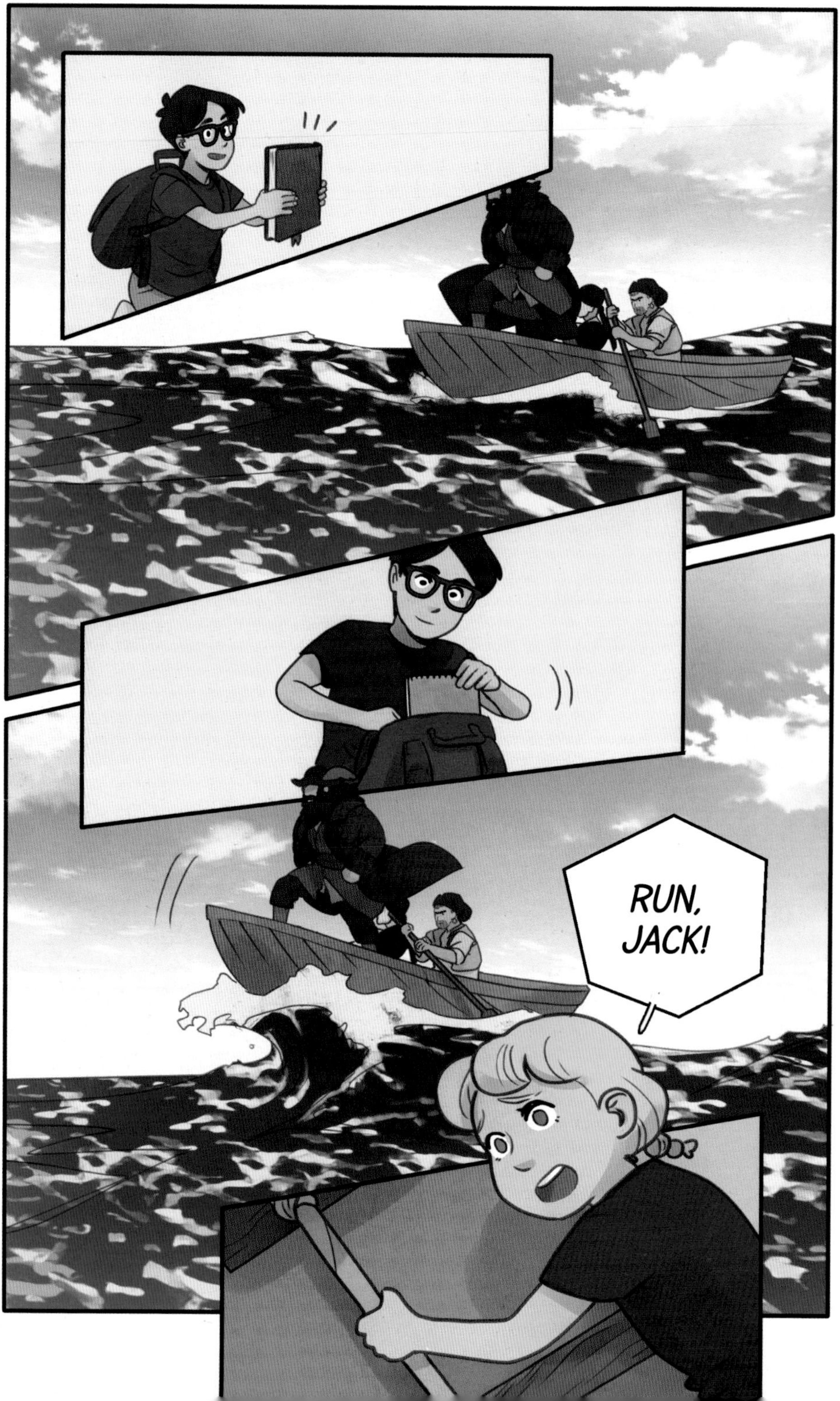
RUN, JACK!

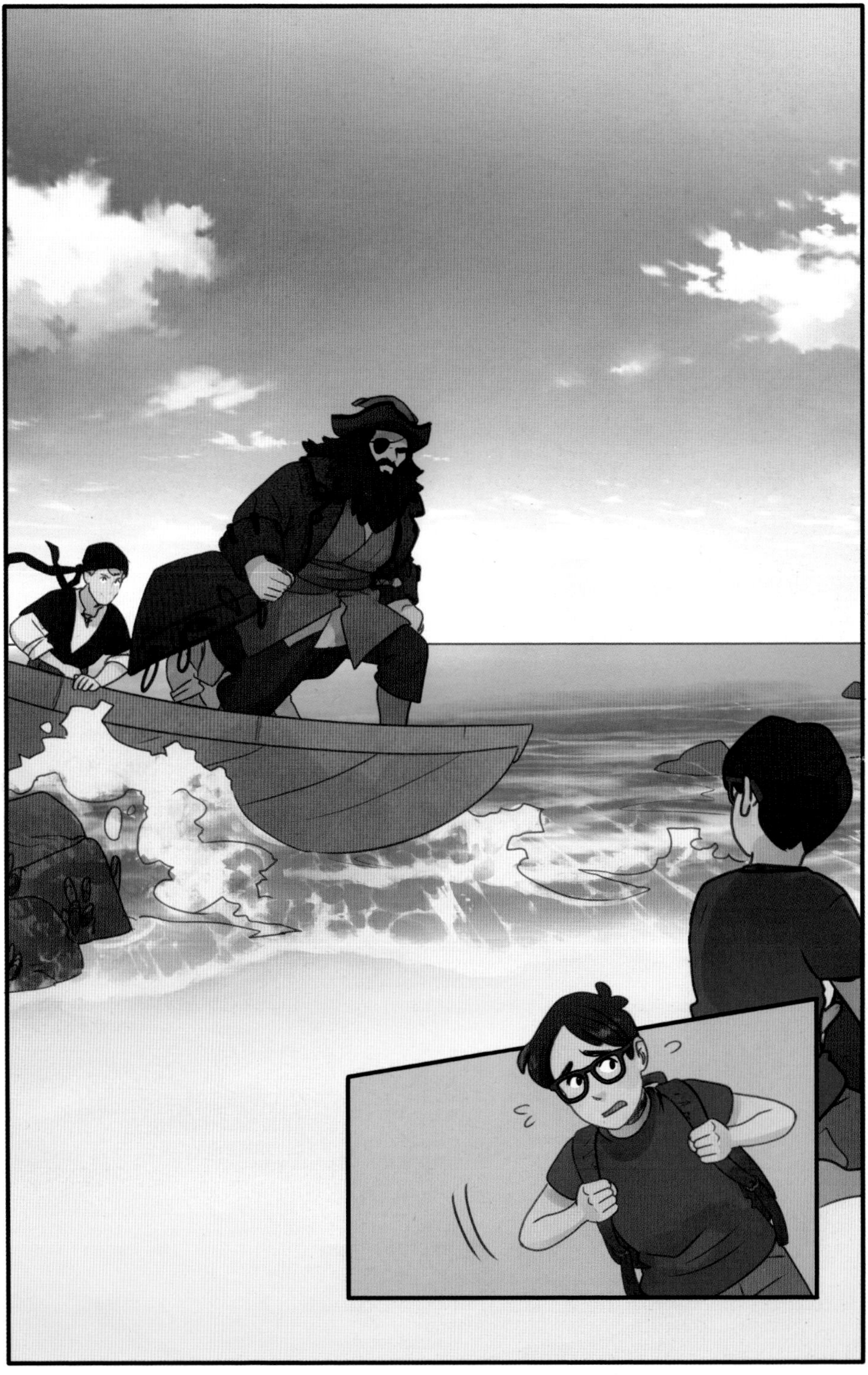

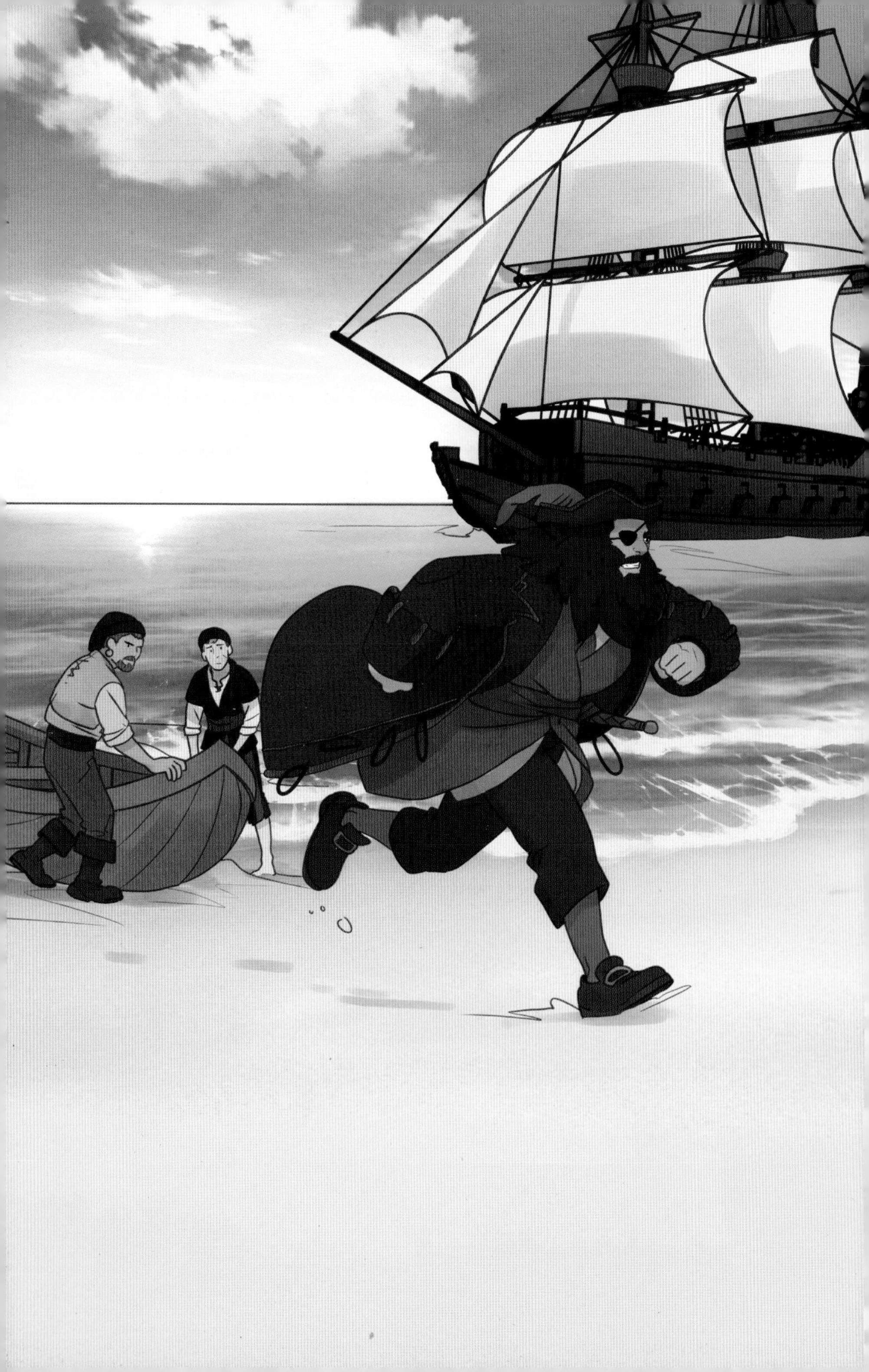

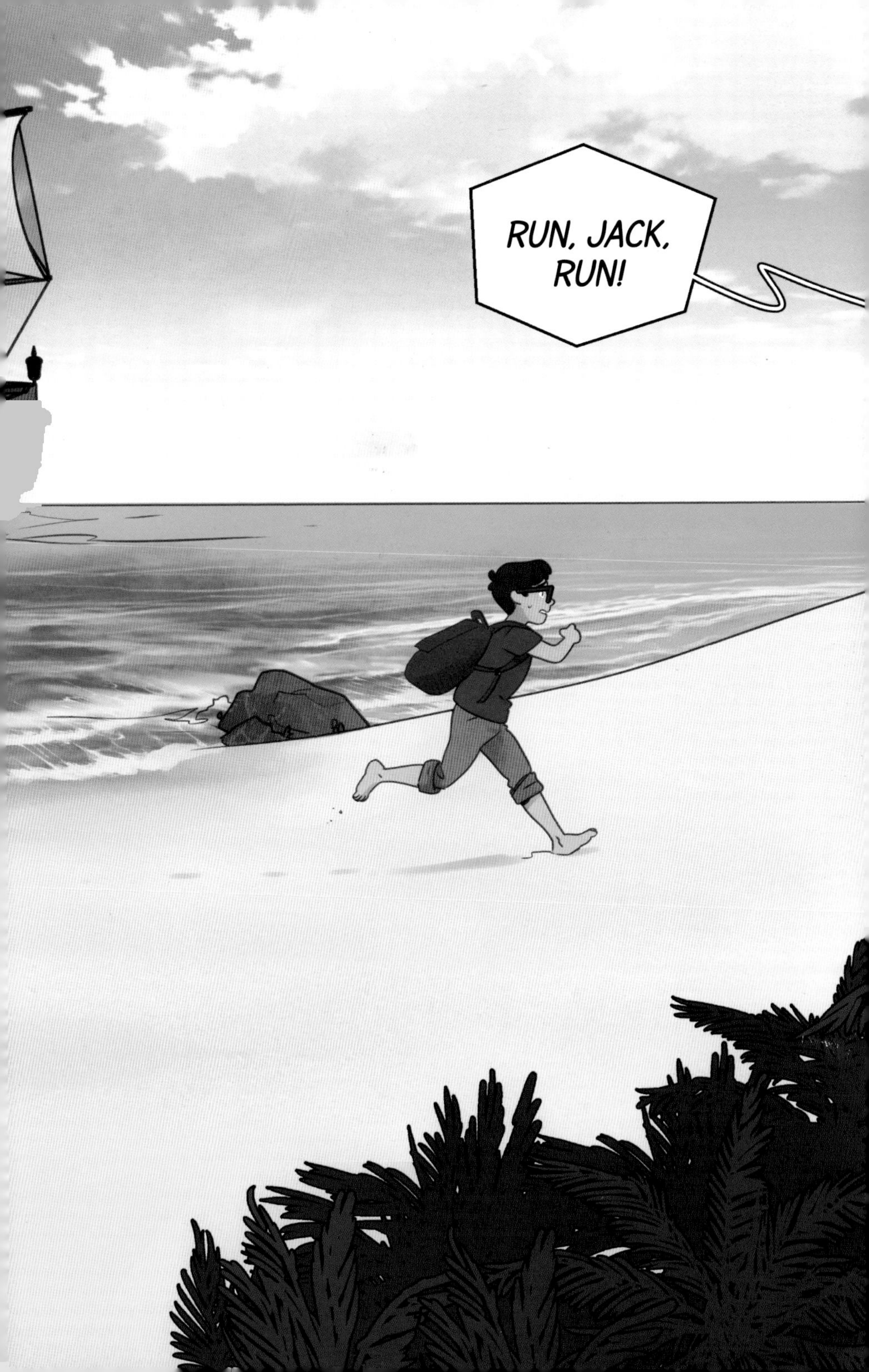
RUN, JACK, RUN!

CHAPTER FOUR

Vile Booty

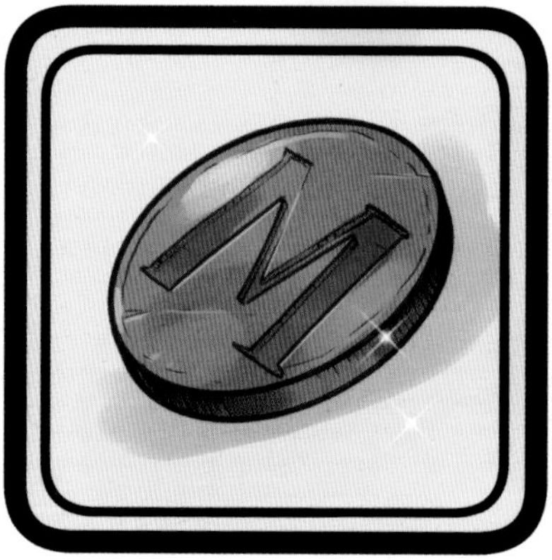
M

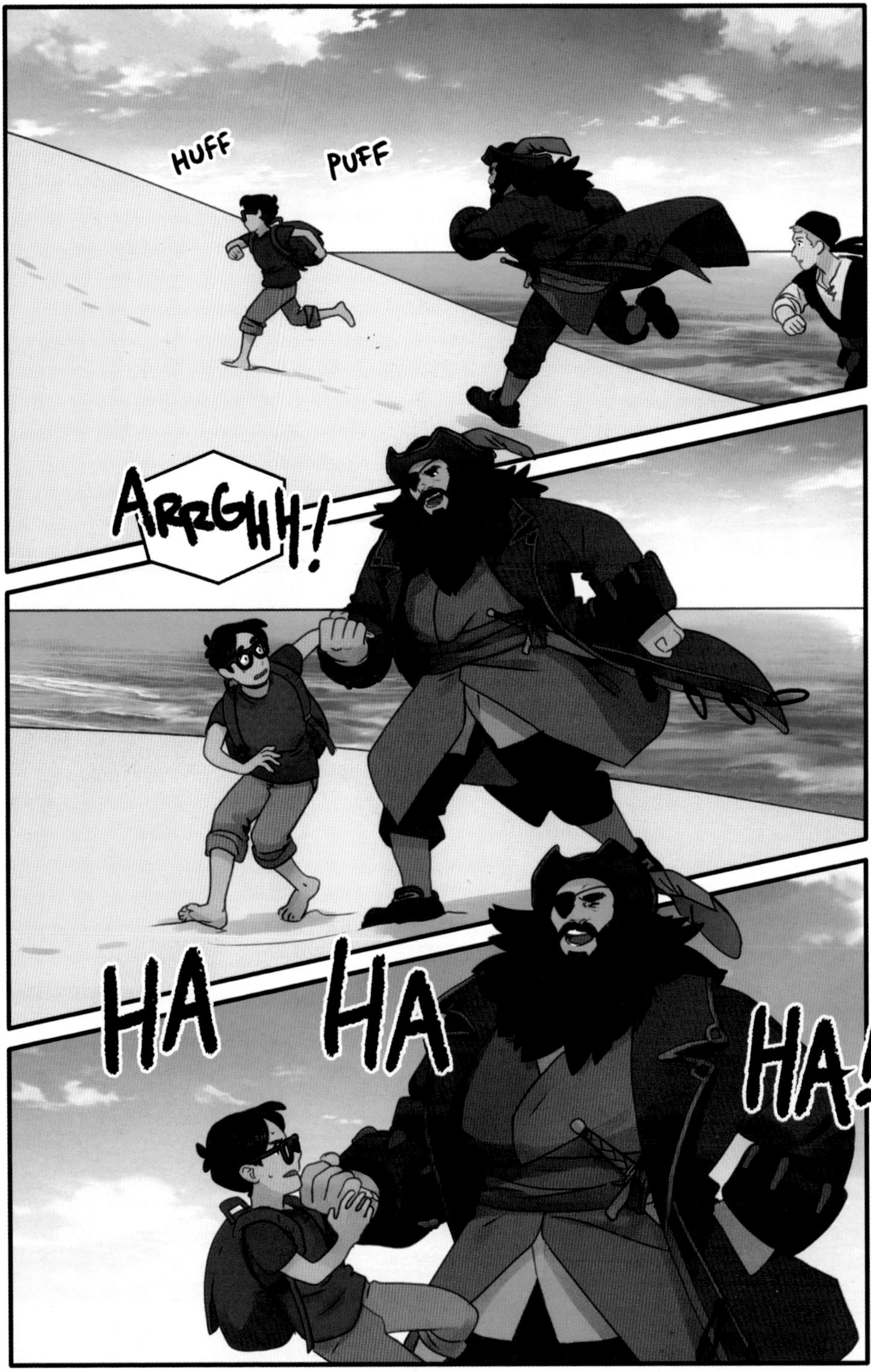
HUFF
PUFF
ARRGHH!
HA HA HA!

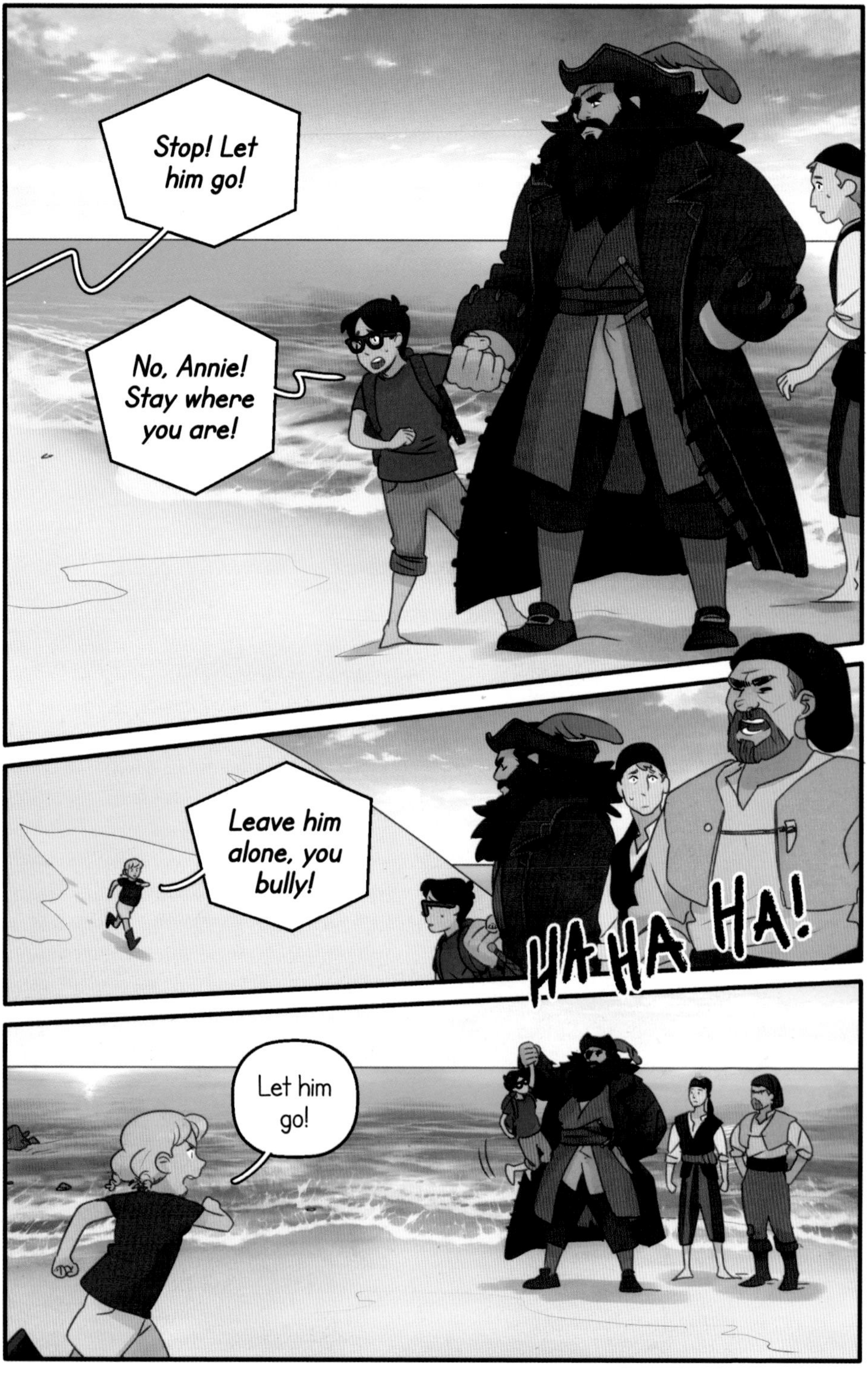

Stop! Let him go!
No, Annie! Stay where you are!
Leave him alone, you bully!
HA HA HA!
Let him go!

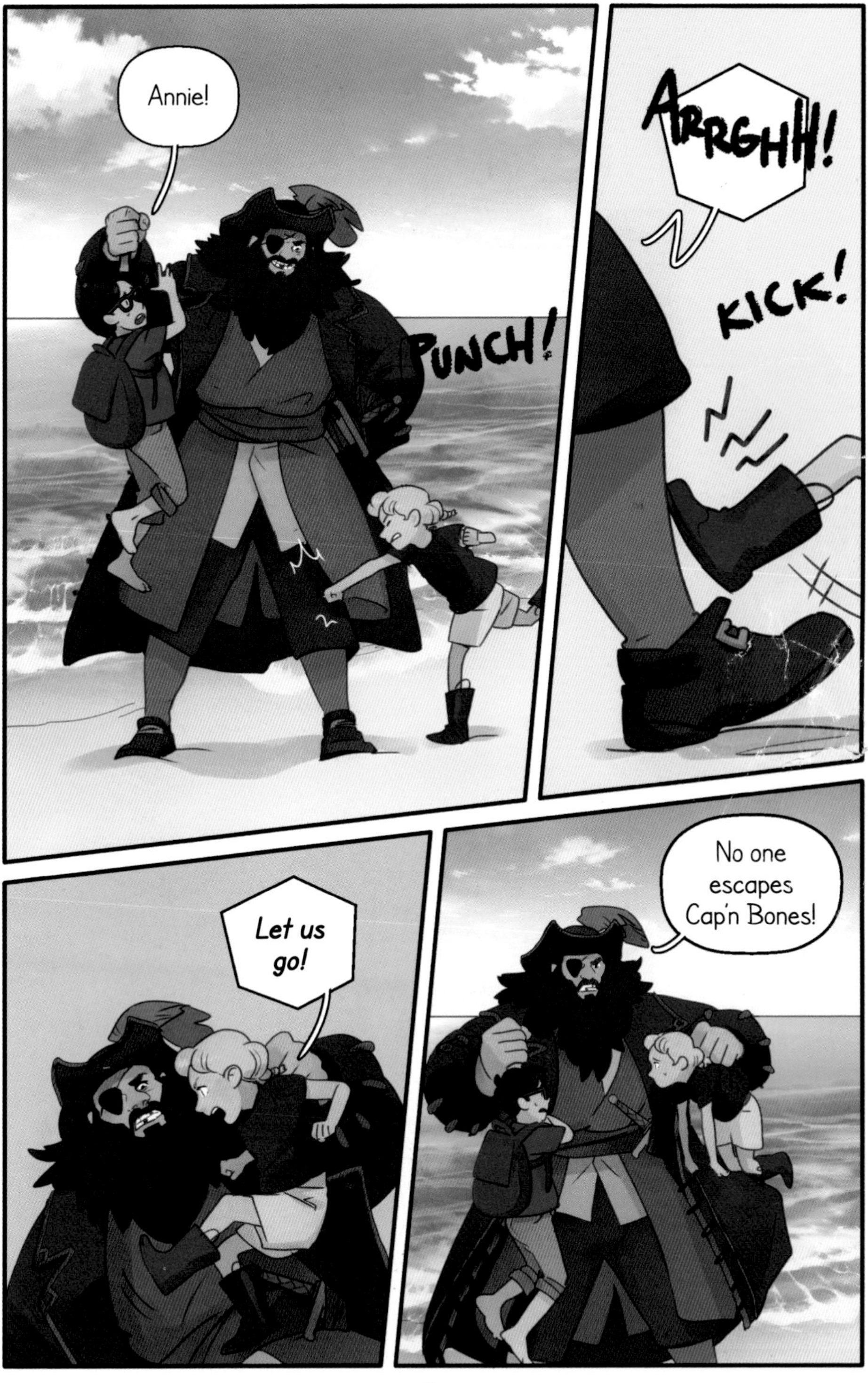
Annie!
PUNCH!
ARRGHH!
KICK!
Let us go!
No one escapes Cap'n Bones!

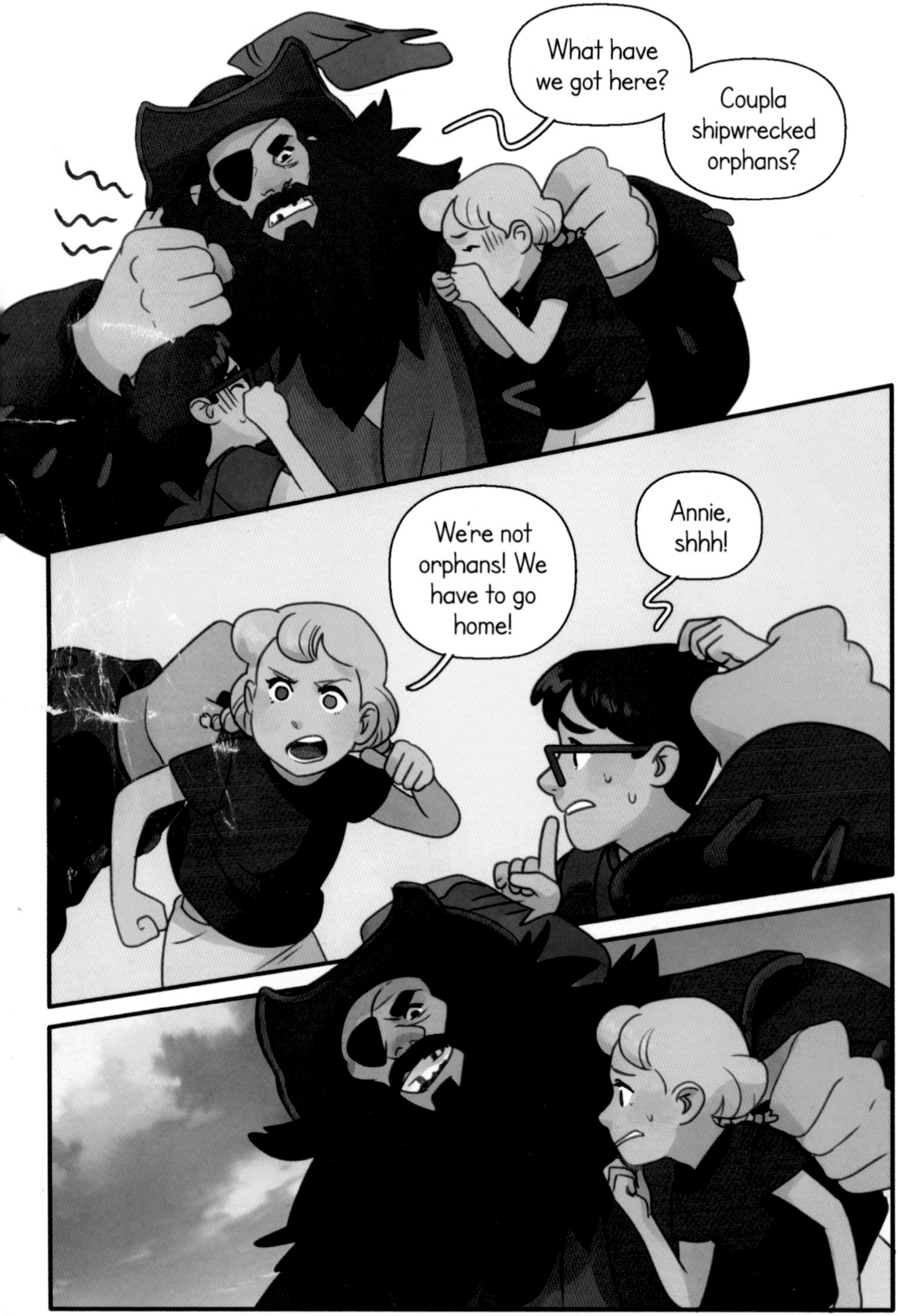
What have we got here?
Coupla shipwrecked orphans?
We're not orphans! We have to go home!
Annie, shhh!

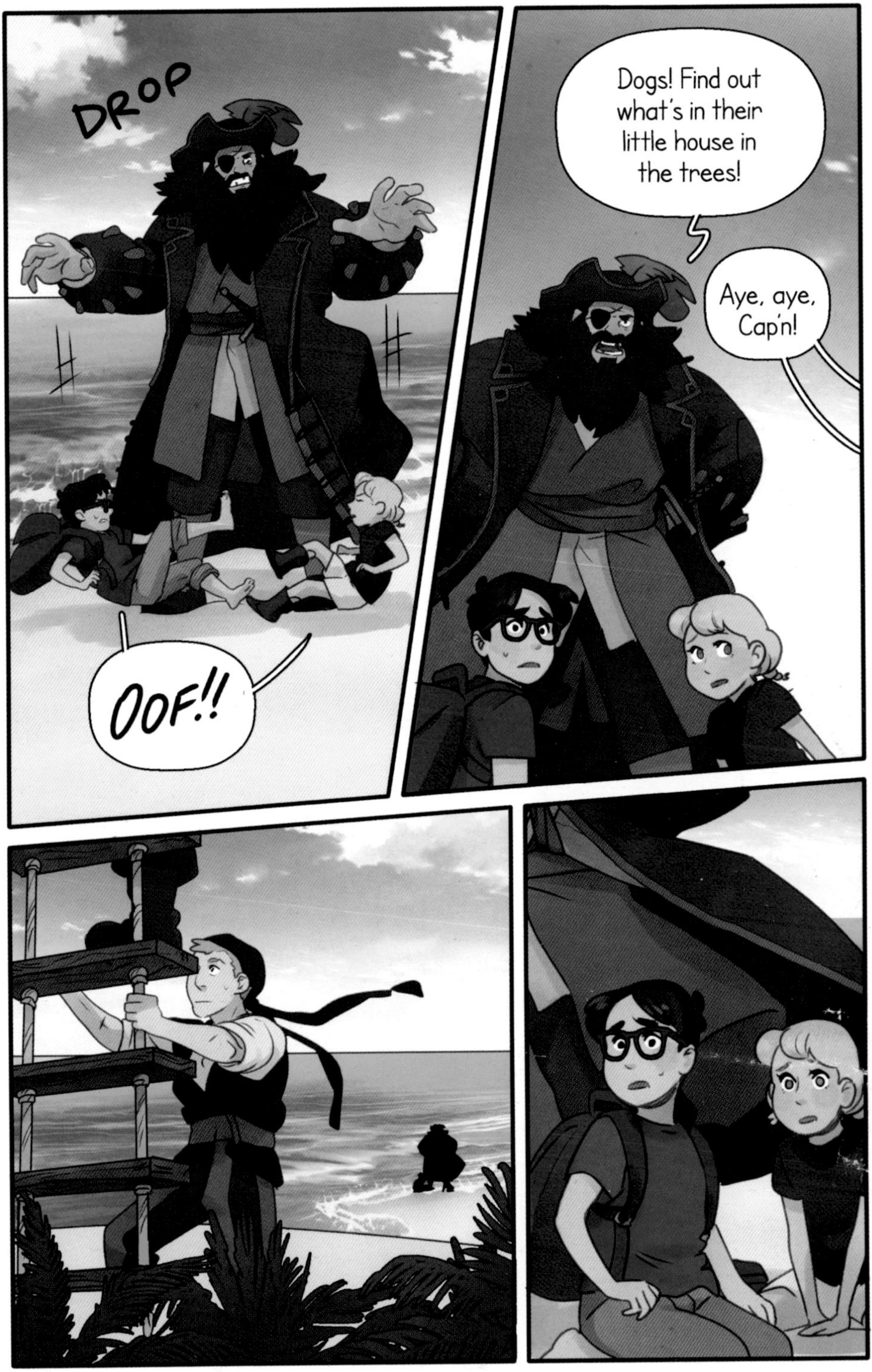
DROP
OOF!!
Dogs! Find out what's in their little house in the trees!
Aye, aye, Cap'n!

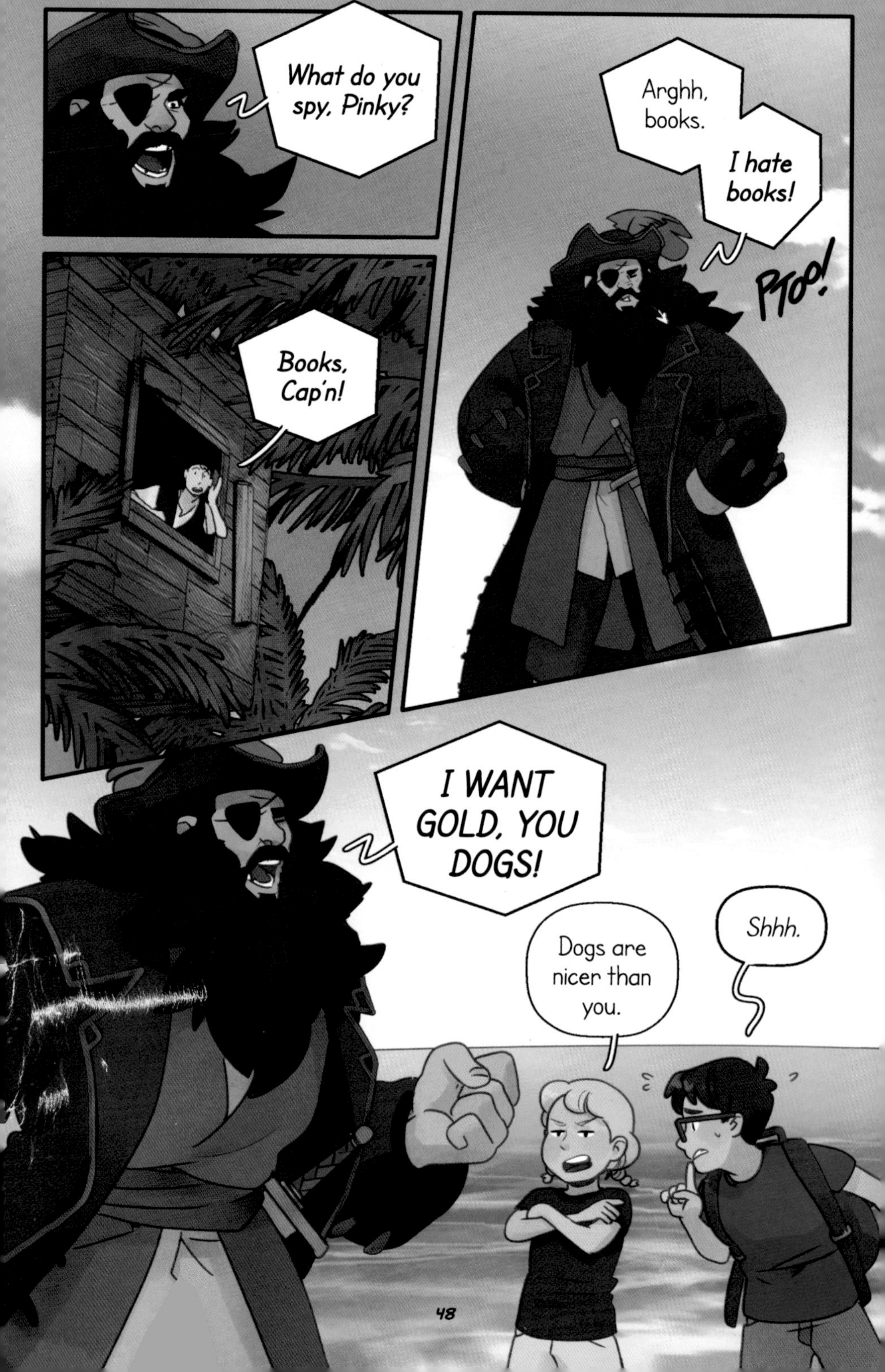
What do you spy, Pinky?
Arghh, books.
I hate books!
PTOO!
Books, Cap'n!
I WANT GOLD, YOU DOGS!
Dogs are nicer than you.
Shhh.

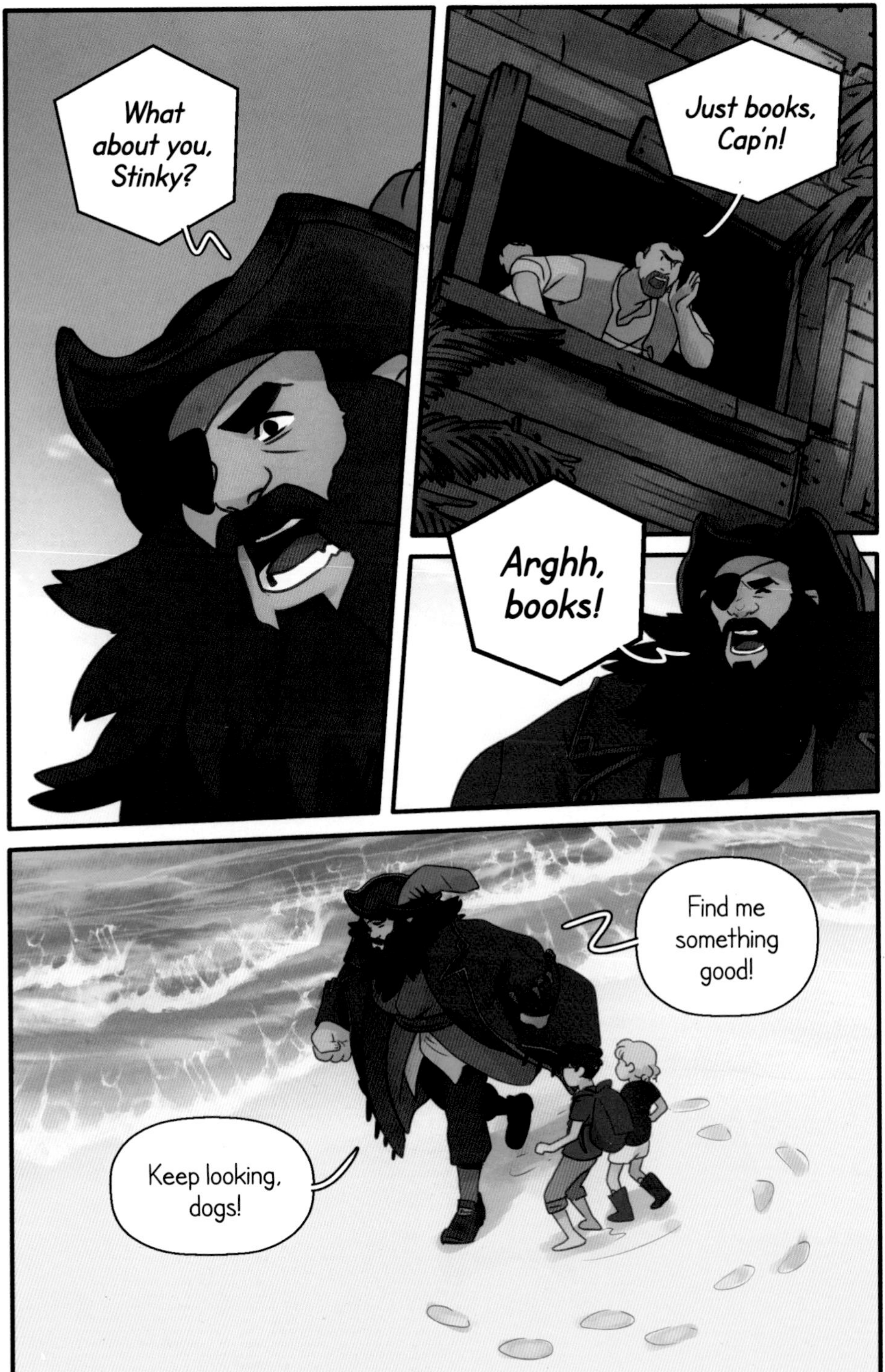
What about you, Stinky?
Just books, Cap'n!
Arghh, books!
Find me something good!
Keep looking, dogs!

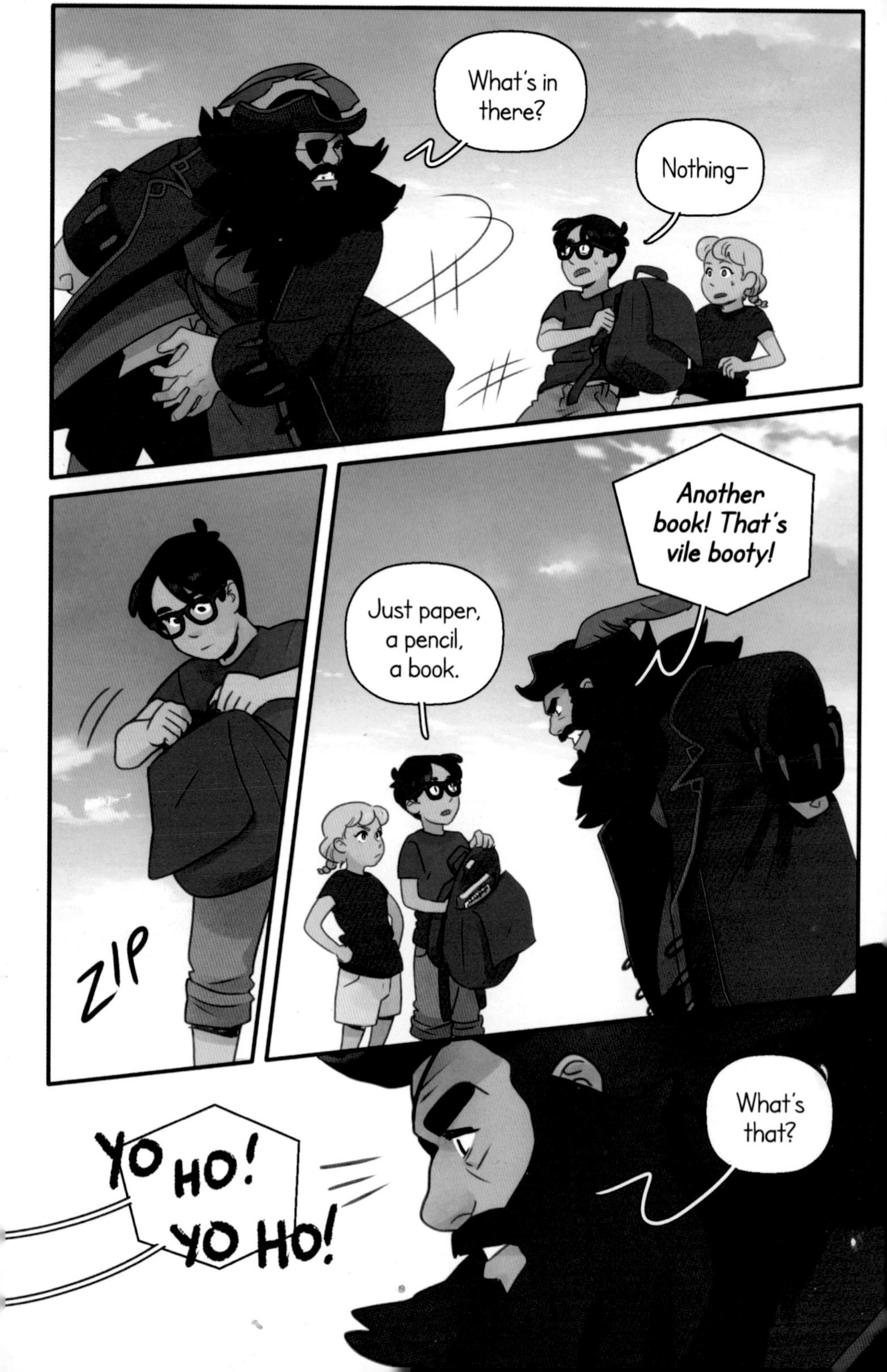
What's in there?
Nothing–
Another book! That's vile booty!
ZIP
Just paper, a pencil, a book.
YO HO! YO HO!
What's that?

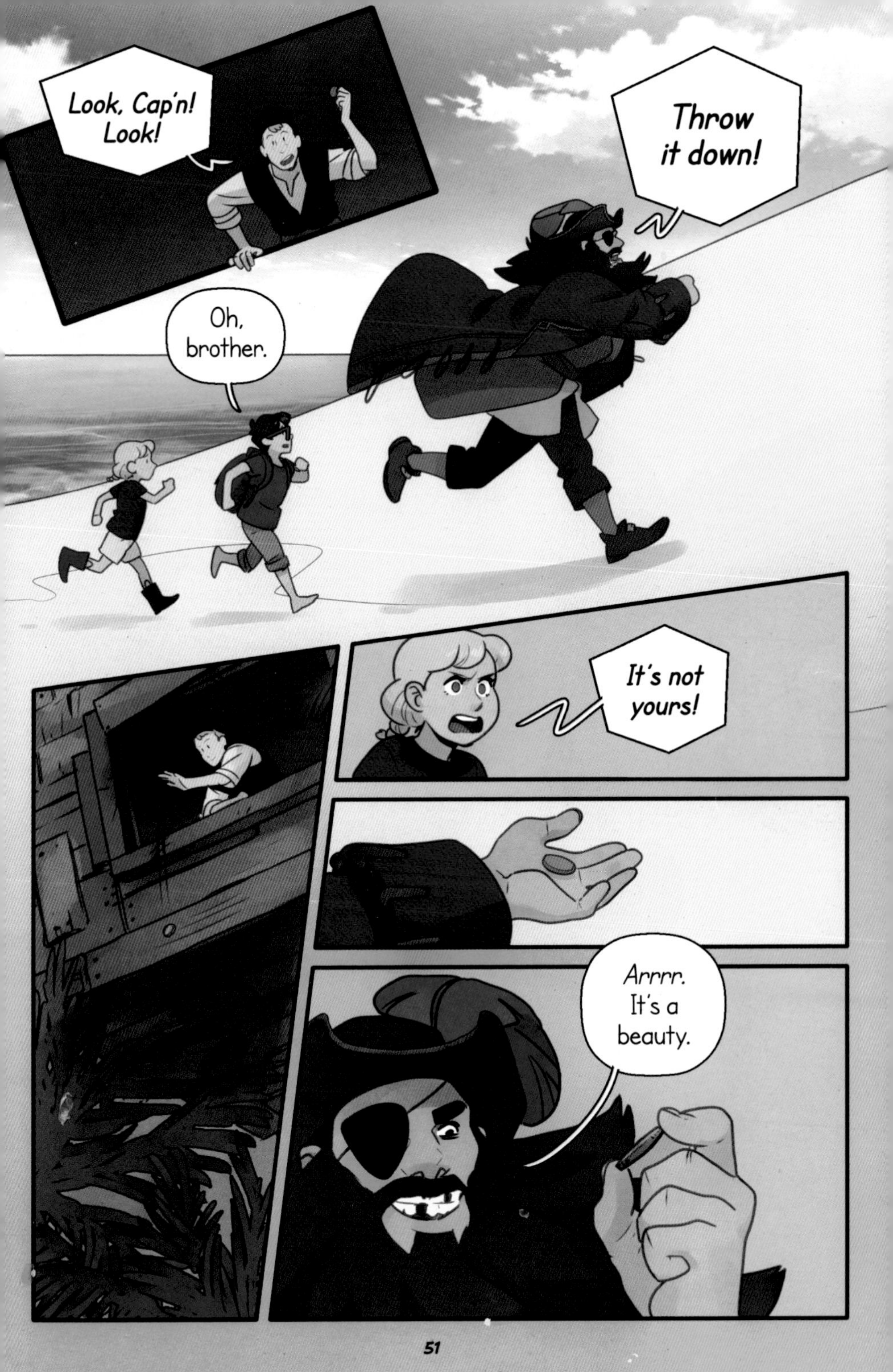
Look, Cap'n! Look!
Throw it down!
Oh, brother.
It's not yours!
Arrrr. It's a beauty.

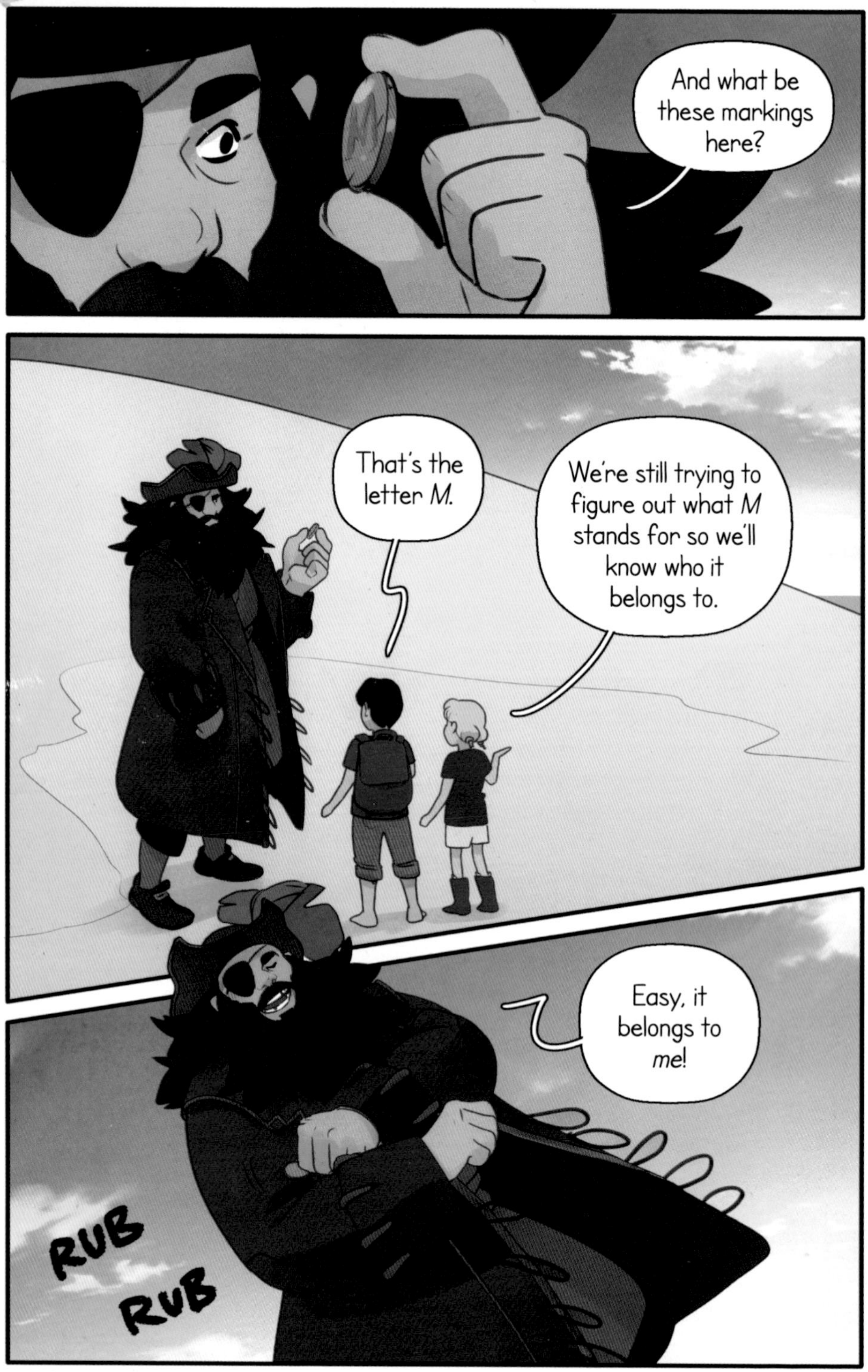
And what be these markings here?
That's the letter *M*.
We're still trying to figure out what *M* stands for so we'll know who it belongs to.
Easy, it belongs to *me*!
RUB RUB

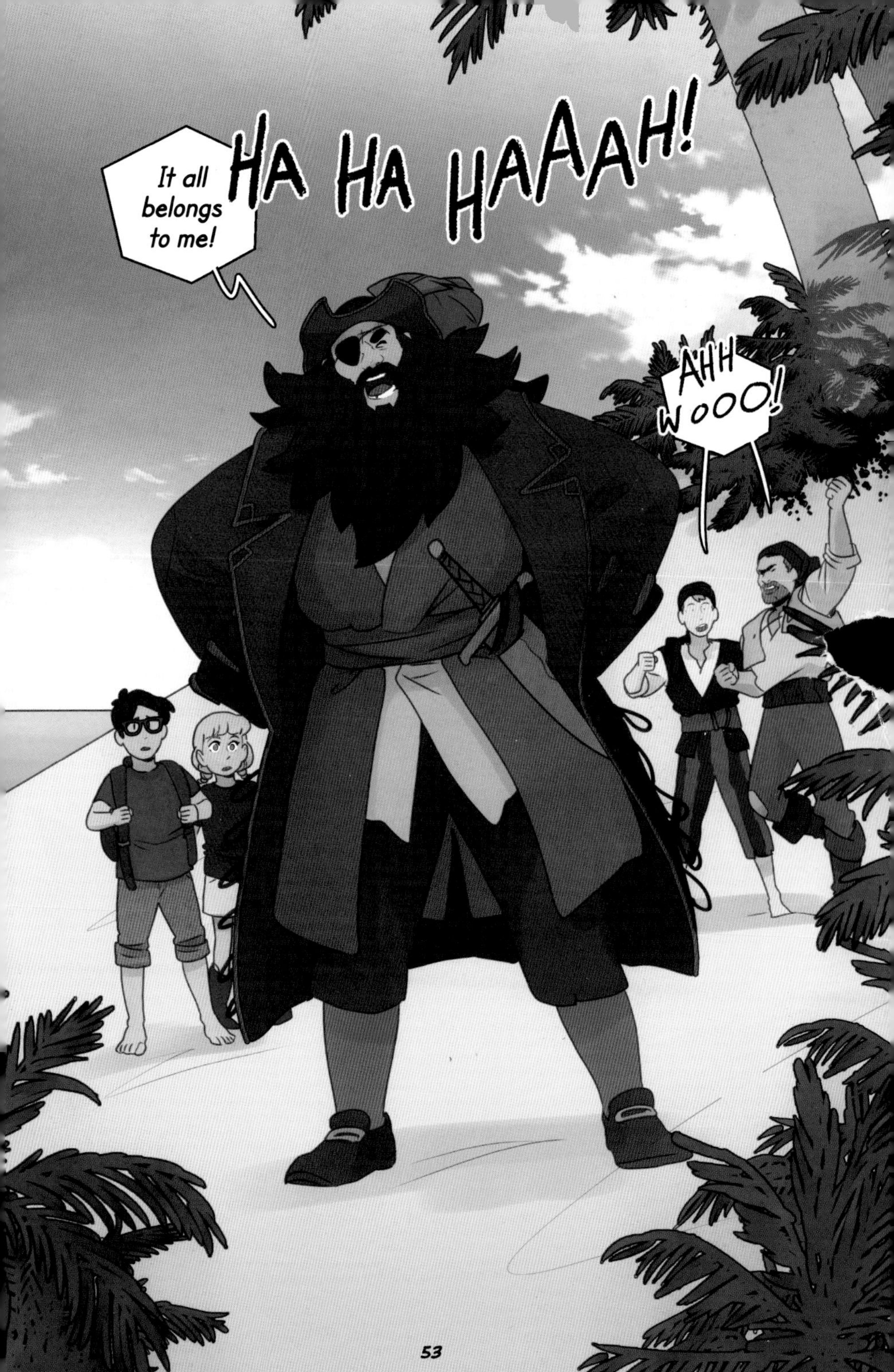
HA HA HAAAH!
It all belongs to me!
AHH WOOO!

CHAPTER FIVE
The Kid's Treasure

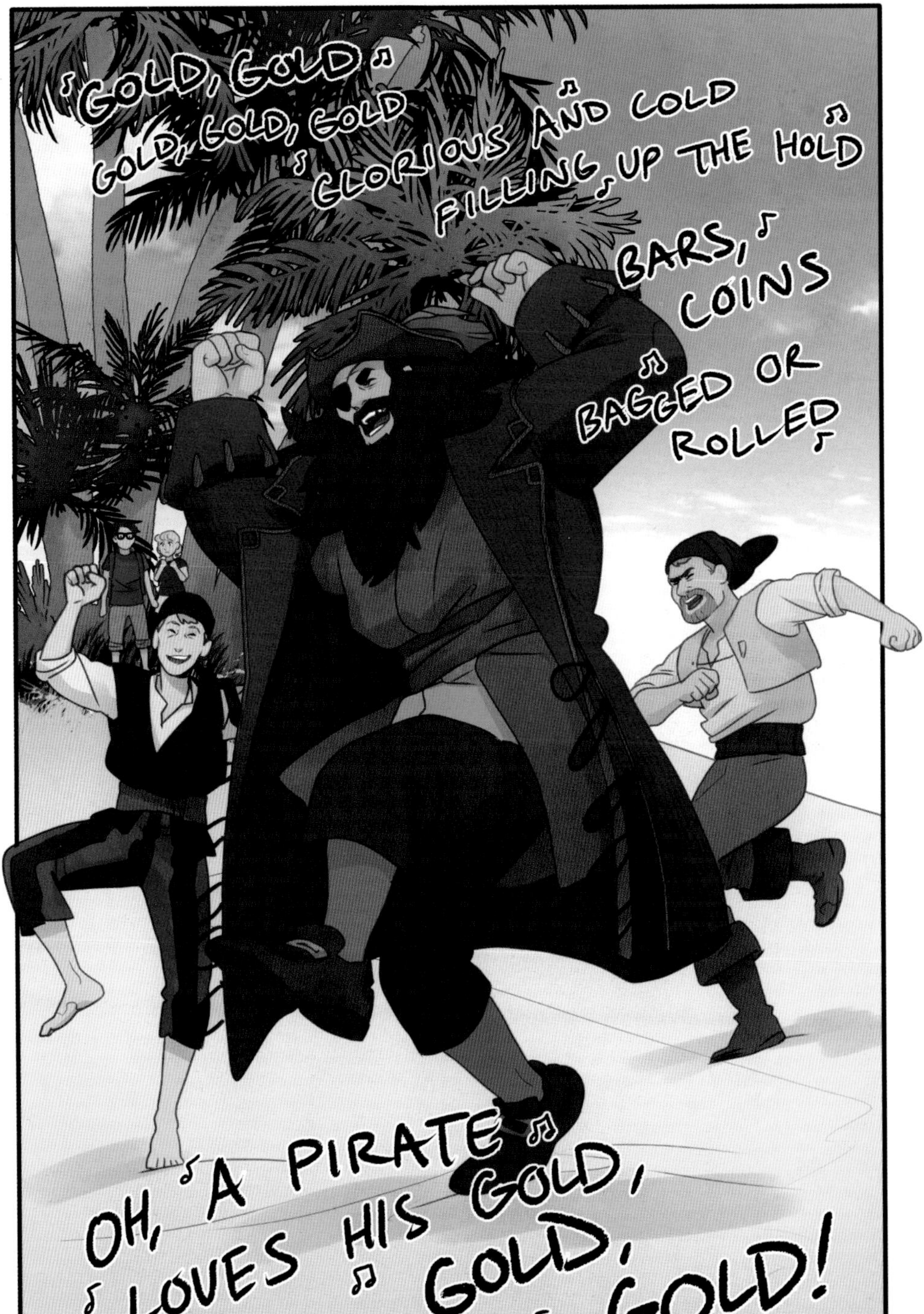
GOLD, GOLD
GOLD, GOLD, GOLD
GLORIOUS AND COLD
FILLING UP THE HOLD
BARS, COINS
BAGGED OR ROLLED
OH, A PIRATE LOVES HIS GOLD, GOLD, GOLD!

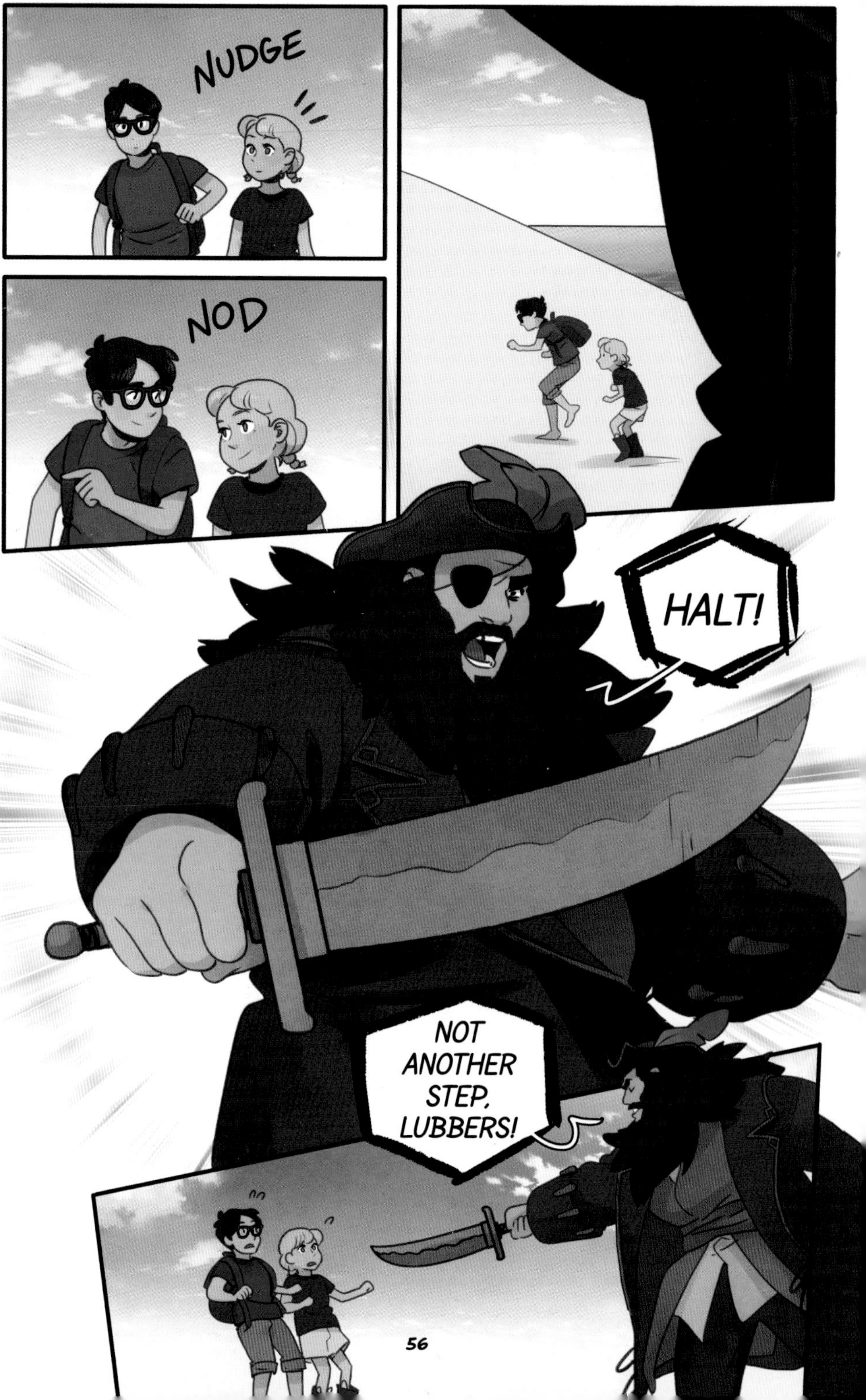
NUDGE
NOD
HALT!
NOT ANOTHER STEP, LUBBERS!

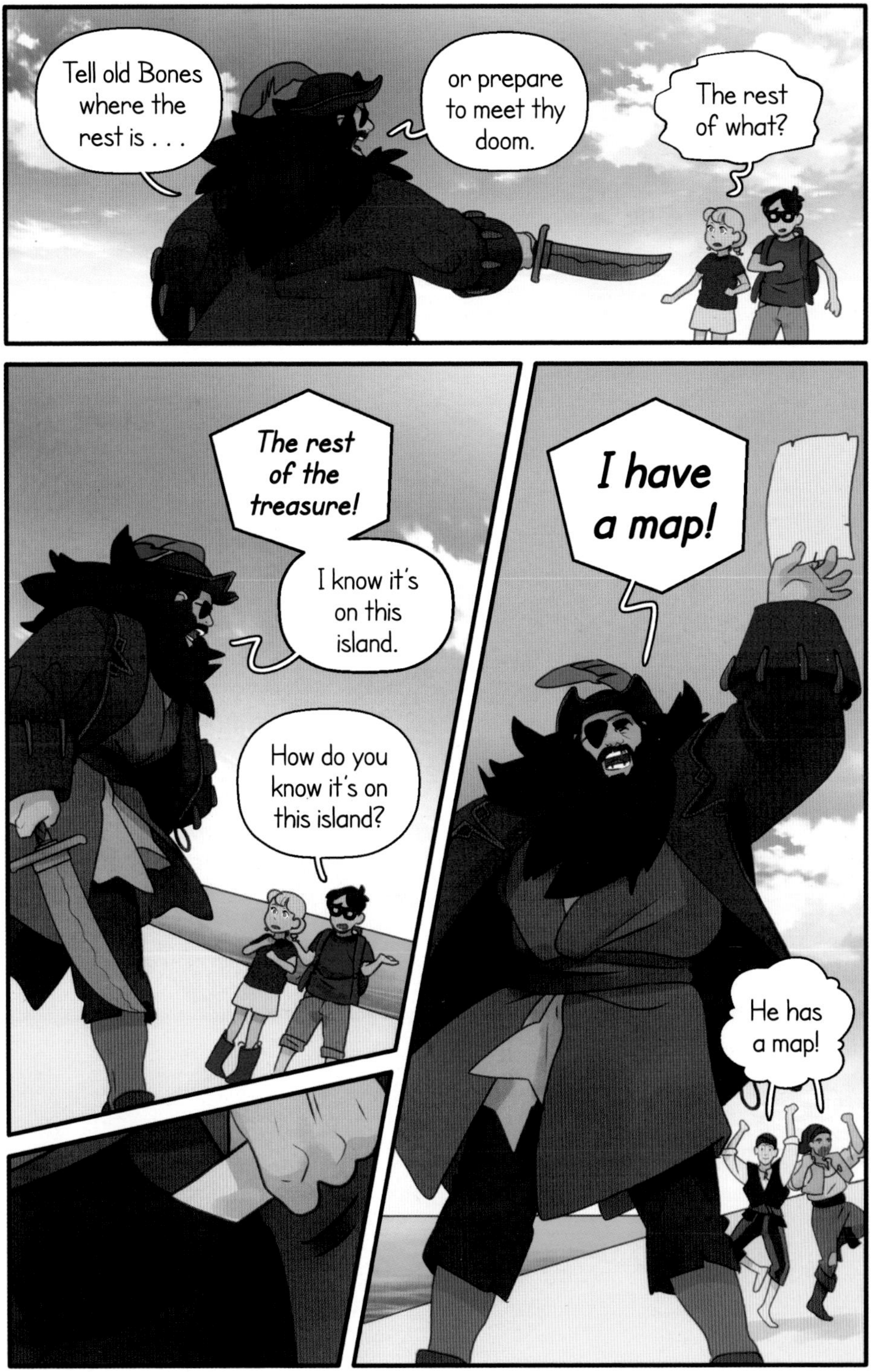
Tell old Bones where the rest is . . .
or prepare to meet thy doom.
The rest of what?
The rest of the treasure!
I know it's on this island.
How do you know it's on this island?
I have a map!
He has a map!

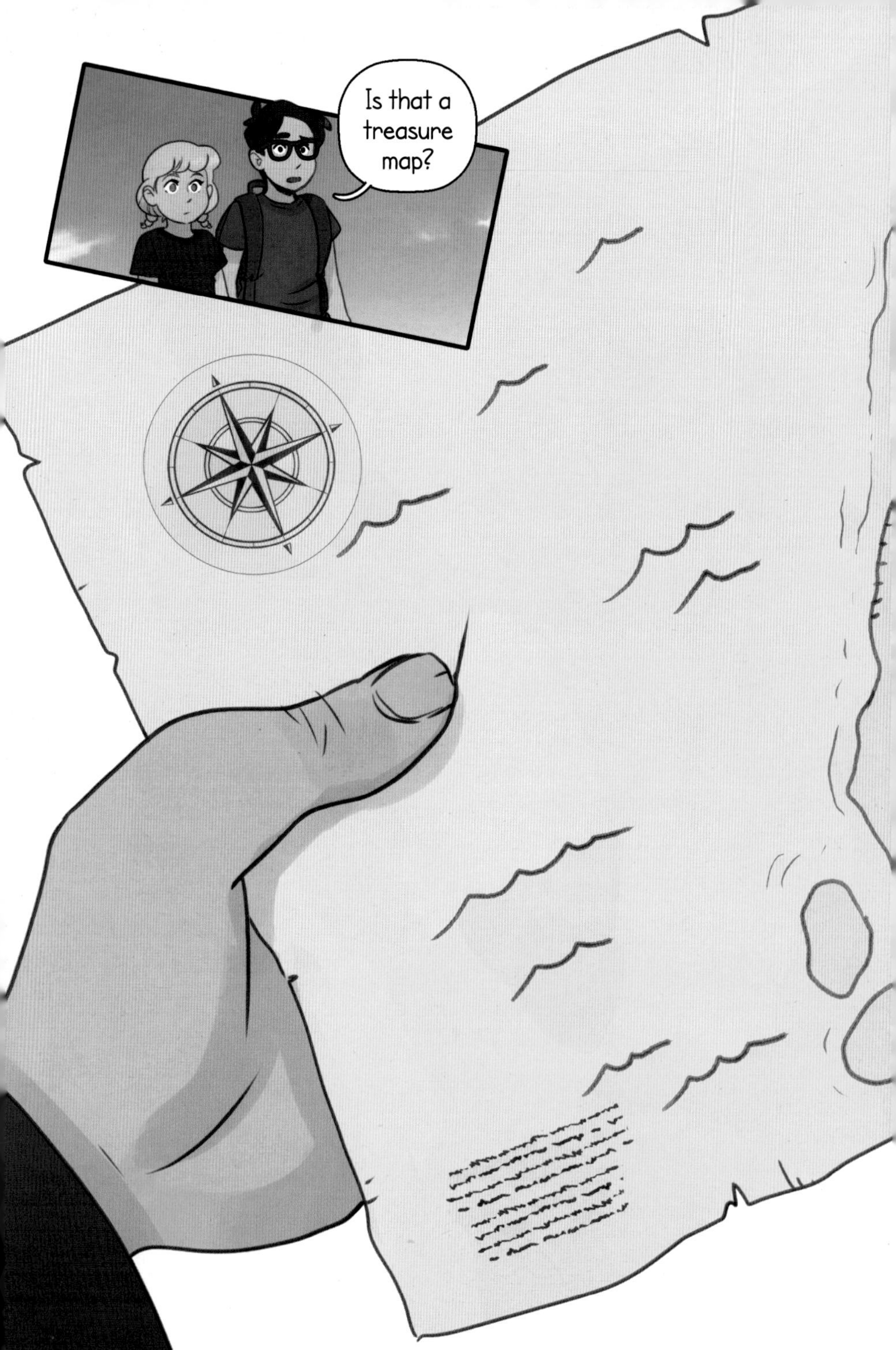
Is that a treasure map?

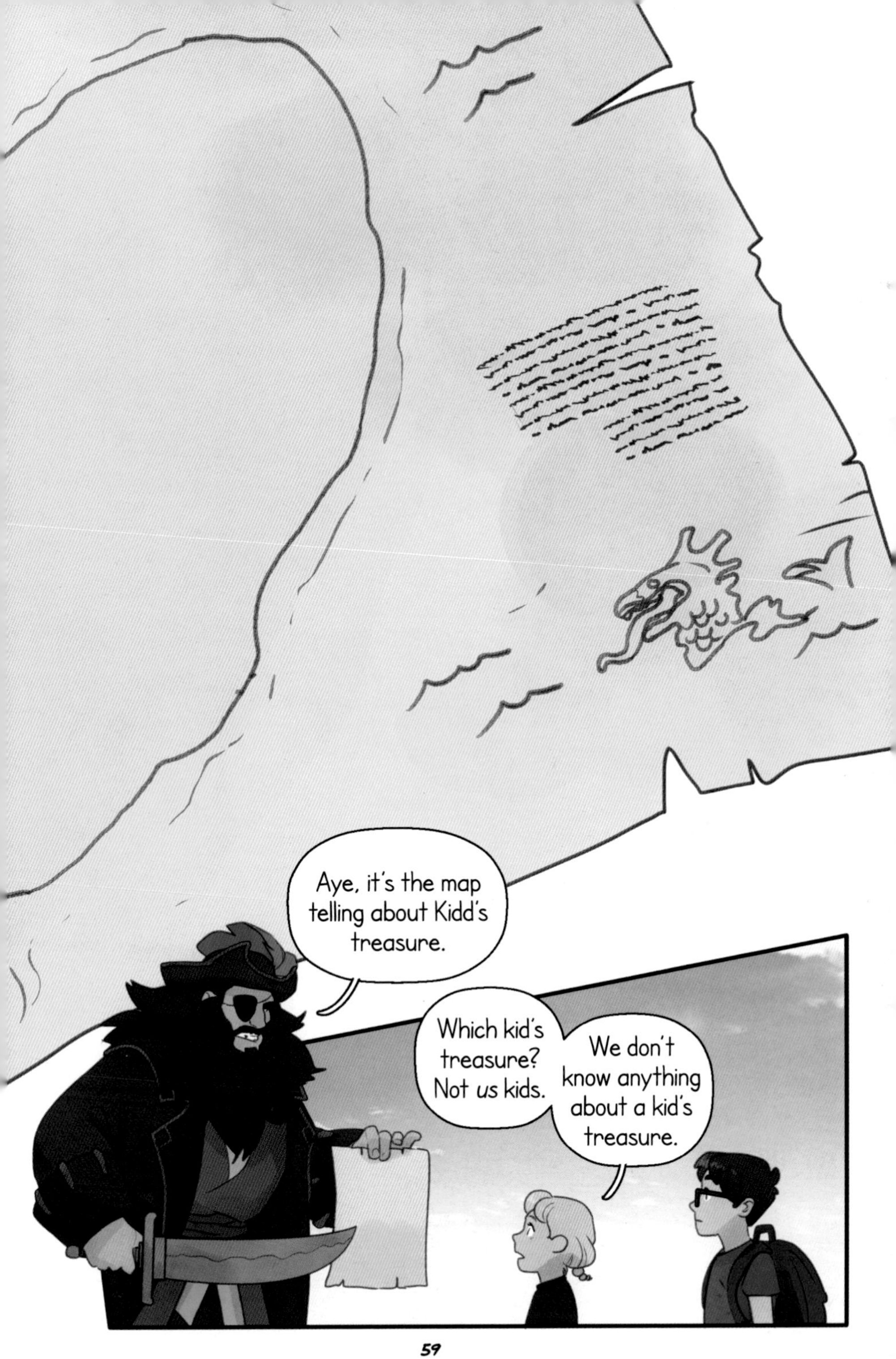

Aye, it's the map telling about Kidd's treasure.
Which kid's treasure? Not *us* kids.
We don't know anything about a kid's treasure.

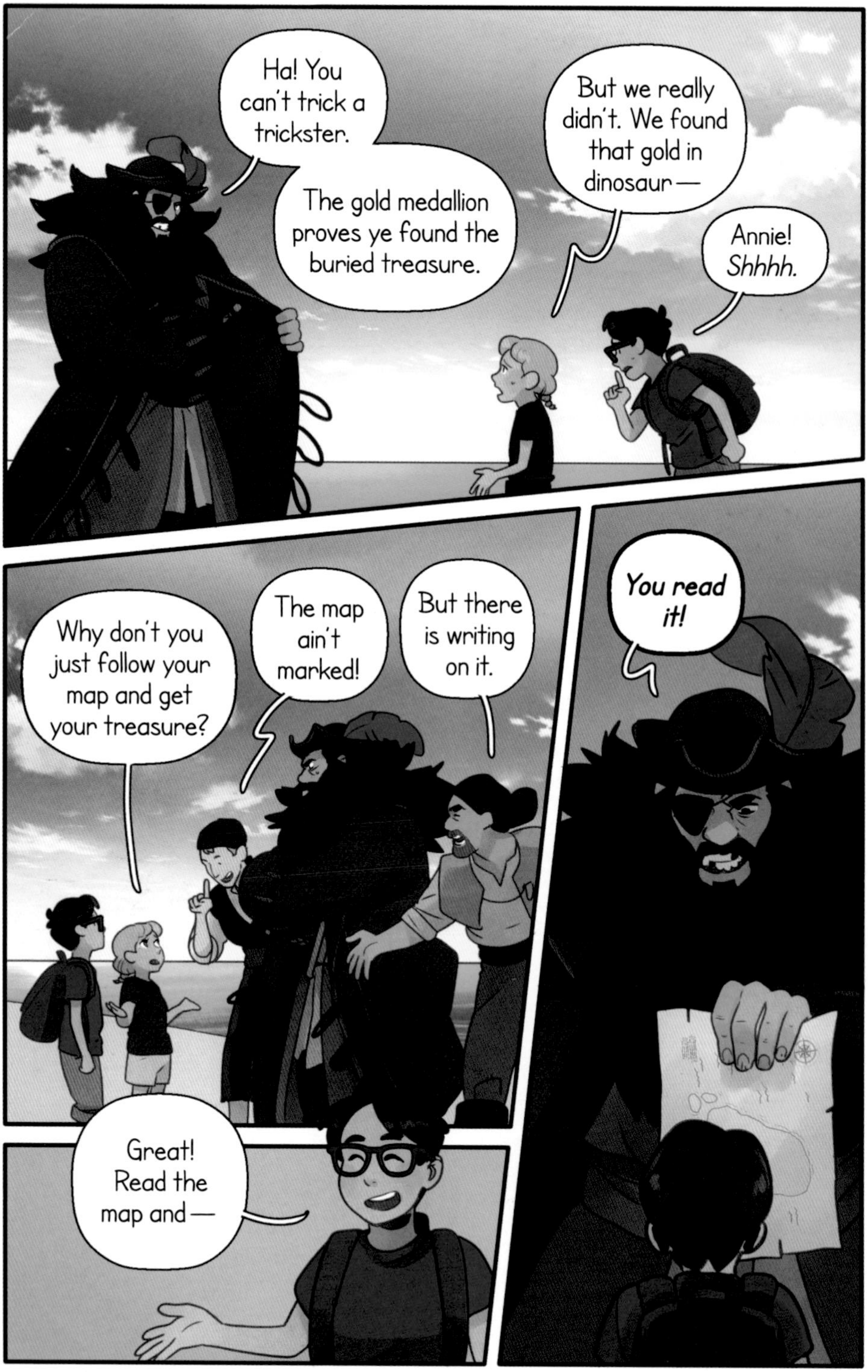

Ha! You can't trick a trickster.
The gold medallion proves ye found the buried treasure.
But we really didn't. We found that gold in dinosaur—
Annie! *Shhhh.*
Why don't you just follow your map and get your treasure?
The map ain't marked!
But there is writing on it.
Great! Read the map and—
You read it!

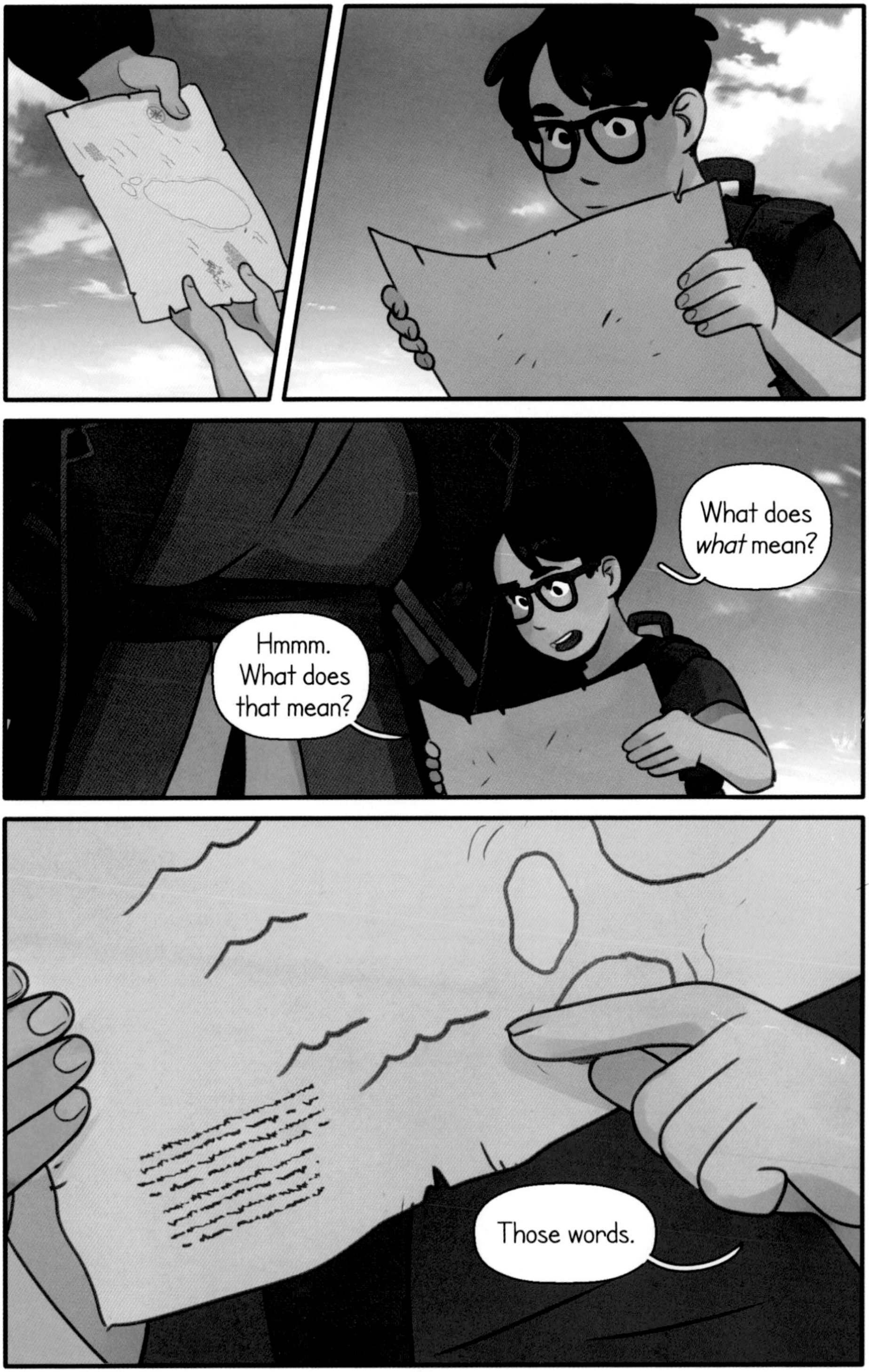
What does
what mean?
Hmmm.
What does
that mean?
Those words.

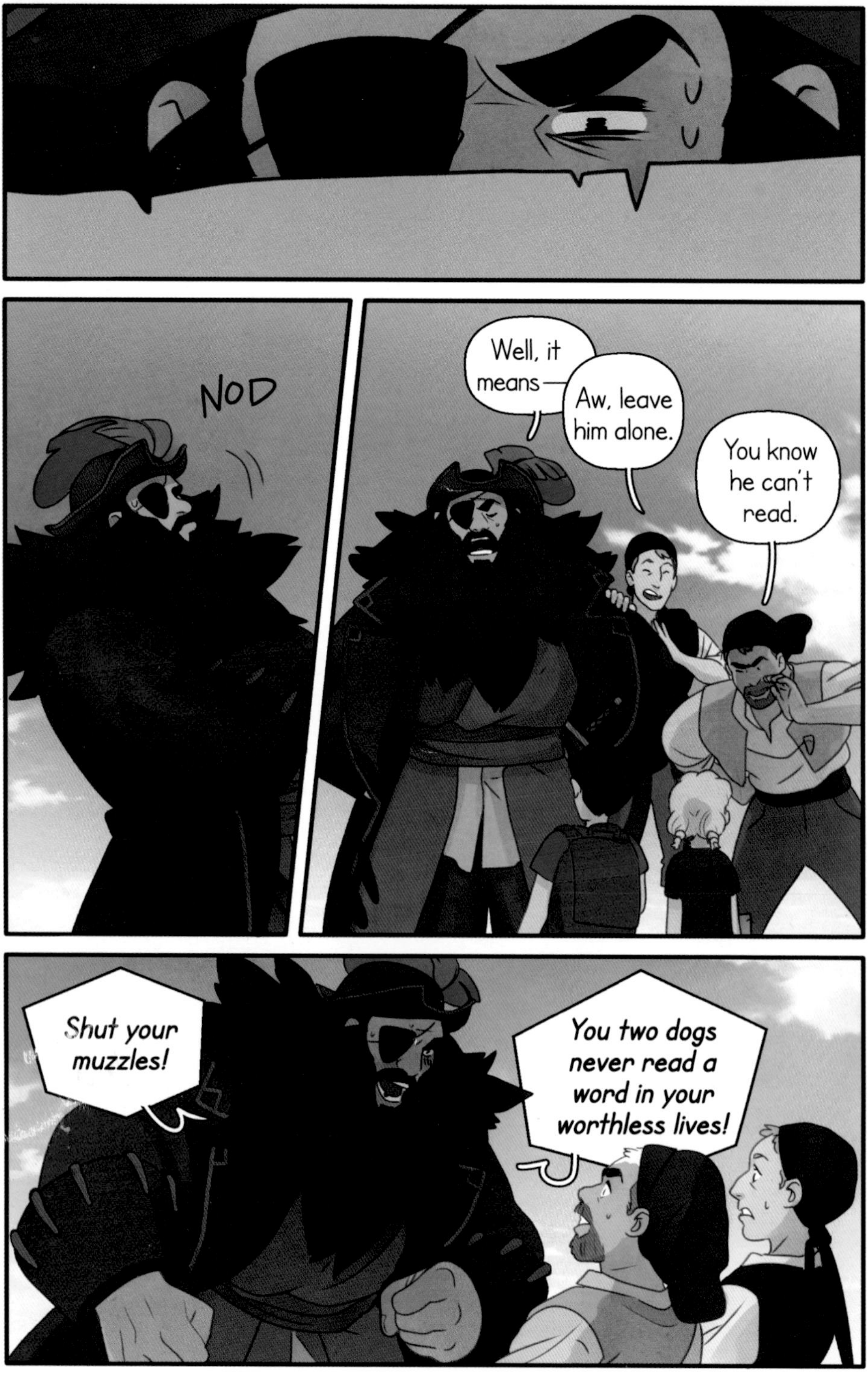
NOD
Well, it means—
Aw, leave him alone.
You know he can't read.
Shut your muzzles!
You two dogs never read a word in your worthless lives!

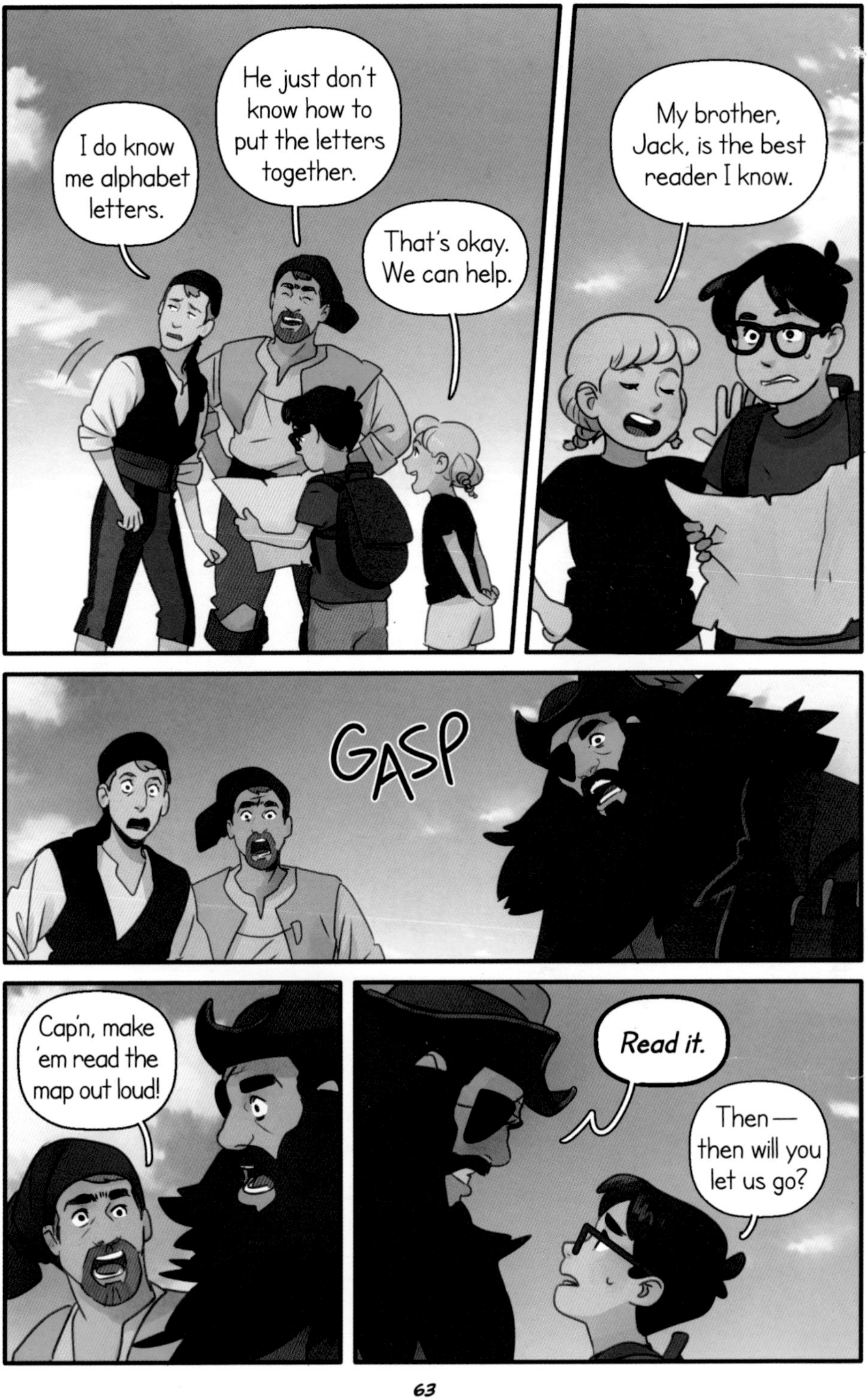
I do know me alphabet letters.
He just don't know how to put the letters together.
That's okay. We can help.
My brother, Jack, is the best reader I know.
GASP
Cap'n, make 'em read the map out loud!
Read it.
Then— then will you let us go?

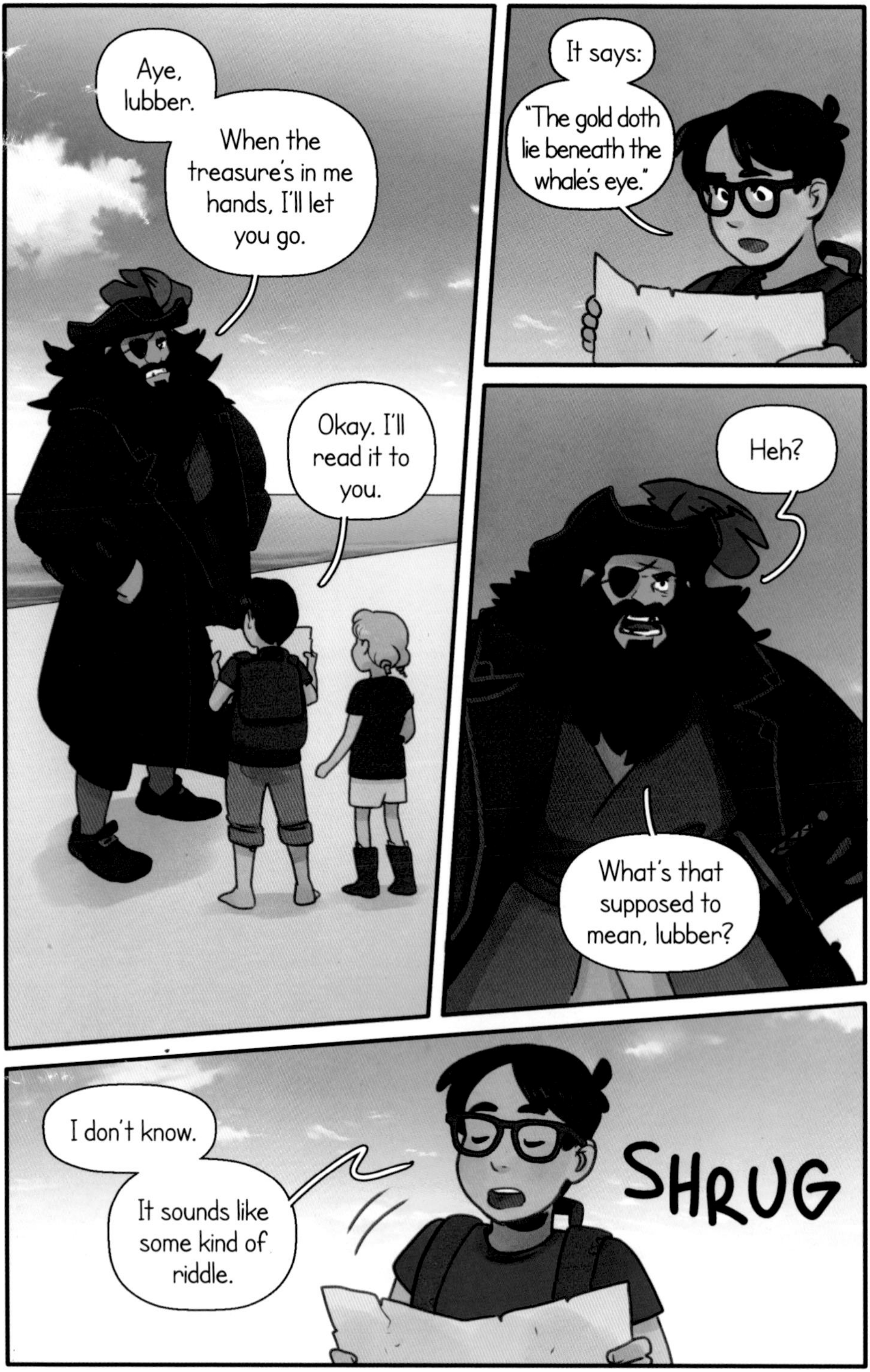
Aye, lubber.
When the treasure's in me hands, I'll let you go.
Okay. I'll read it to you.
It says:
"The gold doth lie beneath the whale's eye."
Heh?
What's that supposed to mean, lubber?
I don't know.
It sounds like some kind of riddle.
SHRUG

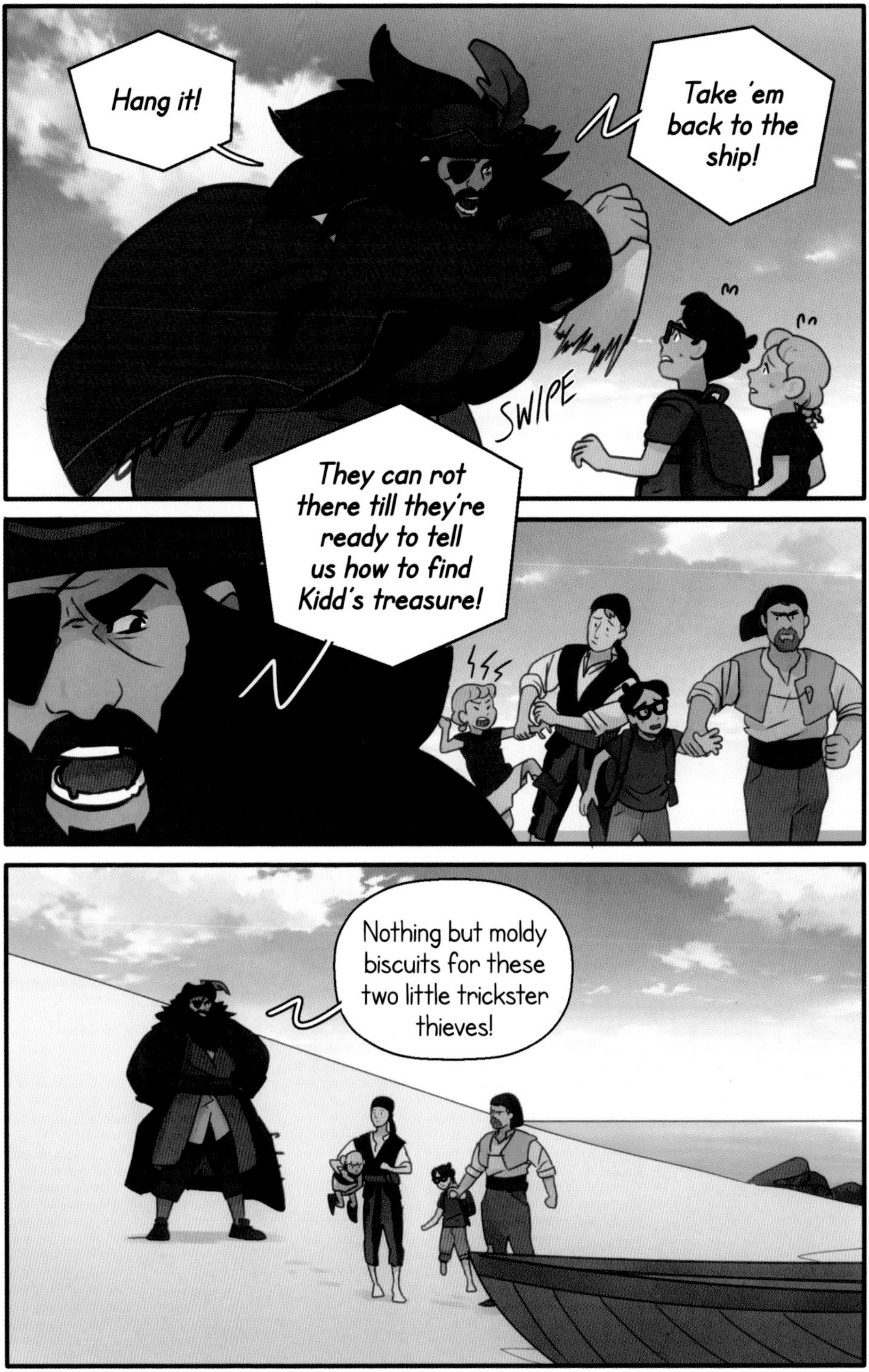
Hang it!
Take 'em back to the ship!
SWIPE
They can rot there till they're ready to tell us how to find Kidd's treasure!
Nothing but moldy biscuits for these two little trickster thieves!

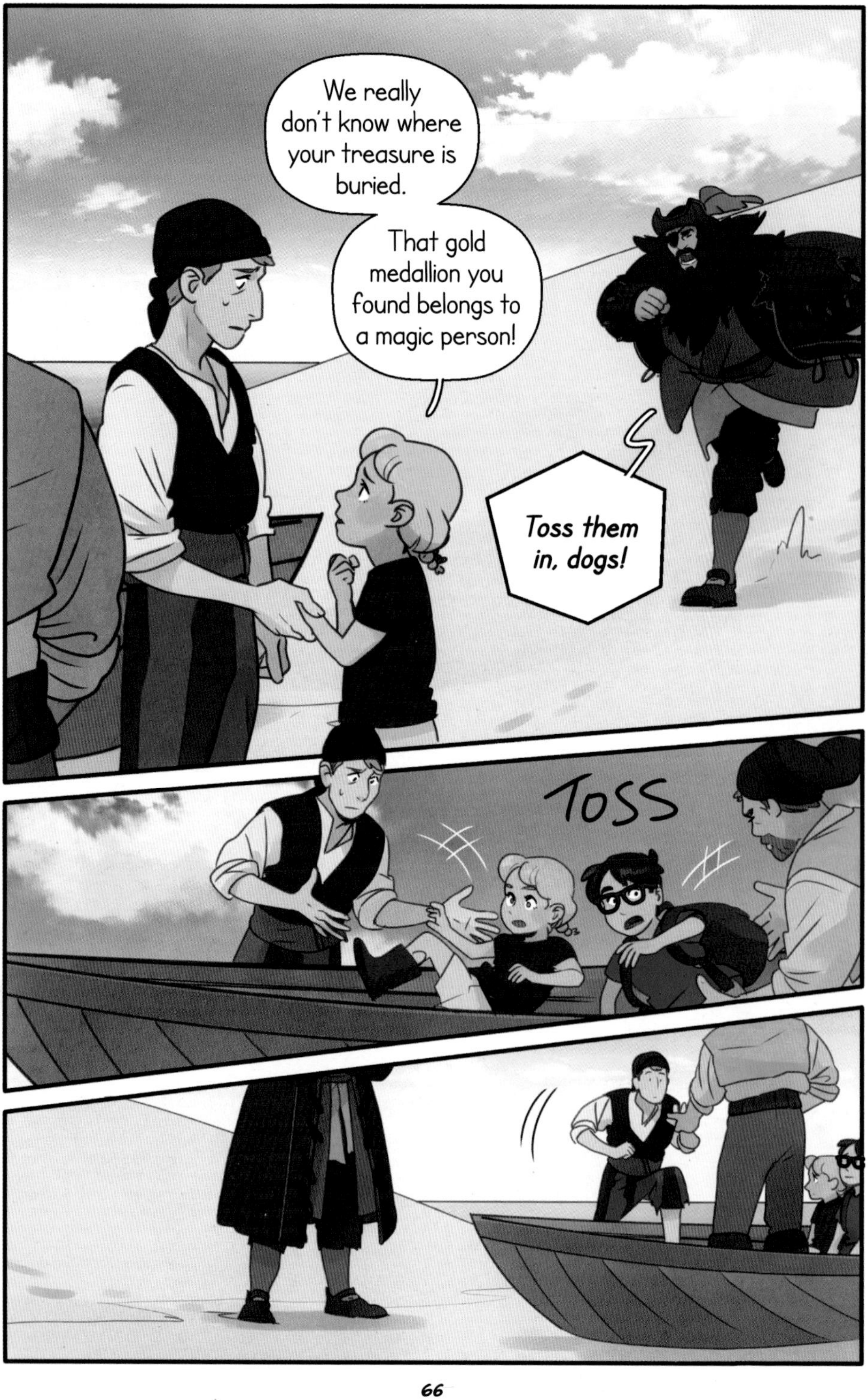
We really don't know where your treasure is buried.
That gold medallion you found belongs to a magic person!
Toss them in, dogs!
TOSS

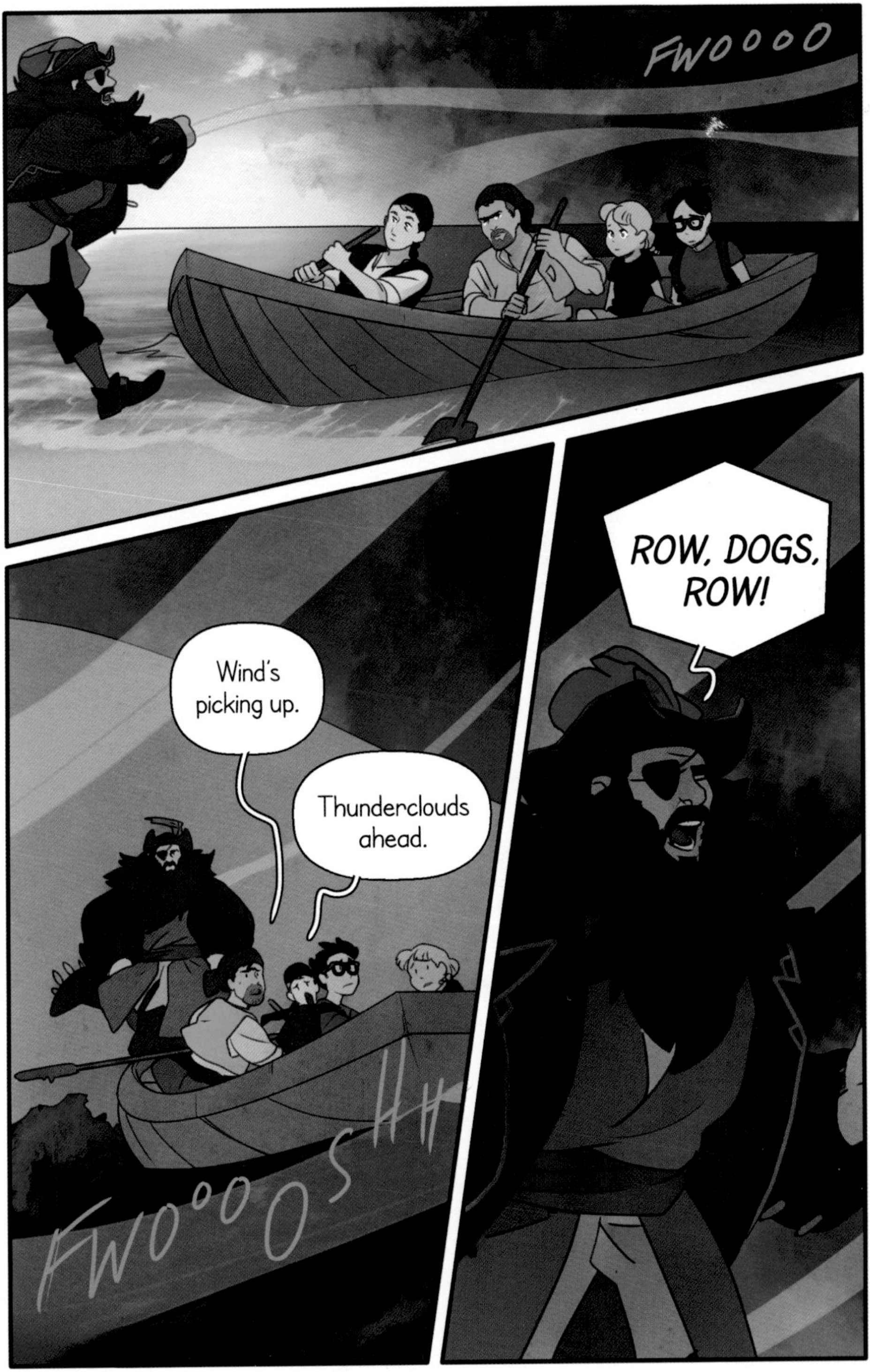
FWOOOO
Wind's picking up.
Thunderclouds ahead.
FWOOOOSHH
ROW, DOGS, ROW!

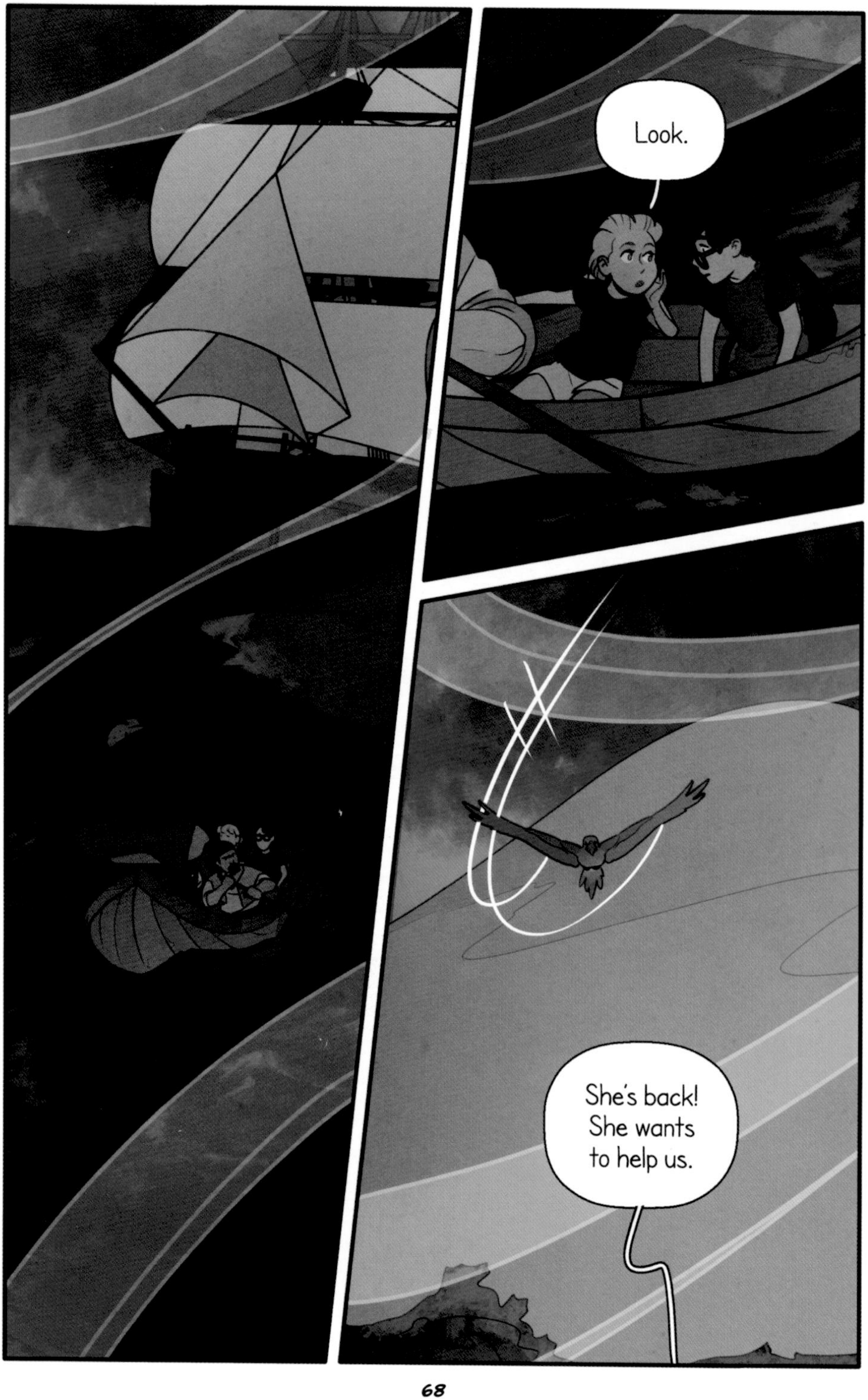
Look.
She's back!
She wants
to help us.

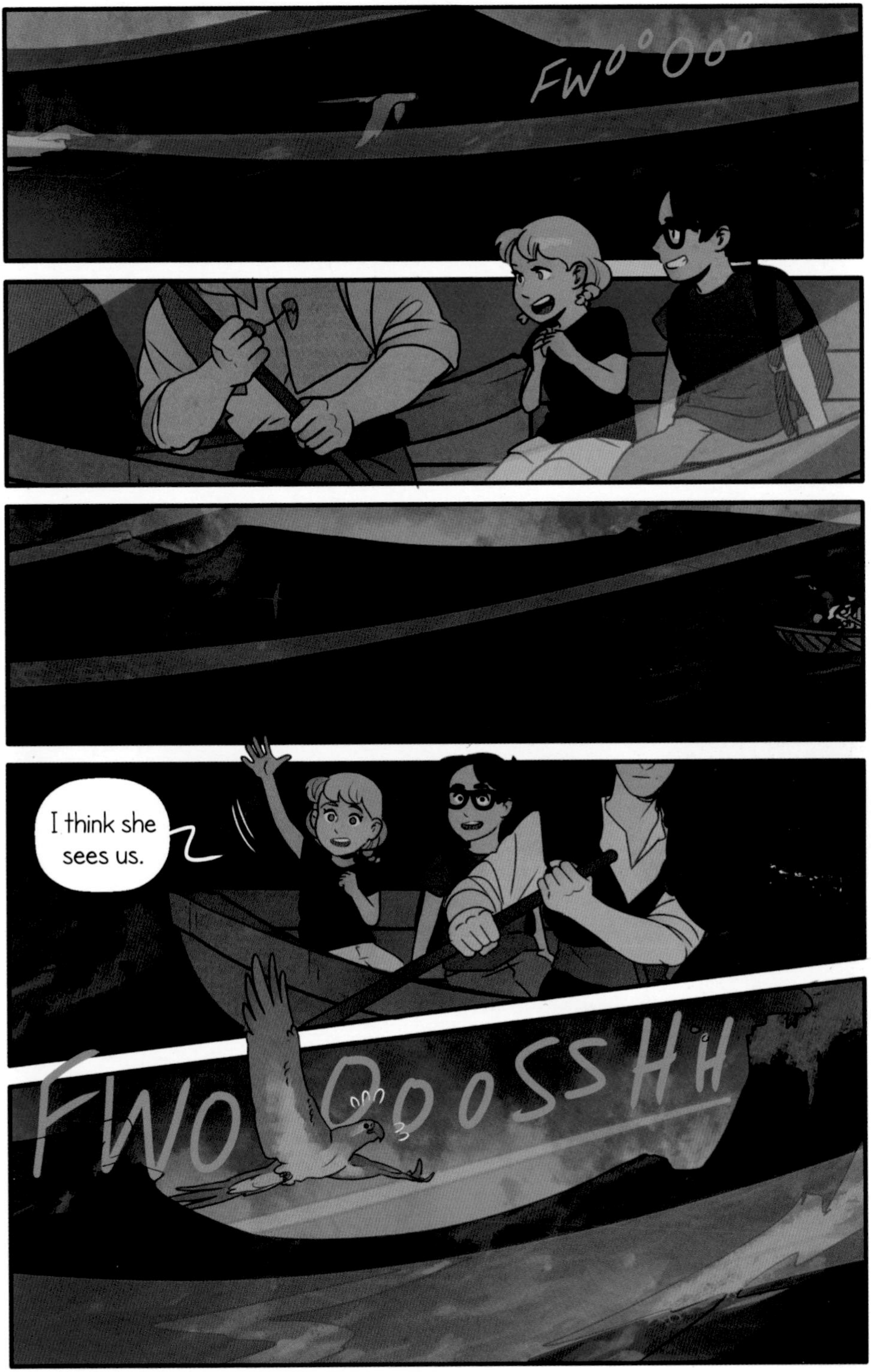
FWOOOO
I think she sees us.
FWOOOOSSHH

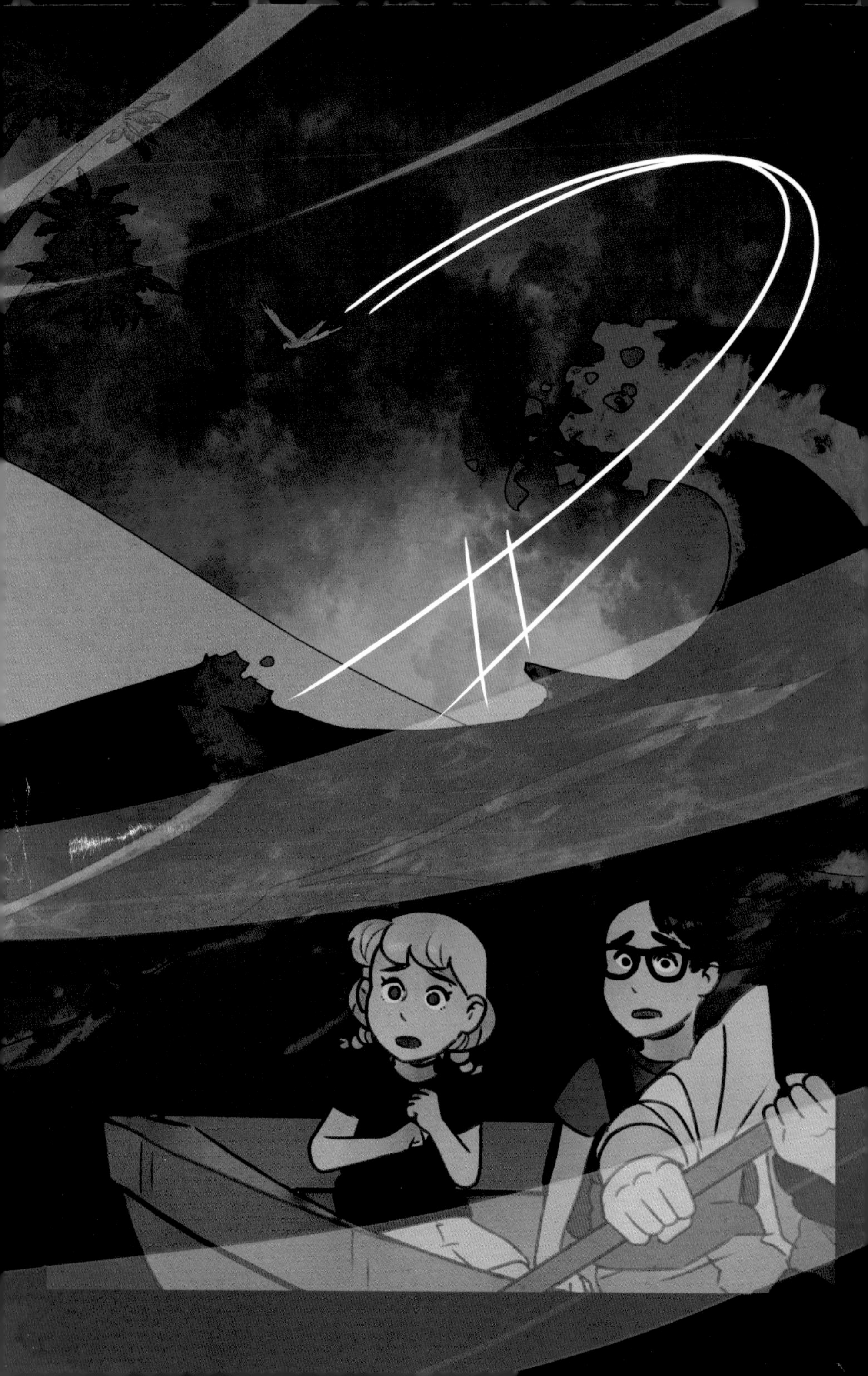

CHAPTER SIX
The Whale's Eye

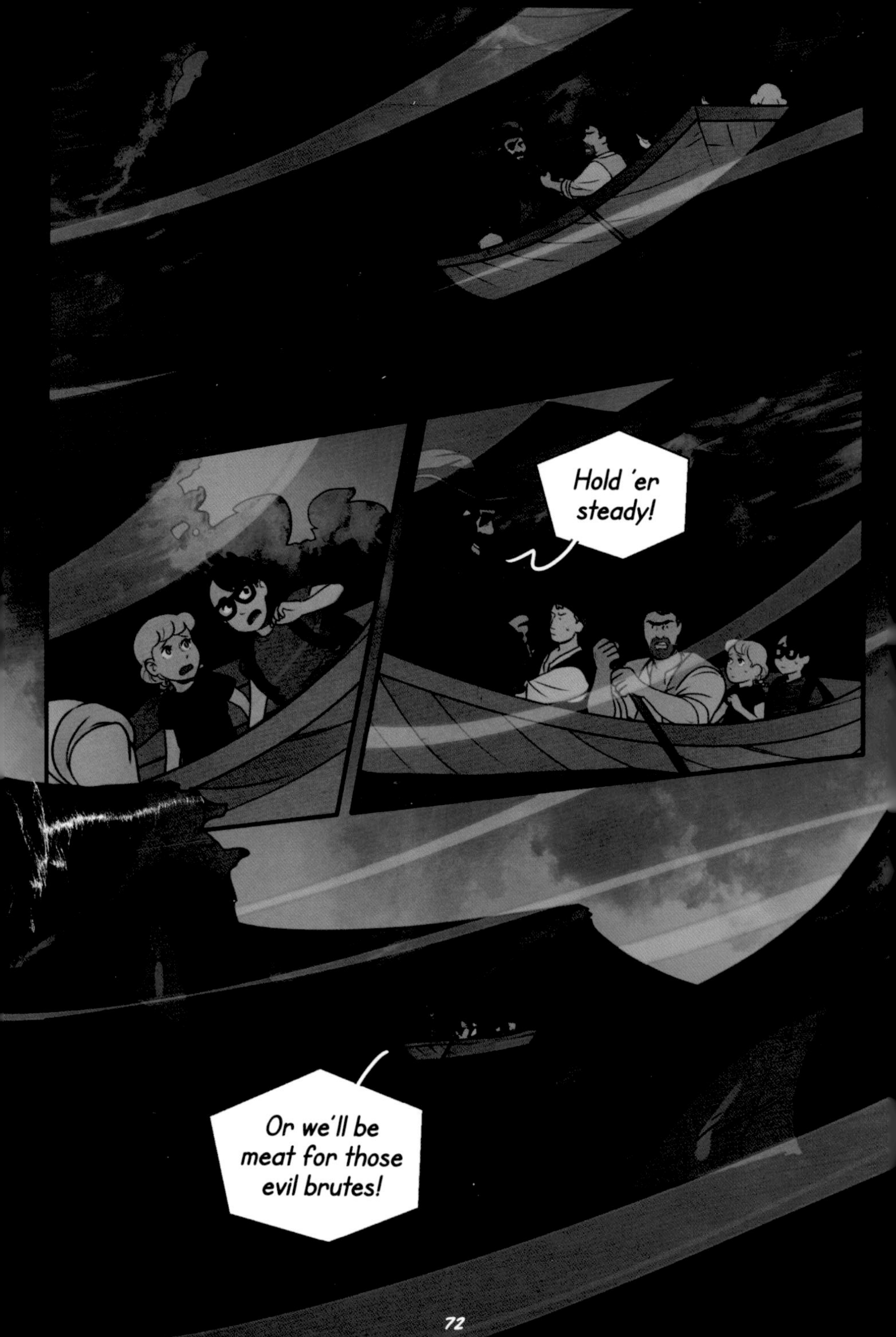
Hold 'er steady!
Or we'll be meat for those evil brutes!

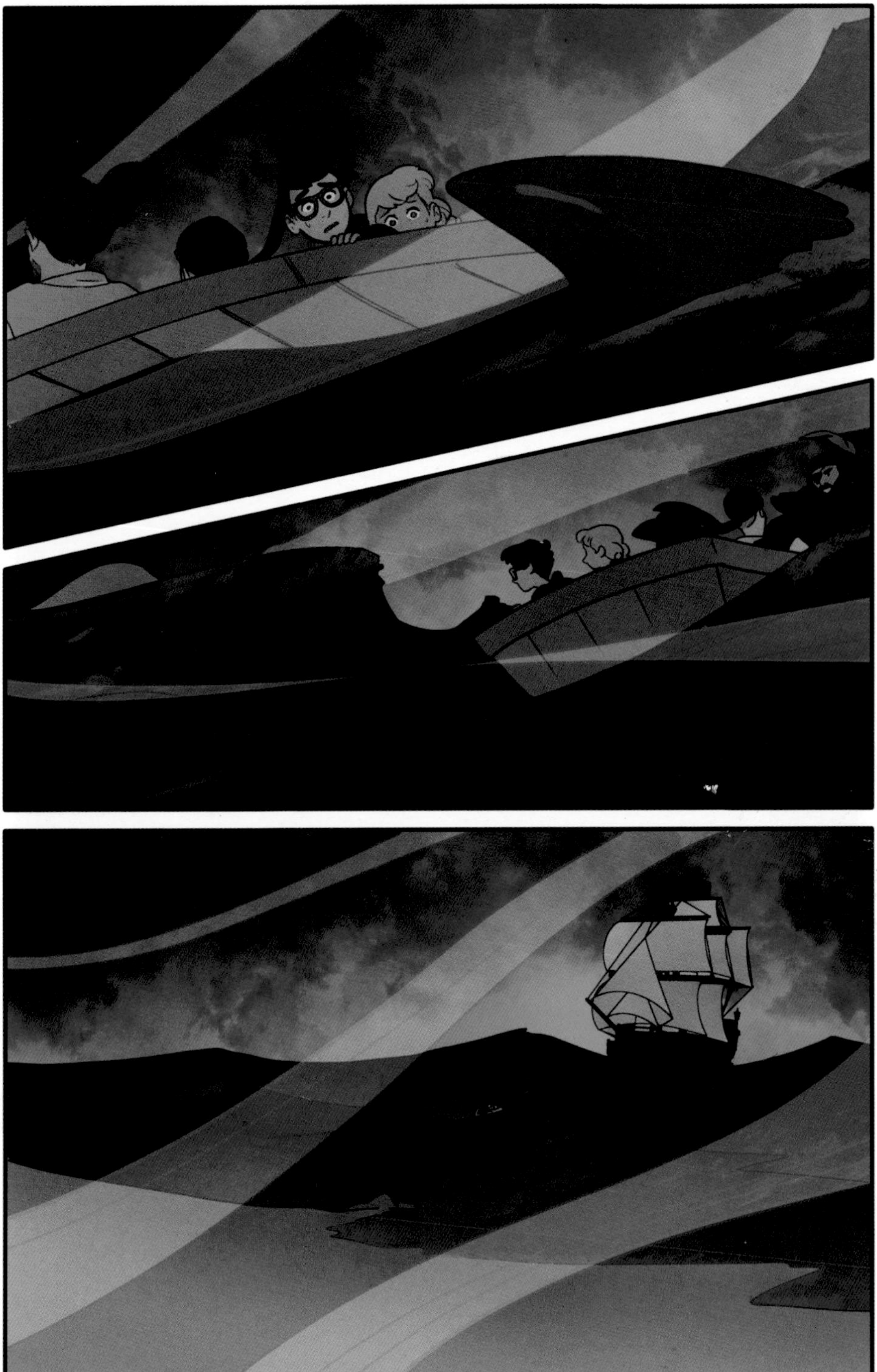

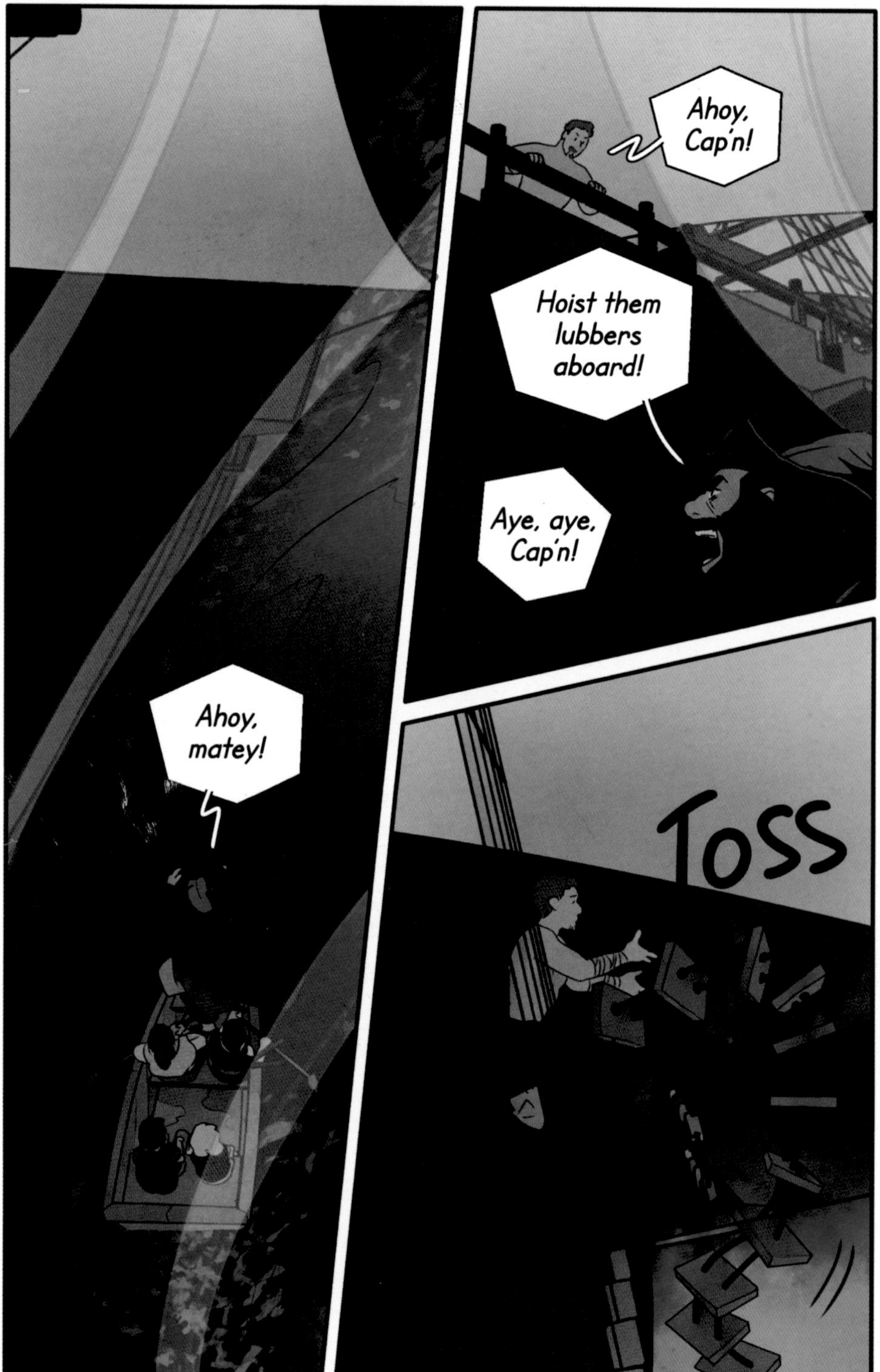
Ahoy, matey!
Ahoy, Cap'n!
Hoist them lubbers aboard!
Aye, aye, Cap'n!
TOSS

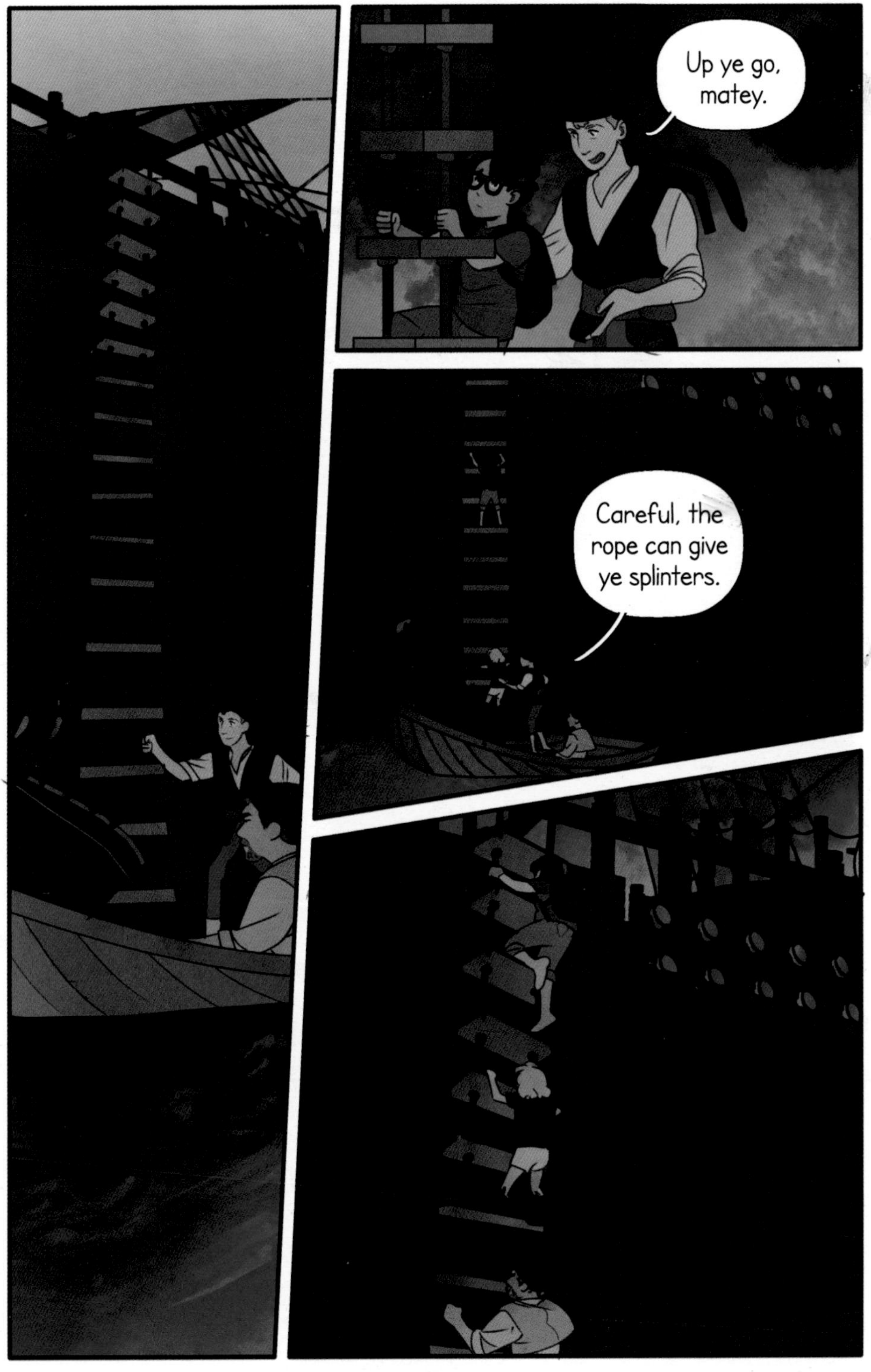
Up ye go, matey.
Careful, the rope can give ye splinters.

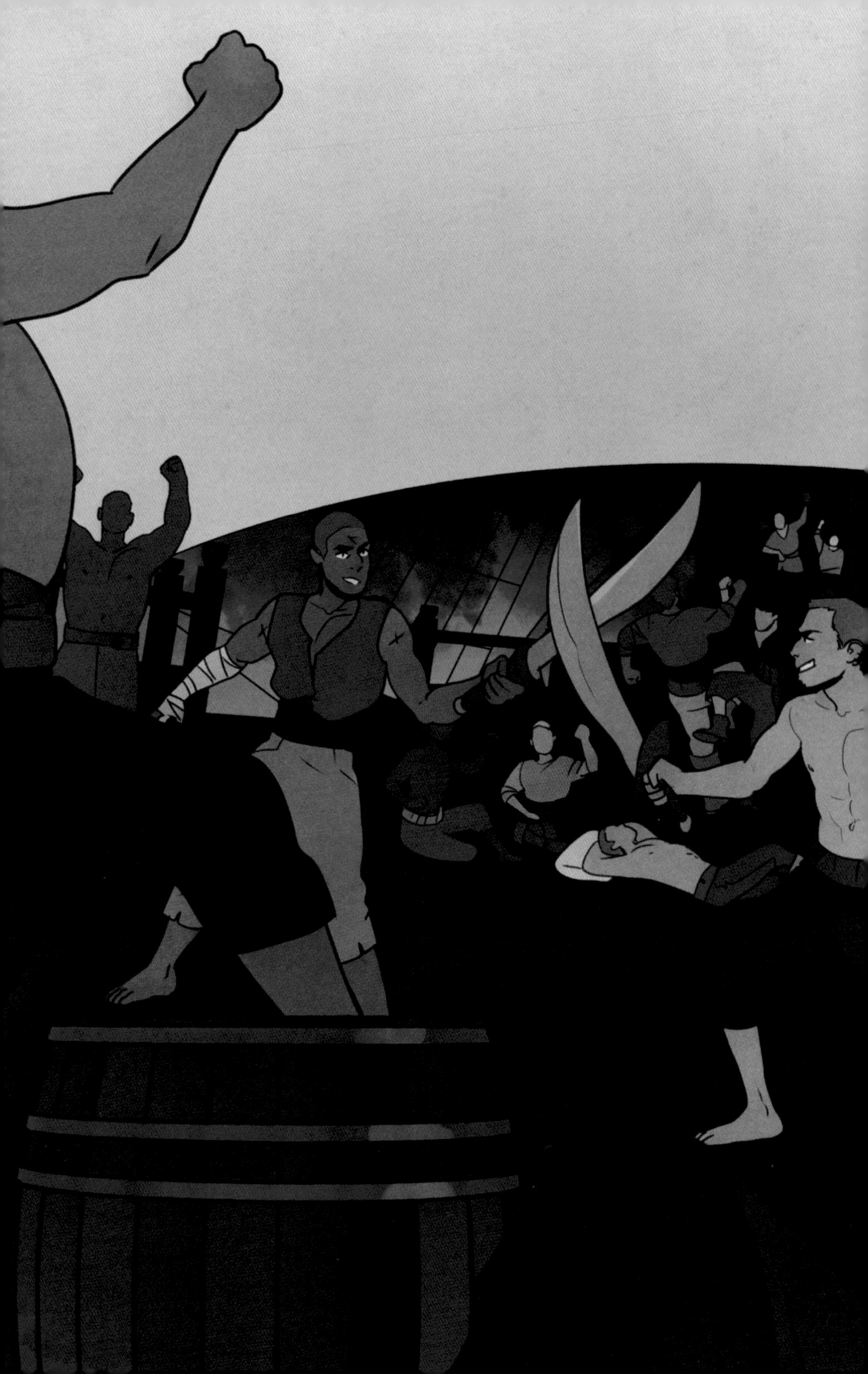

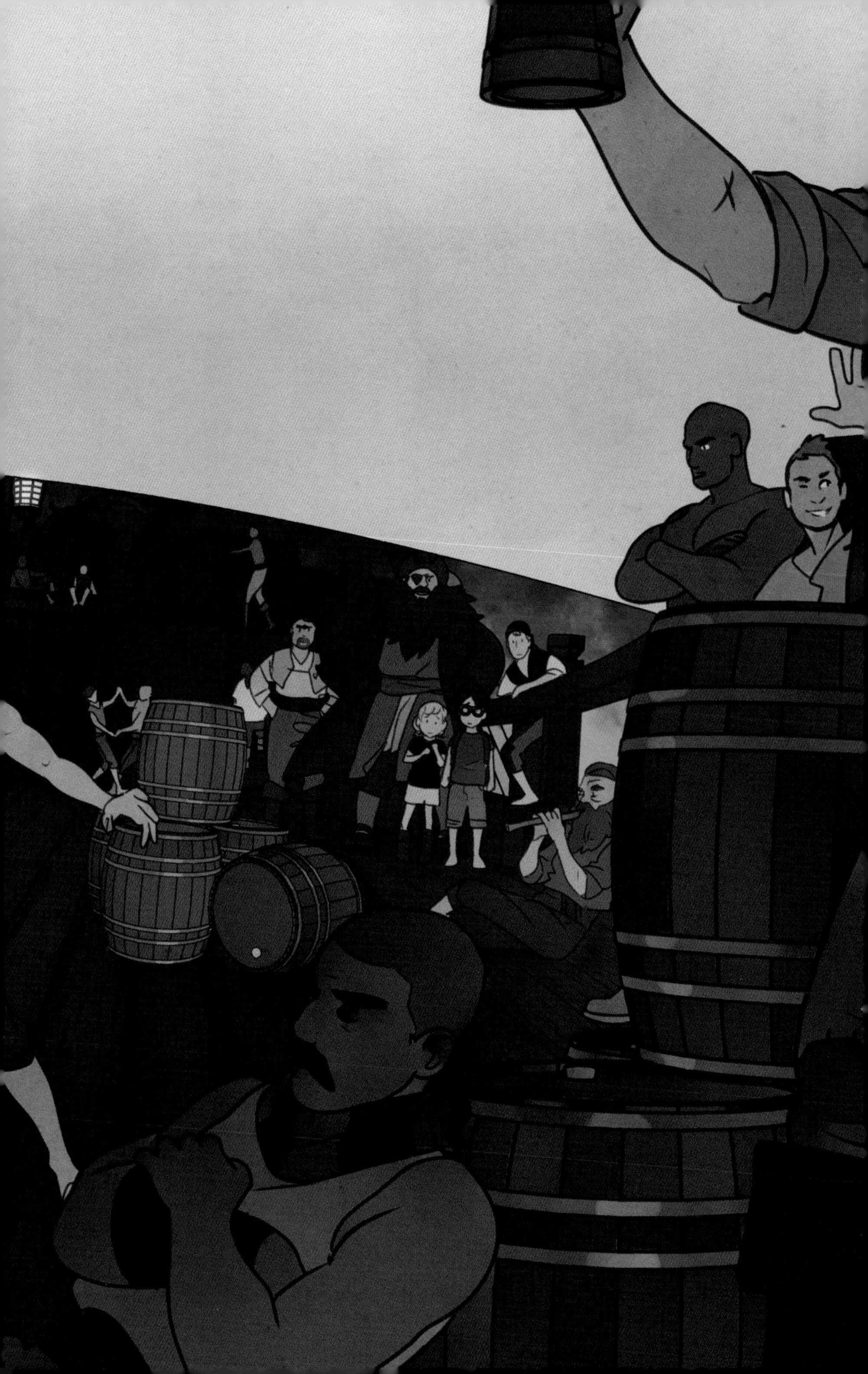

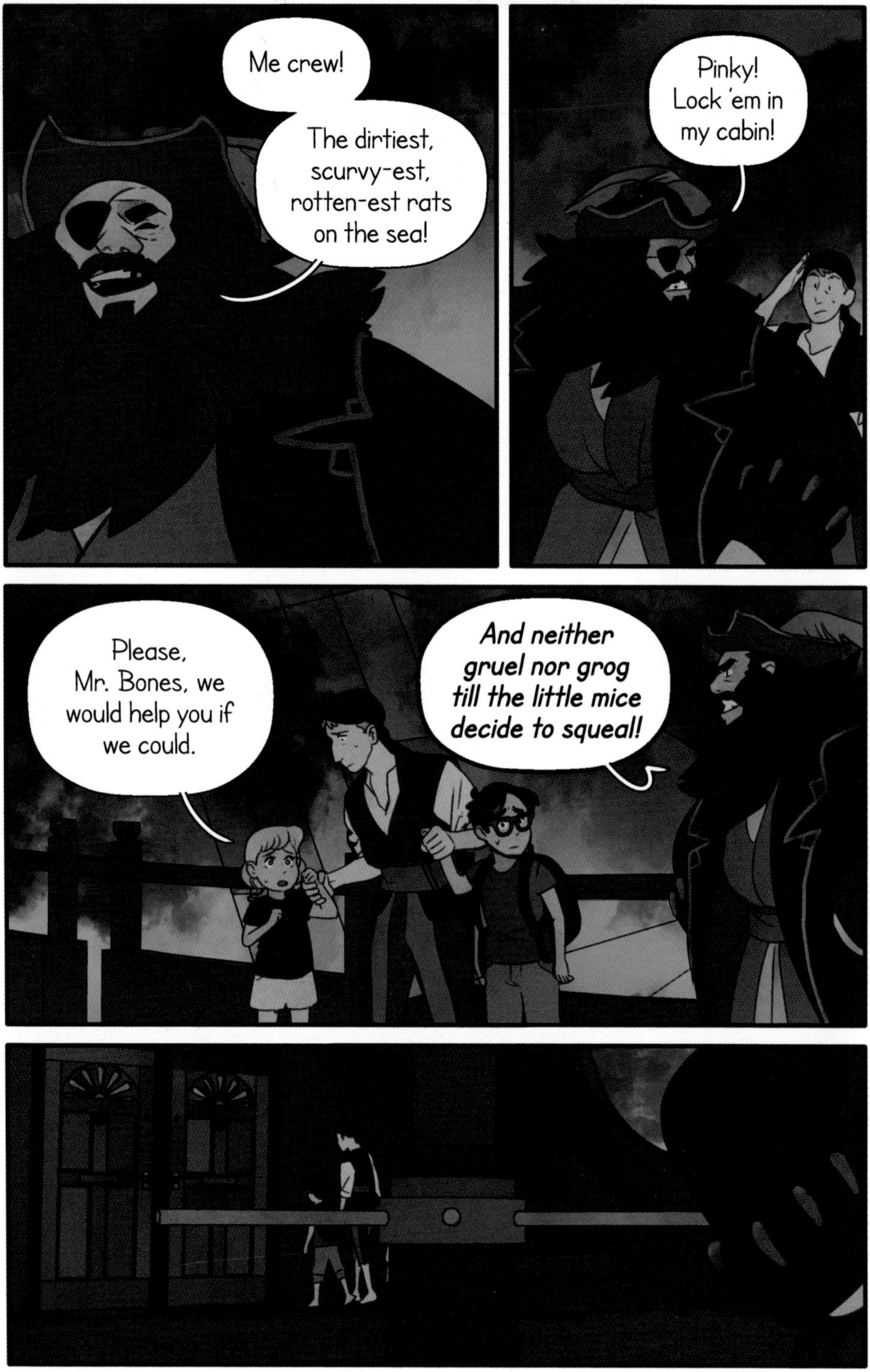
Me crew!
The dirtiest, scurvy-est, rotten-est rats on the sea!
Pinky! Lock 'em in my cabin!
Please, Mr. Bones, we would help you if we could.
And neither gruel nor grog till the little mice decide to squeal!

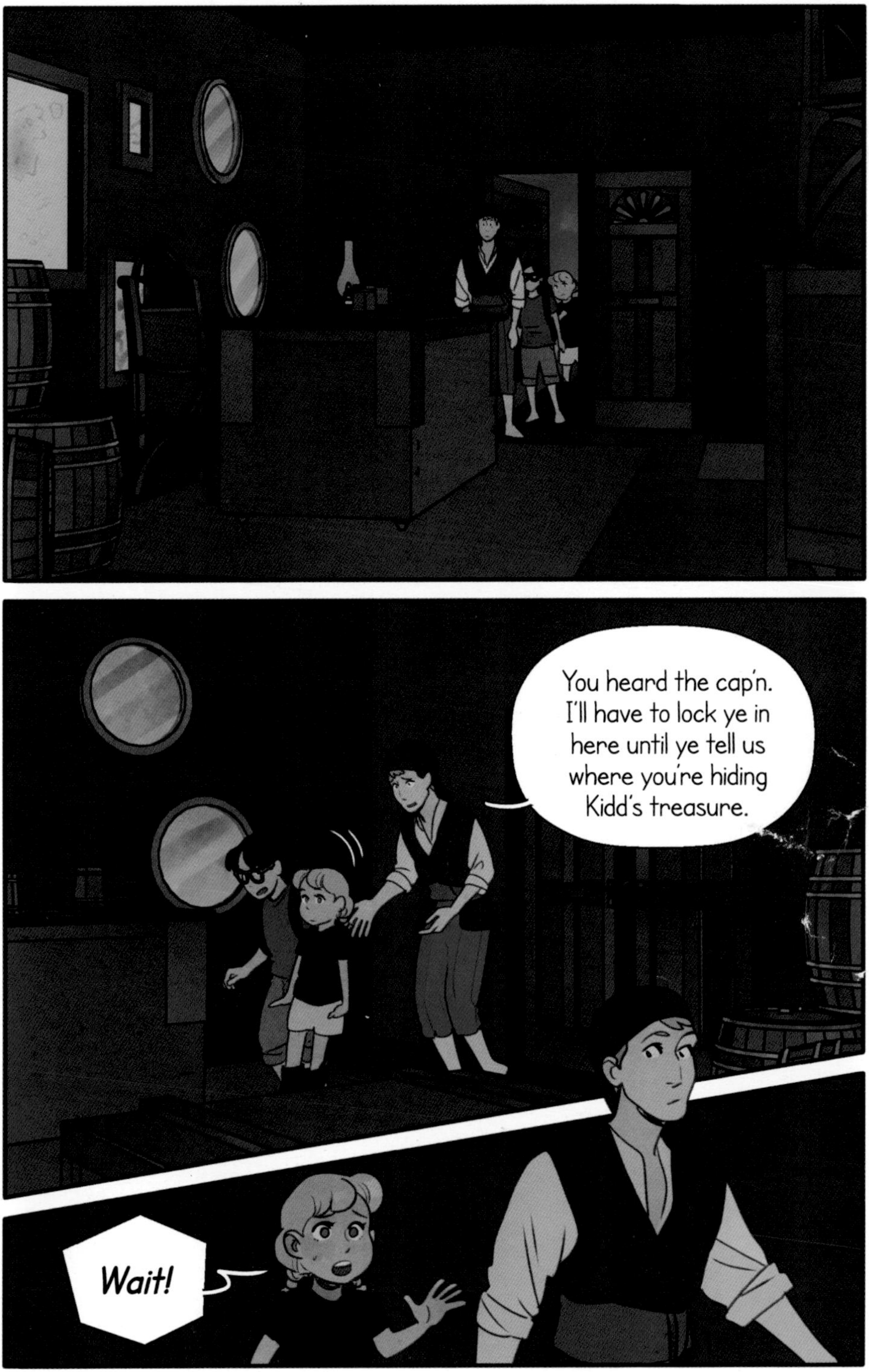
You heard the cap'n. I'll have to lock ye in here until ye tell us where you're hiding Kidd's treasure.
Wait!

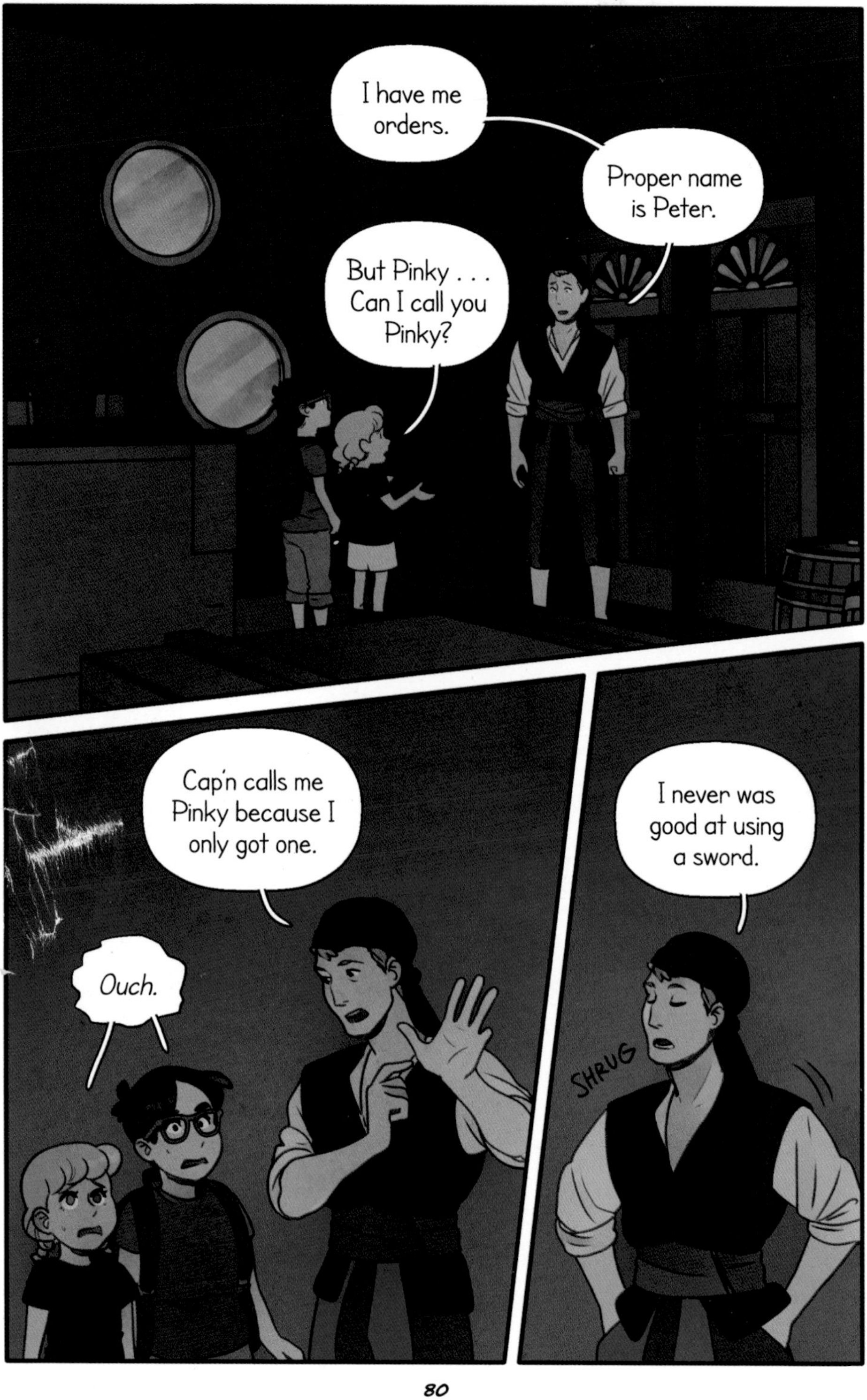
I have me orders.
Proper name is Peter.
But Pinky . . . Can I call you Pinky?
Cap'n calls me Pinky because I only got one.
Ouch.
I never was good at using a sword.
SHRUG

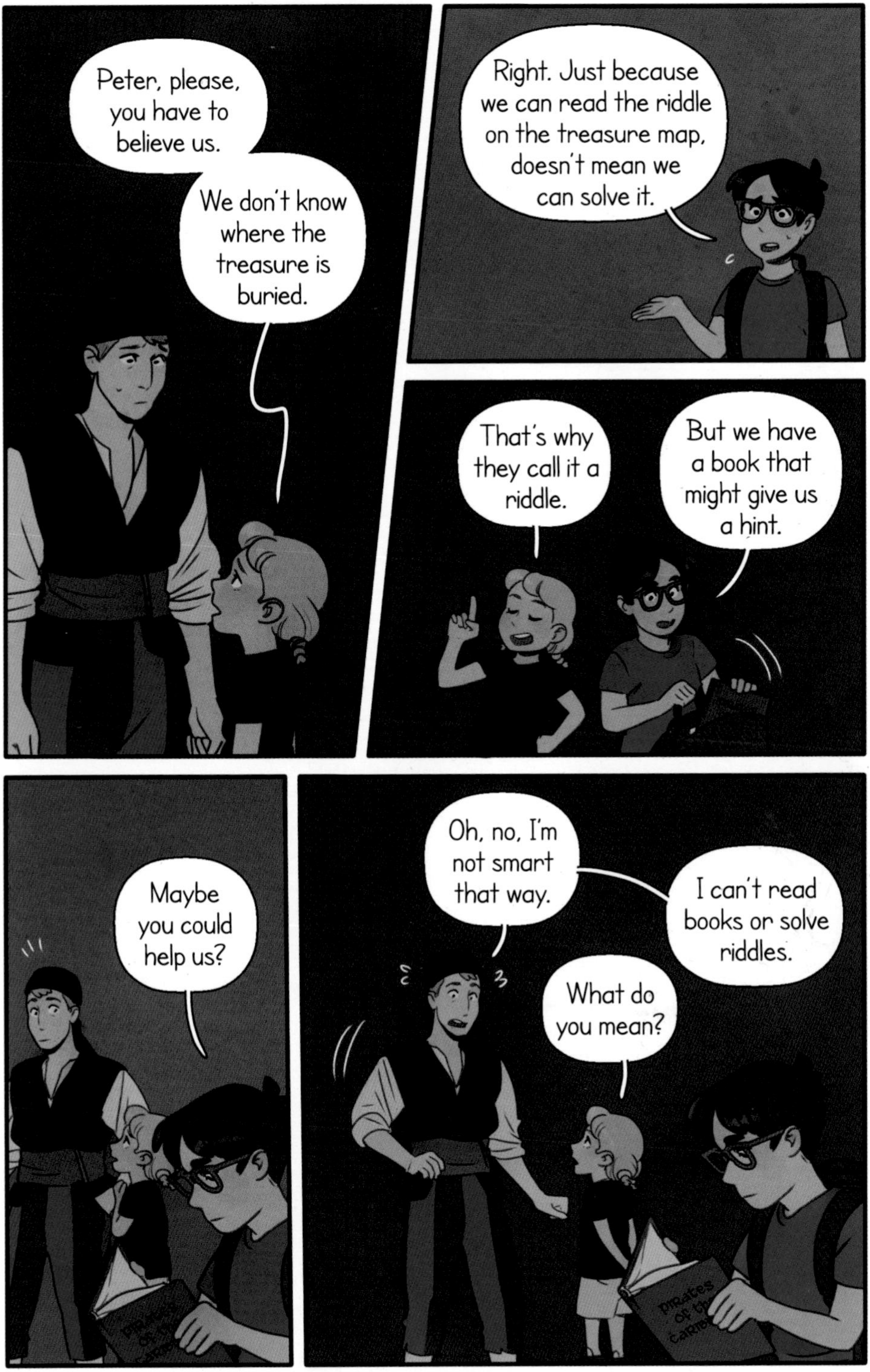
Peter, please, you have to believe us.
We don't know where the treasure is buried.
Right. Just because we can read the riddle on the treasure map, doesn't mean we can solve it.
That's why they call it a riddle.
But we have a book that might give us a hint.
Maybe you could help us?
Oh, no, I'm not smart that way.
I can't read books or solve riddles.
What do you mean?

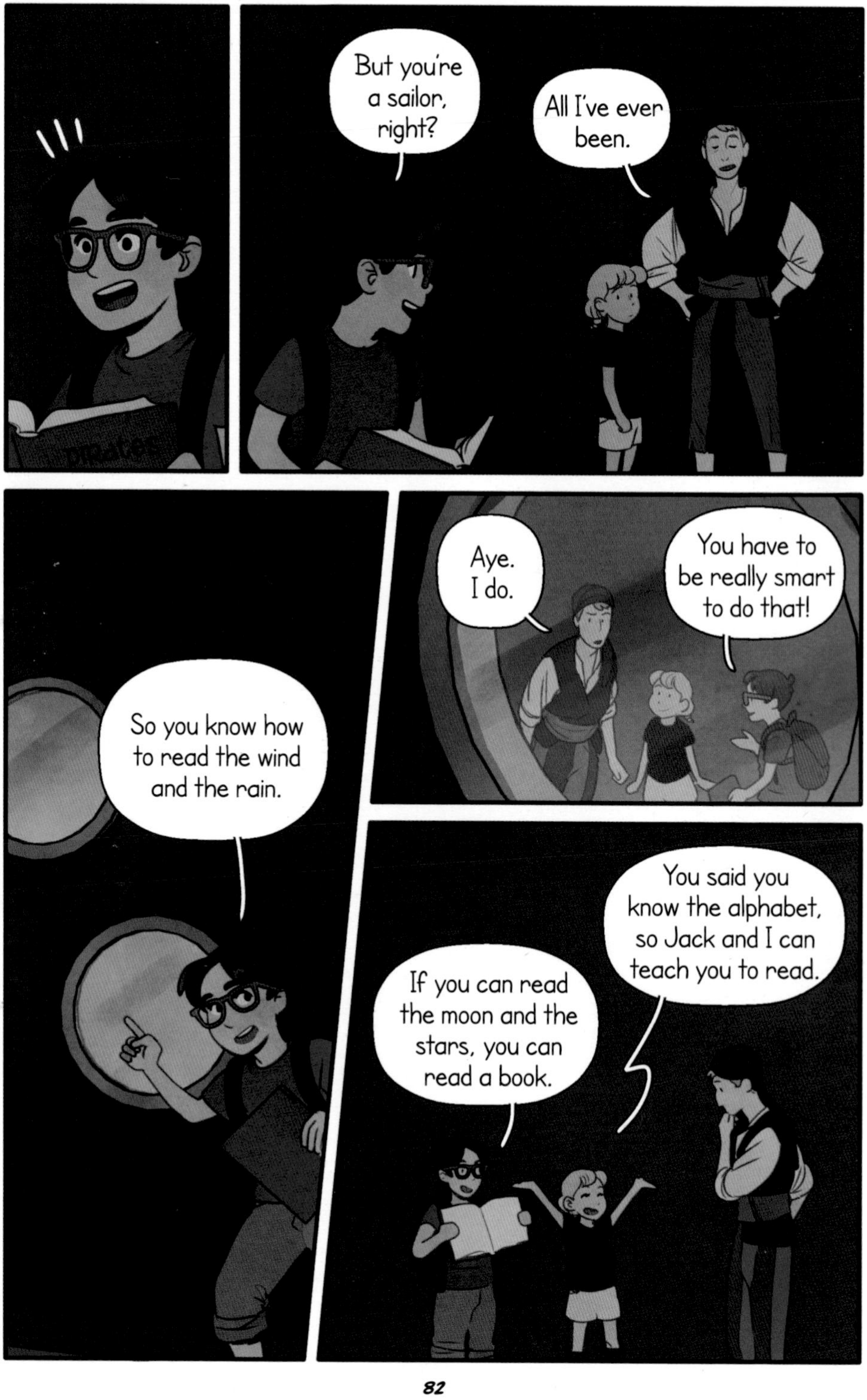
PIRATES
But you're a sailor, right?
All I've ever been.
So you know how to read the wind and the rain.
Aye. I do.
You have to be really smart to do that!
If you can read the moon and the stars, you can read a book.
You said you know the alphabet, so Jack and I can teach you to read.

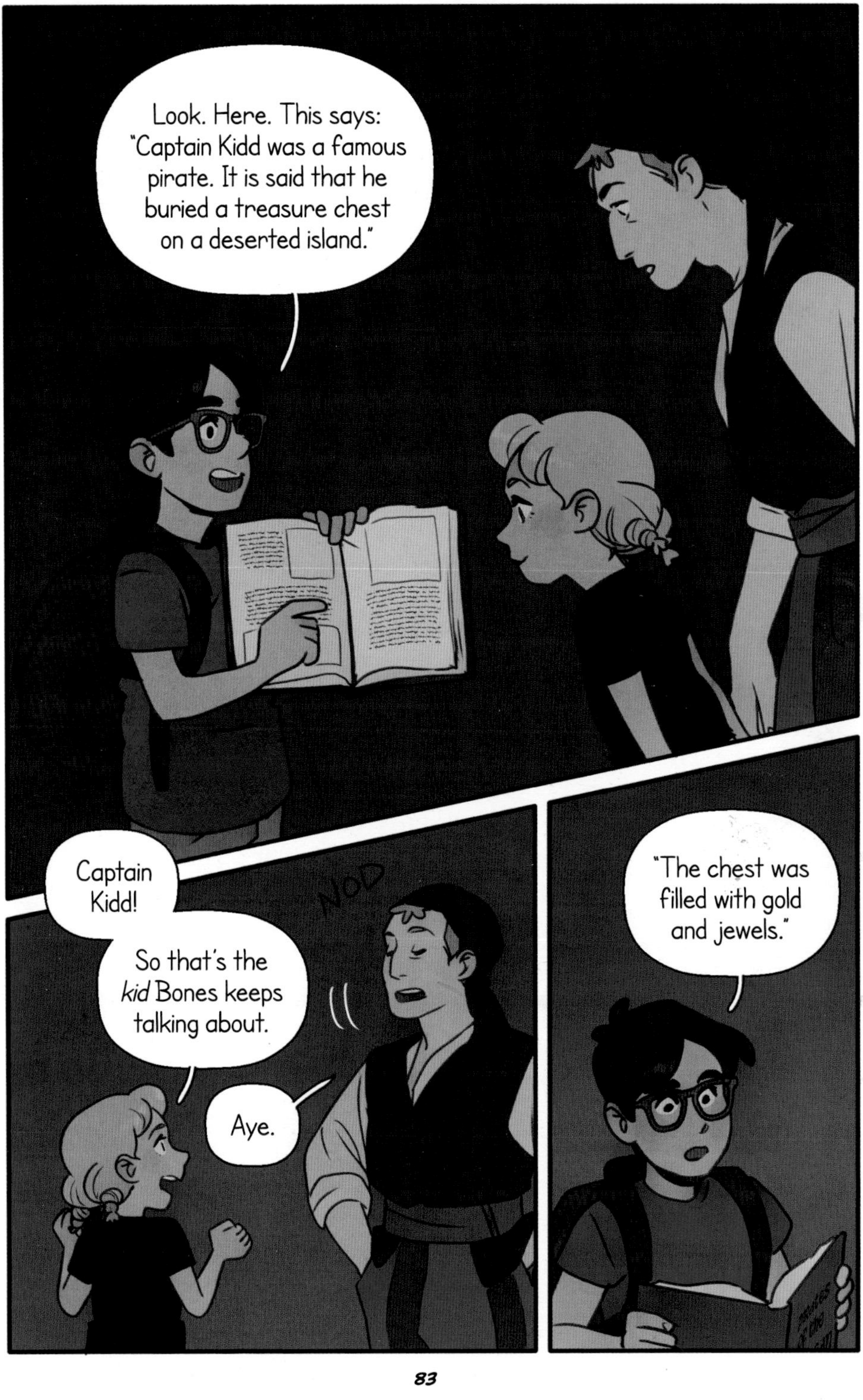

Look. Here. This says: "Captain Kidd was a famous pirate. It is said that he buried a treasure chest on a deserted island."
Captain Kidd!
So that's the *kid* Bones keeps talking about.
NOD
Aye.
"The chest was filled with gold and jewels."

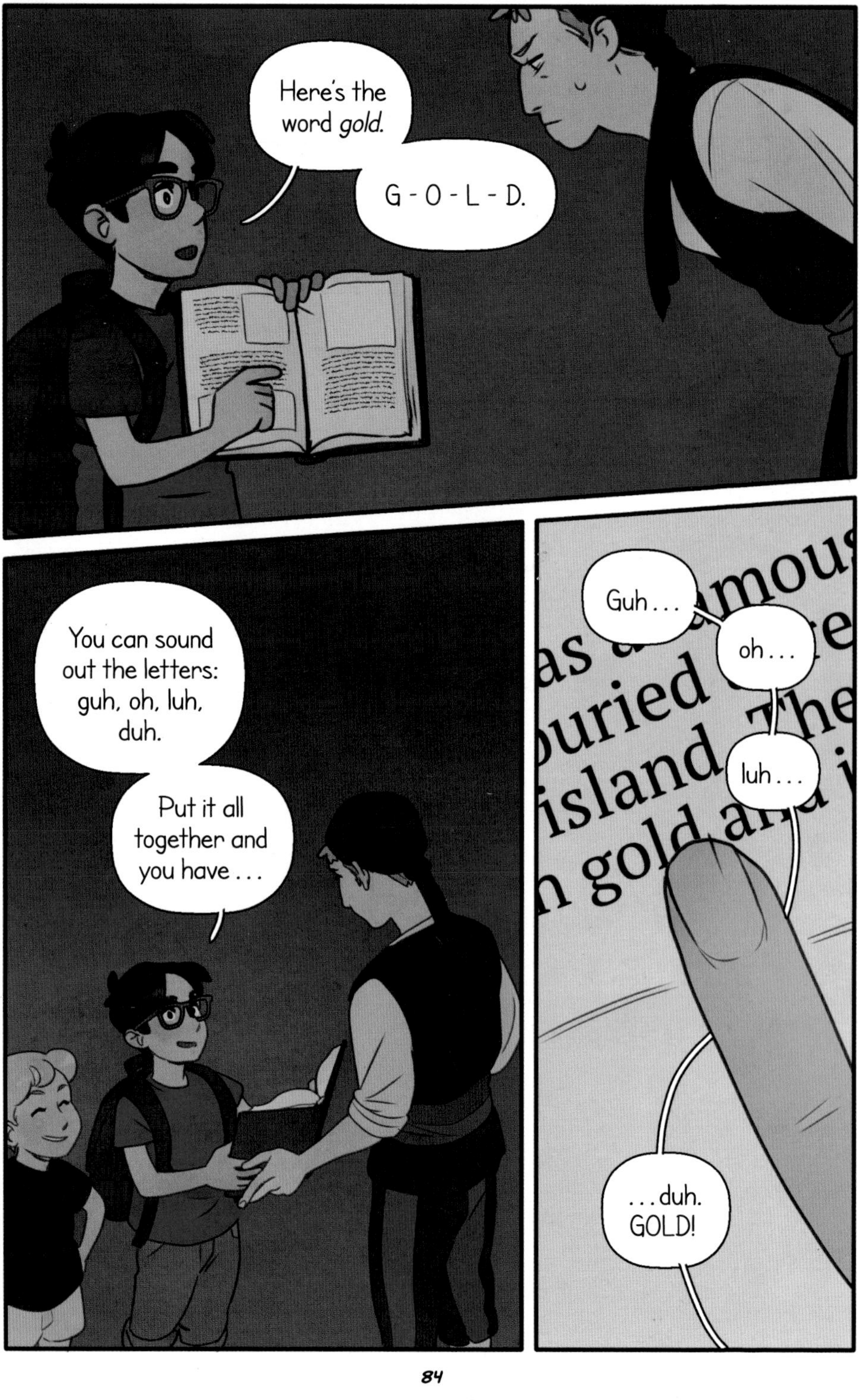
Here's the word *gold.*
G - O - L - D.
You can sound out the letters: guh, oh, luh, duh.
Put it all together and you have . . .
Guh . . .
oh . . .
luh . . .
. . . duh. GOLD!

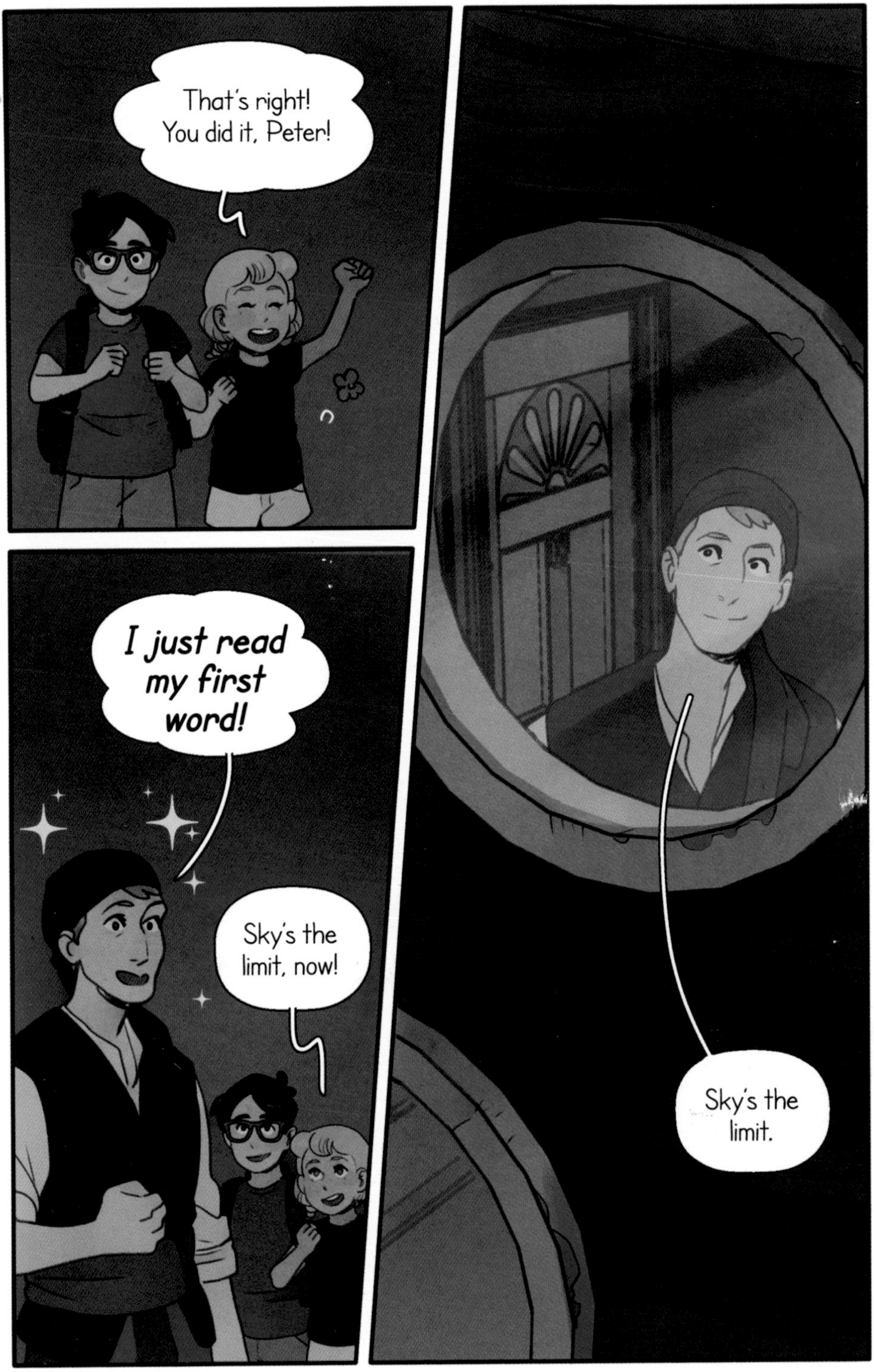
That's right! You did it, Peter!
I just read my first word!
Sky's the limit, now!
Sky's the limit.

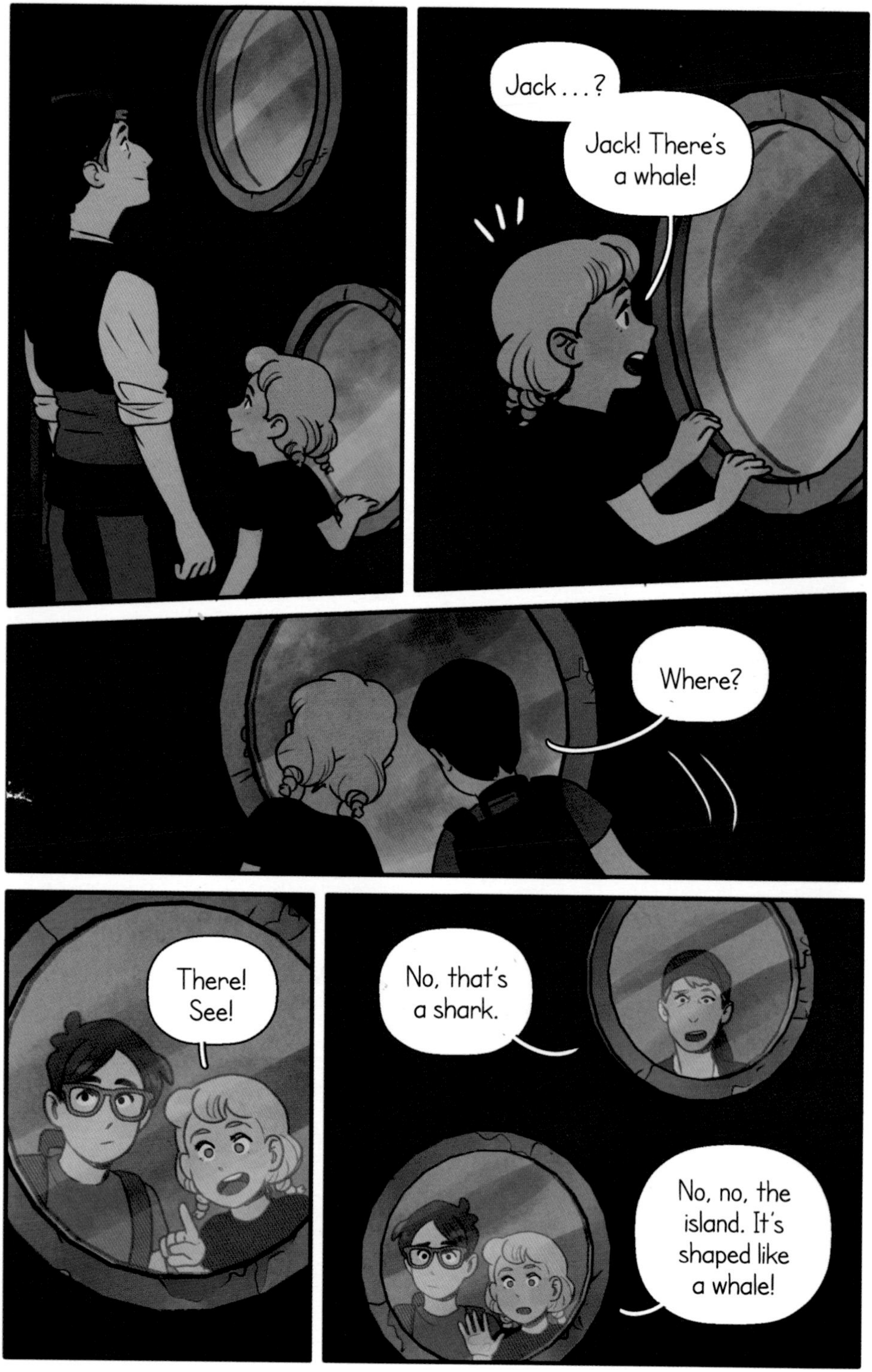
Jack . . . ?
Jack! There's a whale!
Where?
There! See!
No, that's a shark.
No, no, the island. It's shaped like a whale!

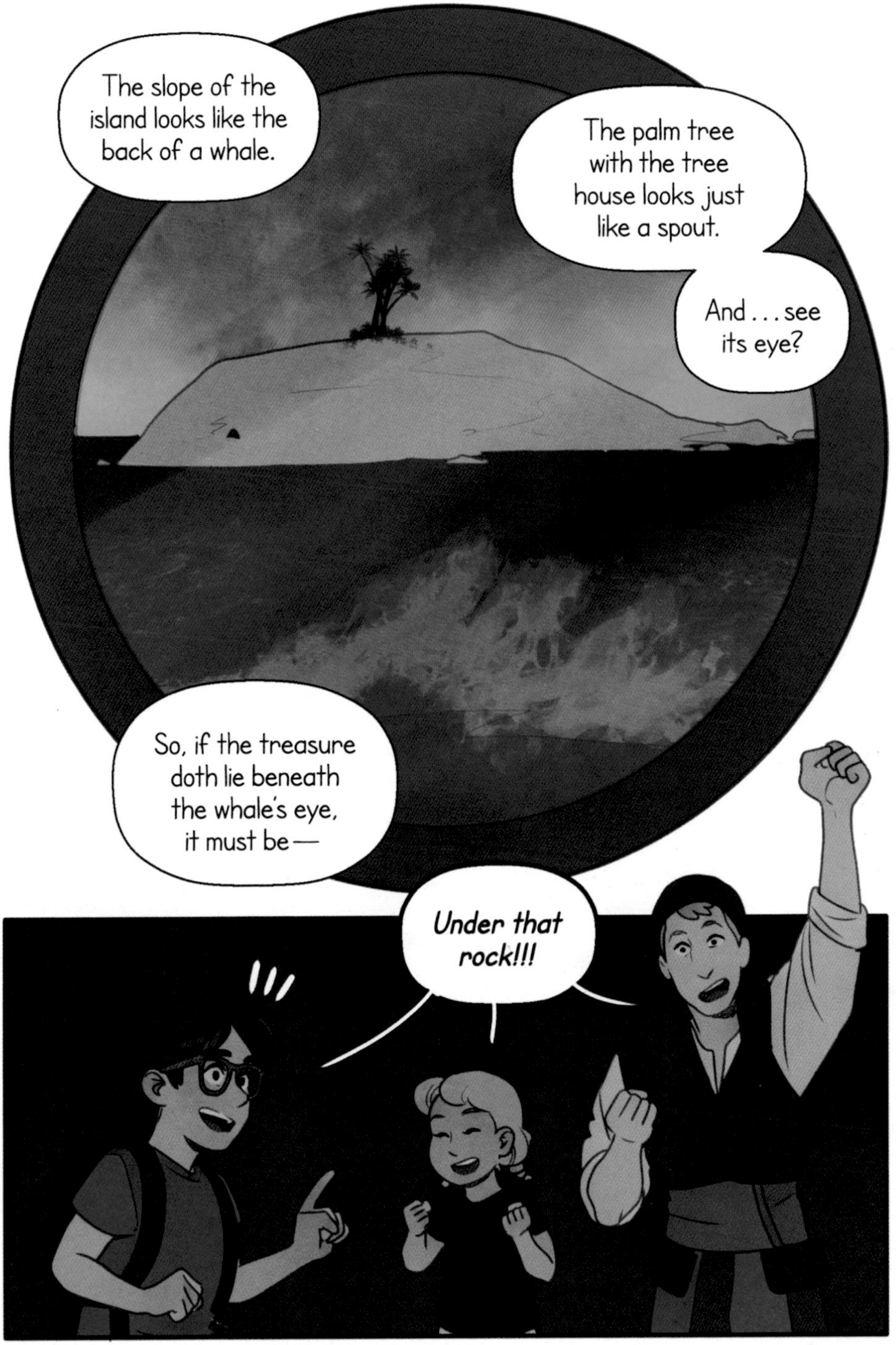
The slope of the island looks like the back of a whale.
The palm tree with the tree house looks just like a spout.
And . . . see its eye?
So, if the treasure doth lie beneath the whale's eye, it must be—
!!!
Under that rock!!!

CHAPTER SEVEN
Gale's a-Blowin'

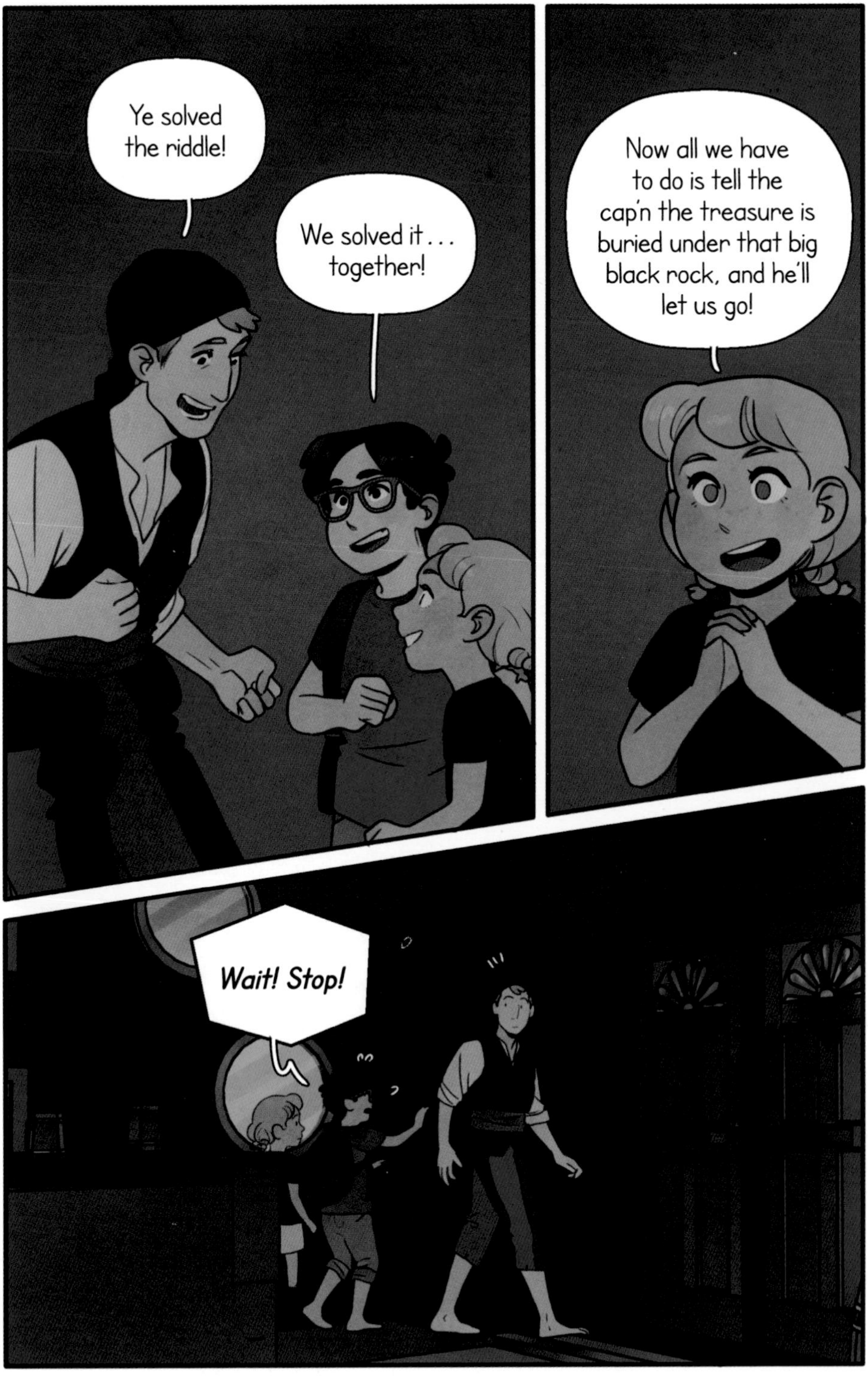
Ye solved the riddle!
We solved it . . . together!
Now all we have to do is tell the cap'n the treasure is buried under that big black rock, and he'll let us go!
Wait! Stop!

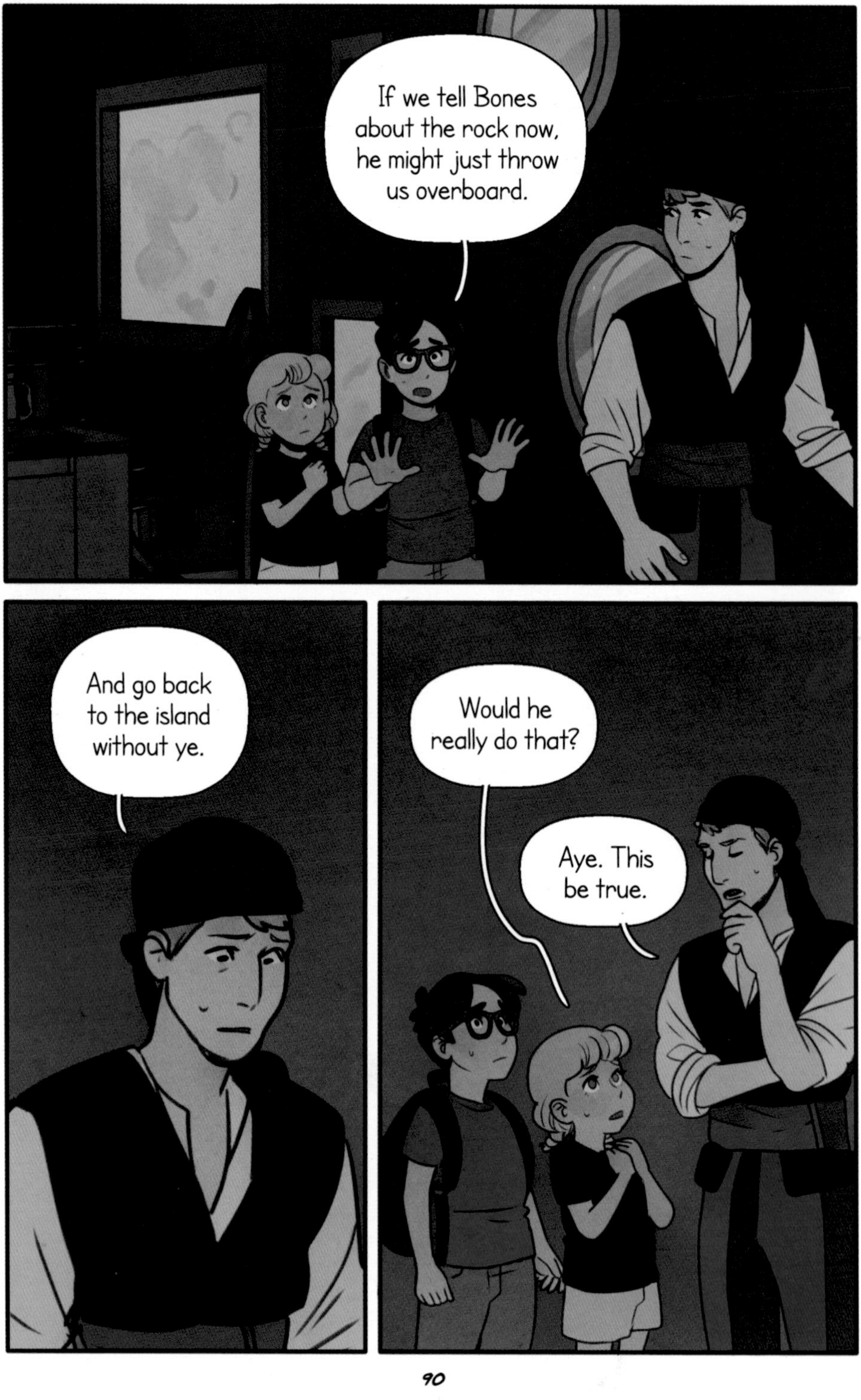
If we tell Bones about the rock now, he might just throw us overboard.
And go back to the island without ye.
Would he really do that?
Aye. This be true.

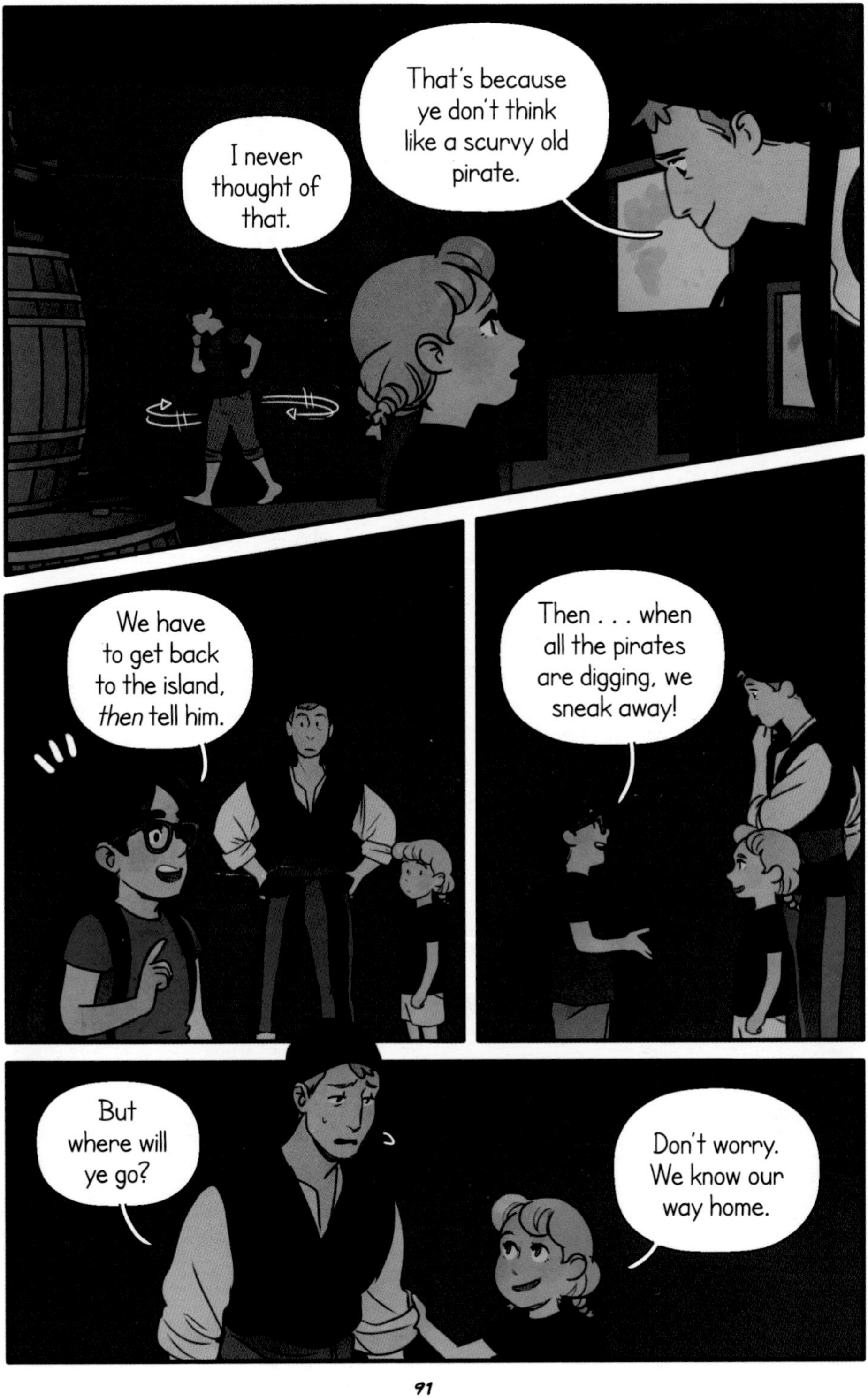
I never thought of that.
That's because ye don't think like a scurvy old pirate.
We have to get back to the island, *then* tell him.
Then . . . when all the pirates are digging, we sneak away!
But where will ye go?
Don't worry. We know our way home.

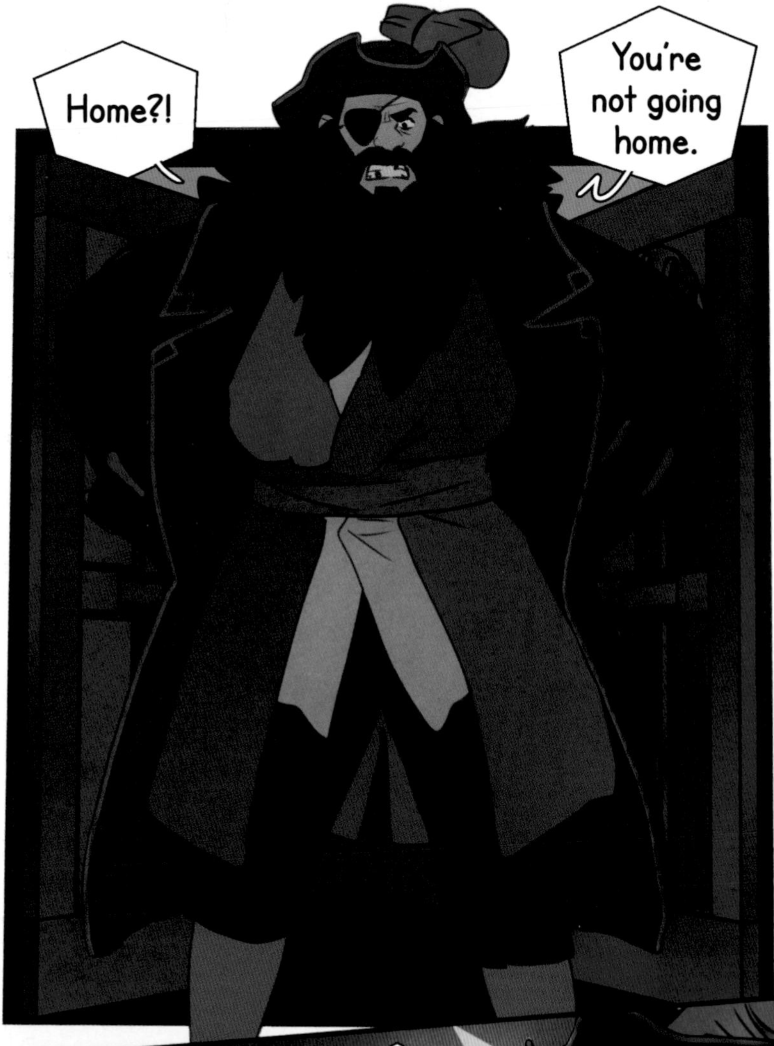
Home?!
You're not going home.

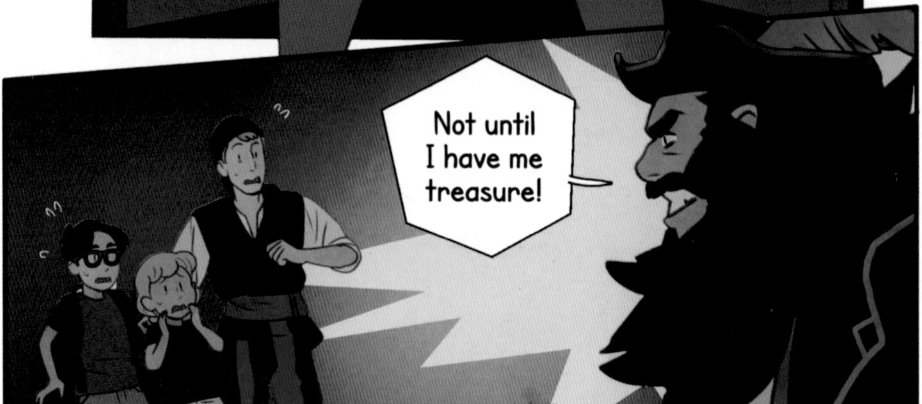
Not until I have me treasure!

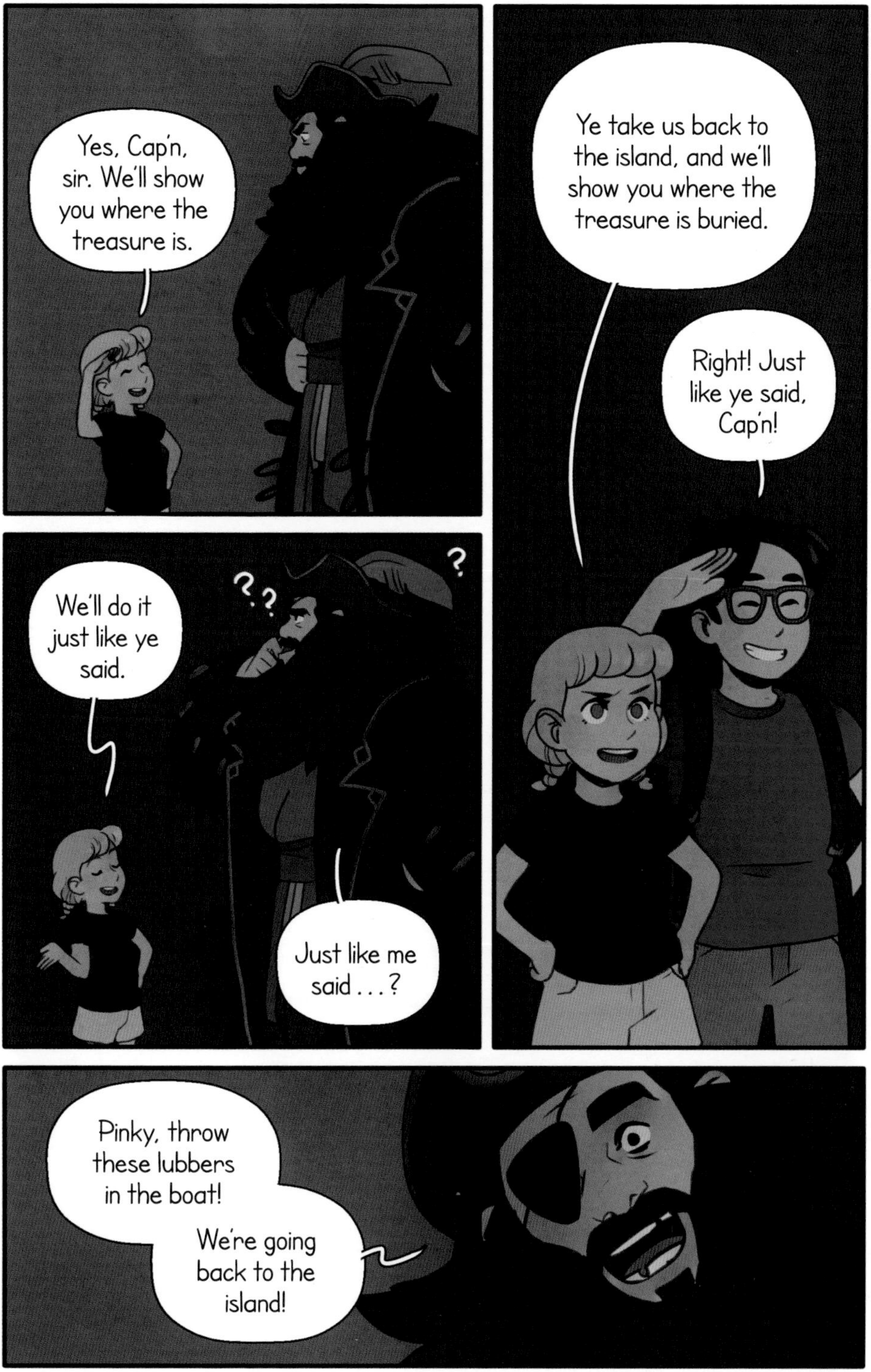
Yes, Cap'n, sir. We'll show you where the treasure is.
Ye take us back to the island, and we'll show you where the treasure is buried.
Right! Just like ye said, Cap'n!
We'll do it just like ye said.
? ? ?
Just like me said . . . ?
Pinky, throw these lubbers in the boat!
We're going back to the island!

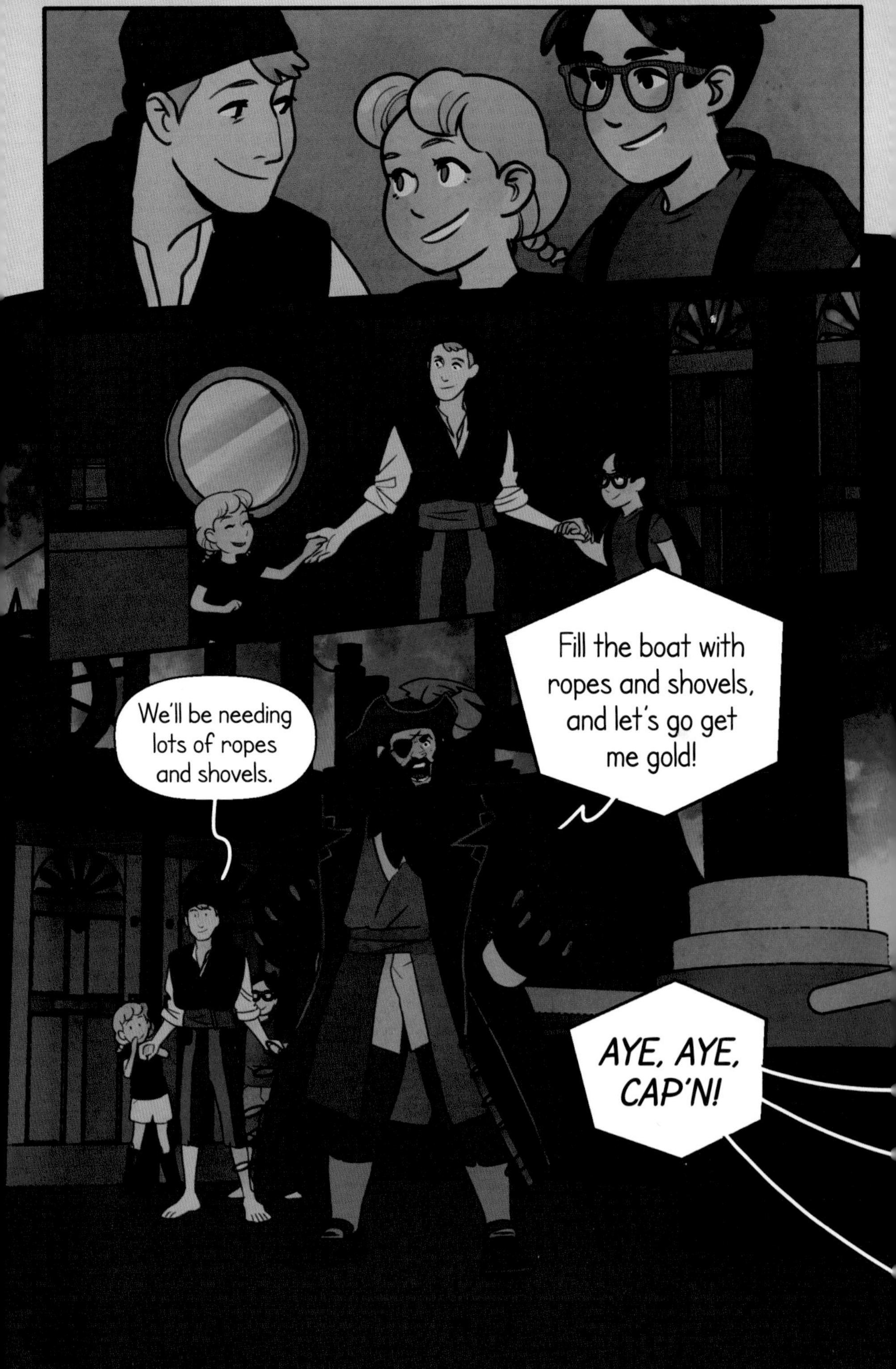
We'll be needing lots of ropes and shovels.
Fill the boat with ropes and shovels, and let's go get me gold!
AYE, AYE, CAP'N!

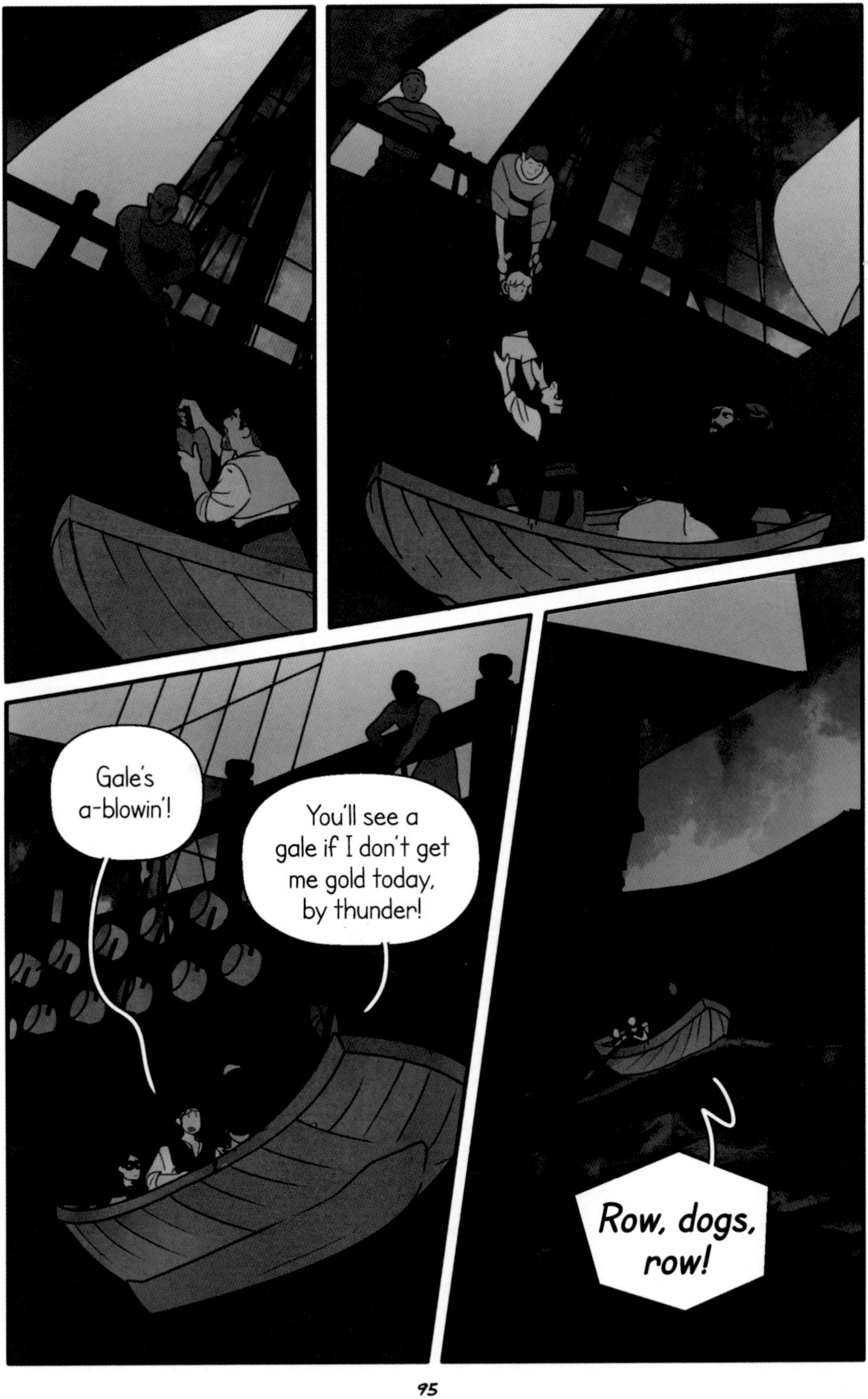
Gale's a-blowin'!
You'll see a gale if I don't get me gold today, by thunder!
Row, dogs, row!

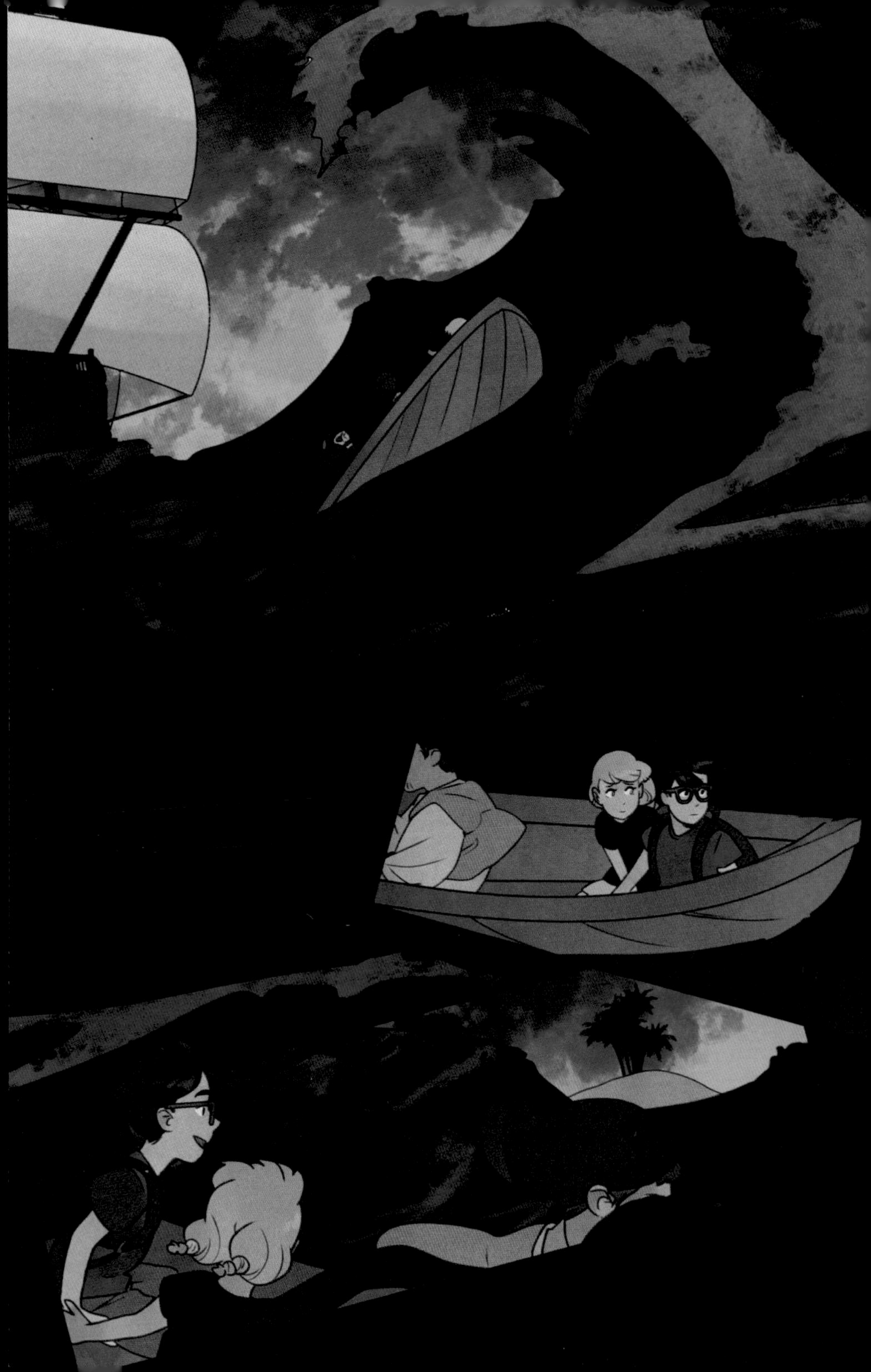

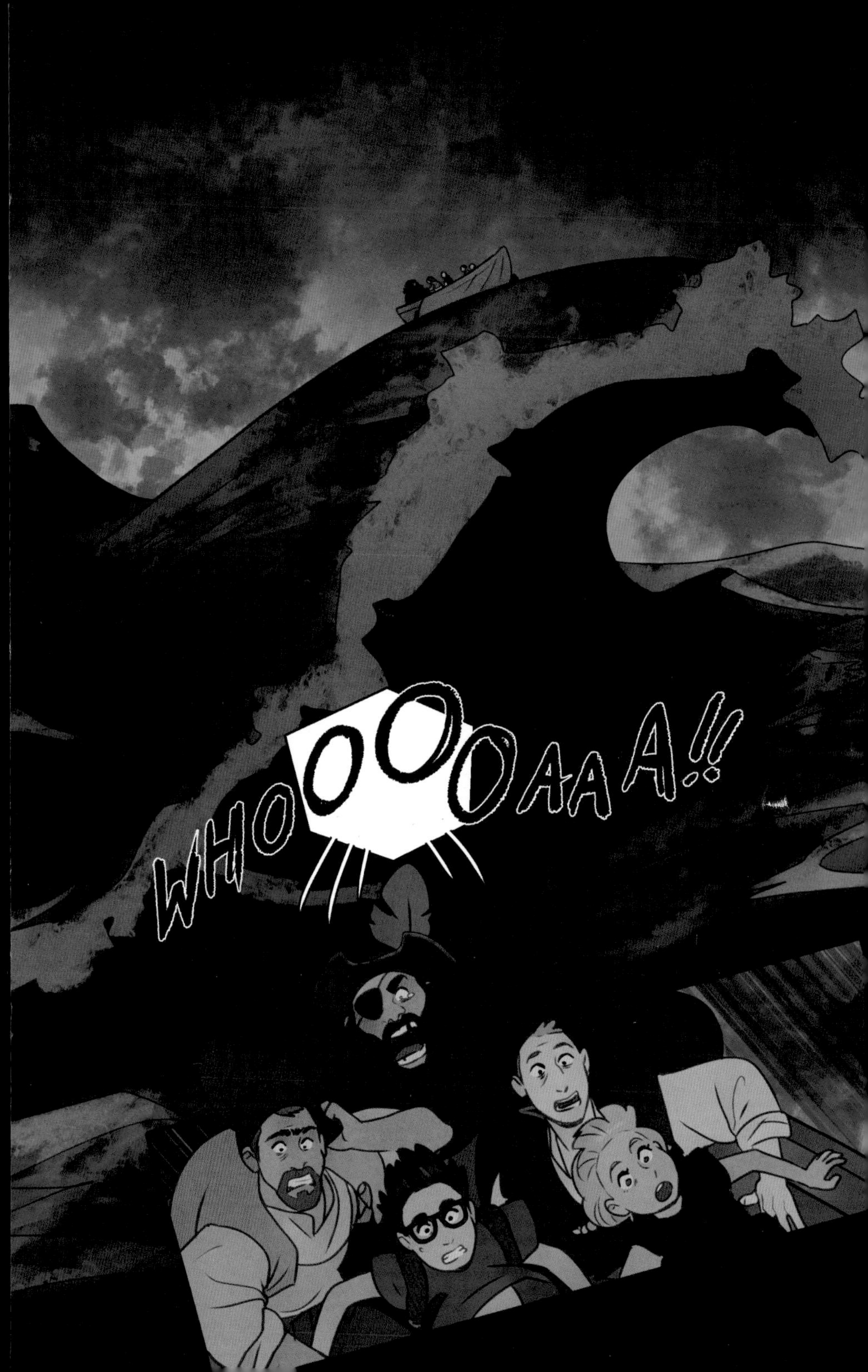
WHOOOOAAA!!

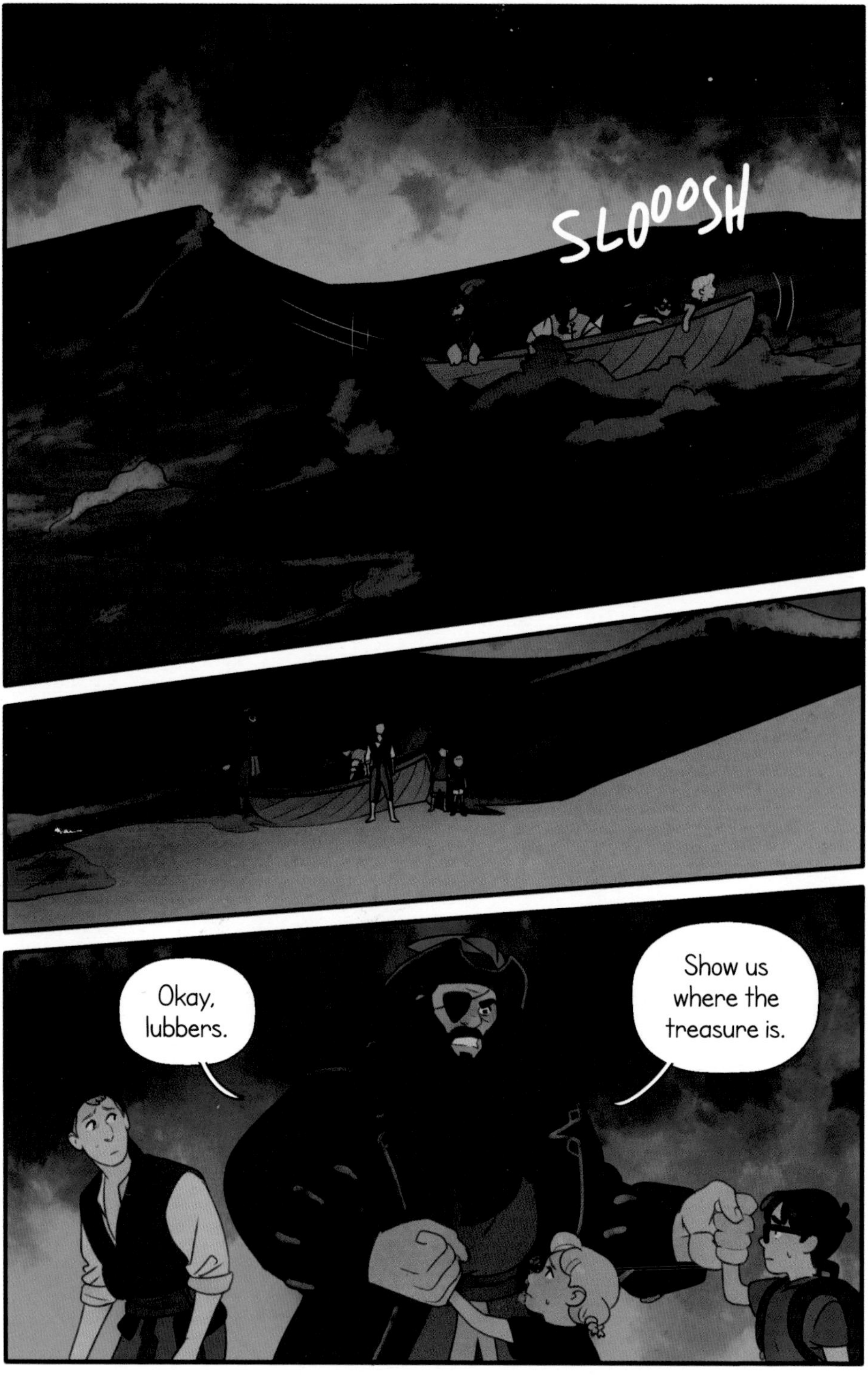
SLOOOSH
Okay, lubbers.
Show us where the treasure is.

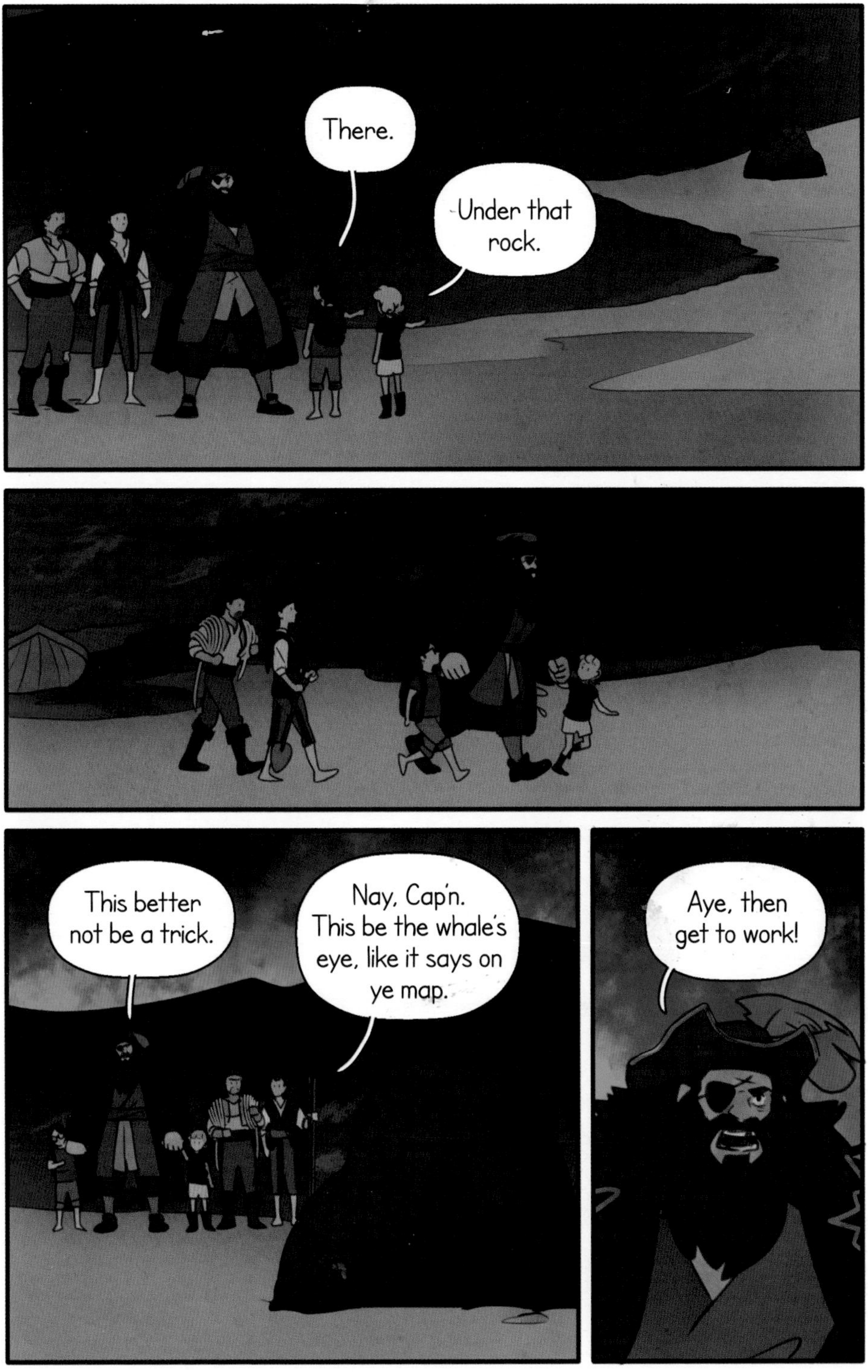
There.
Under that rock.
This better not be a trick.
Nay, Cap'n. This be the whale's eye, like it says on ye map.
Aye, then get to work!

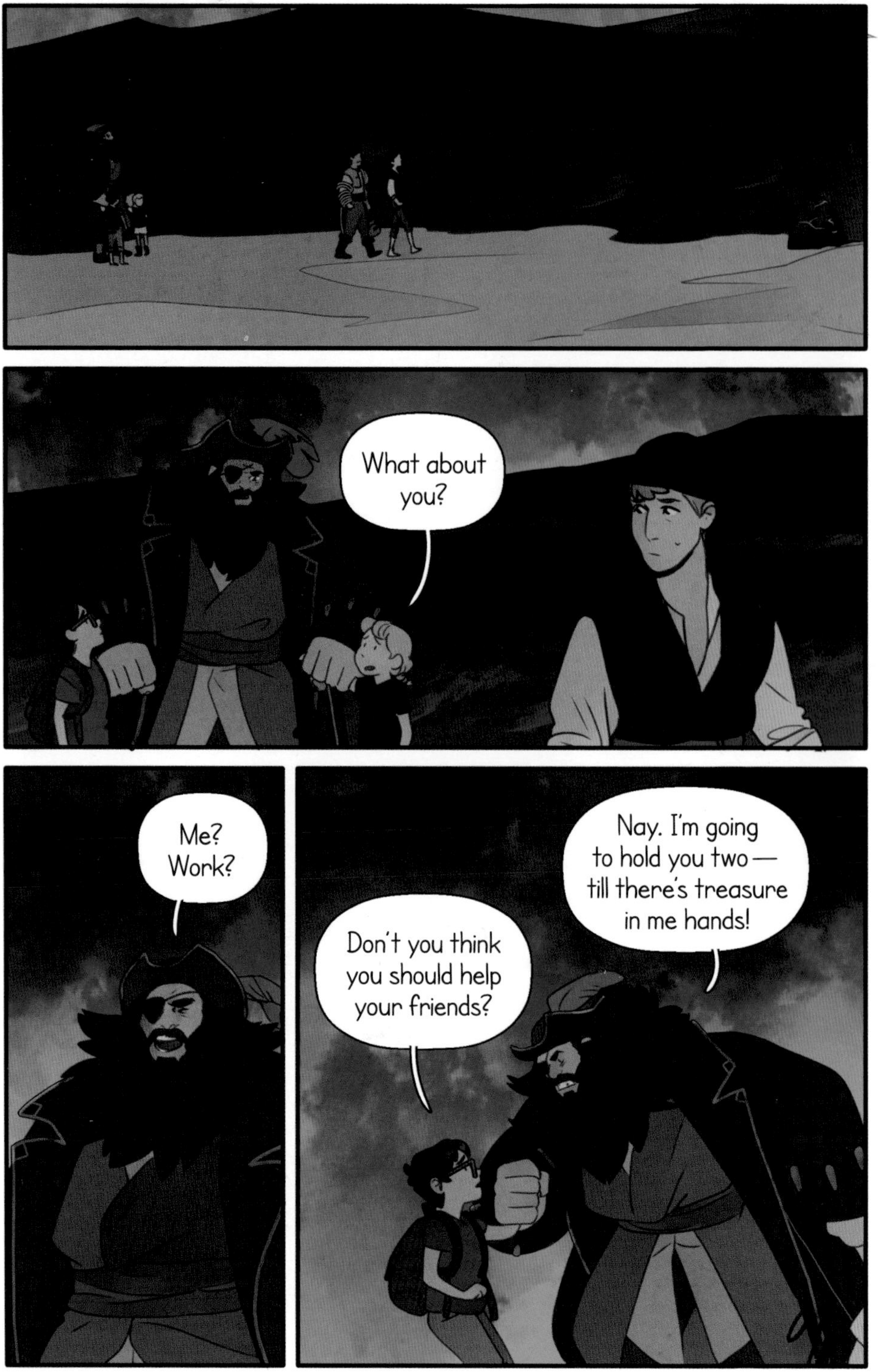
What about you?
Me? Work?
Nay. I'm going to hold you two — till there's treasure in me hands!
Don't you think you should help your friends?

CHAPTER EIGHT
Dig, Dogs, Dig

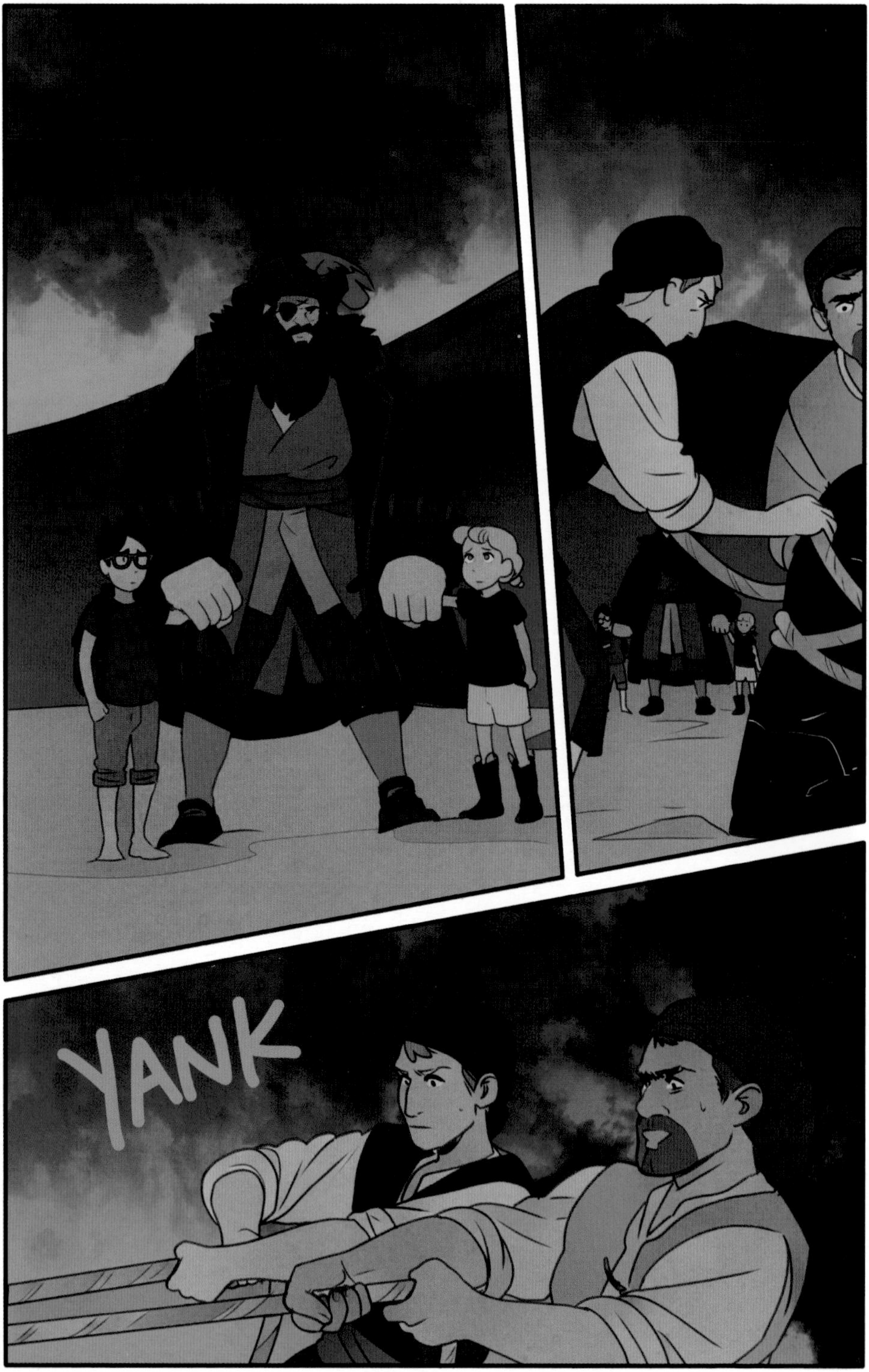
YANK

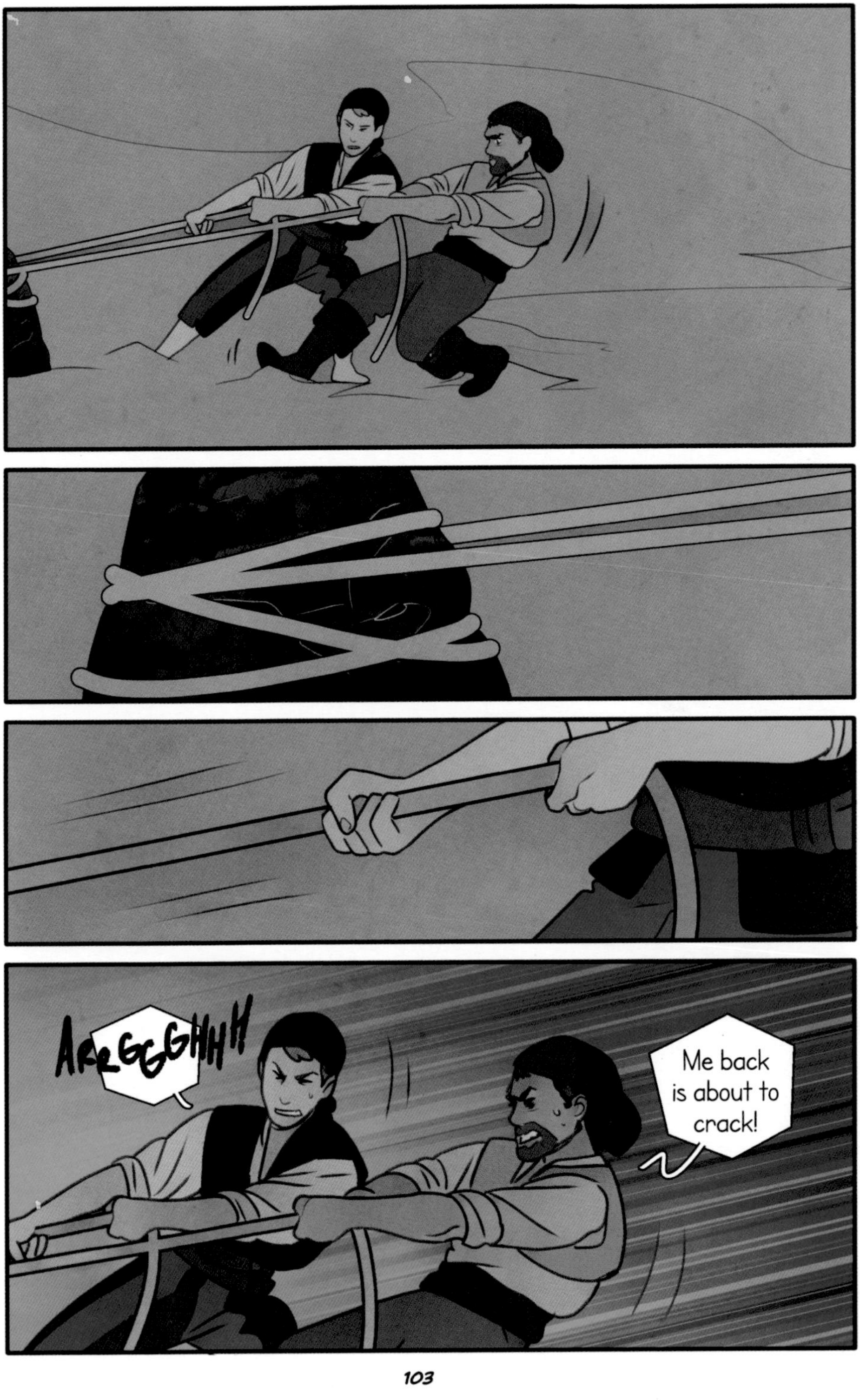
ARRGGGHHH!
Me back is about to crack!

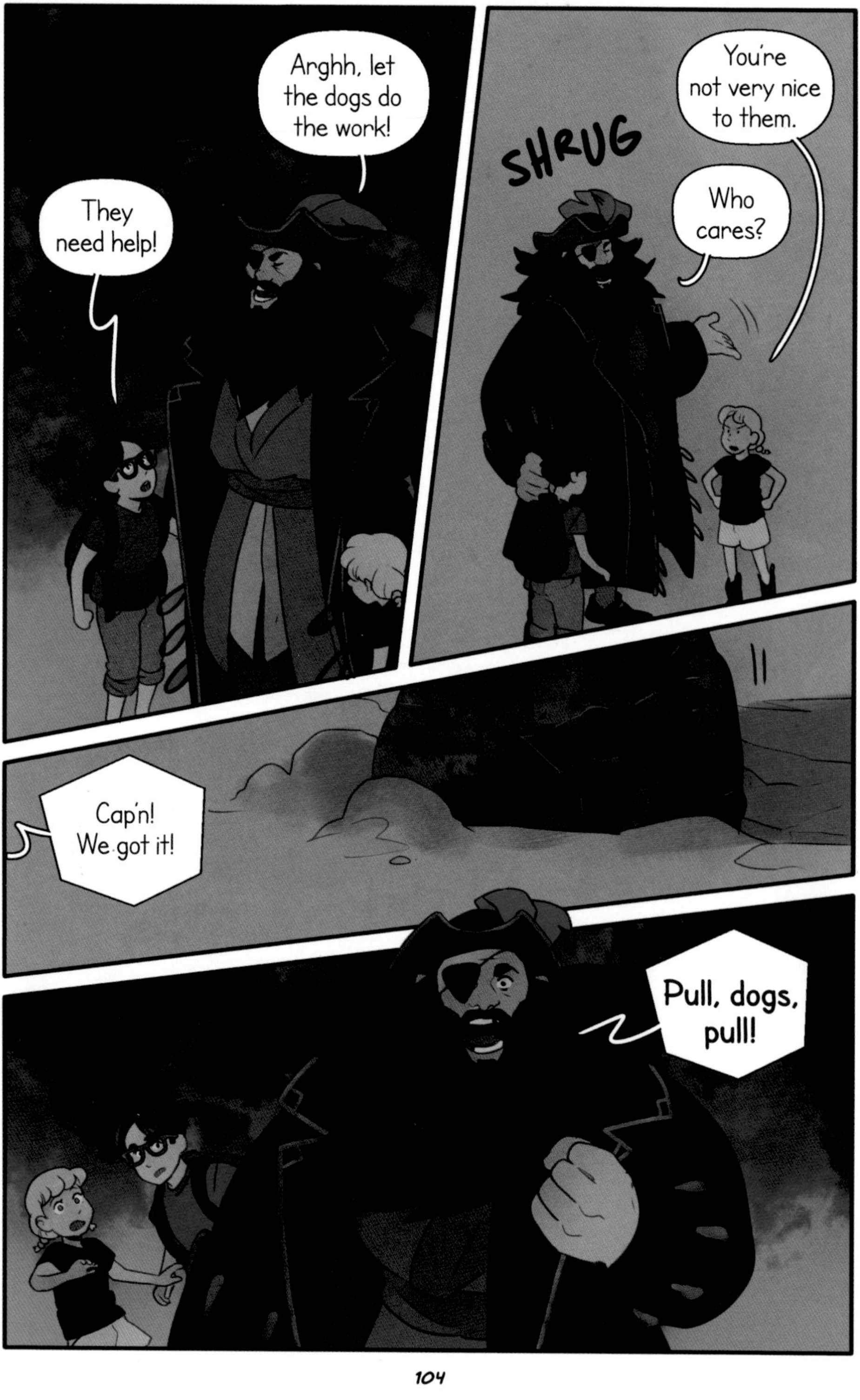
Arghh, let the dogs do the work!
They need help!
SHRUG
You're not very nice to them.
Who cares?
Cap'n! We got it!
Pull, dogs, pull!

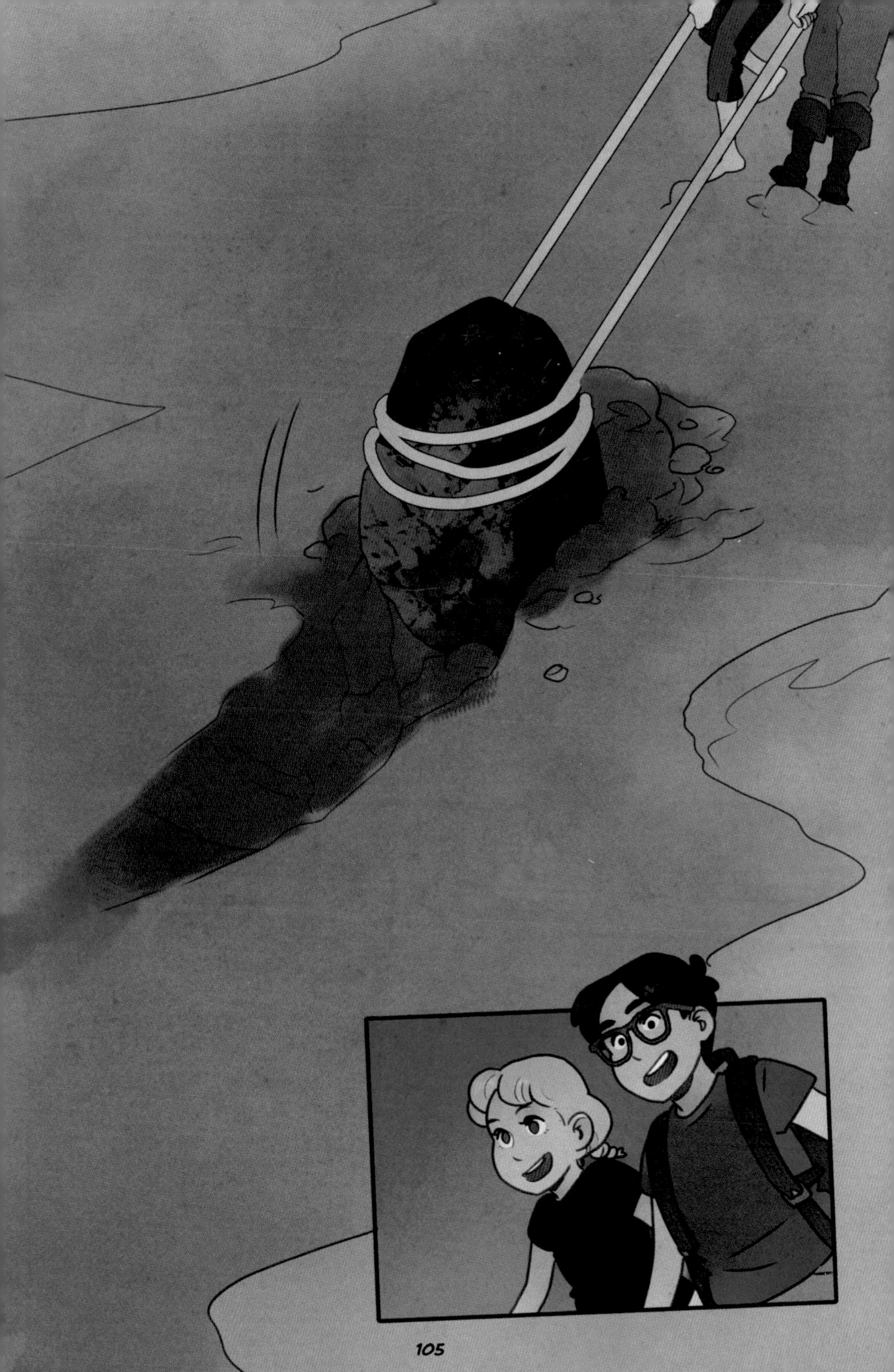

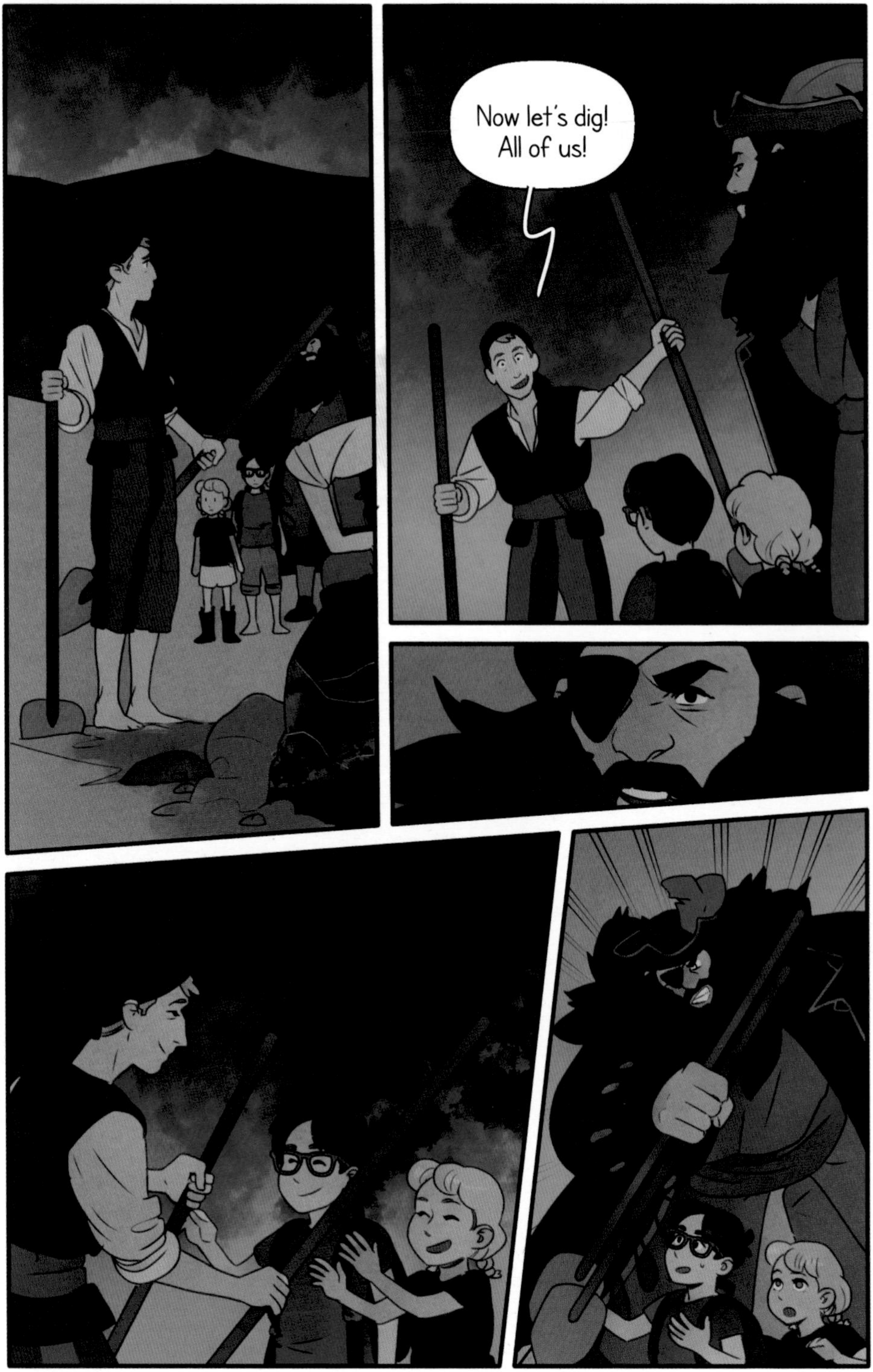
Now let's dig!
All of us!

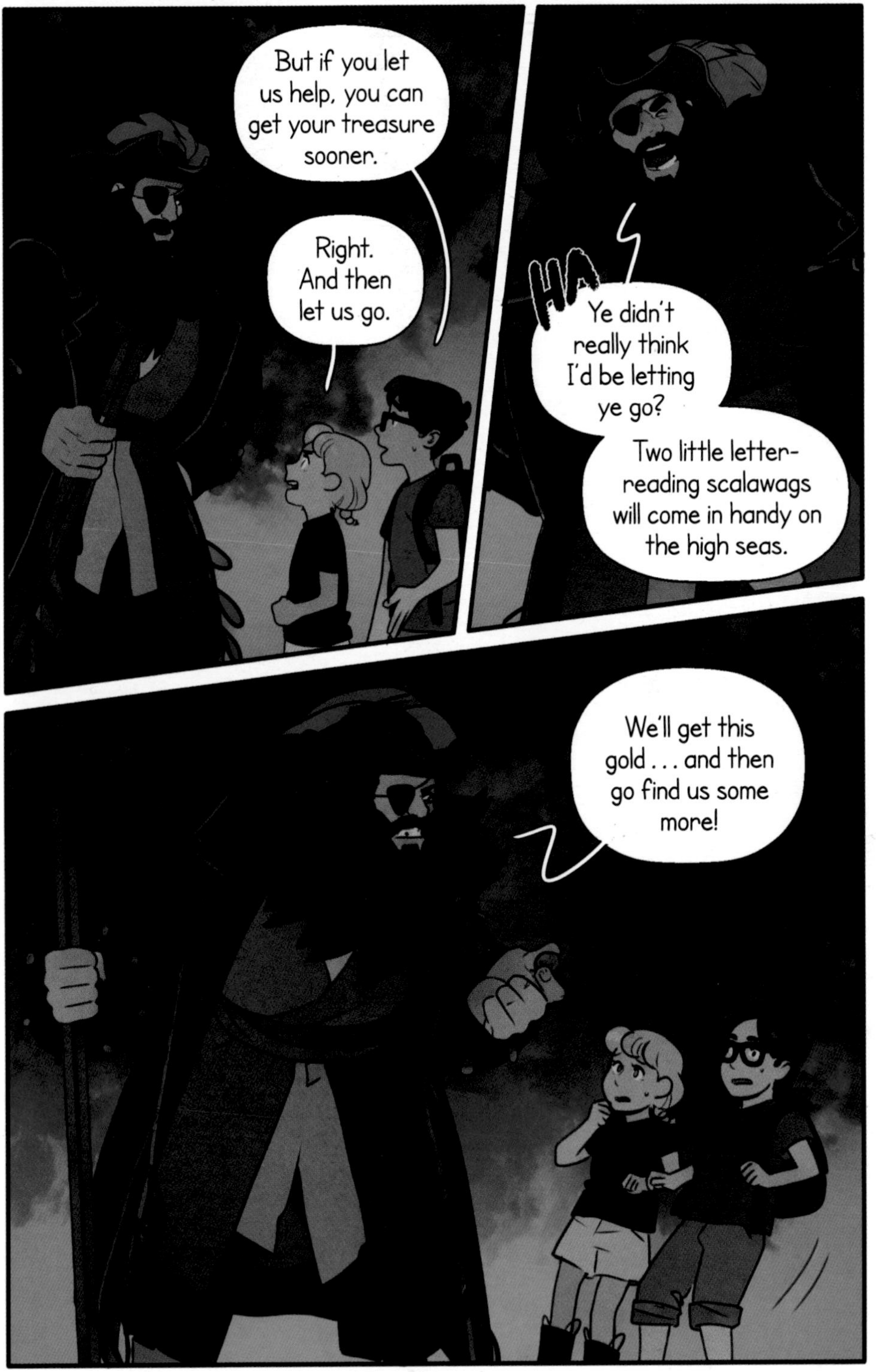
But if you let us help, you can get your treasure sooner.
Right. And then let us go.
HA
Ye didn't really think I'd be letting ye go?
Two little letter-reading scalawags will come in handy on the high seas.
We'll get this gold . . . and then go find us some more!

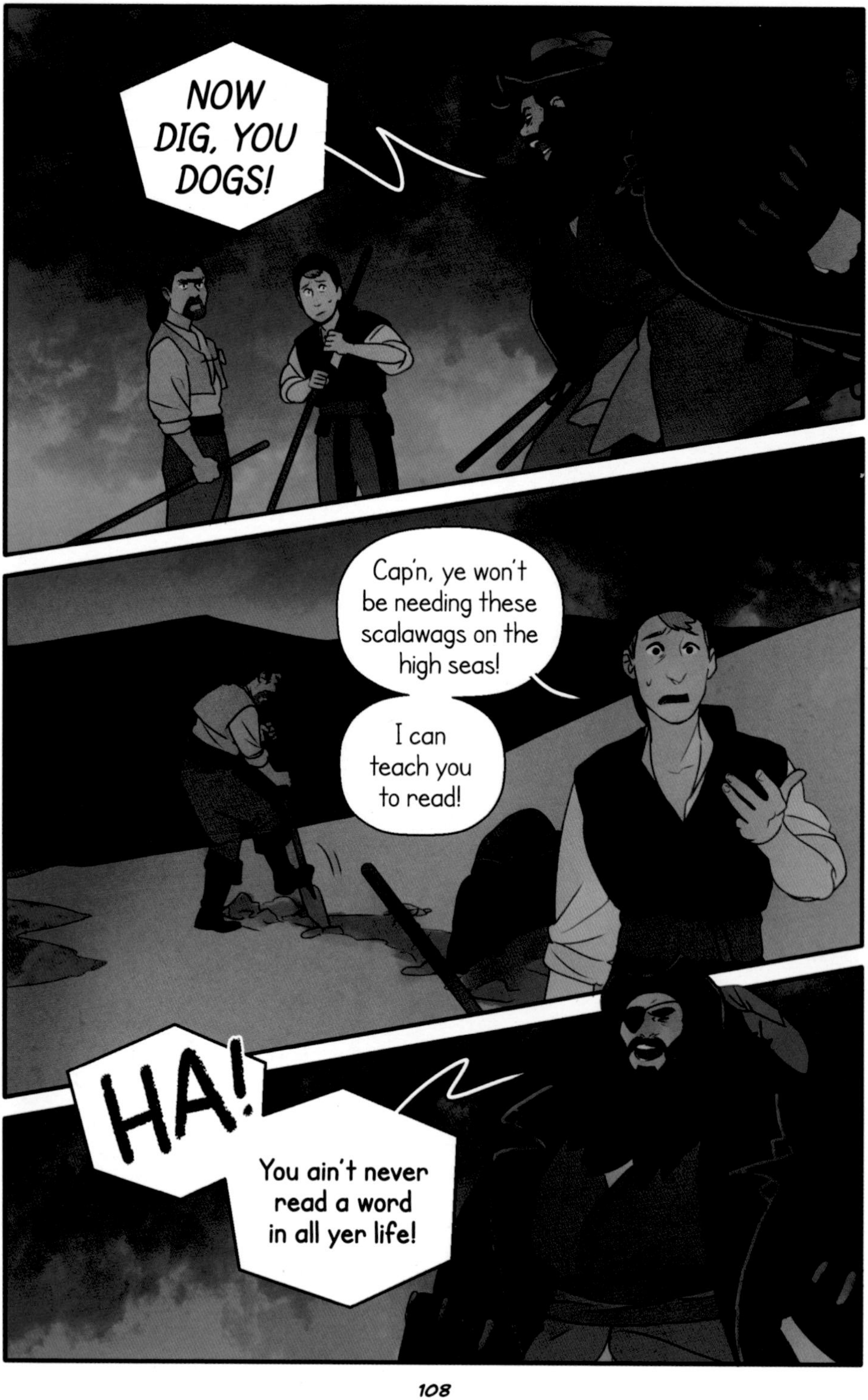
NOW DIG, YOU DOGS!
Cap'n, ye won't be needing these scalawags on the high seas!
I can teach you to read!
HA!
You ain't never read a word in all yer life!

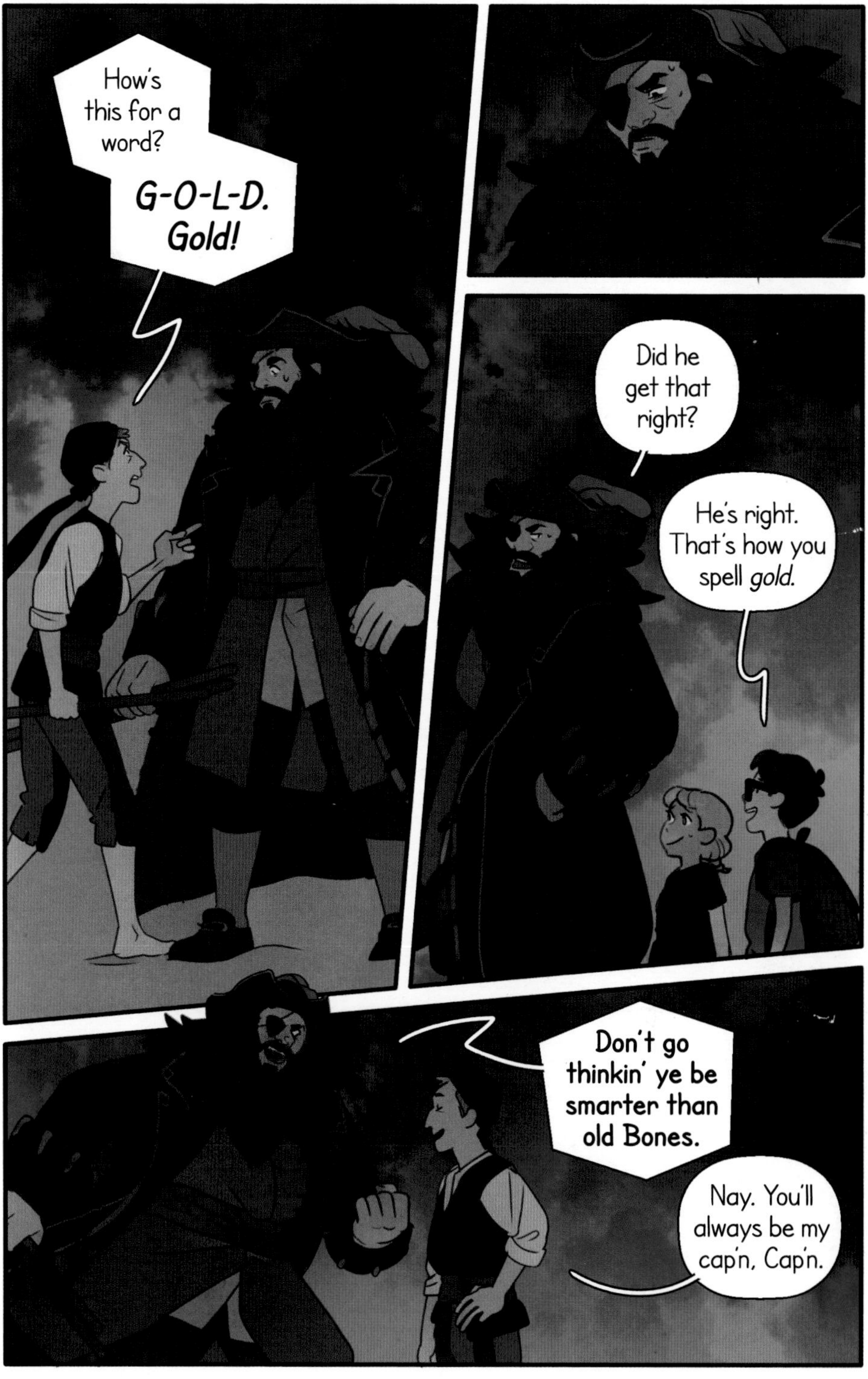
How's this for a word?
G-O-L-D. Gold!
Did he get that right?
He's right. That's how you spell *gold.*
Don't go thinkin' ye be smarter than old Bones.
Nay. You'll always be my cap'n, Cap'n.

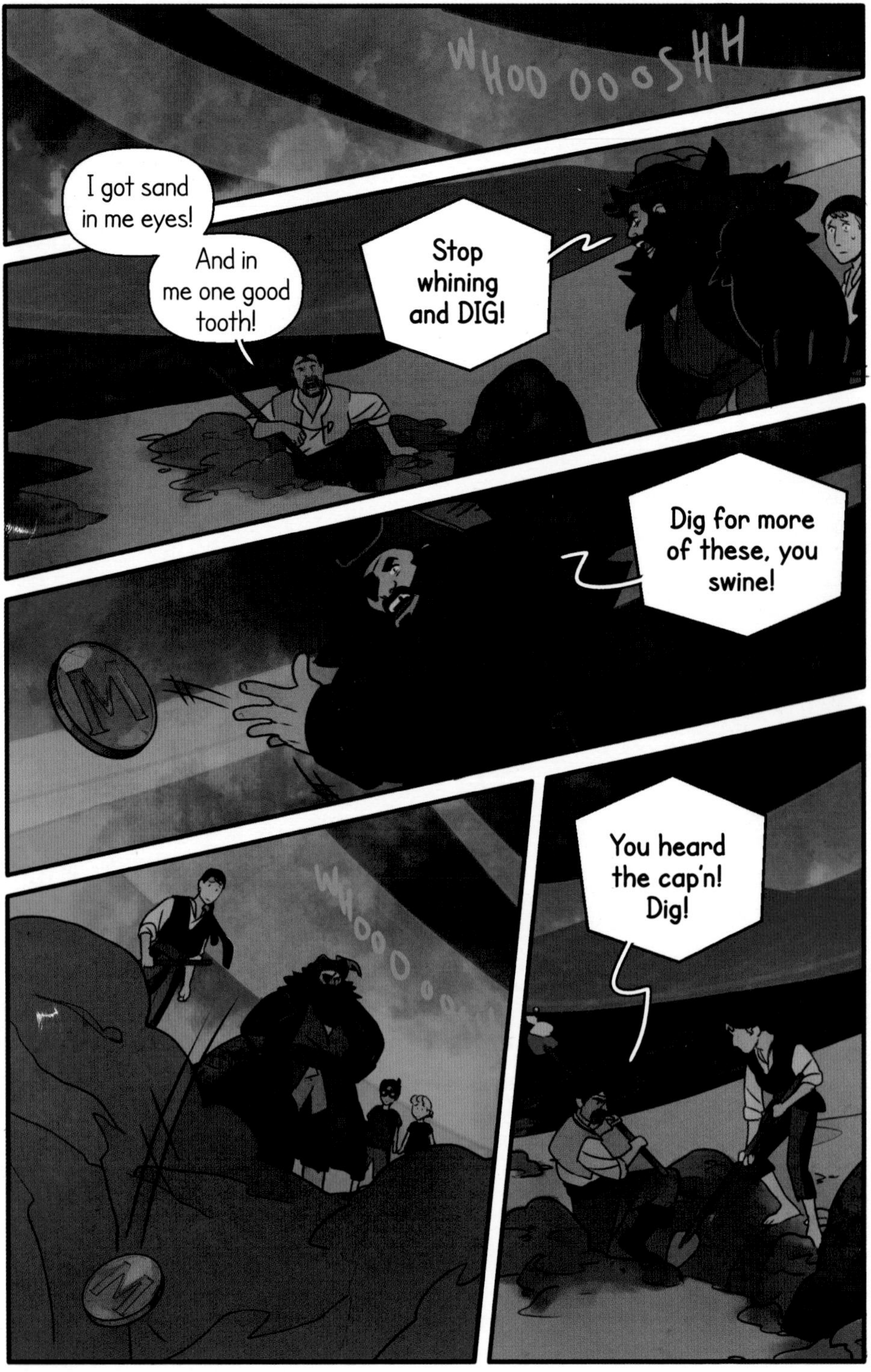
WHOOOOOSHH
I got sand in me eyes!
And in me one good tooth!
Stop whining and DIG!
Dig for more of these, you swine!
WHOOOOO
You heard the cap'n! Dig!

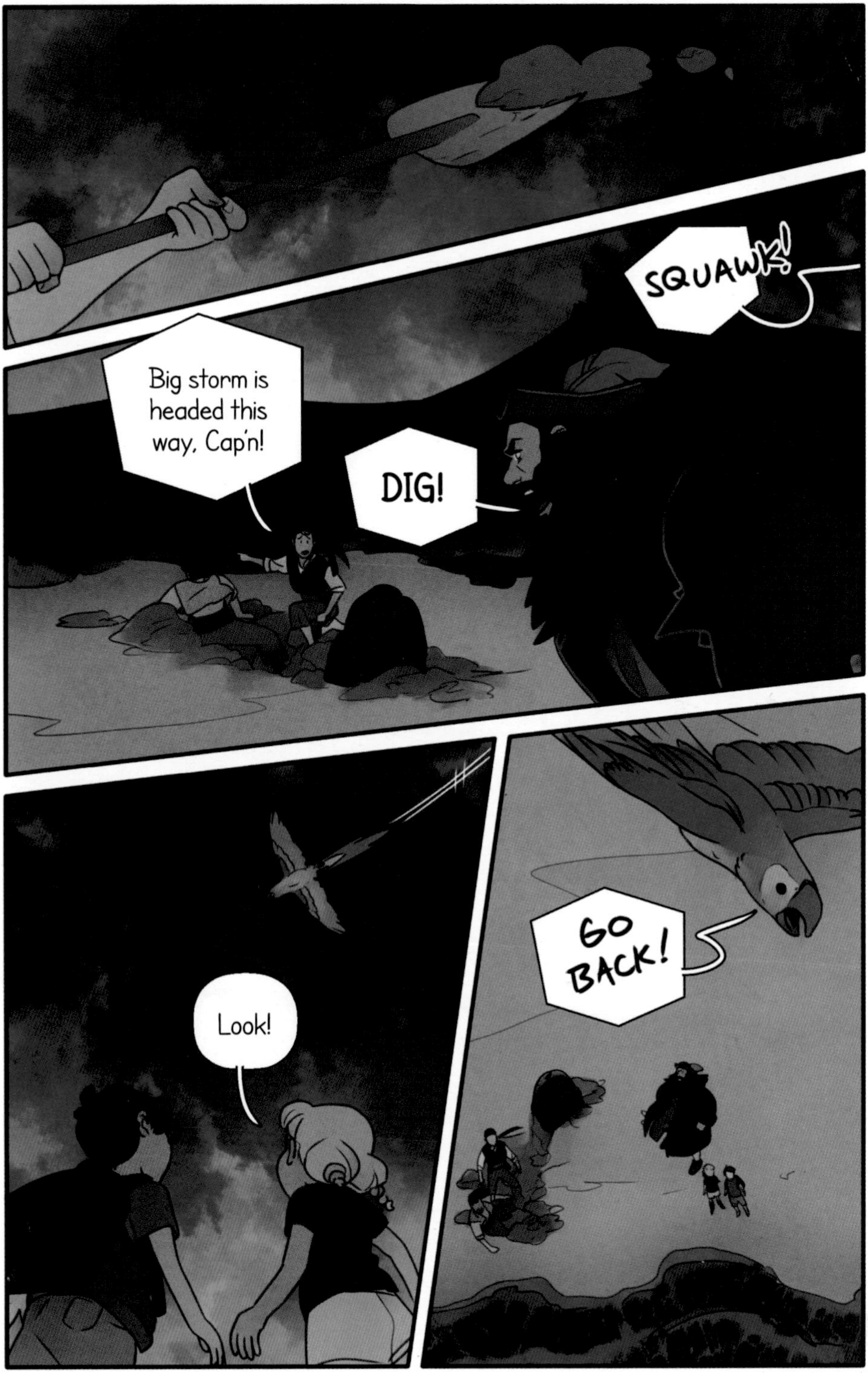
SQUAWK!
Big storm is headed this way, Cap'n!
DIG!
Look!
GO BACK!

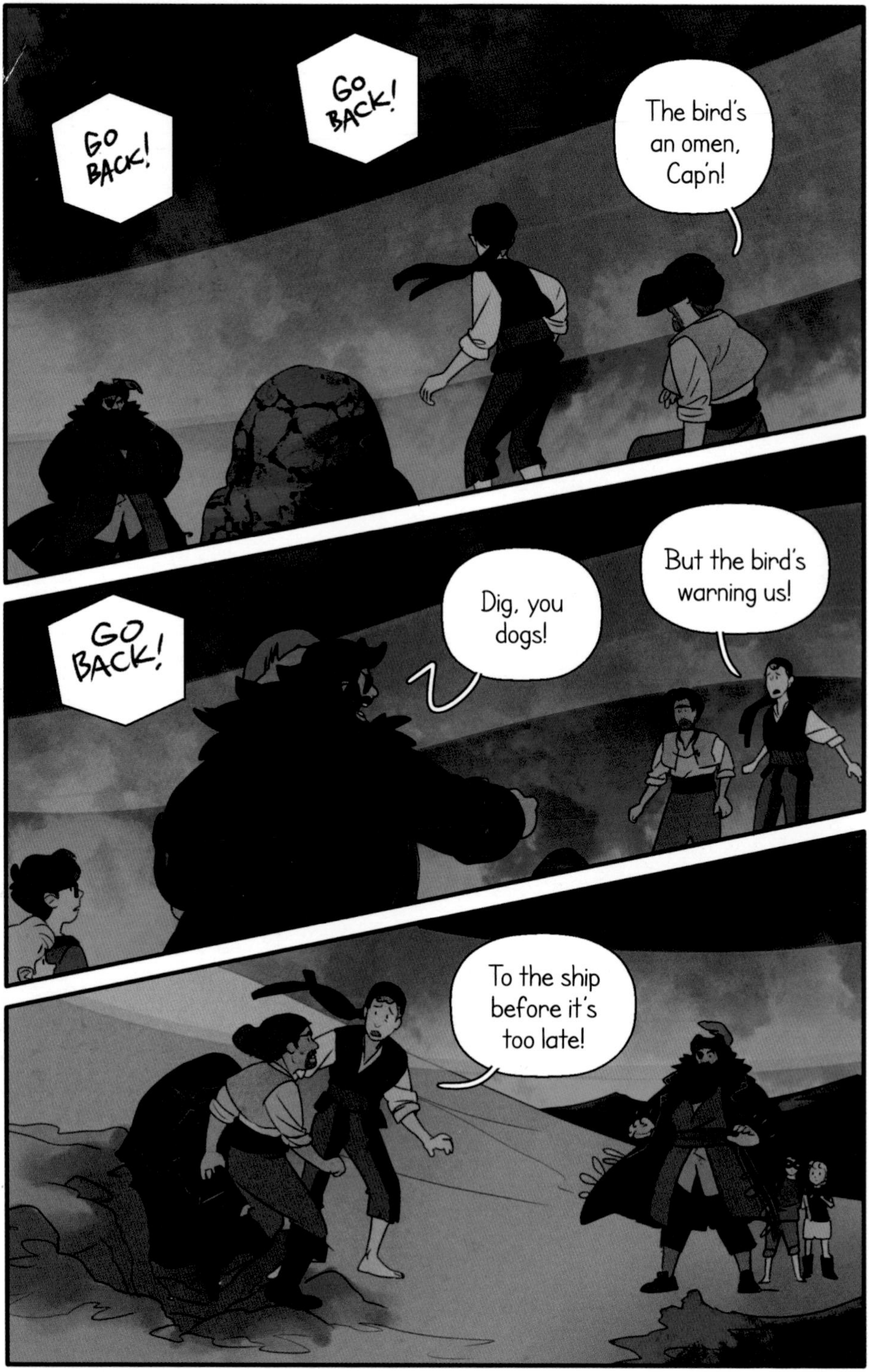
GO BACK!
GO BACK!
The bird's an omen, Cap'n!
GO BACK!
Dig, you dogs!
But the bird's warning us!
To the ship before it's too late!

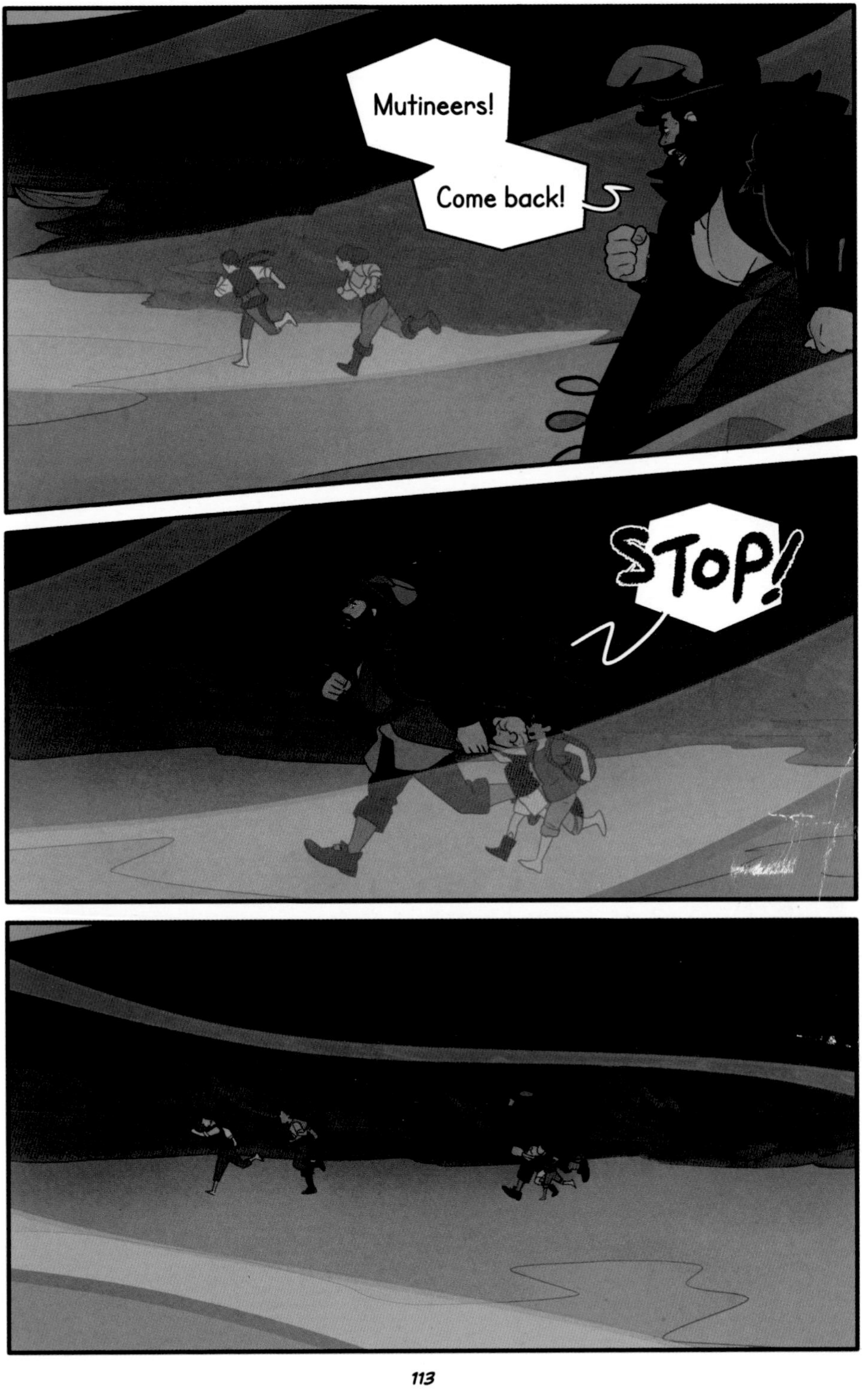
Mutineers!
Come back!
STOP!

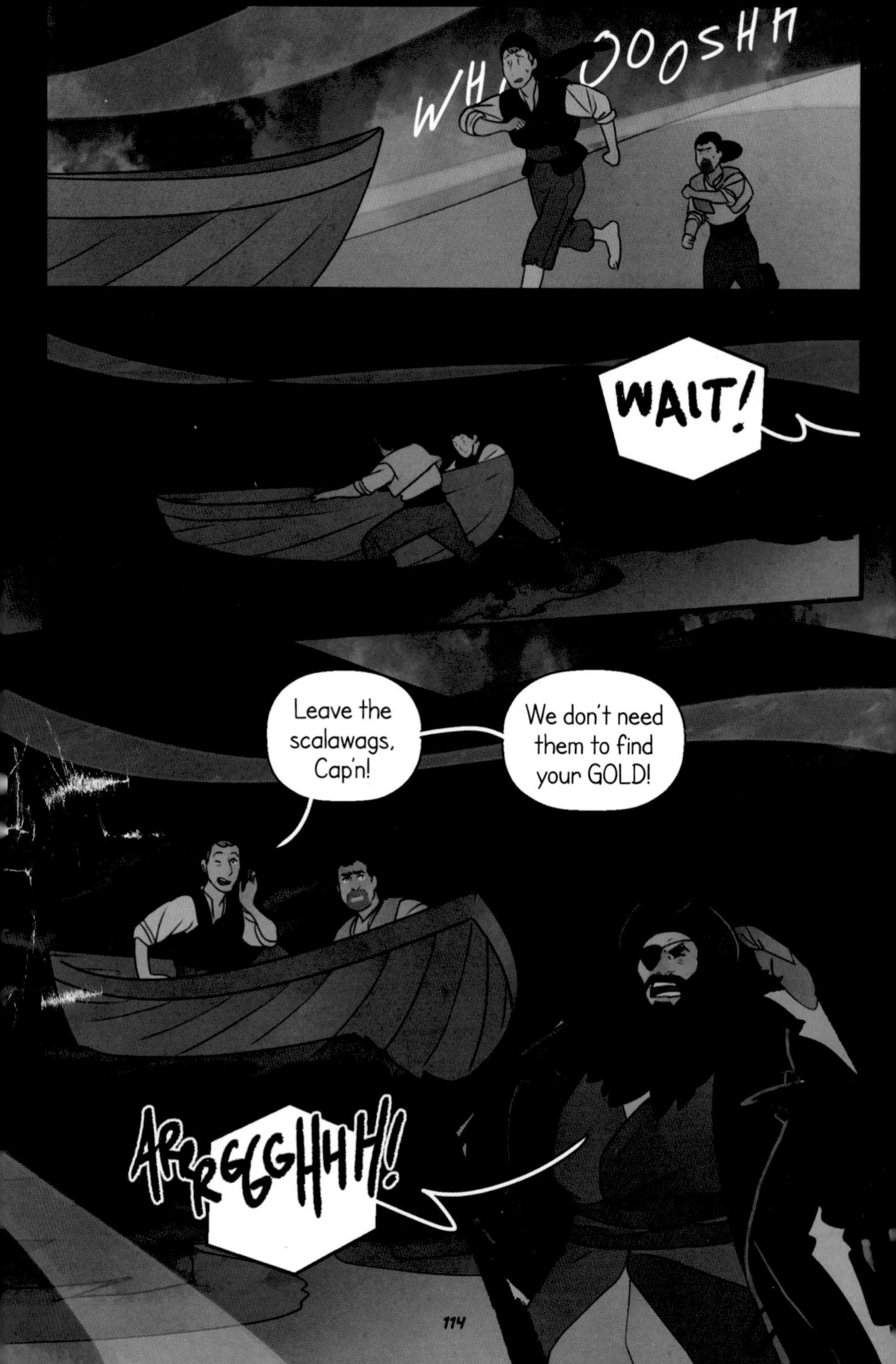
WHOOOOSHM
WAIT!
Leave the scalawags, Cap'n!
We don't need them to find your GOLD!
ARRRGGHHH!

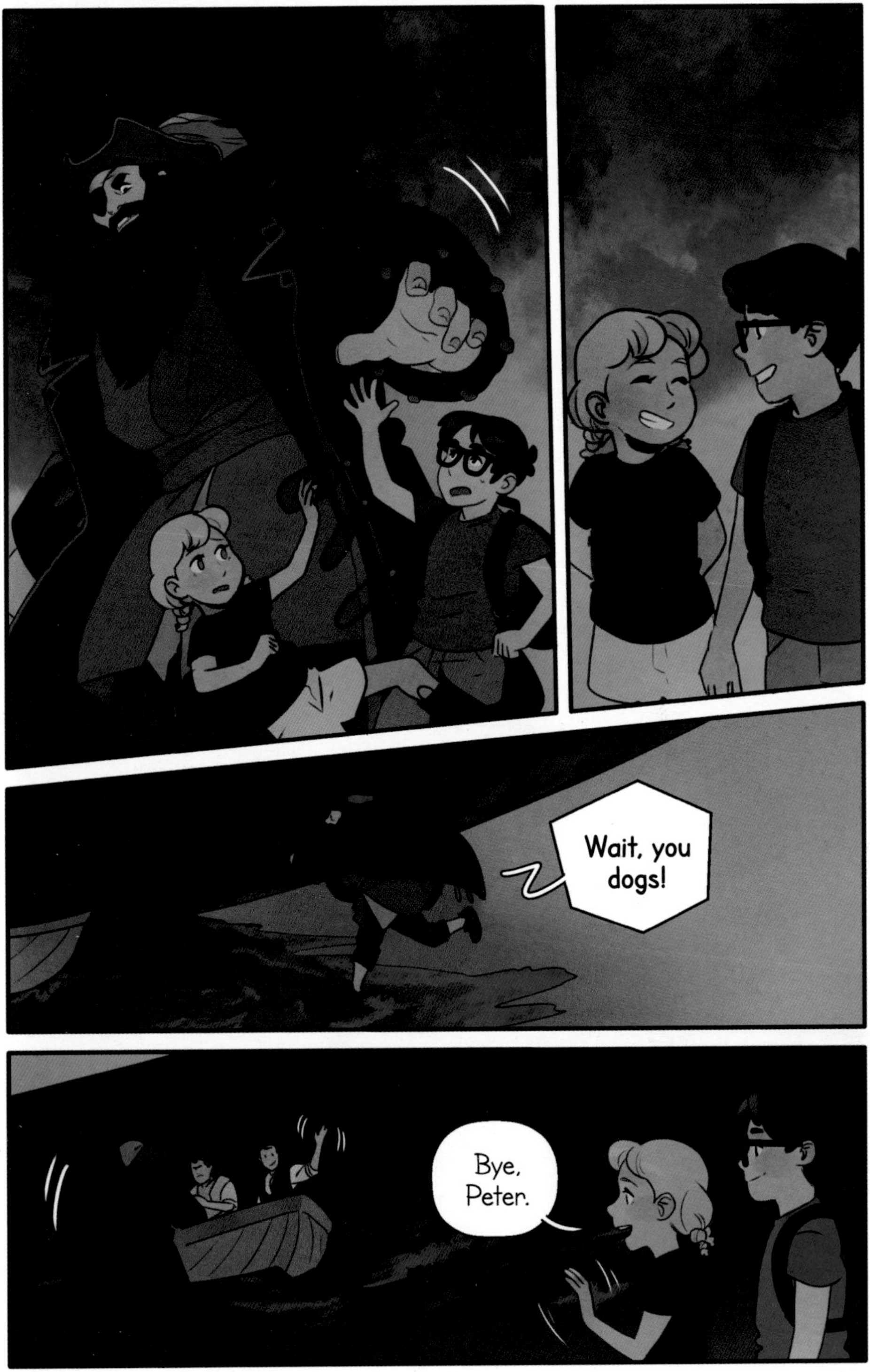
Wait, you dogs!
Bye, Peter.

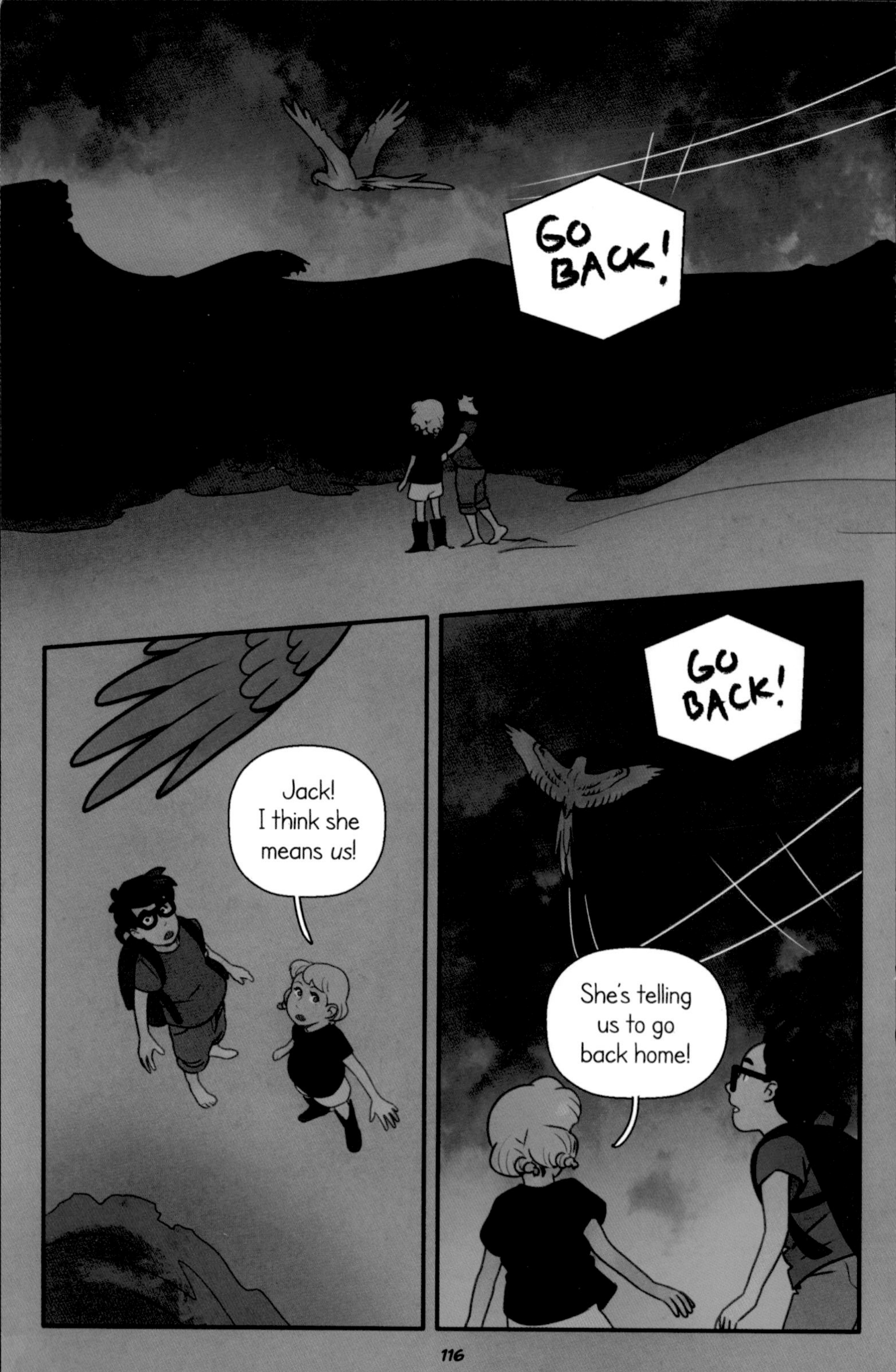
GO BACK!
GO BACK!
Jack! I think she means *us*!
She's telling us to go back home!

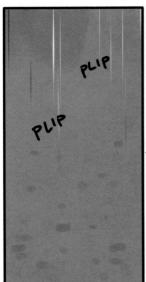

PLIP
PLIP

PLIP
PLIP
PLIP
PLIP
PLIP

Let's go!

You go!
I have to get
the medallion!

Get the
Pennsylvania
book ready!
Hurry!

Okay!
And *you*
hurry!

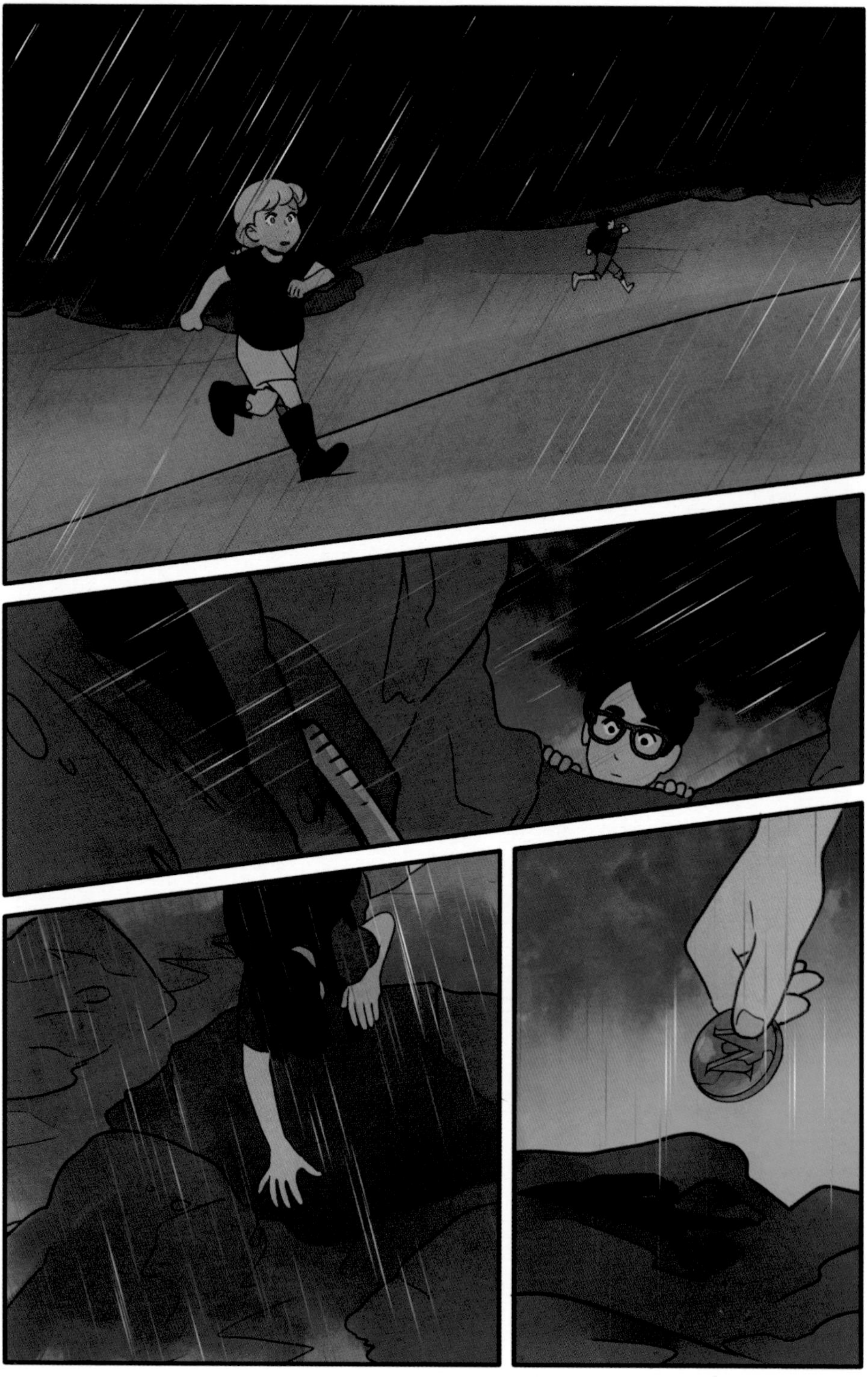

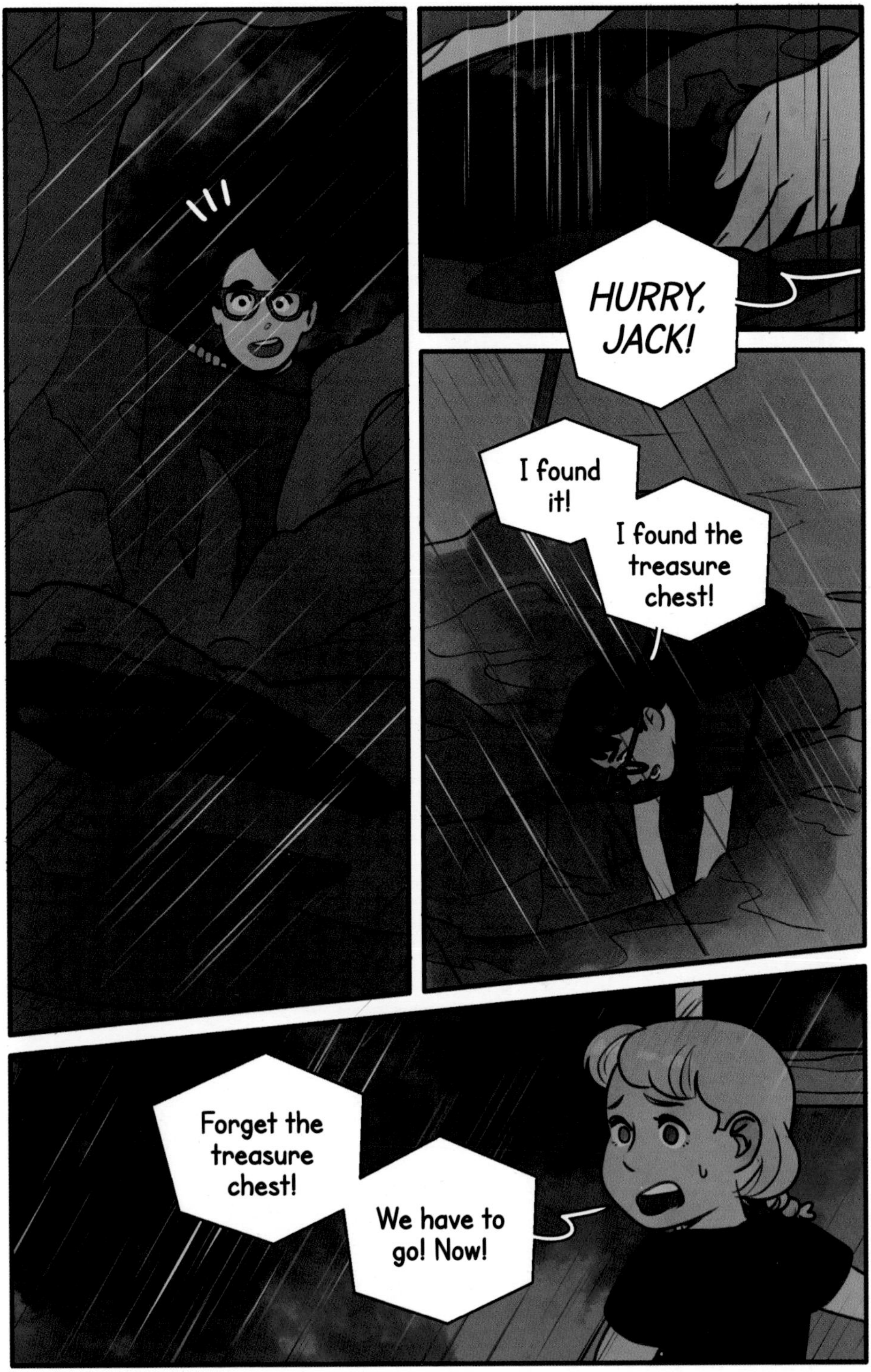
HURRY, JACK!
I found it!
I found the treasure chest!
Forget the treasure chest!
We have to go! Now!

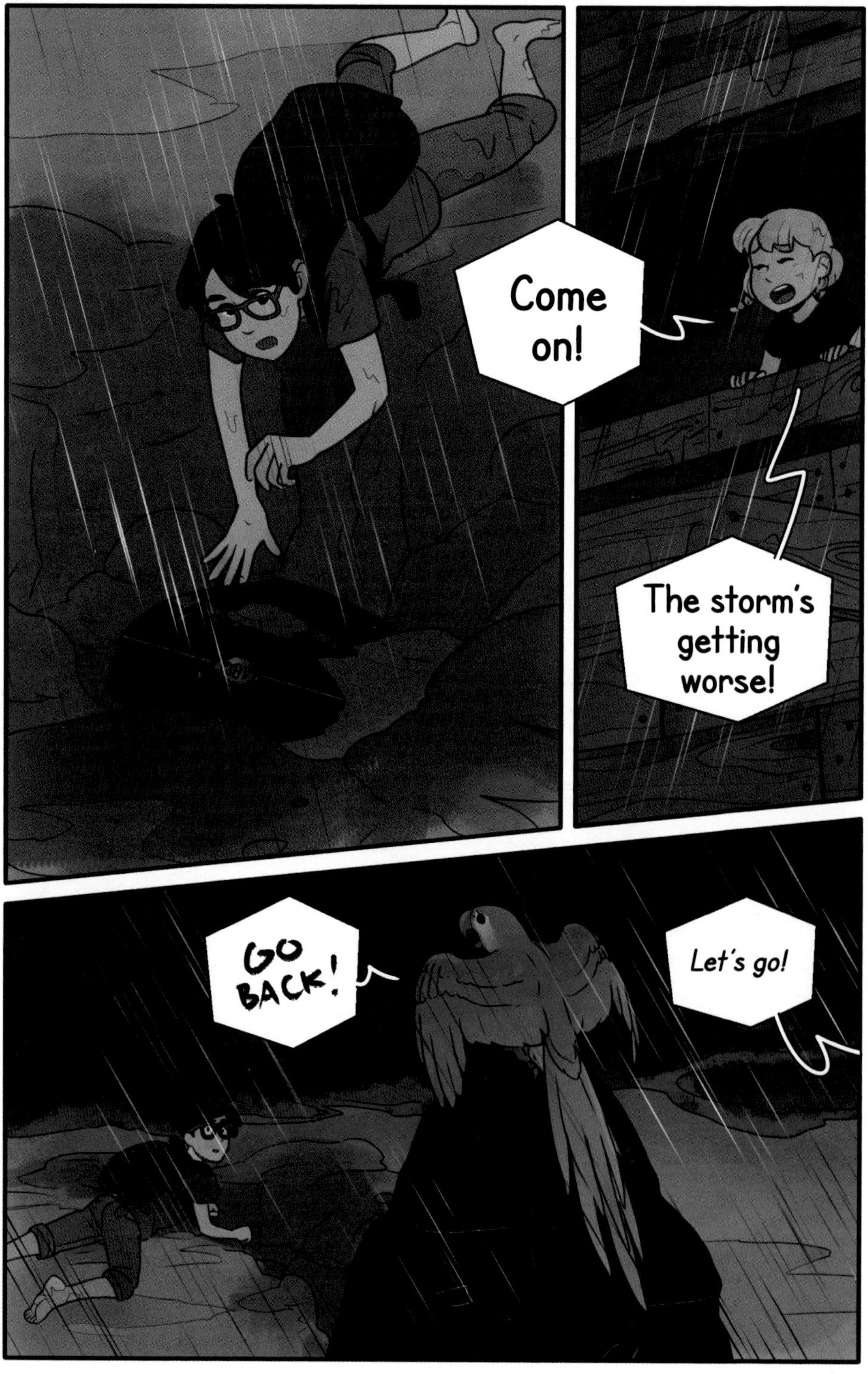
Come on!
The storm's getting worse!
GO BACK!
Let's go!

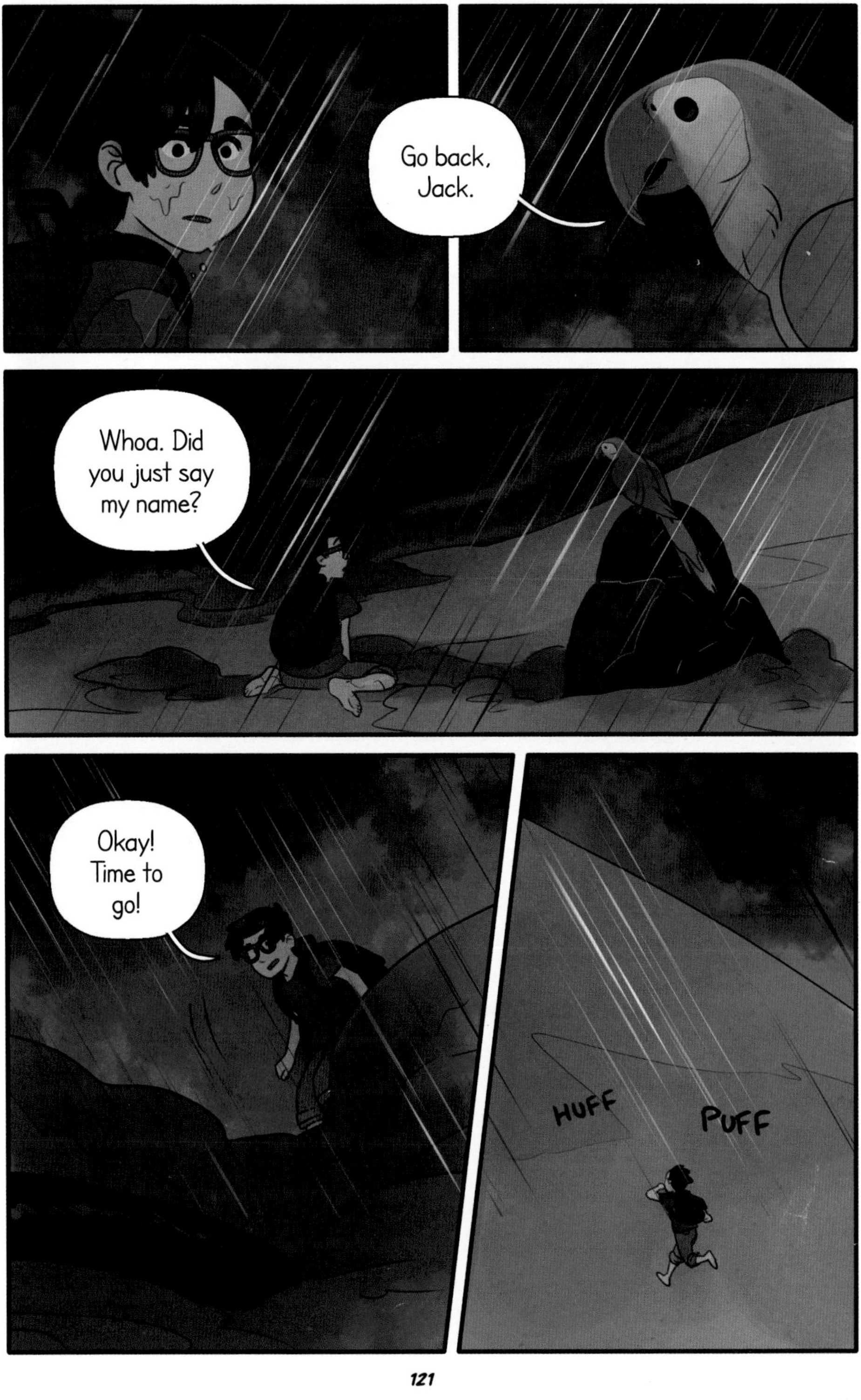
Go back, Jack.
Whoa. Did you just say my name?
Okay! Time to go!
HUFF
PUFF

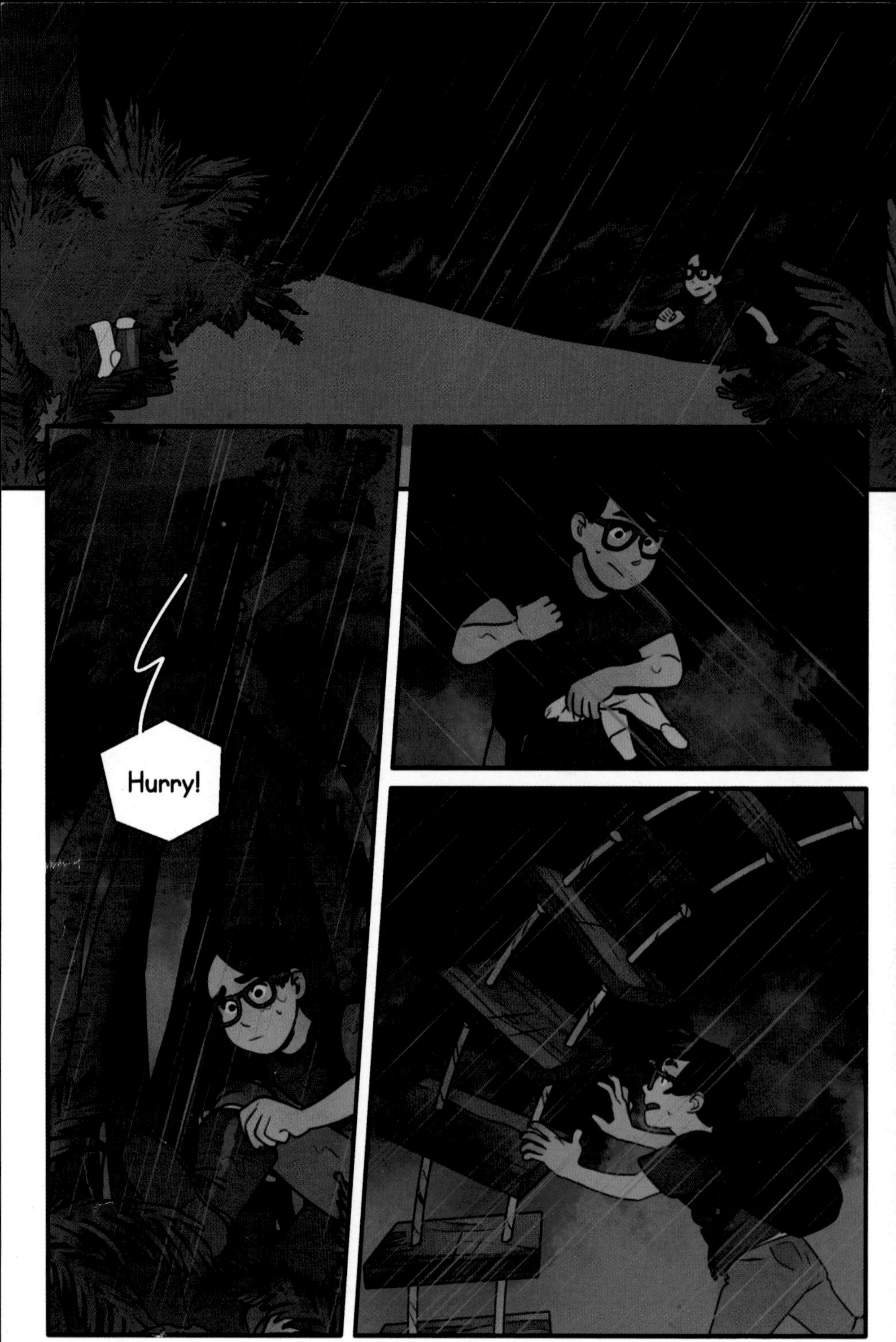
Hurry!

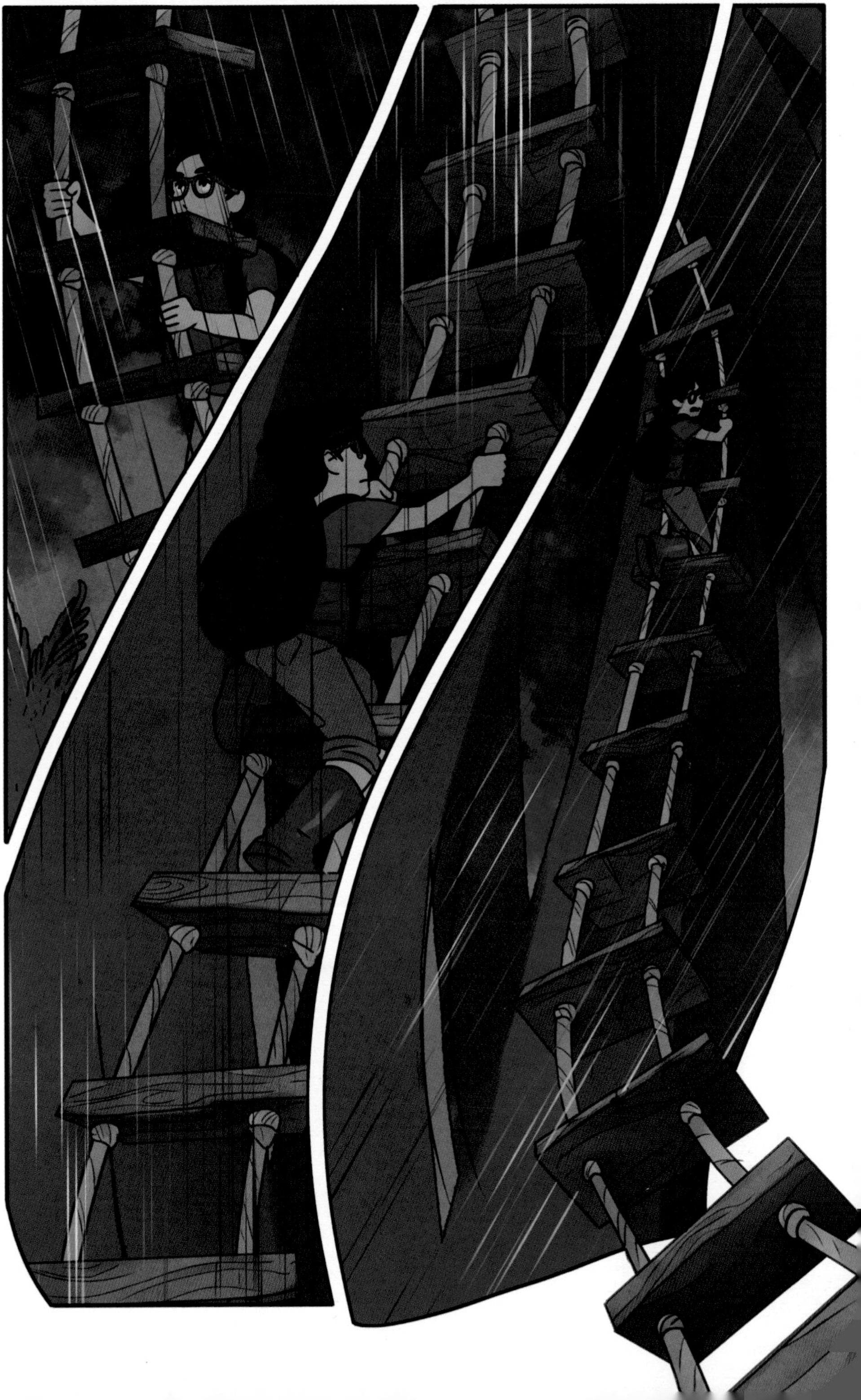

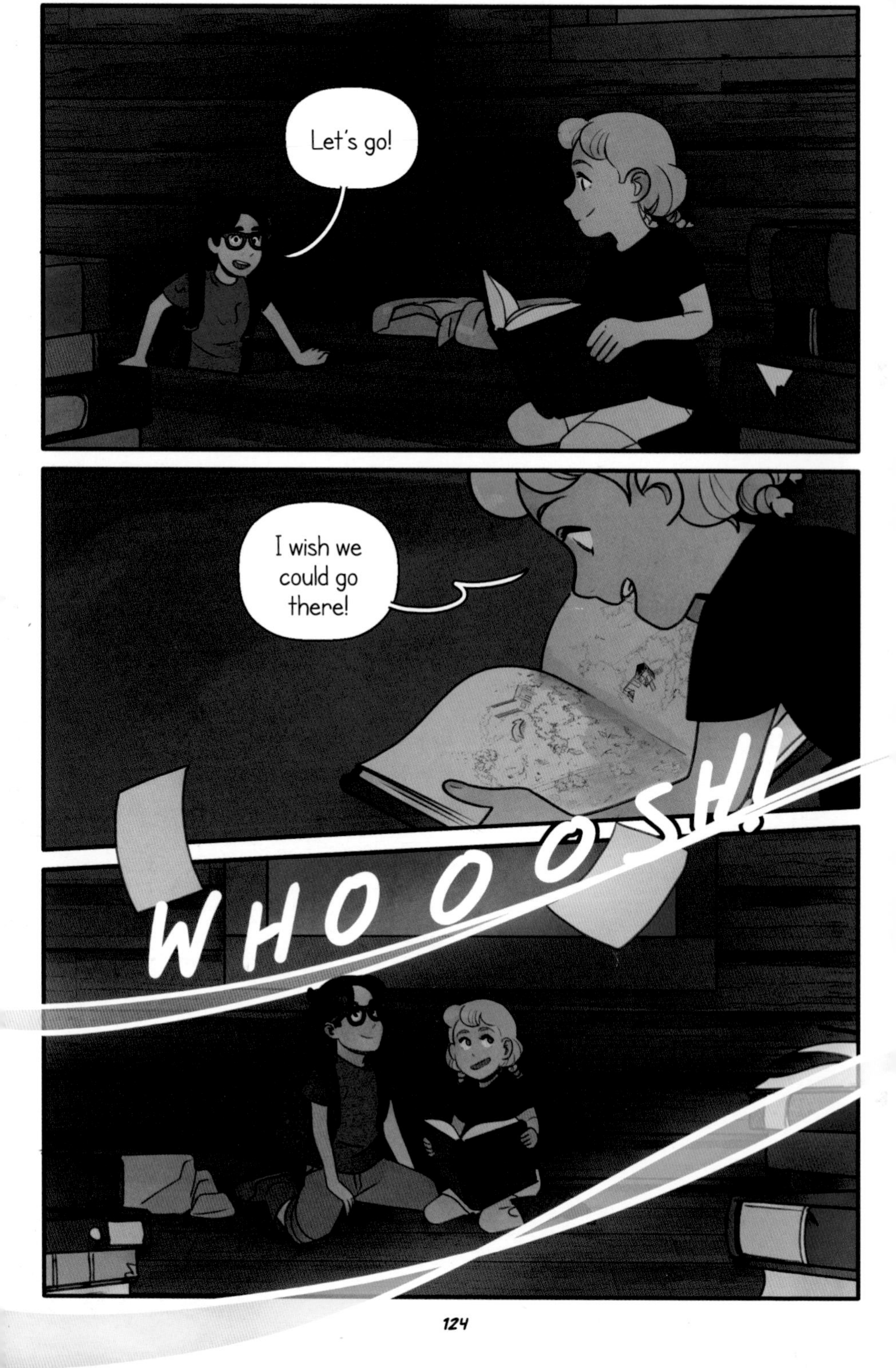
Let's go!
I wish we could go there!
WHOOOOSH!

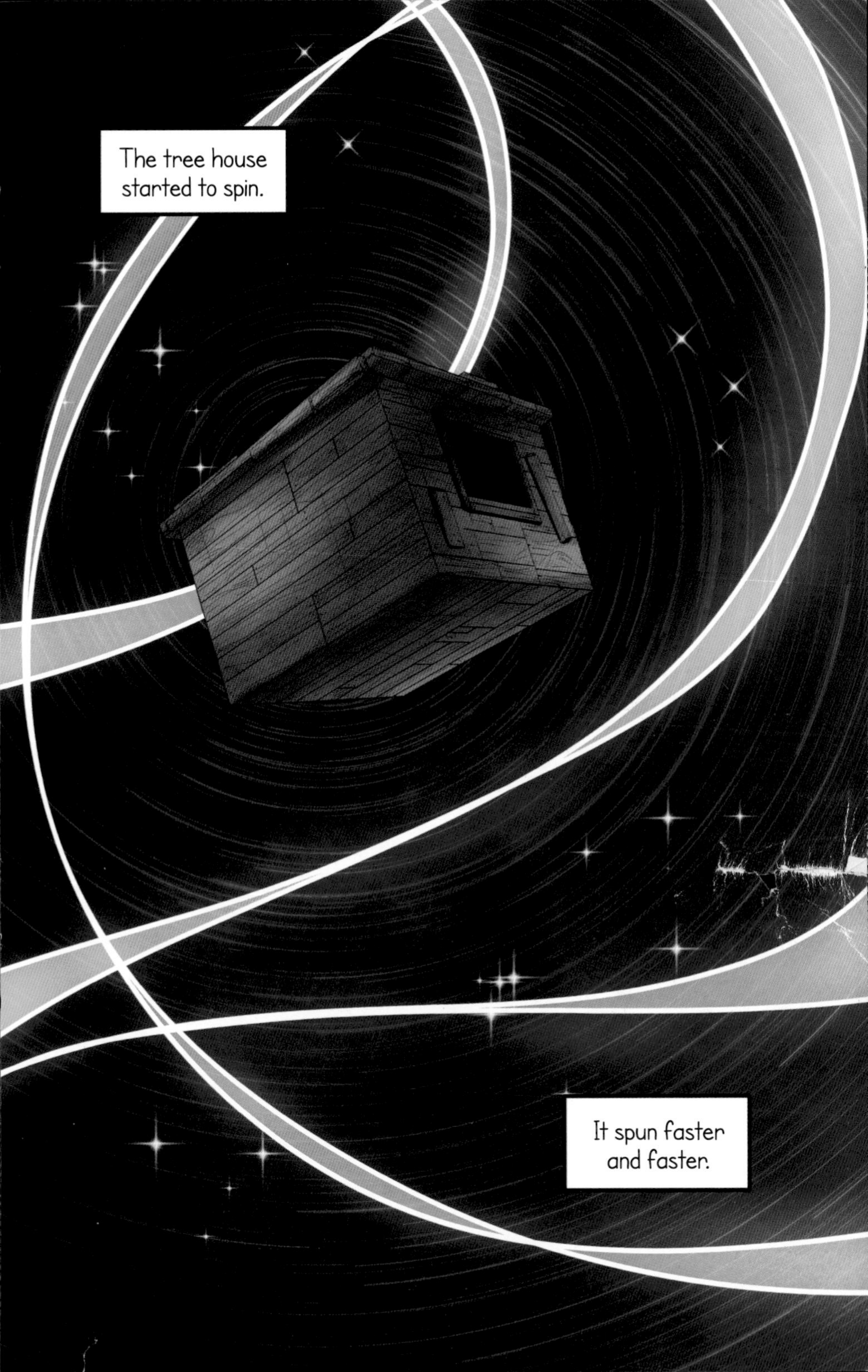
The tree house started to spin.
It spun faster and faster.

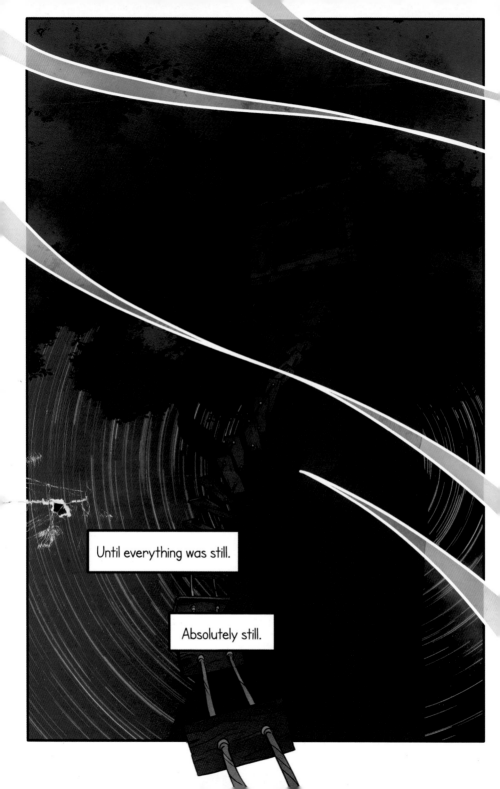

Until everything was still.

Absolutely still.

CHAPTER NINE
The Mysterious M

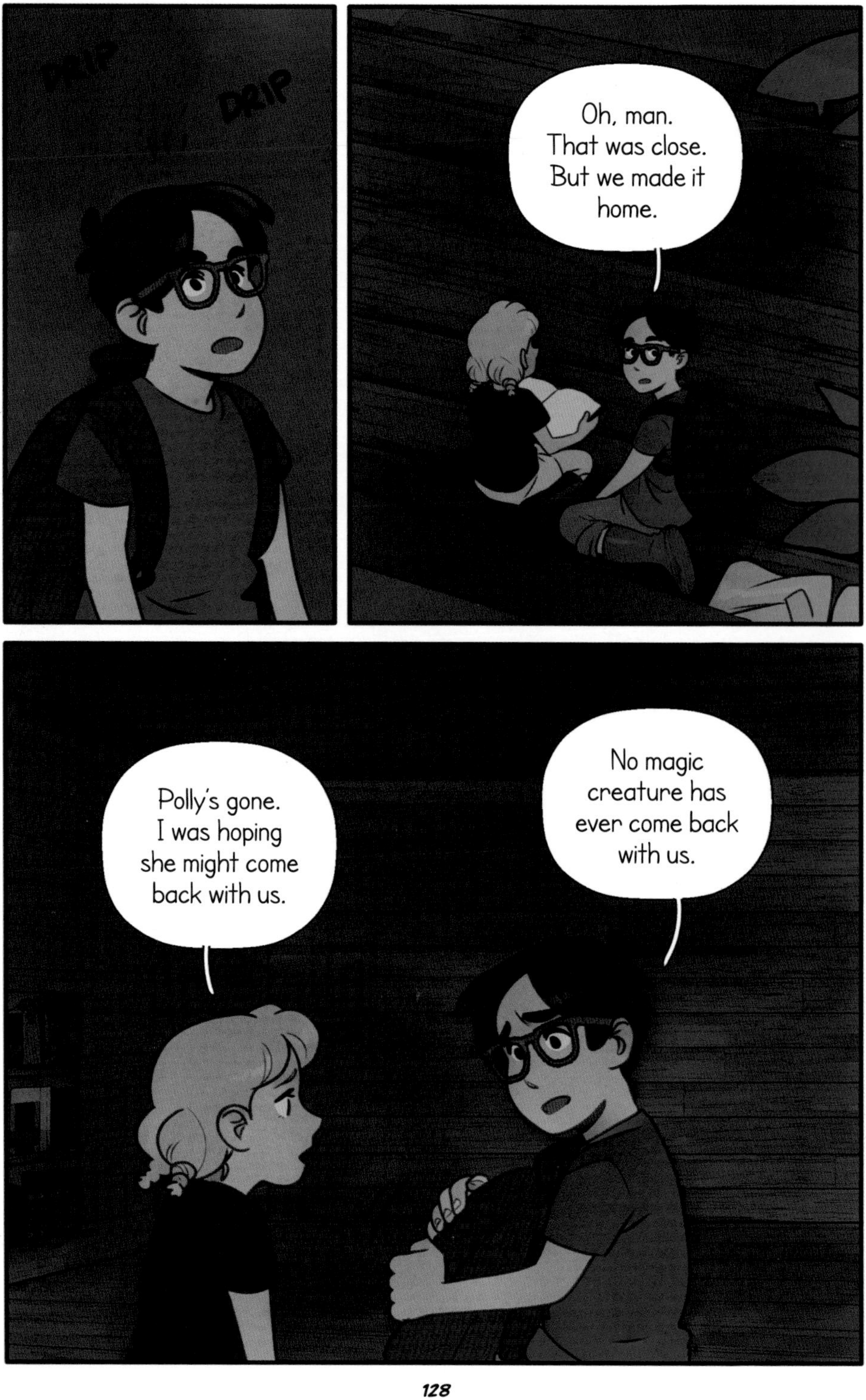
DRIP
DRIP
Oh, man. That was close. But we made it home.
Polly's gone. I was hoping she might come back with us.
No magic creature has ever come back with us.

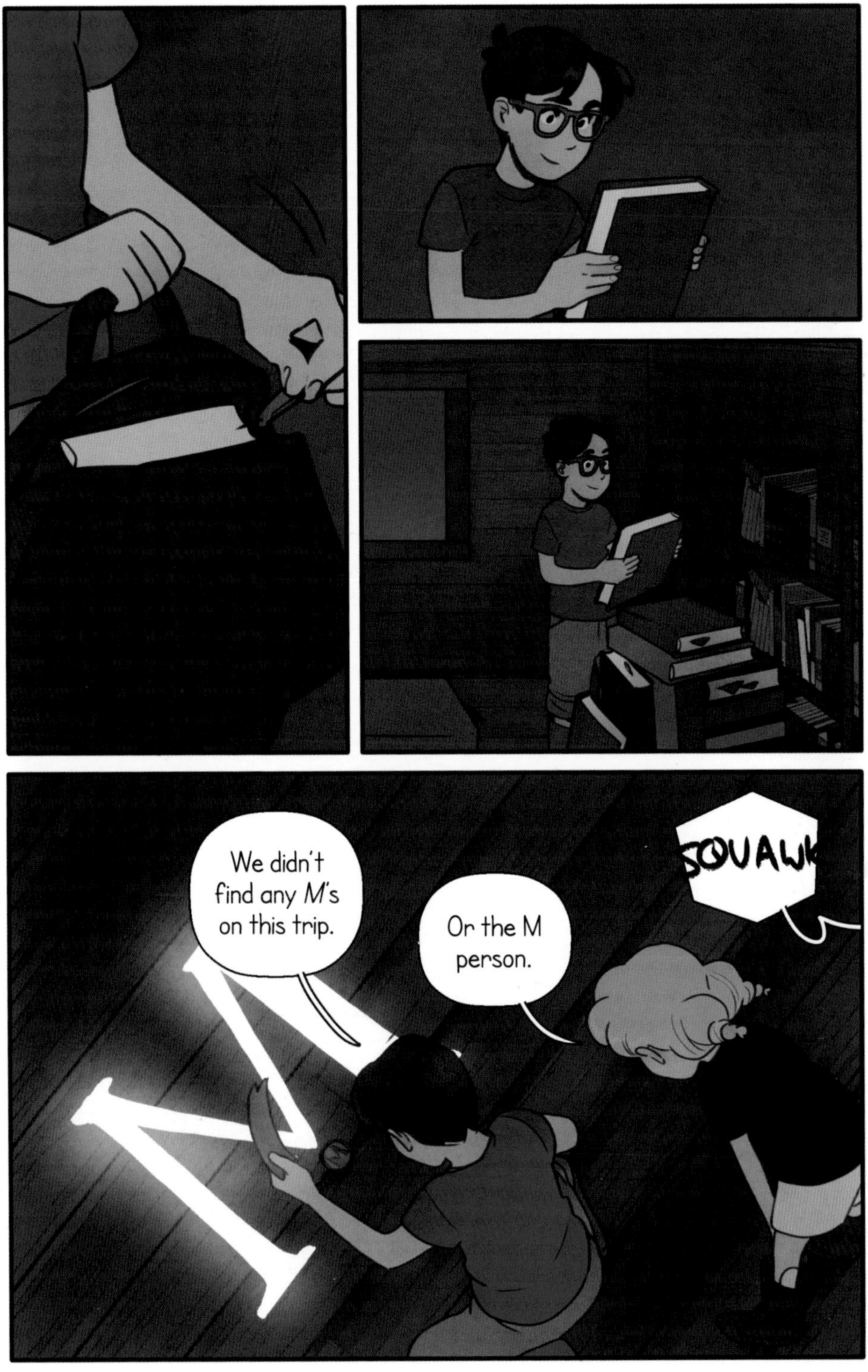
We didn't find any *M*'s on this trip.
Or the M person.
SQUAWK

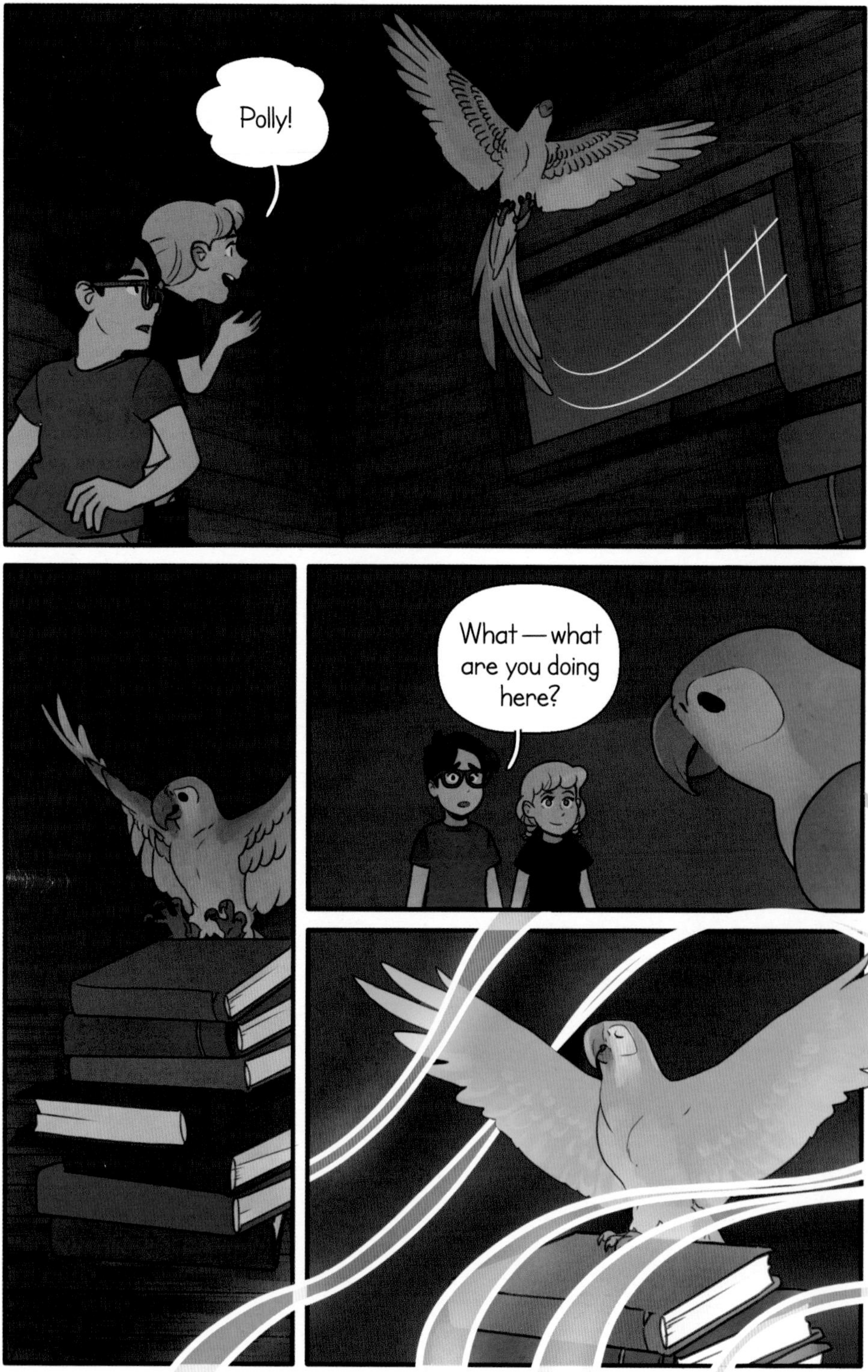
Polly!
What—what are you doing here?

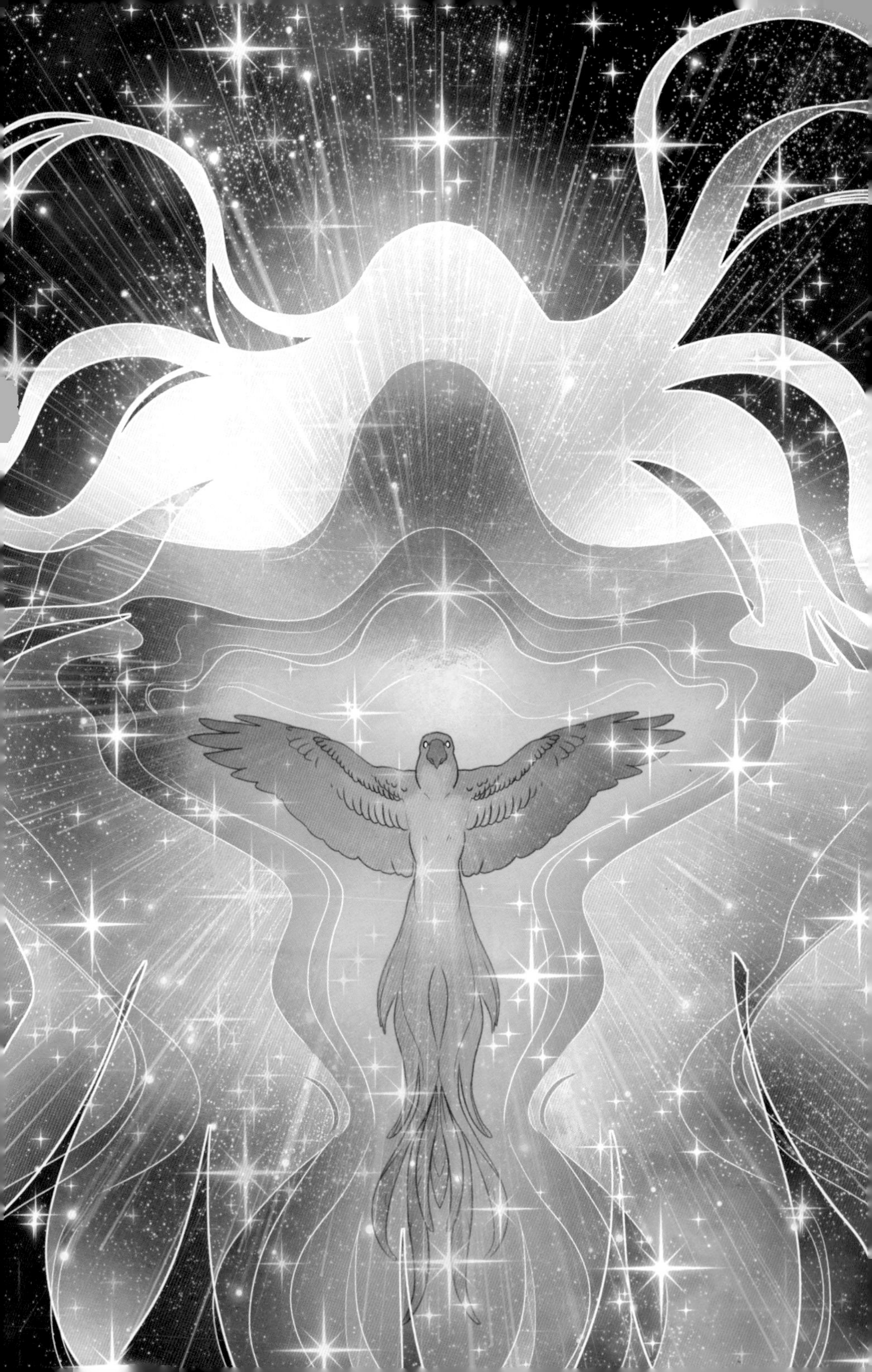

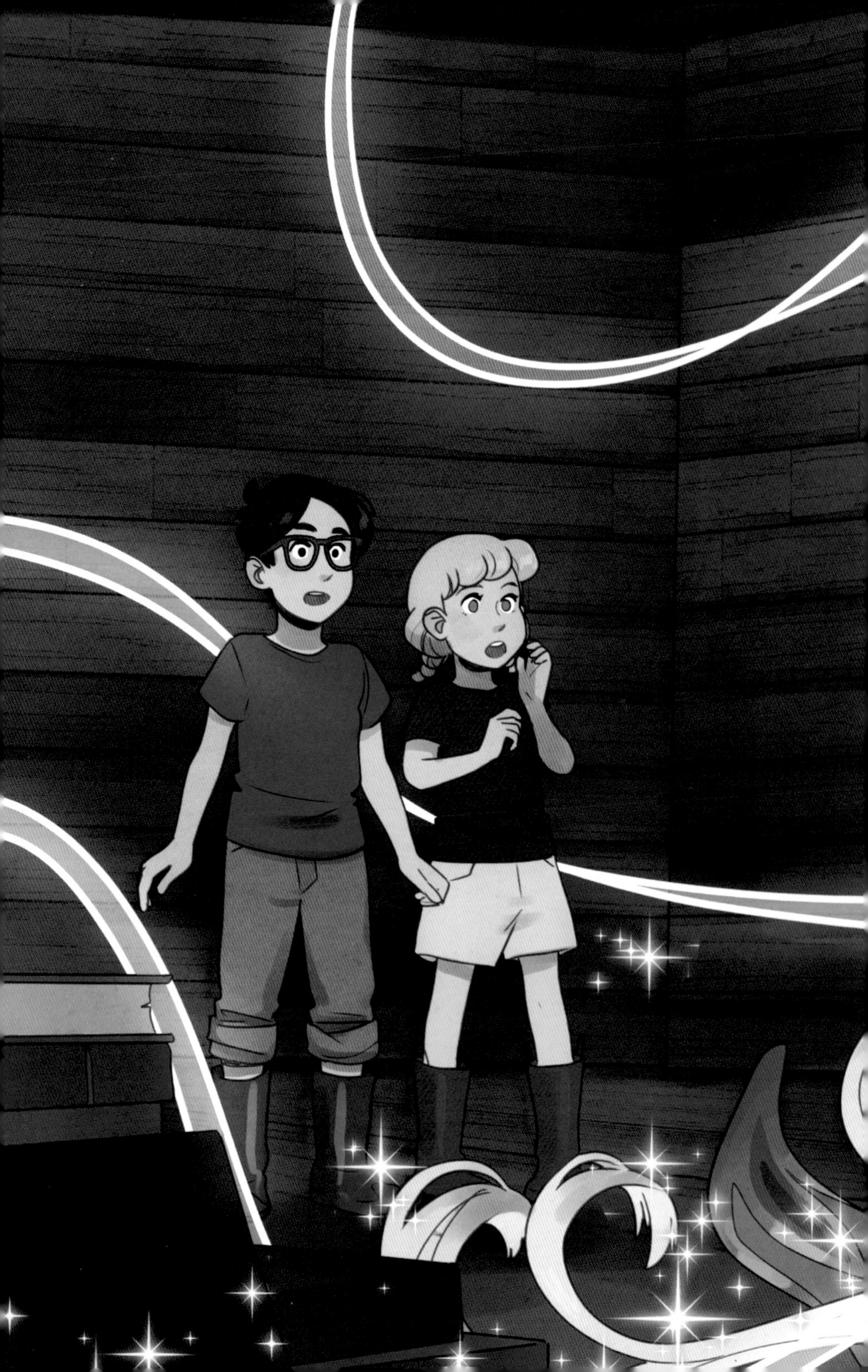

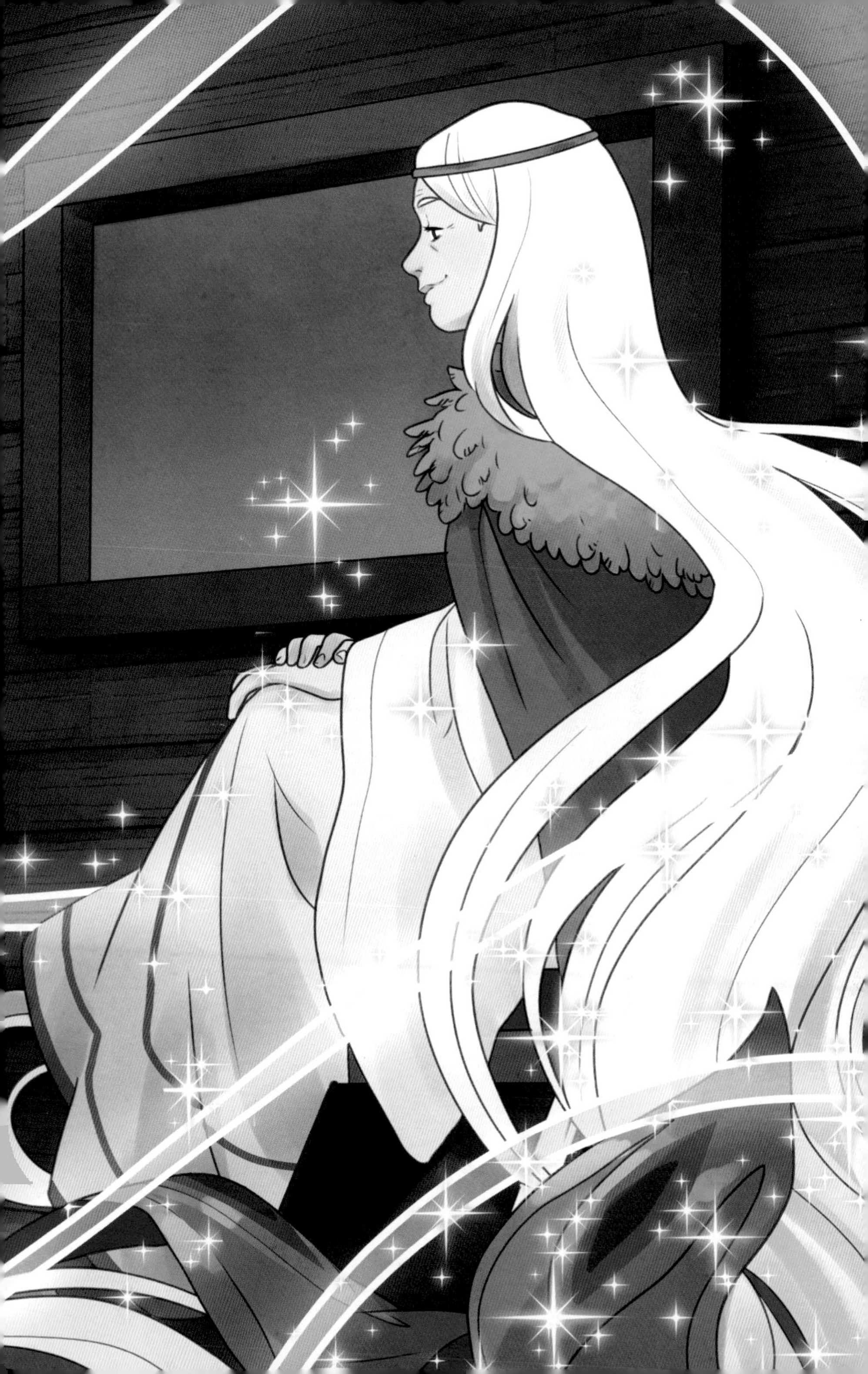

CHAPTER TEN
Treasure Again

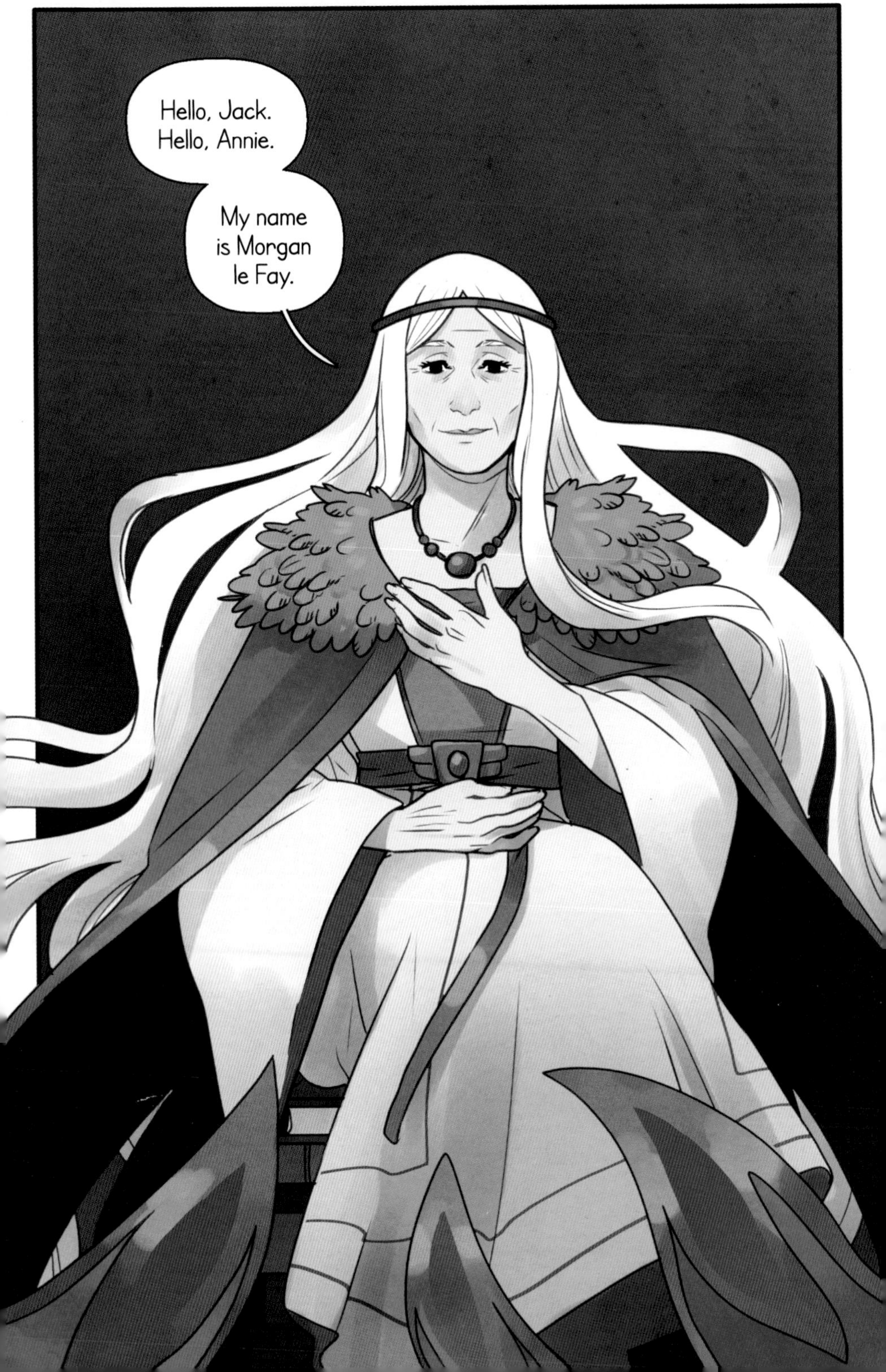
Hello, Jack.
Hello, Annie.
My name is Morgan le Fay.

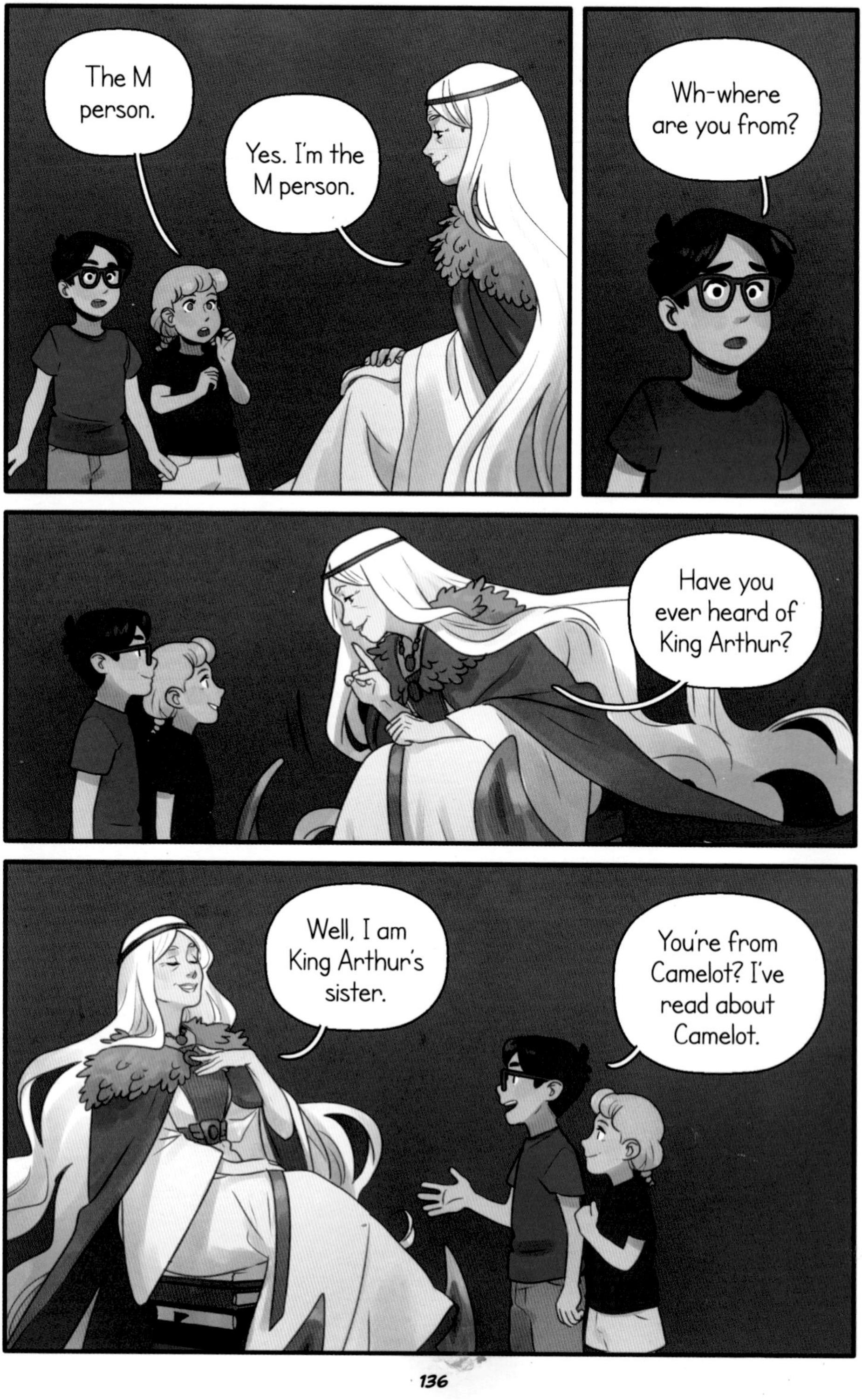

The M person.
Yes. I'm the M person.
Wh-where are you from?
Have you ever heard of King Arthur?
Well, I am King Arthur's sister.
You're from Camelot? I've read about Camelot.

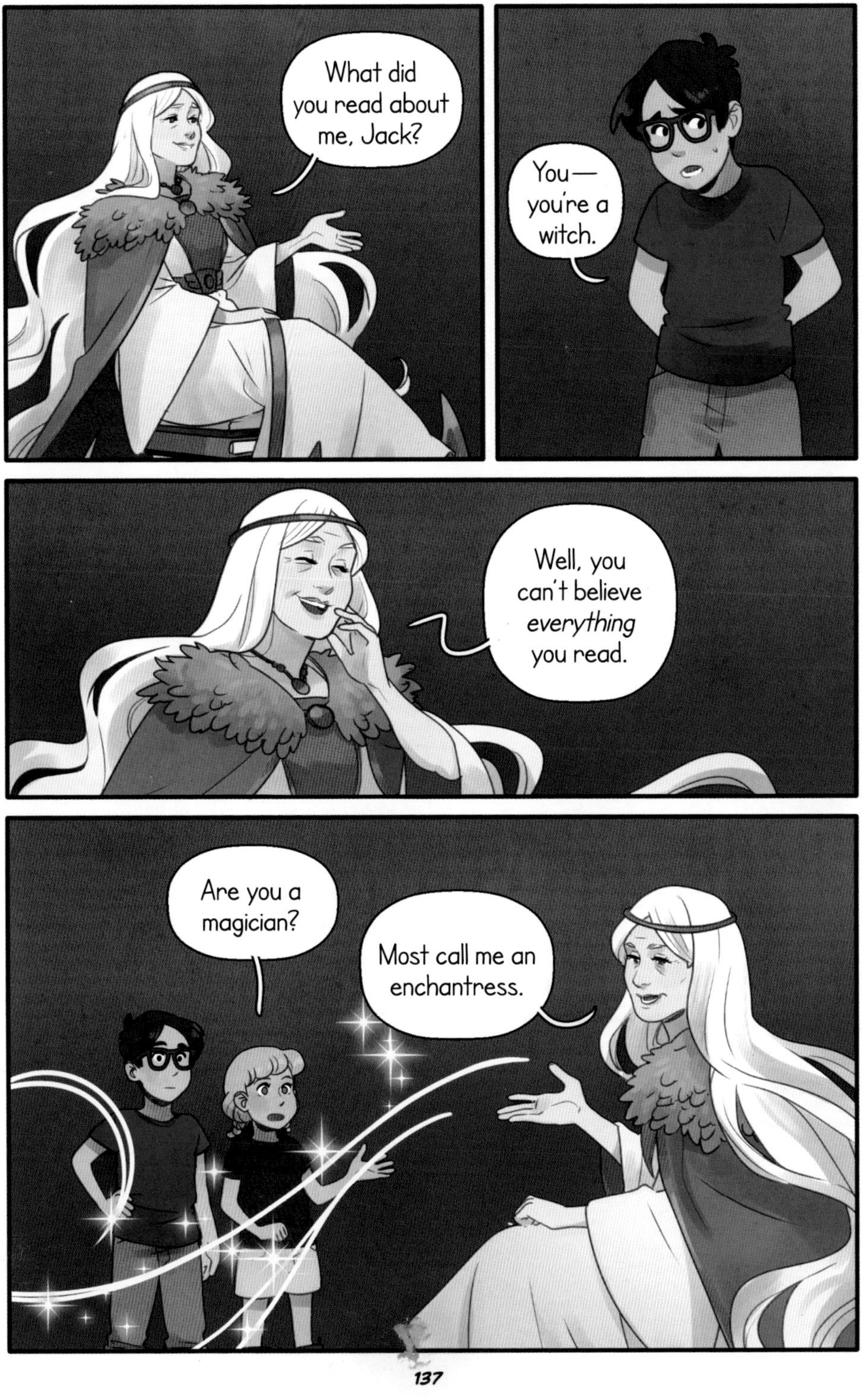
What did you read about me, Jack?
You— you're a witch.
Well, you can't believe *everything* you read.
Are you a magician?
Most call me an enchantress.

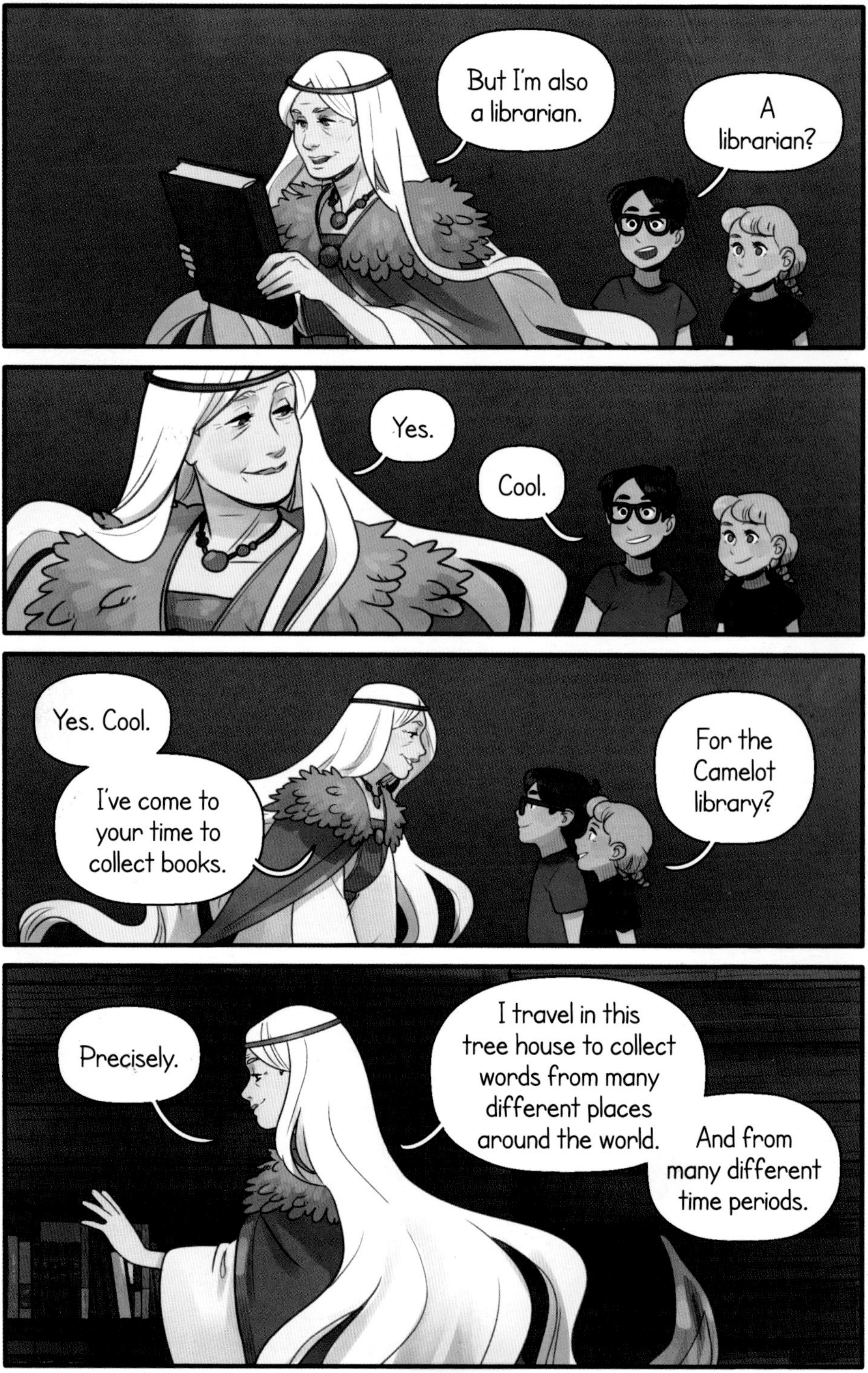
But I'm also a librarian.
A librarian?
Yes.
Cool.
Yes. Cool.
I've come to your time to collect books.
For the Camelot library?
Precisely.
I travel in this tree house to collect words from many different places around the world.
And from many different time periods.

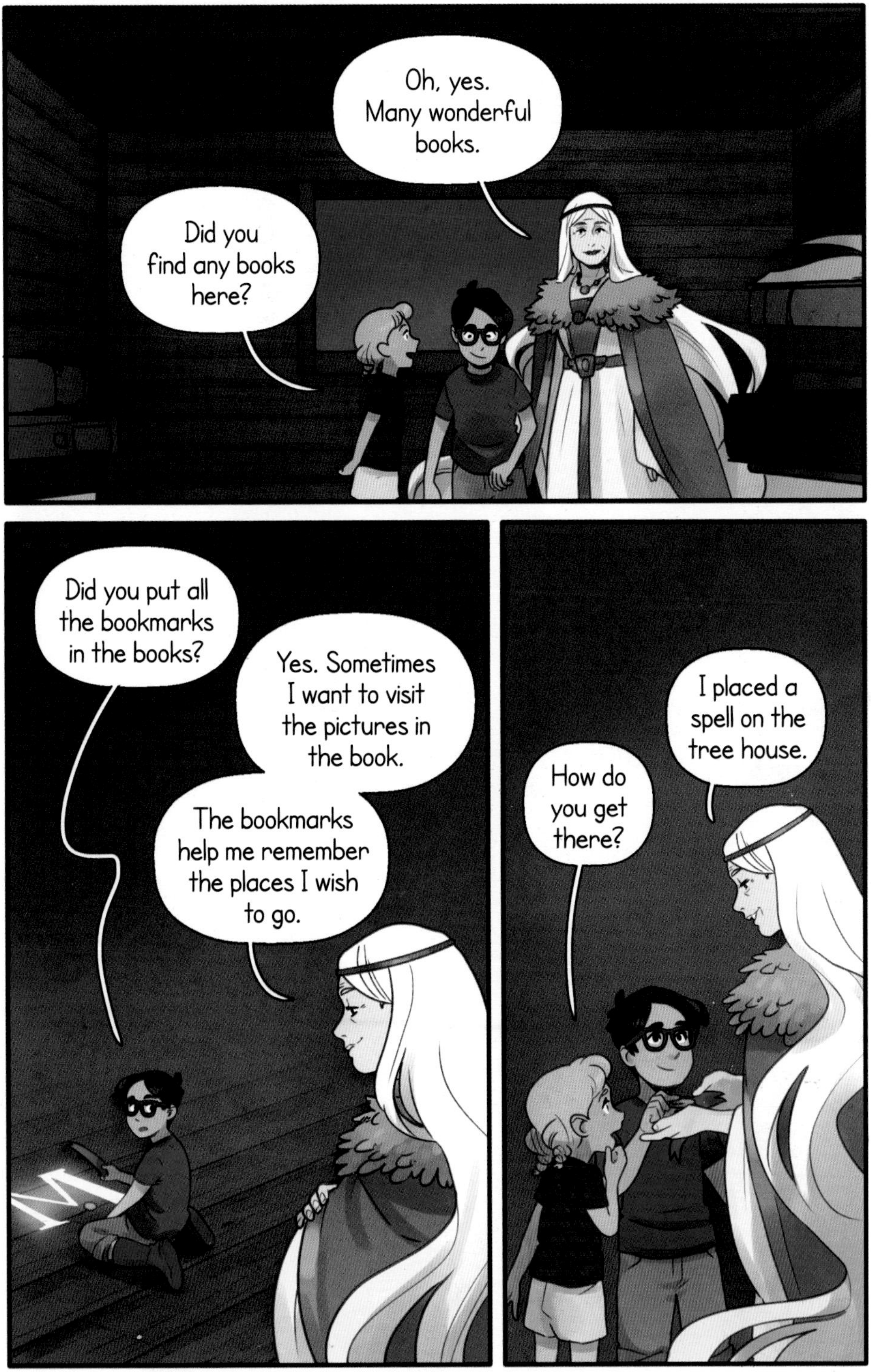
Oh, yes. Many wonderful books.
Did you find any books here?
Did you put all the bookmarks in the books?
Yes. Sometimes I want to visit the pictures in the book.
The bookmarks help me remember the places I wish to go.
How do you get there?
I placed a spell on the tree house.

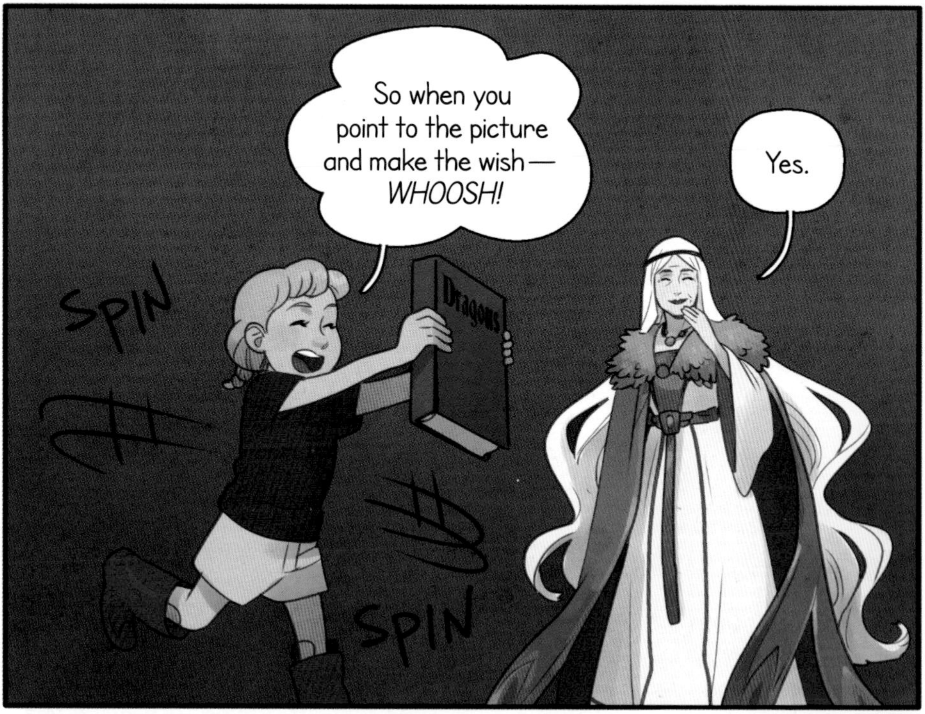
So when you point to the picture and make the wish— *WHOOSH!*
Yes.
Dragons
SPIN
SPIN

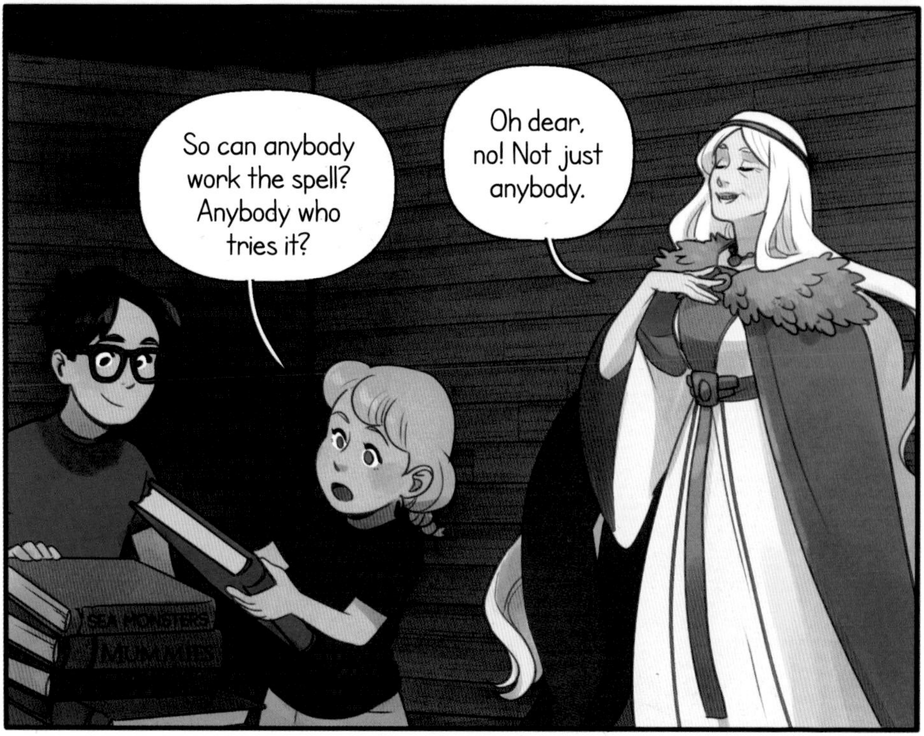
So can anybody work the spell? Anybody who tries it?
Oh dear, no! Not just anybody.
SEA MONSTERS
MUMMIES

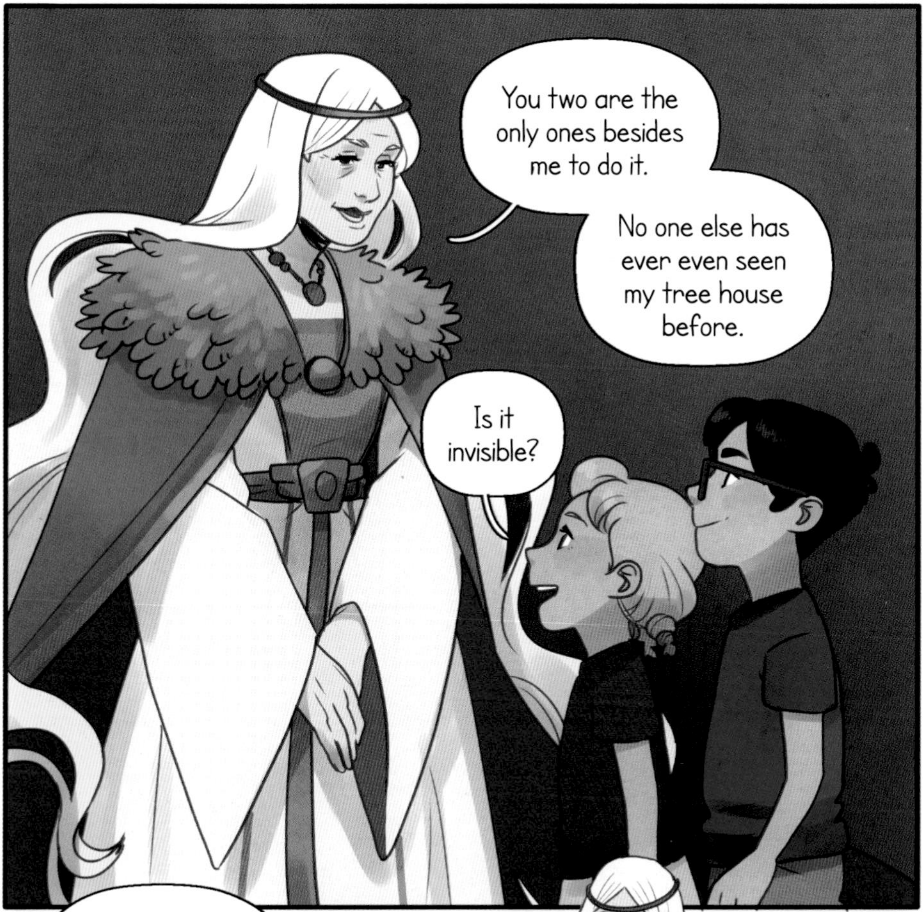
You two are the only ones besides me to do it.
No one else has ever even seen my tree house before.
Is it invisible?

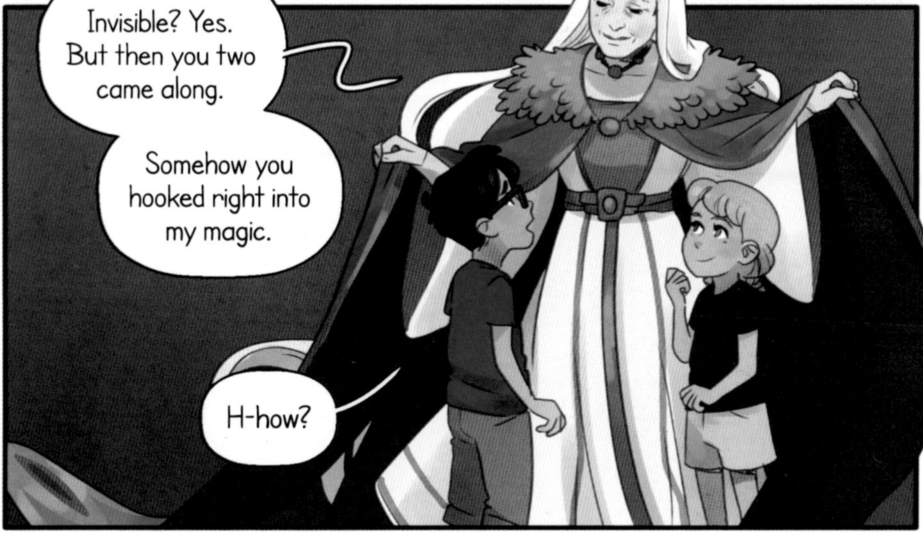
Invisible? Yes. But then you two came along.
Somehow you hooked right into my magic.
H-how?

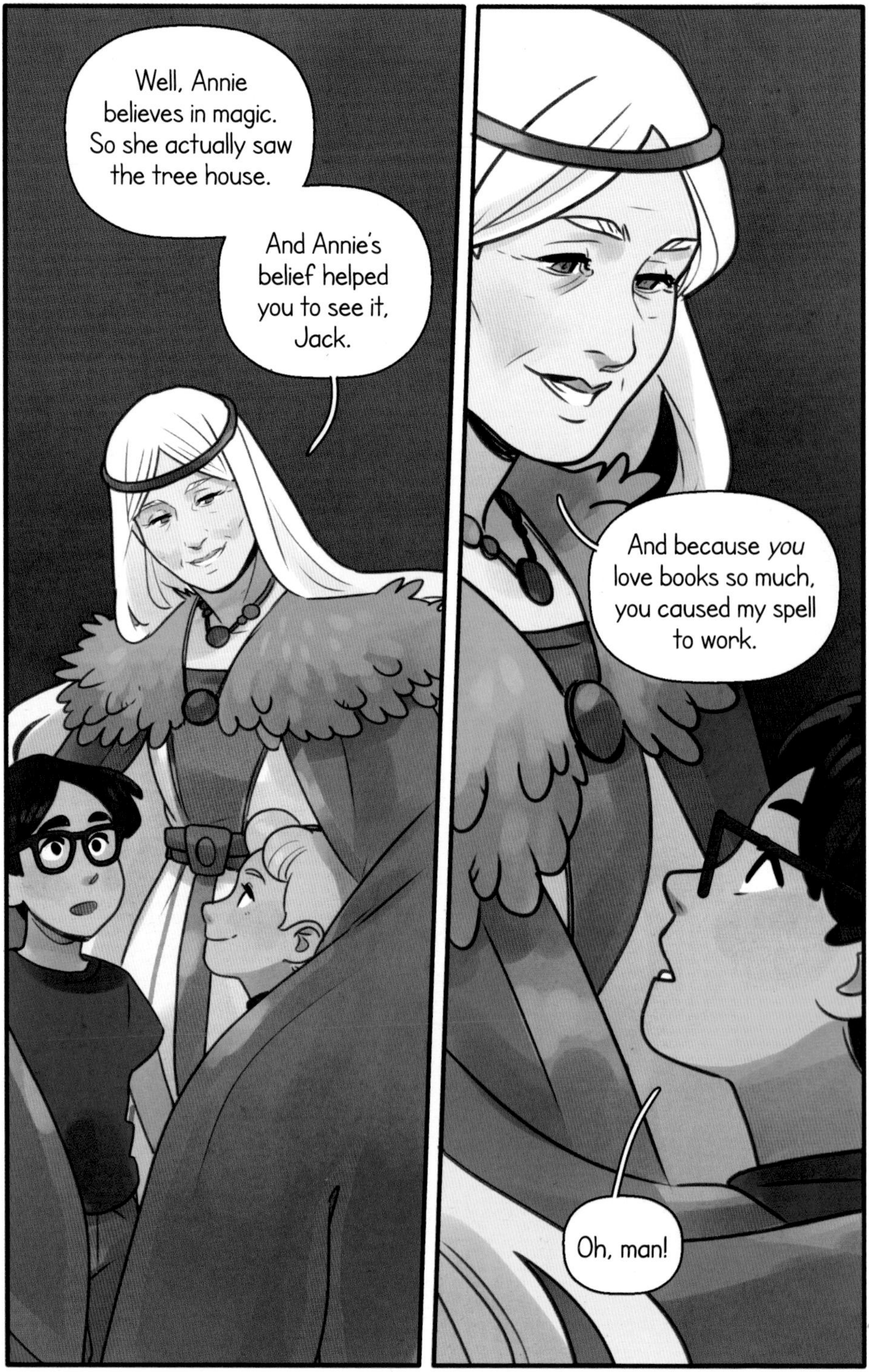
Well, Annie believes in magic. So she actually saw the tree house.
And Annie's belief helped you to see it, Jack.
And because *you* love books so much, you caused my spell to work.
Oh, man!

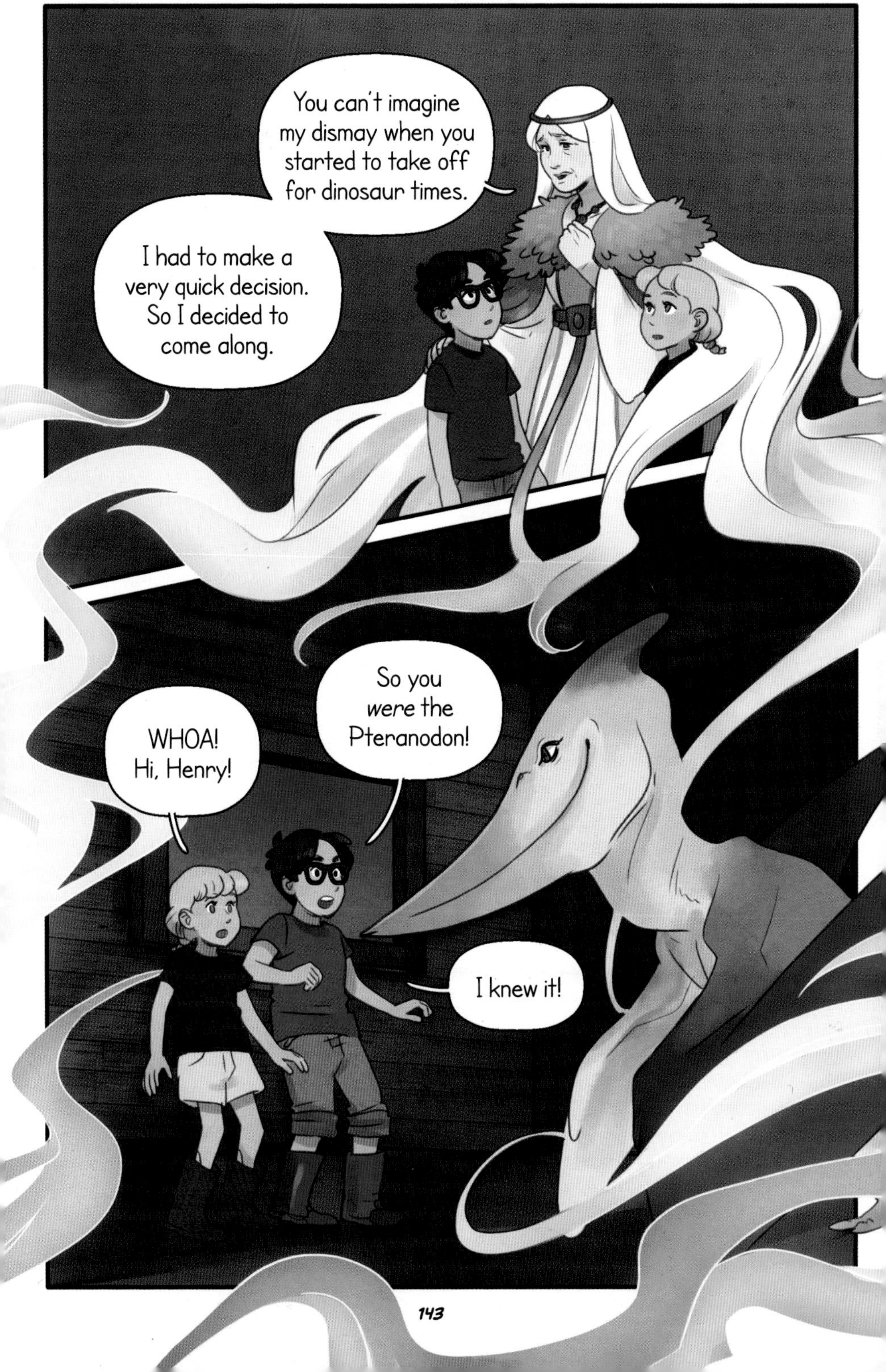
You can't imagine my dismay when you started to take off for dinosaur times.
I had to make a very quick decision. So I decided to come along.
WHOA! Hi, Henry!
So you *were* the Pteranodon!
I knew it!

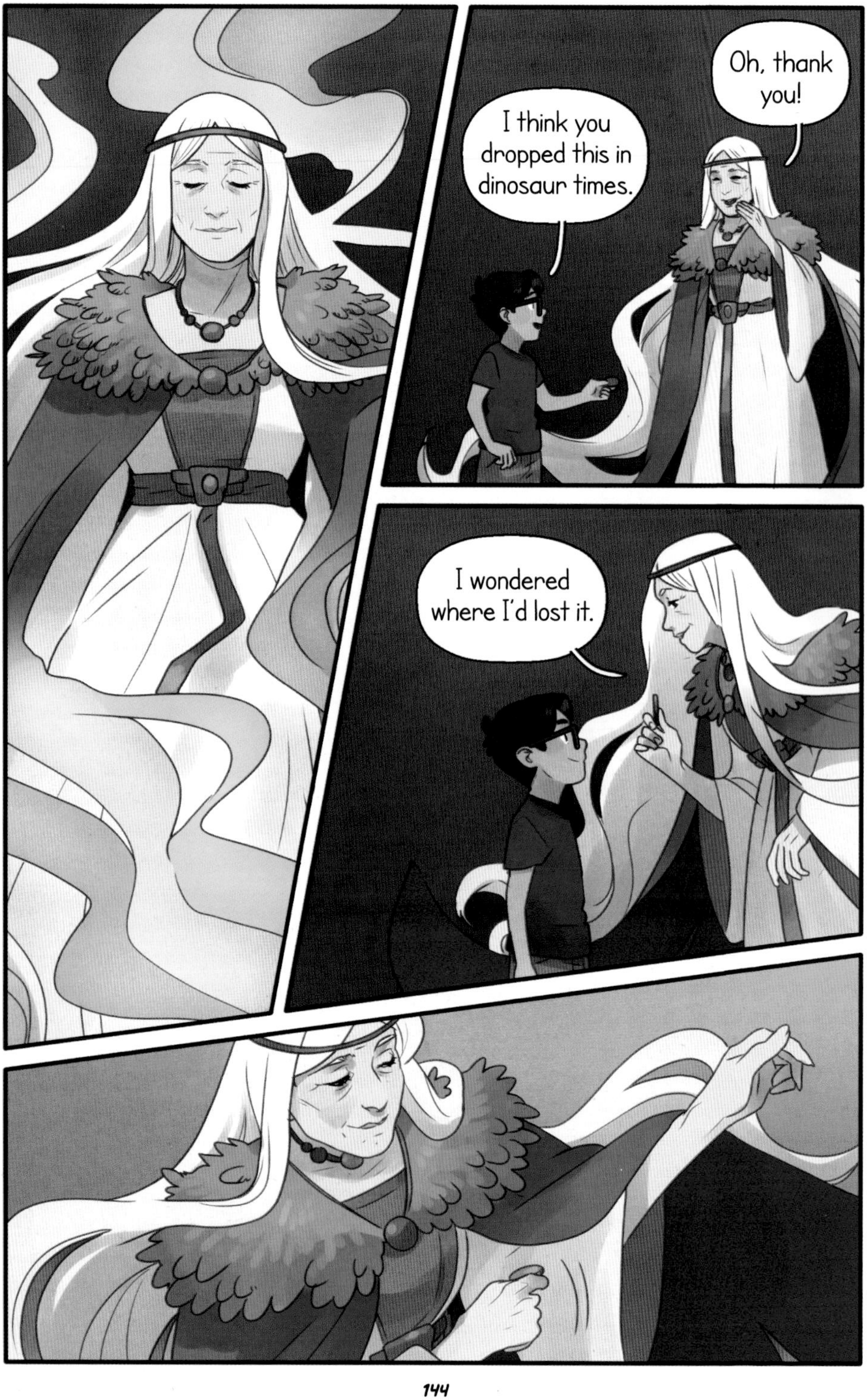
I think you dropped this in dinosaur times.
Oh, thank you!
I wondered where I'd lost it.

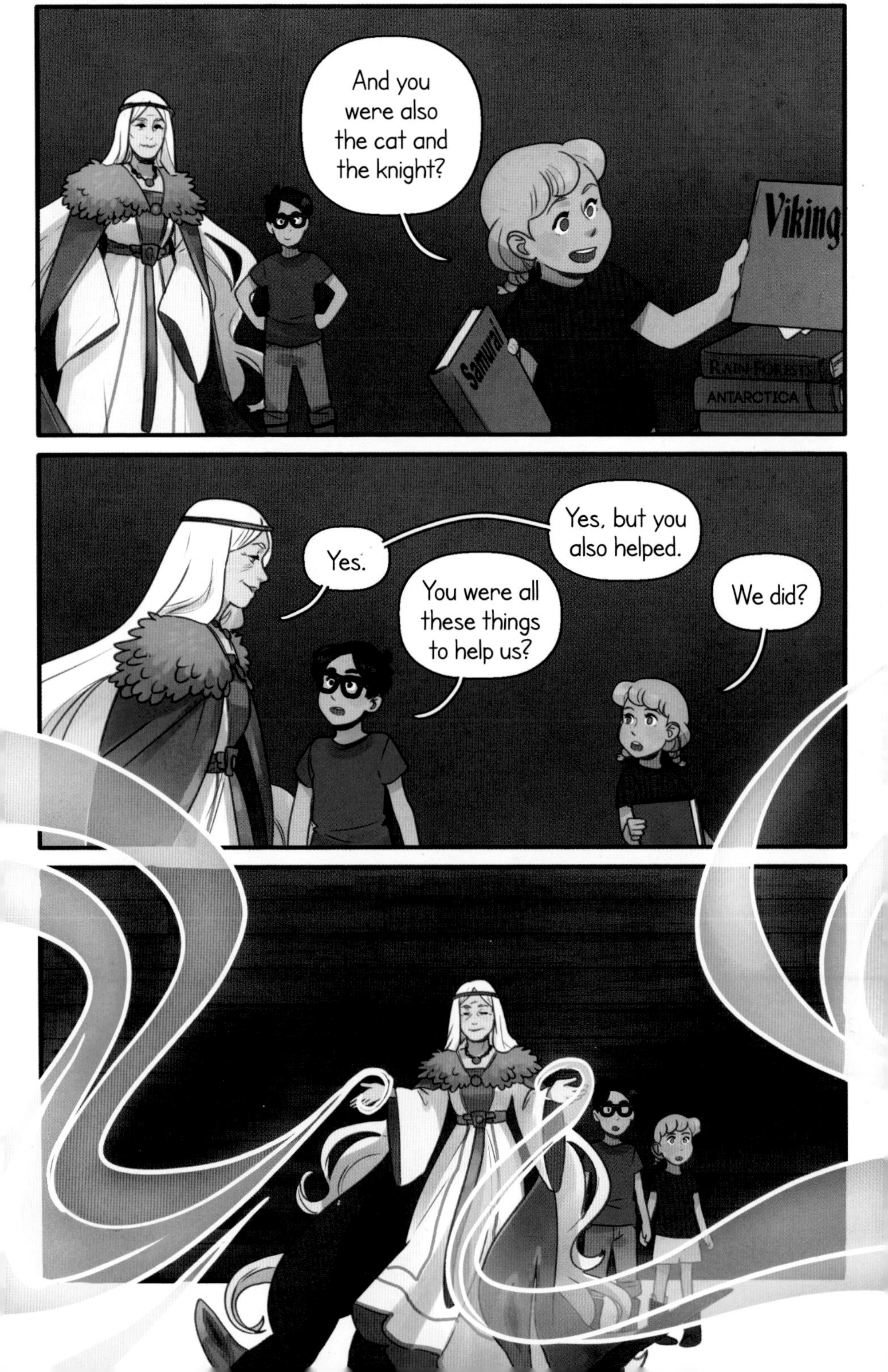
And you were also the cat and the knight?
Viking
Samurai
RAIN FORESTS
ANTARCTICA
Yes.
Yes, but you also helped.
You were all these things to help us?
We did?

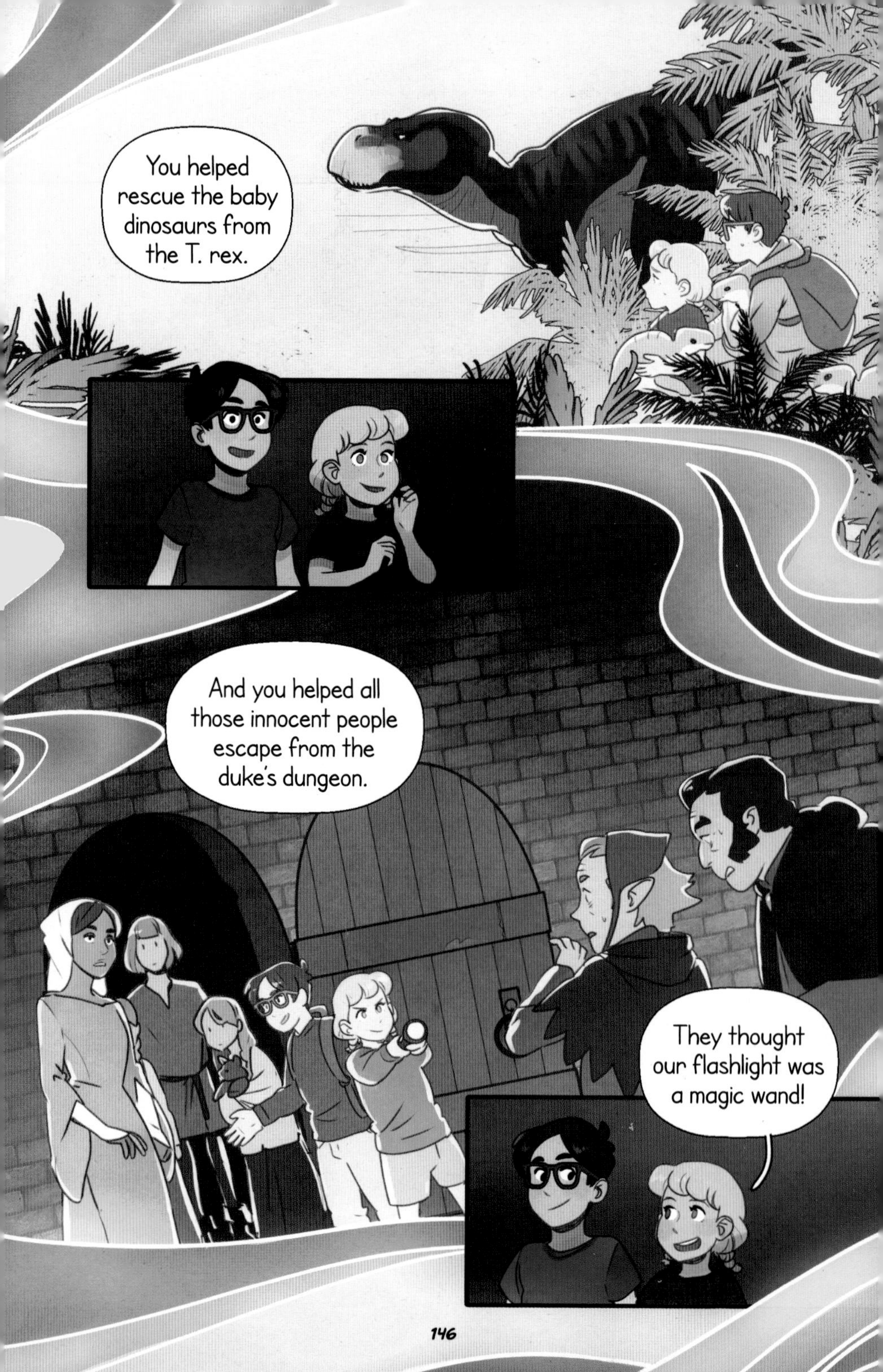
You helped rescue the baby dinosaurs from the T. rex.
And you helped all those innocent people escape from the duke's dungeon.
They thought our flashlight was a magic wand!

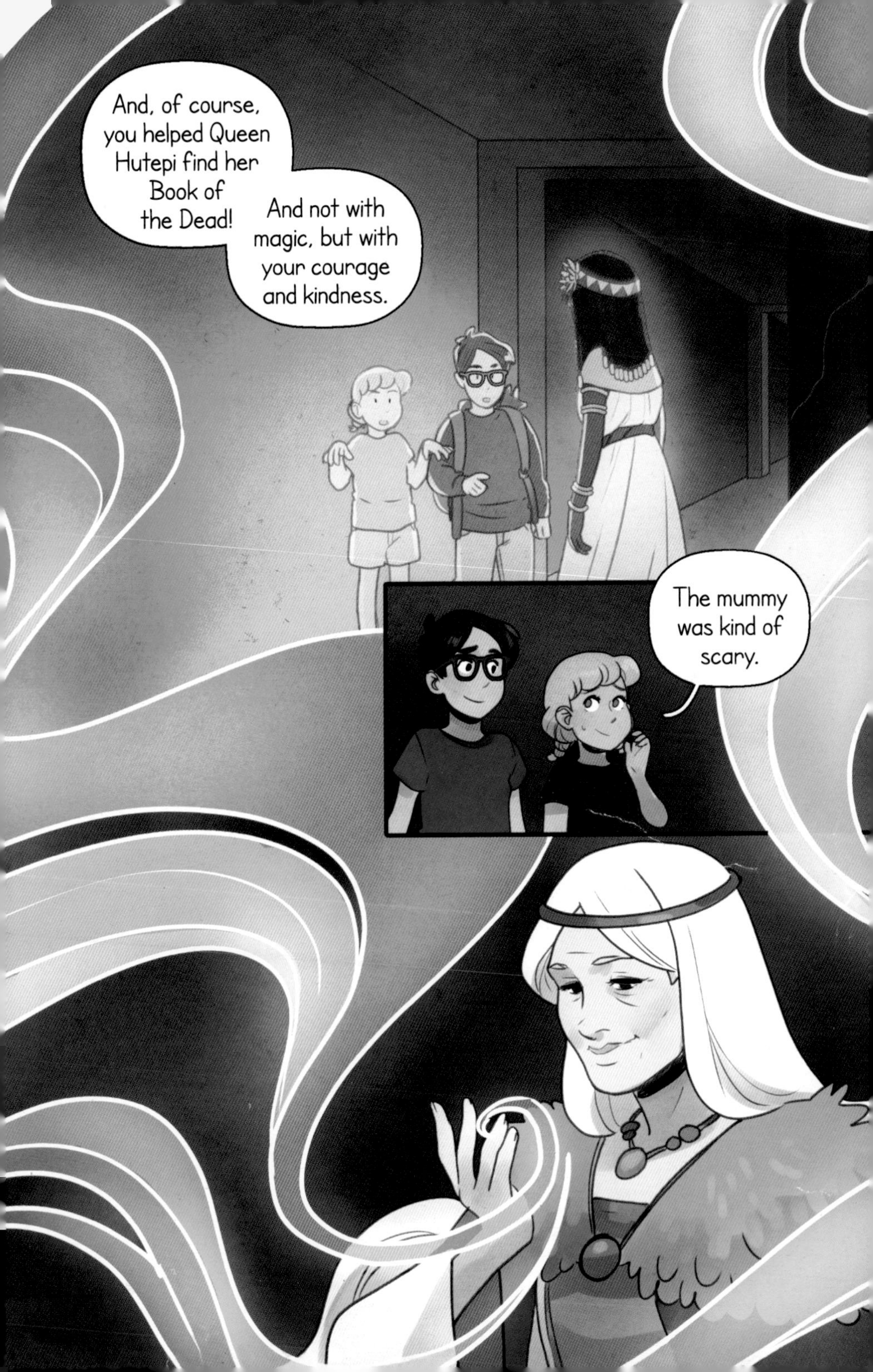
And, of course, you helped Queen Hutepi find her Book of the Dead!
And not with magic, but with your courage and kindness.
The mummy was kind of scary.

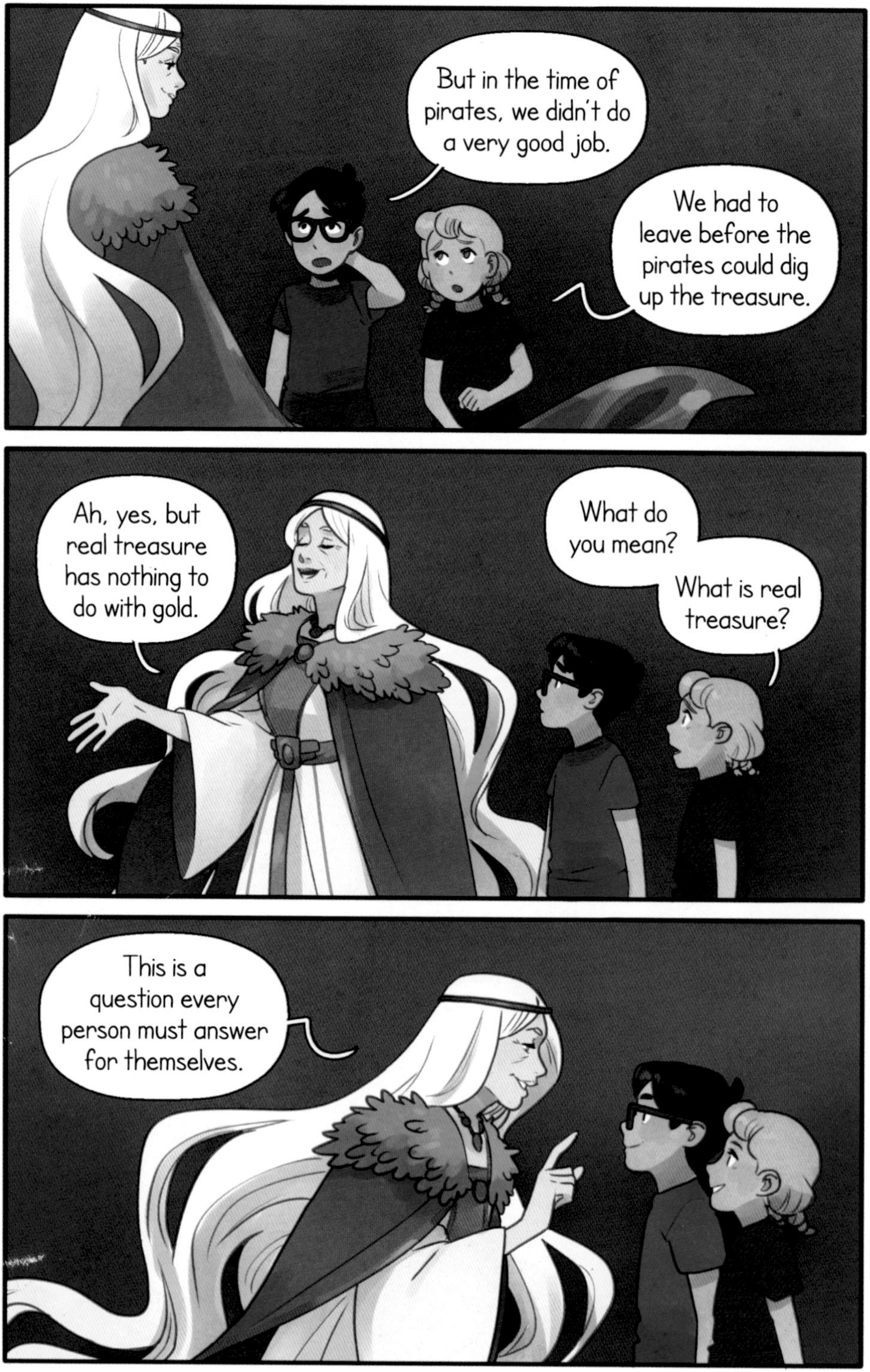

But in the time of pirates, we didn't do a very good job.
We had to leave before the pirates could dig up the treasure.
Ah, yes, but real treasure has nothing to do with gold.
What do you mean?
What is real treasure?
This is a question every person must answer for themselves.

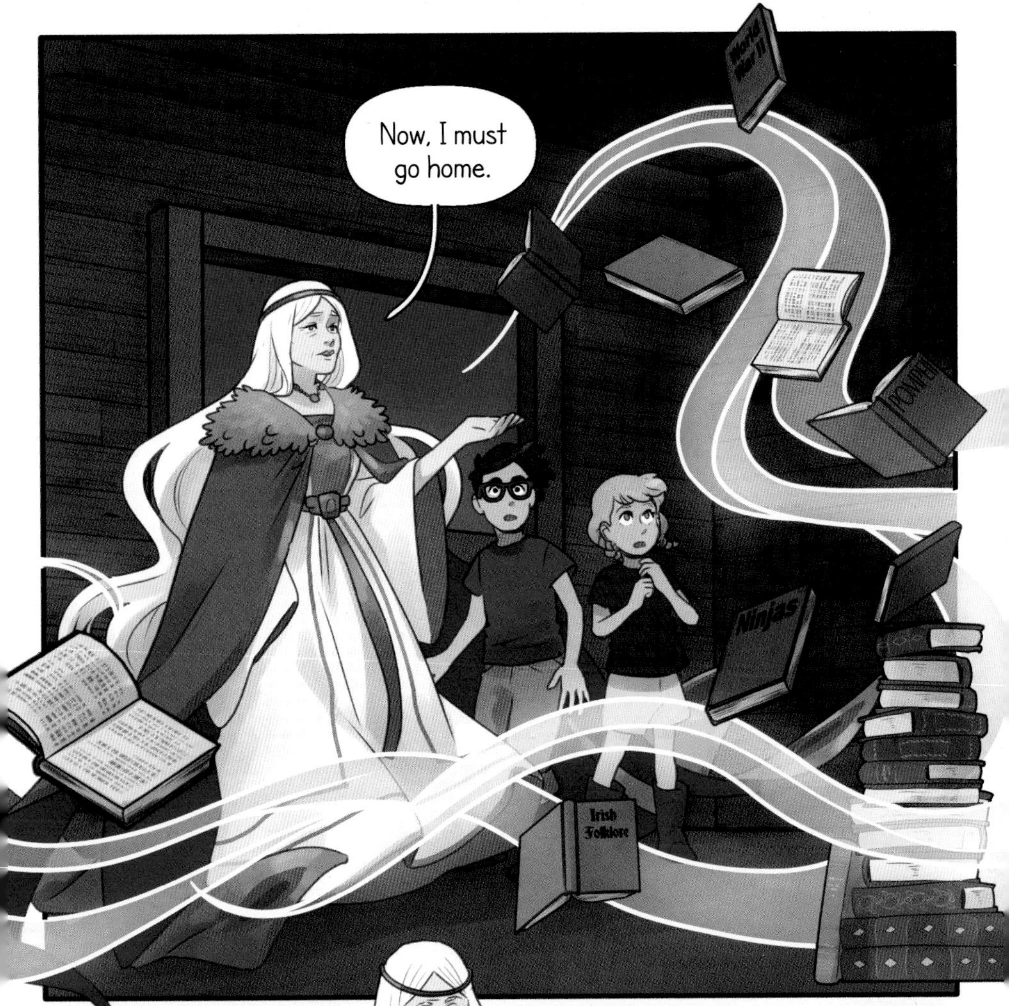
Now, I must go home.
World War II
POMPEII
Ninjas
Irish Folklore

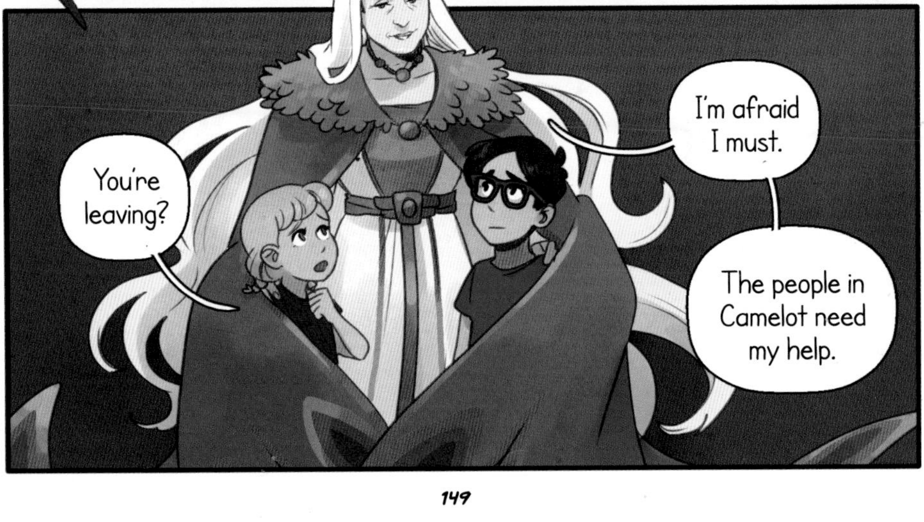
You're leaving?
I'm afraid I must.
The people in Camelot need my help.

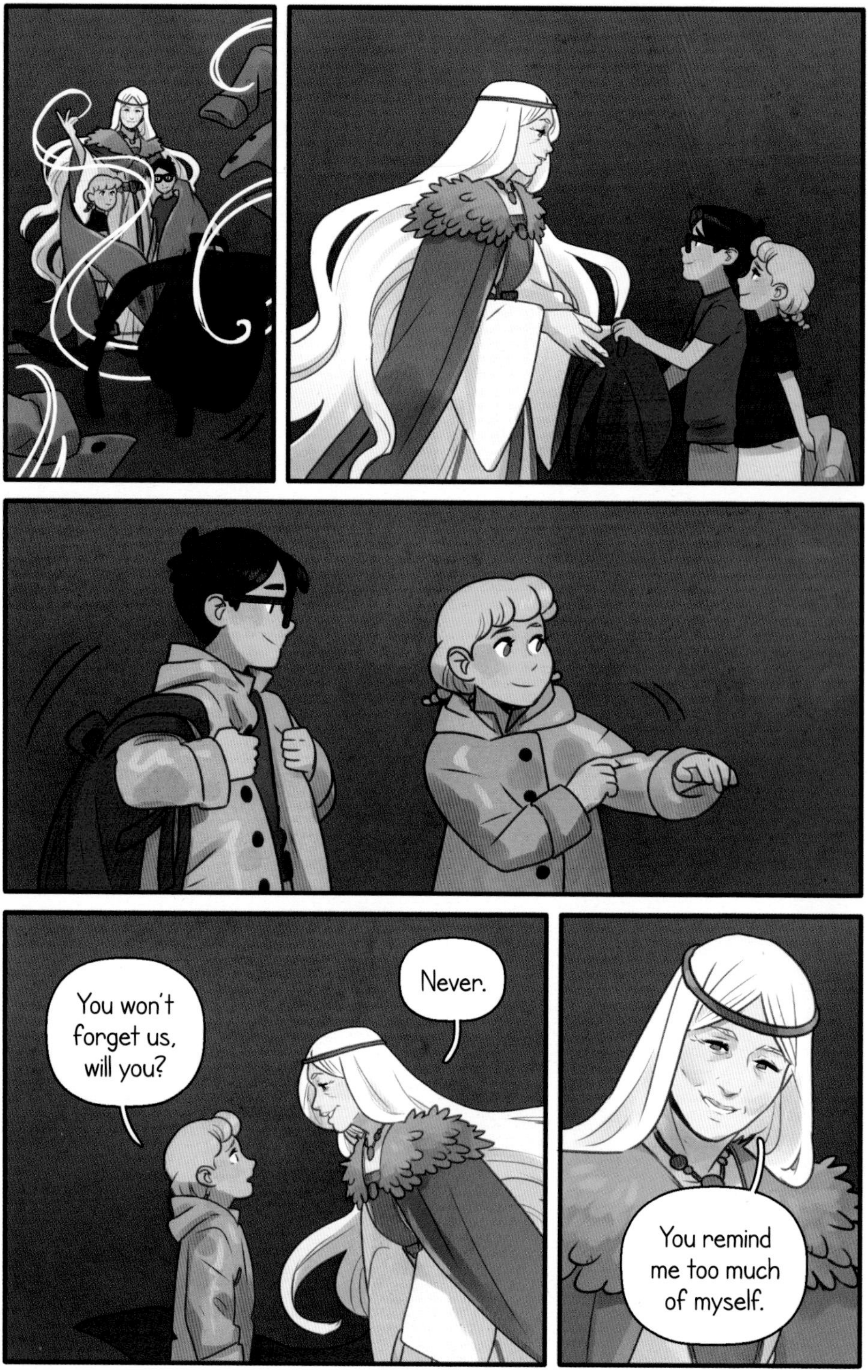
You won't forget us, will you?
Never.
You remind me too much of myself.

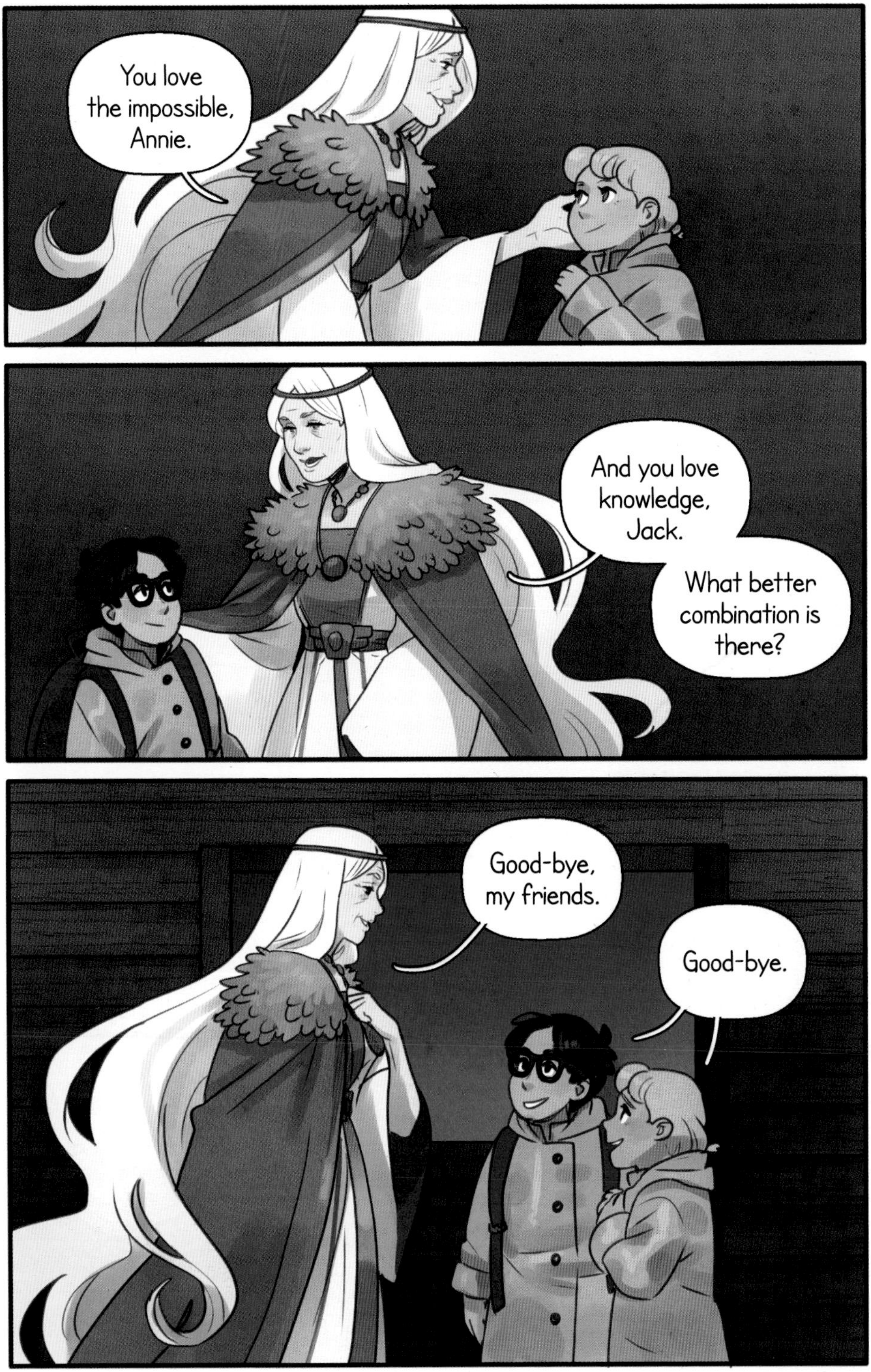
You love the impossible, Annie.
And you love knowledge, Jack.
What better combination is there?
Good-bye, my friends.
Good-bye.

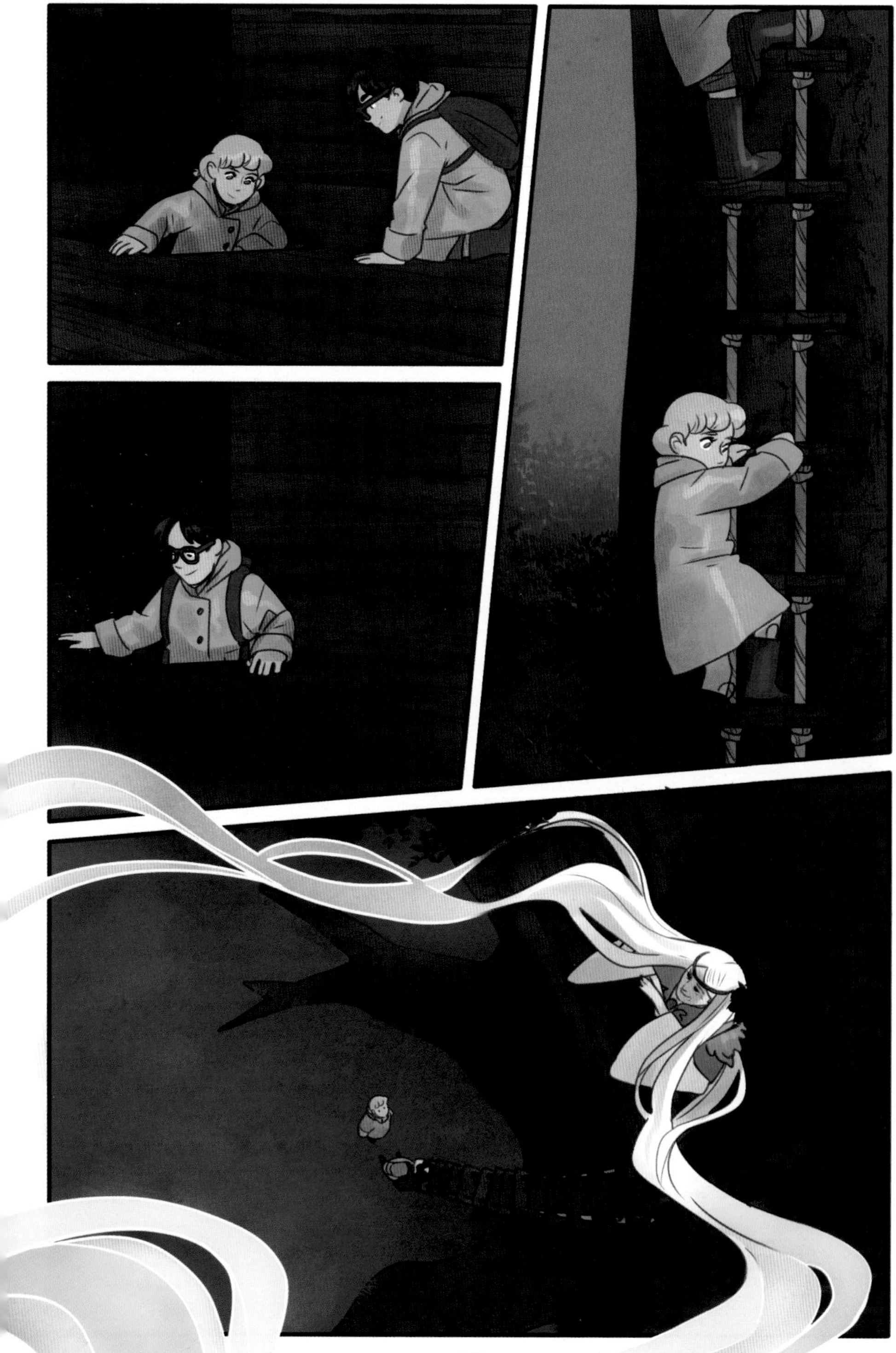

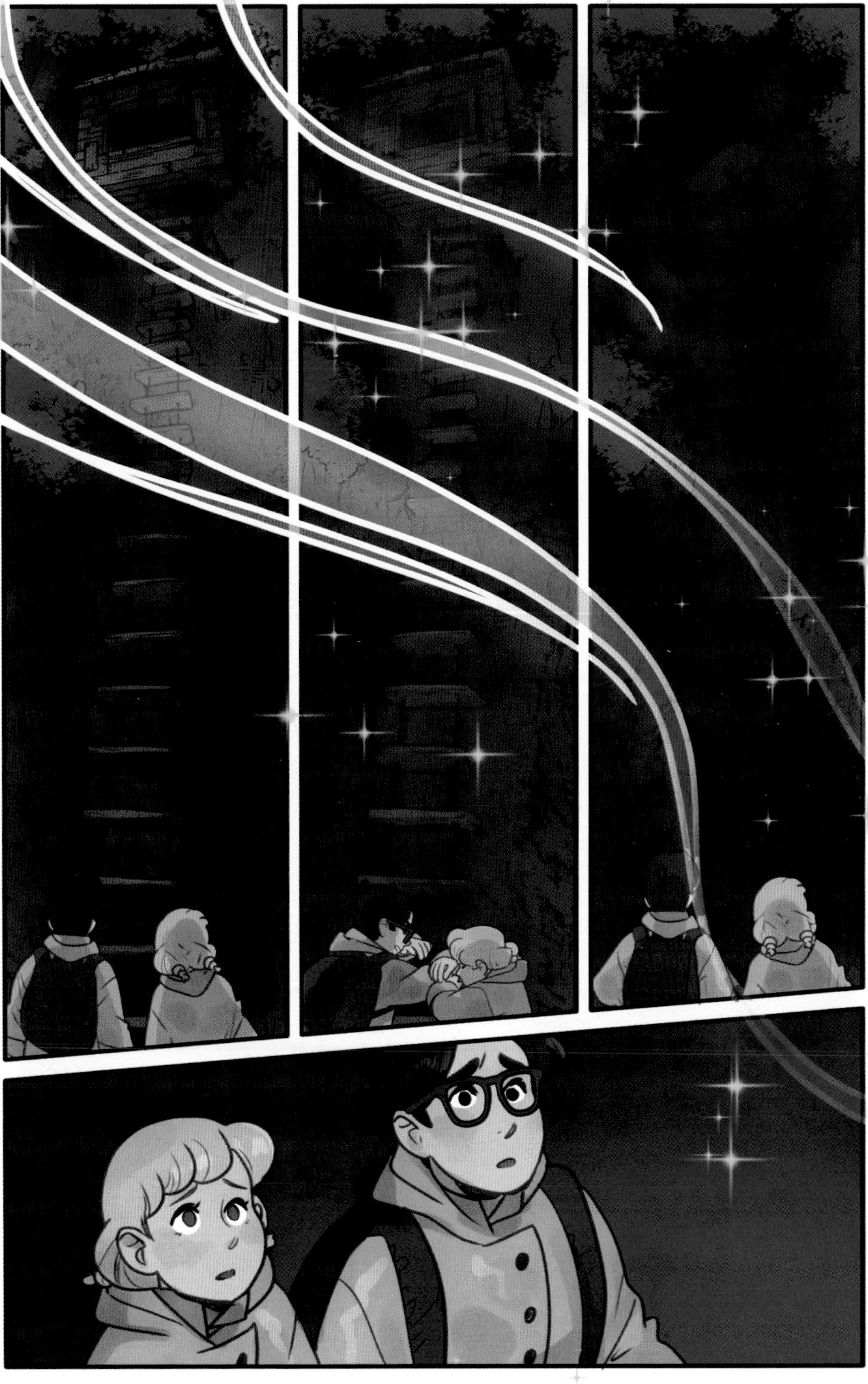

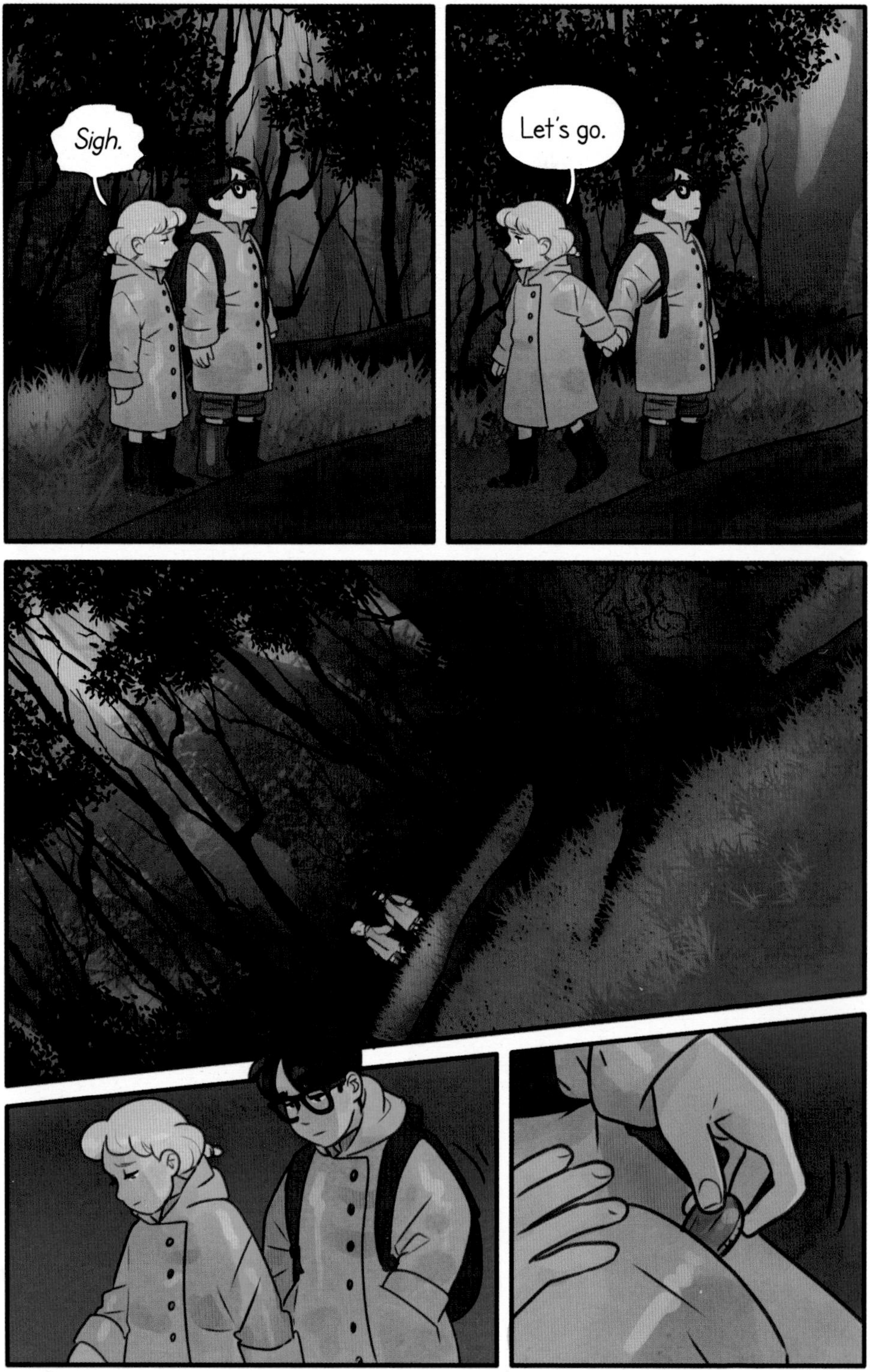
Sigh.
Let's go.

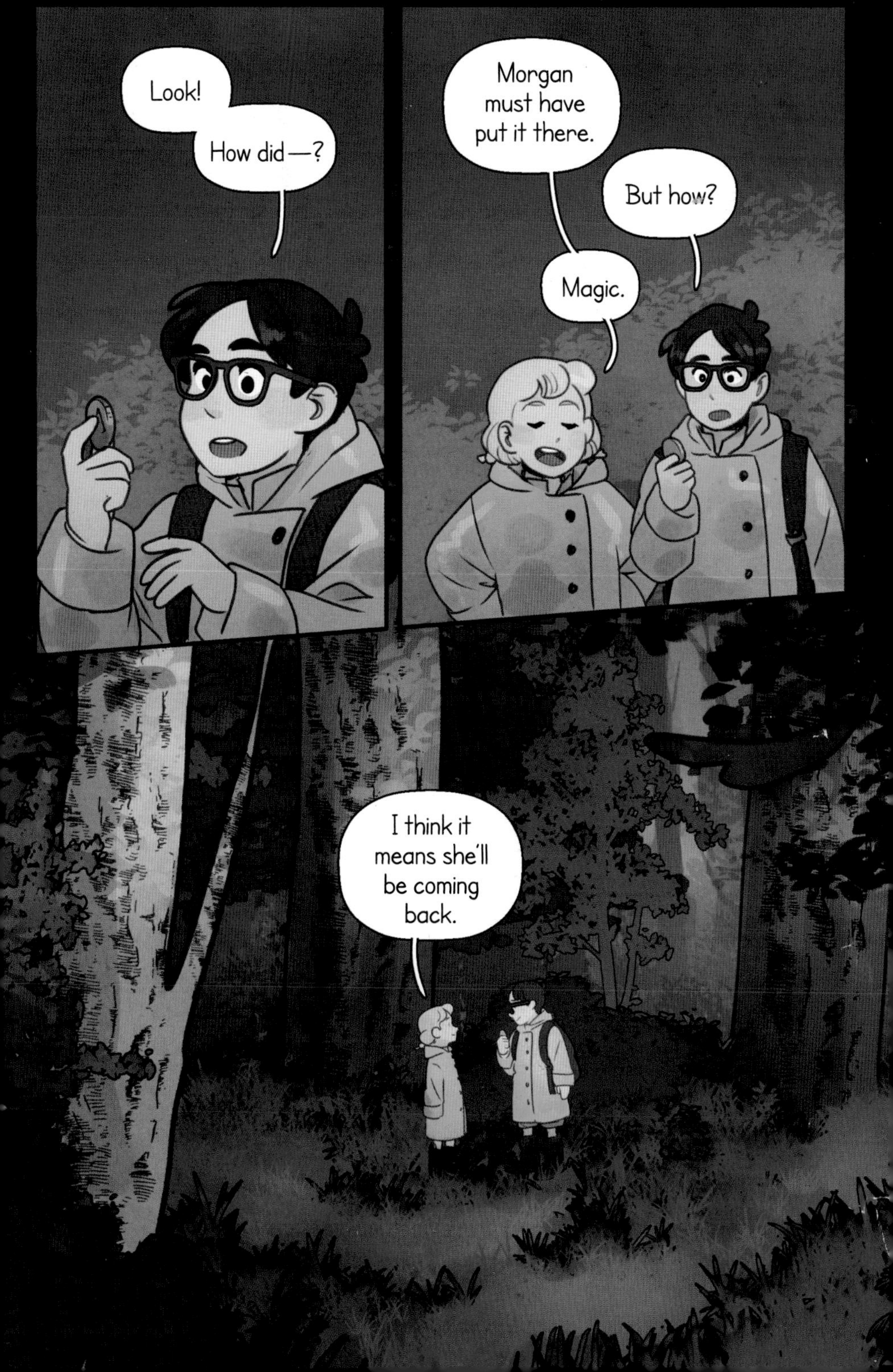
Look!
How did—?
Morgan must have put it there.
But how?
Magic.
I think it means she'll be coming back.

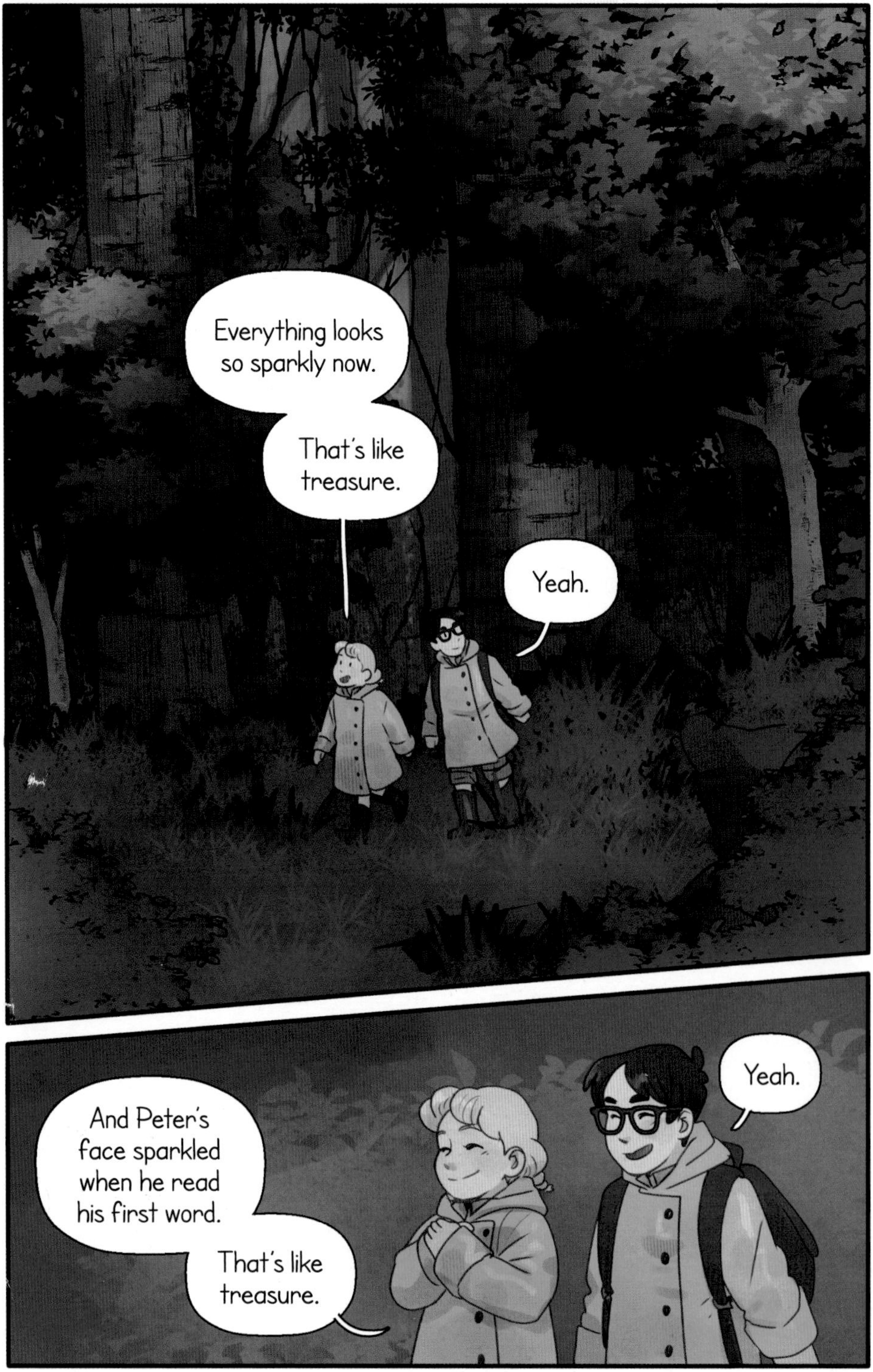
Everything looks so sparkly now.
That's like treasure.
Yeah.
And Peter's face sparkled when he read his first word.
That's like treasure.
Yeah.

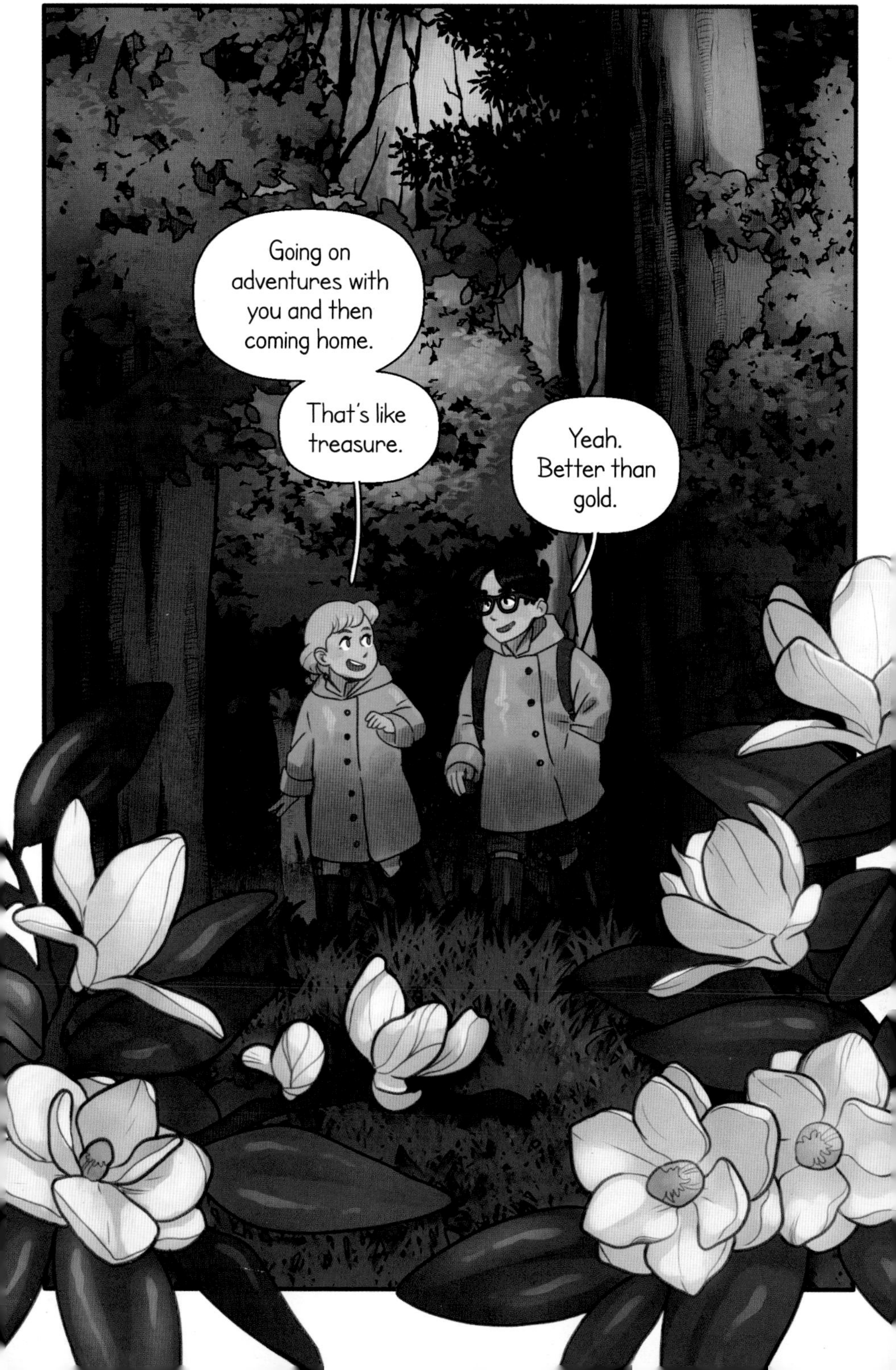
Going on adventures with you and then coming home.
That's like treasure.
Yeah. Better than gold.

Don't miss another adventure in the Magic Tree House where Jack and Annie get whisked away to ancient Egypt!

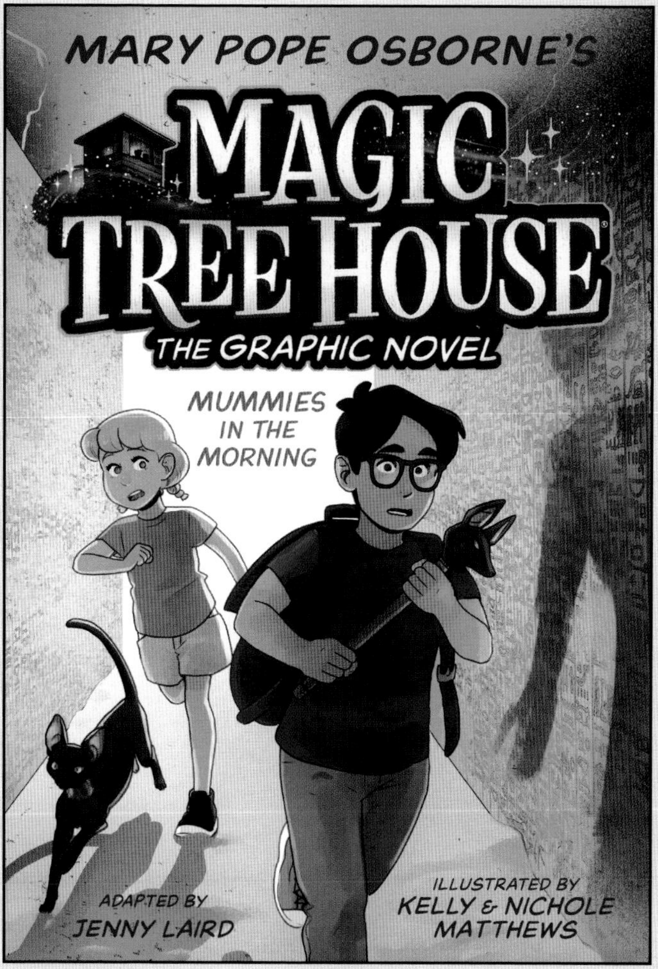
MARY POPE OSBORNE'S
MAGIC TREE HOUSE
THE GRAPHIC NOVEL
MUMMIES IN THE MORNING
ADAPTED BY JENNY LAIRD
ILLUSTRATED BY KELLY & NICHOLE MATTHEWS

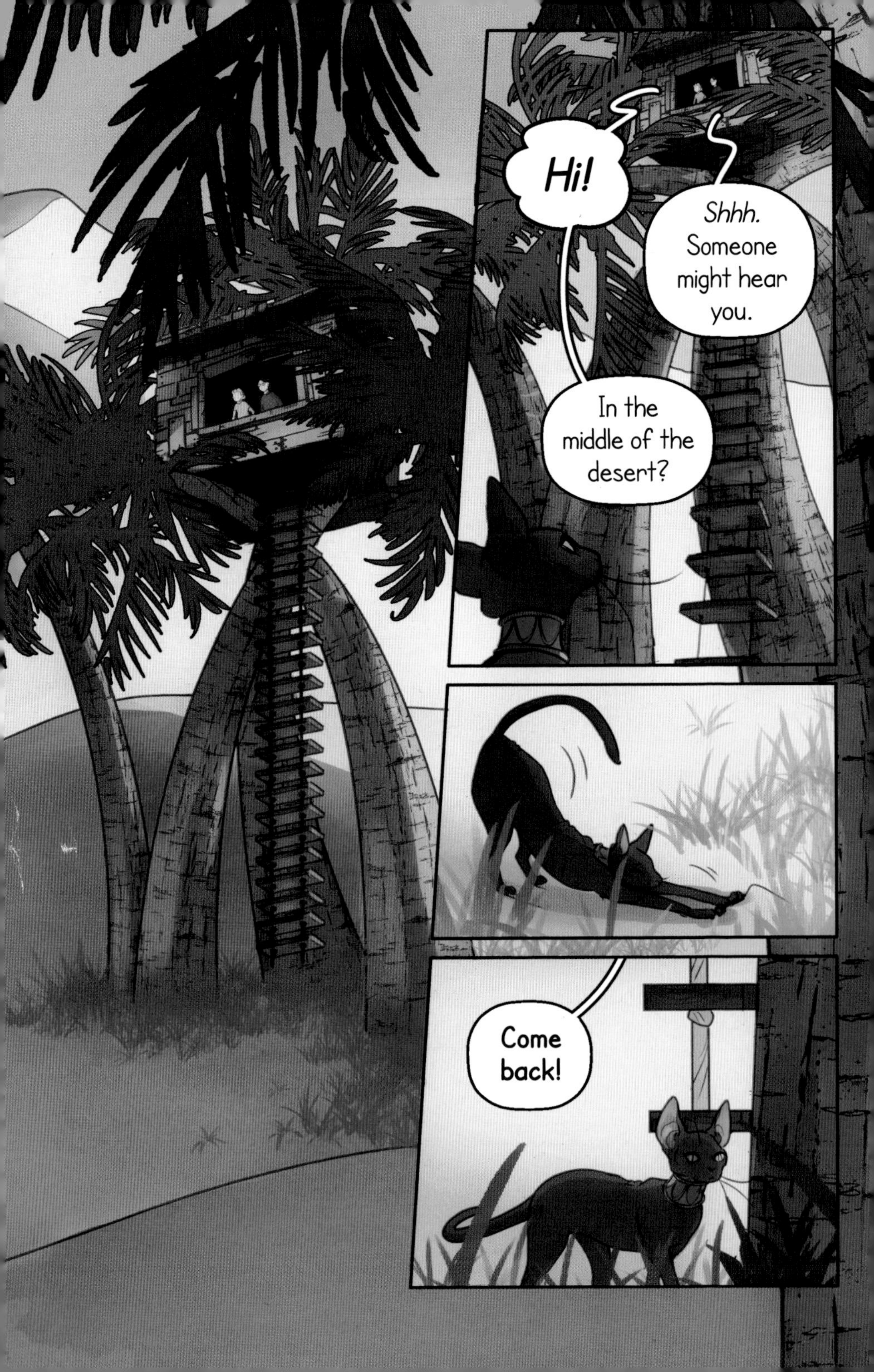
Hi!
Shhh. Someone might hear you.
In the middle of the desert?
Come back!

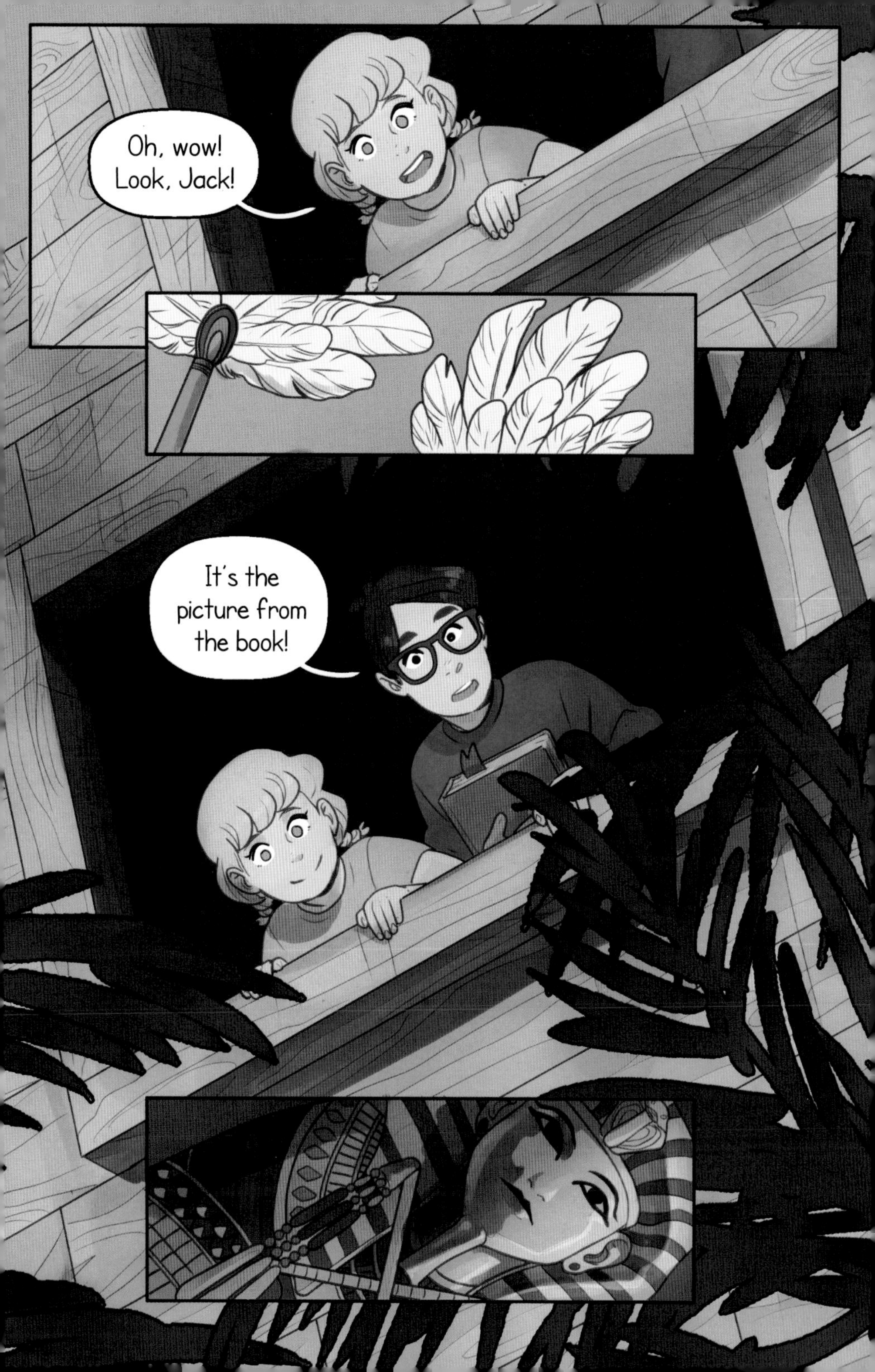
Oh, wow! Look, Jack!
It's the picture from the book!

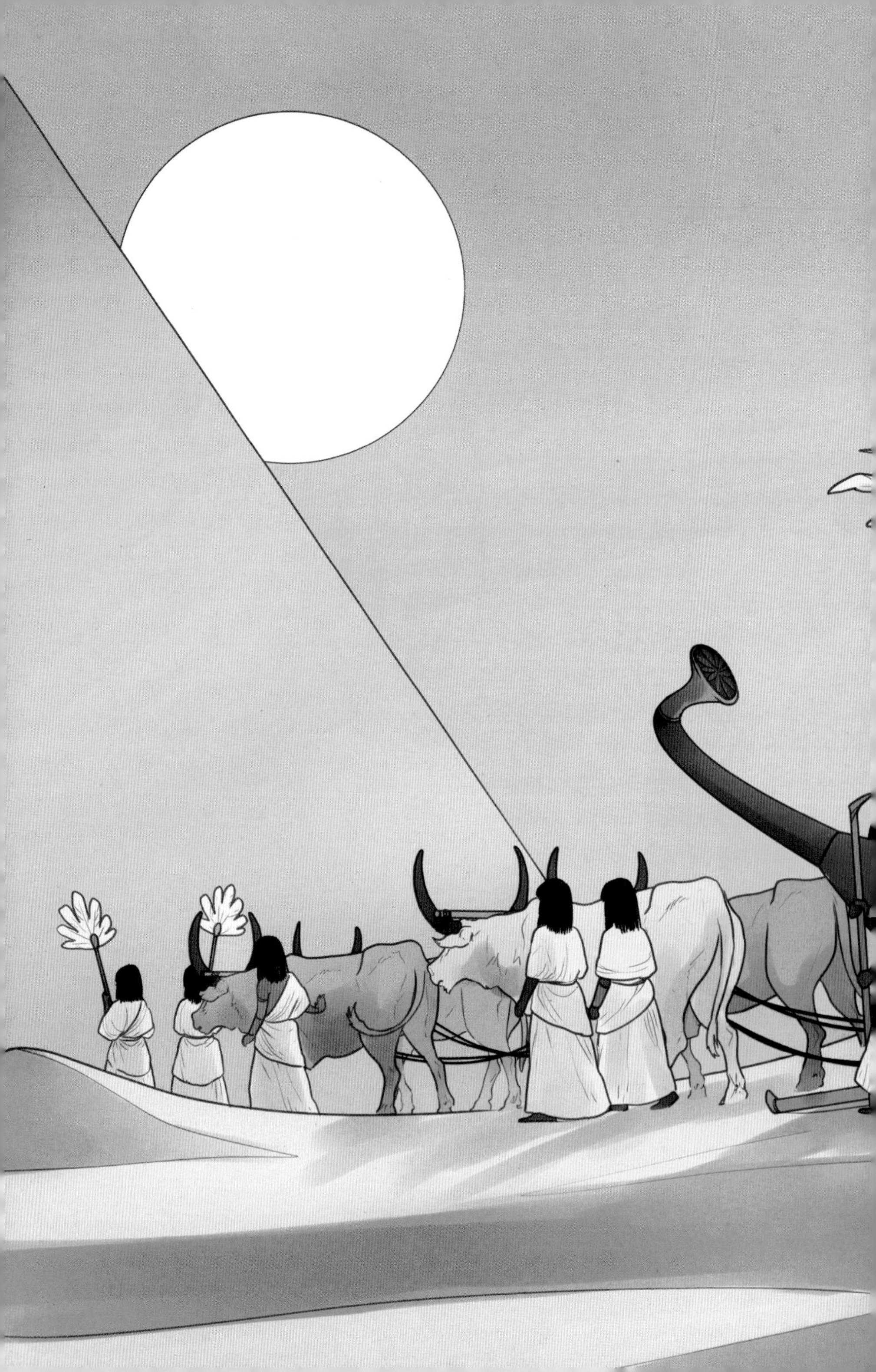

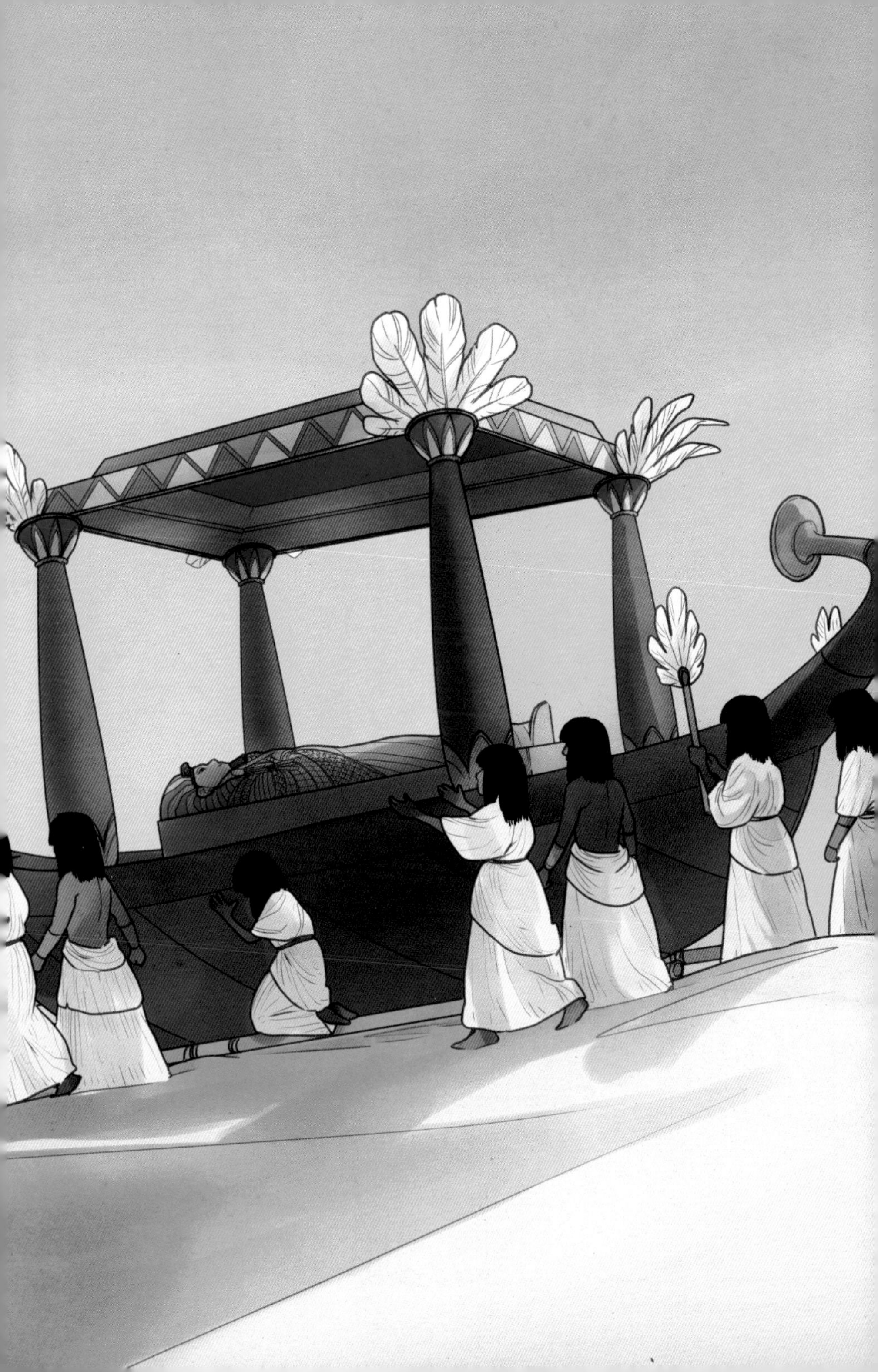

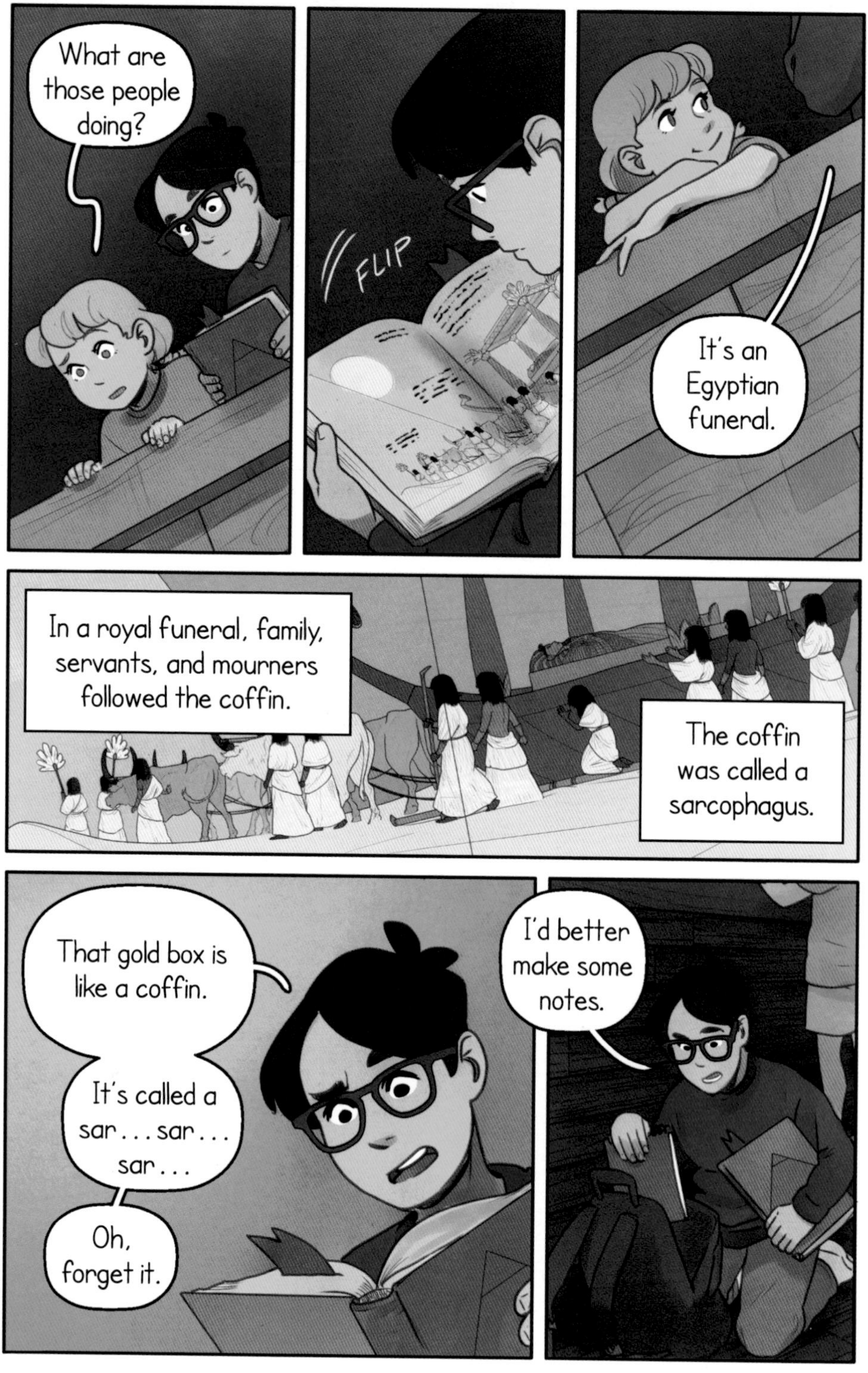

What are those people doing?
FLIP
It's an Egyptian funeral.
In a royal funeral, family, servants, and mourners followed the coffin.
The coffin was called a sarcophagus.
That gold box is like a coffin.
It's called a sar . . . sar . . . sar . . .
Oh, forget it.
I'd better make some notes.

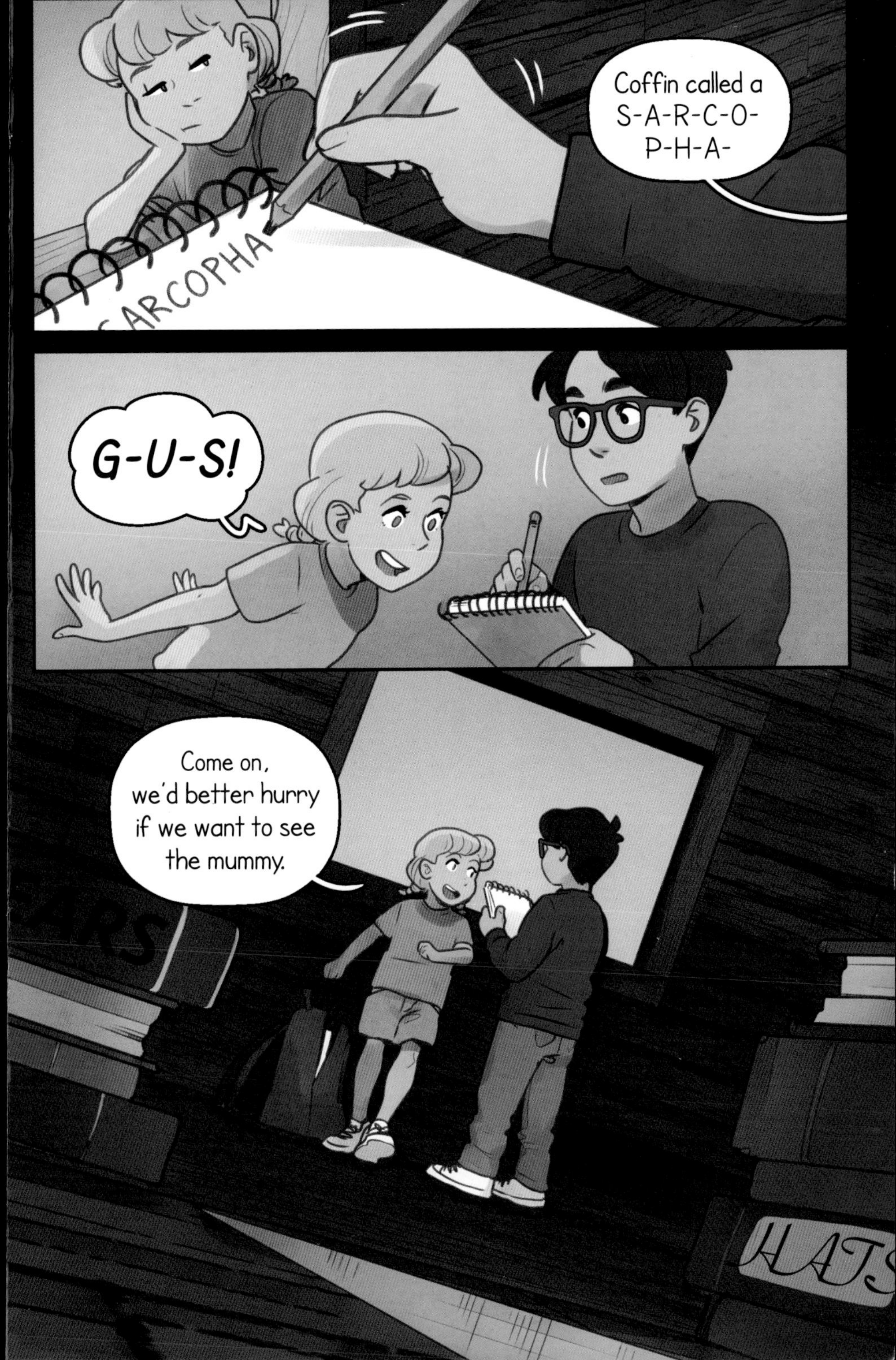
Coffin called a S-A-R-C-O-P-H-A-
G-U-S!
Come on, we'd better hurry if we want to see the mummy.

LET THE MAGIC TREE HOUSE® WHISK YOU AWAY!

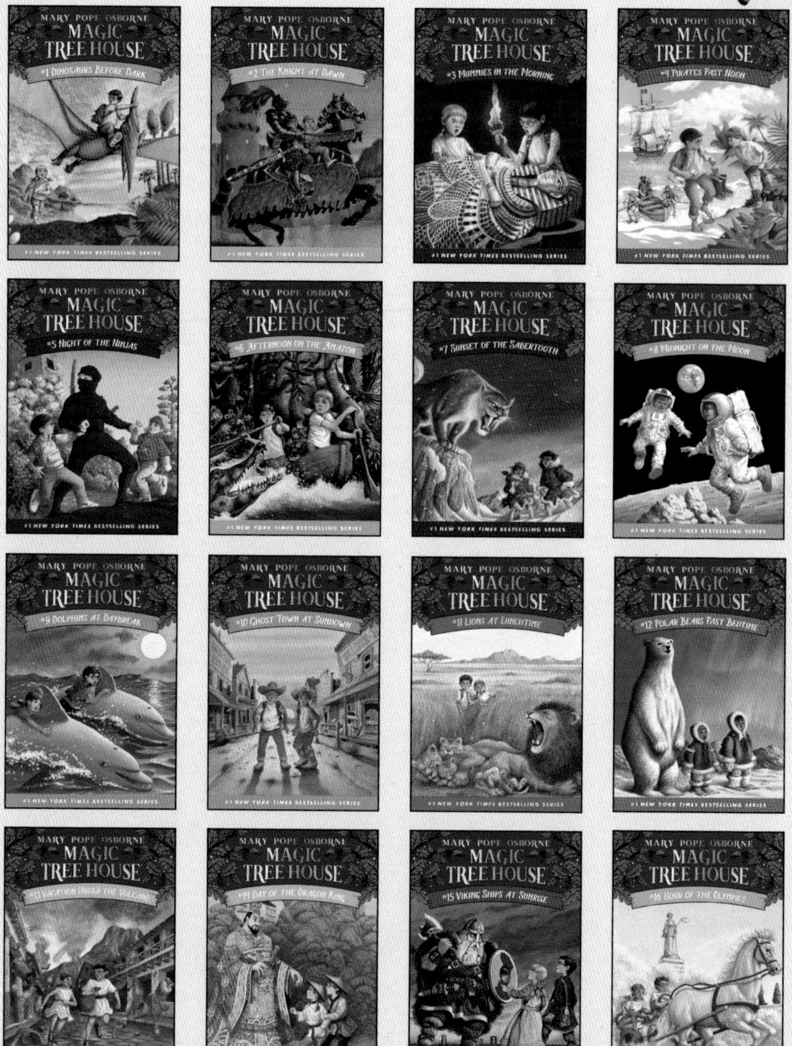
MARY POPE OSBORNE
MAGIC TREE HOUSE
#1 DINOSAURS BEFORE DARK
#1 NEW YORK TIMES BESTSELLING SERIES
MARY POPE OSBORNE
MAGIC TREE HOUSE
#2 THE KNIGHT AT DAWN
#1 NEW YORK TIMES BESTSELLING SERIES
MARY POPE OSBORNE
MAGIC TREE HOUSE
#3 MUMMIES IN THE MORNING
#1 NEW YORK TIMES BESTSELLING SERIES
MARY POPE OSBORNE
MAGIC TREE HOUSE
#4 PIRATES PAST NOON
#1 NEW YORK TIMES BESTSELLING SERIES
MARY POPE OSBORNE
MAGIC TREE HOUSE
#5 NIGHT OF THE NINJAS
#1 NEW YORK TIMES BESTSELLING SERIES
MARY POPE OSBORNE
MAGIC TREE HOUSE
#6 AFTERNOON ON THE AMAZON
#1 NEW YORK TIMES BESTSELLING SERIES
MARY POPE OSBORNE
MAGIC TREE HOUSE
#7 SUNSET OF THE SABERTOOTH
#1 NEW YORK TIMES BESTSELLING SERIES
MARY POPE OSBORNE
MAGIC TREE HOUSE
#8 MIDNIGHT ON THE MOON
#1 NEW YORK TIMES BESTSELLING SERIES
MARY POPE OSBORNE
MAGIC TREE HOUSE
#9 DOLPHINS AT DAYBREAK
#1 NEW YORK TIMES BESTSELLING SERIES
MARY POPE OSBORNE
MAGIC TREE HOUSE
#10 GHOST TOWN AT SUNDOWN
#1 NEW YORK TIMES BESTSELLING SERIES
MARY POPE OSBORNE
MAGIC TREE HOUSE
#11 LIONS AT LUNCHTIME
#1 NEW YORK TIMES BESTSELLING SERIES
MARY POPE OSBORNE
MAGIC TREE HOUSE
#12 POLAR BEARS PAST BEDTIME
#1 NEW YORK TIMES BESTSELLING SERIES
MARY POPE OSBORNE
MAGIC TREE HOUSE
#13 VACATION UNDER THE VOLCANO
#1 NEW YORK TIMES BESTSELLING SERIES
MARY POPE OSBORNE
MAGIC TREE HOUSE
#14 DAY OF THE DRAGON KING
#1 NEW YORK TIMES BESTSELLING SERIES
MARY POPE OSBORNE
MAGIC TREE HOUSE
#15 VIKING SHIPS AT SUNRISE
#1 NEW YORK TIMES BESTSELLING SERIES
MARY POPE OSBORNE
MAGIC TREE HOUSE
#16 HOUR OF THE OLYMPICS
#1 NEW YORK TIMES BESTSELLING SERIES

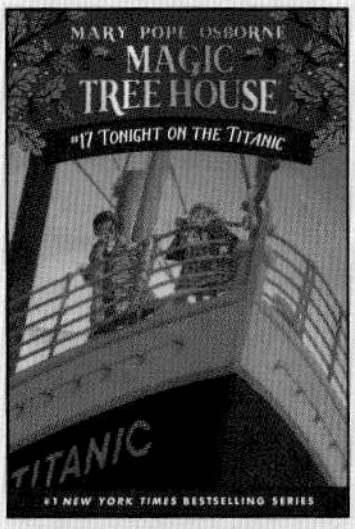
MARY POPE OSBORNE
MAGIC TREE HOUSE
#17 TONIGHT ON THE TITANIC
TITANIC
#1 NEW YORK TIMES BESTSELLING SERIES

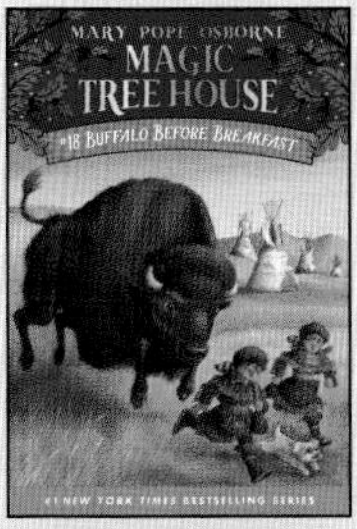
MARY POPE OSBORNE
MAGIC TREE HOUSE
#18 BUFFALO BEFORE BREAKFAST
#1 NEW YORK TIMES BESTSELLING SERIES

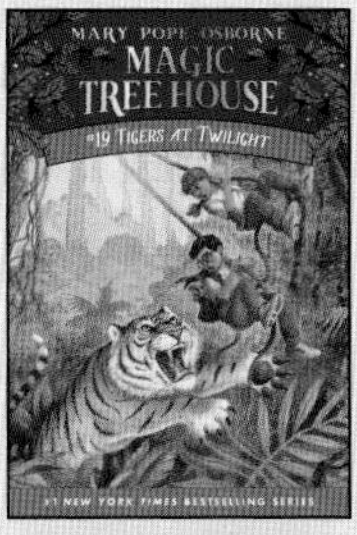
MARY POPE OSBORNE
MAGIC TREE HOUSE
#19 TIGERS AT TWILIGHT
#1 NEW YORK TIMES BESTSELLING SERIES

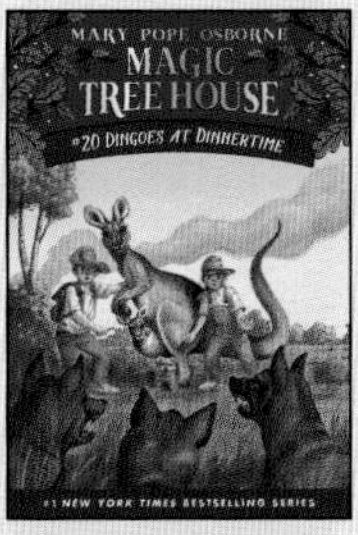
MARY POPE OSBORNE
MAGIC TREE HOUSE
#20 DINGOES AT DINNERTIME
#1 NEW YORK TIMES BESTSELLING SERIES

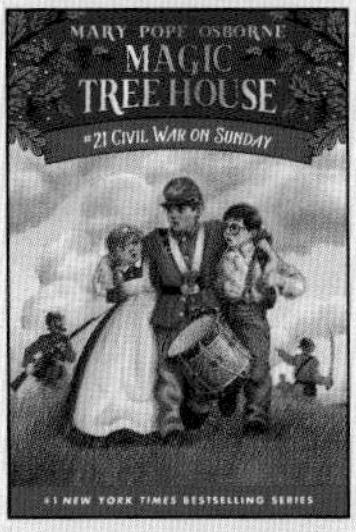
MARY POPE OSBORNE
MAGIC TREE HOUSE
#21 CIVIL WAR ON SUNDAY
#1 NEW YORK TIMES BESTSELLING SERIES

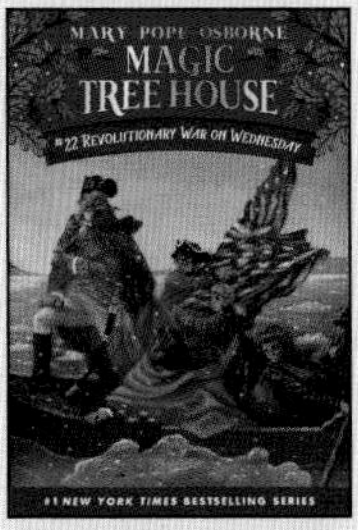
MARY POPE OSBORNE
MAGIC TREE HOUSE
#22 REVOLUTIONARY WAR ON WEDNESDAY
#1 NEW YORK TIMES BESTSELLING SERIES

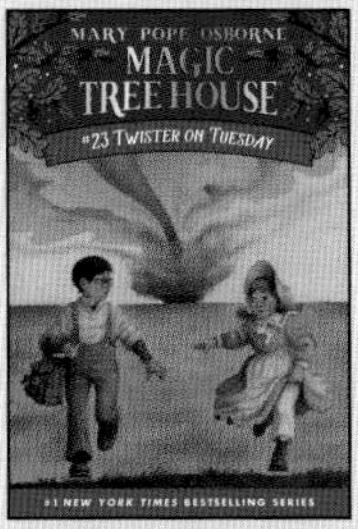
MARY POPE OSBORNE
MAGIC TREE HOUSE
#23 TWISTER ON TUESDAY
#1 NEW YORK TIMES BESTSELLING SERIES

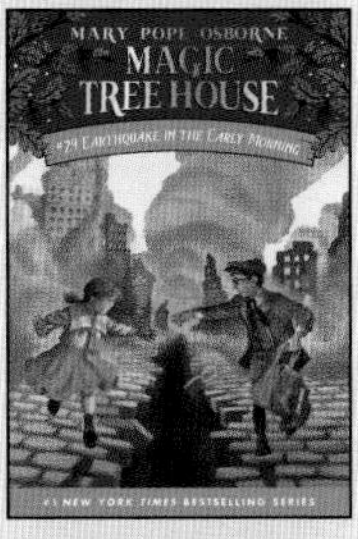
MARY POPE OSBORNE
MAGIC TREE HOUSE
#24 EARTHQUAKE IN THE EARLY MORNING
#1 NEW YORK TIMES BESTSELLING SERIES

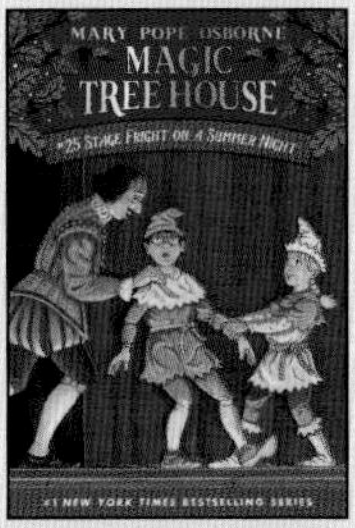
MARY POPE OSBORNE
MAGIC TREE HOUSE
#25 STAGE FRIGHT ON A SUMMER NIGHT
#1 NEW YORK TIMES BESTSELLING SERIES

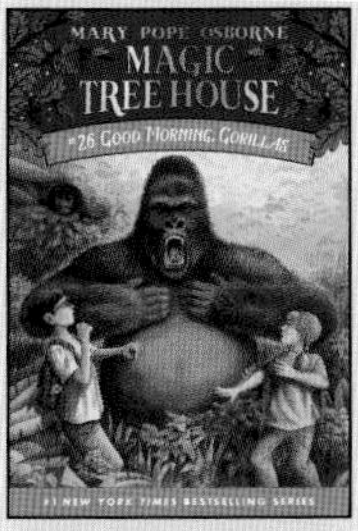
MARY POPE OSBORNE
MAGIC TREE HOUSE
#26 GOOD MORNING, GORILLAS
#1 NEW YORK TIMES BESTSELLING SERIES

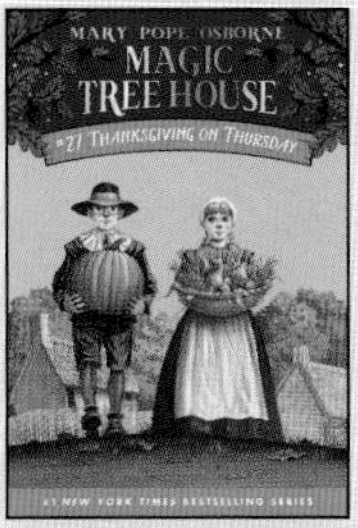
MARY POPE OSBORNE
MAGIC TREE HOUSE
#27 THANKSGIVING ON THURSDAY
#1 NEW YORK TIMES BESTSELLING SERIES

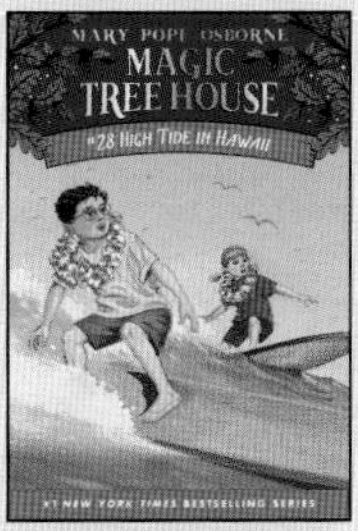
MARY POPE OSBORNE
MAGIC TREE HOUSE
#28 HIGH TIDE IN HAWAII
#1 NEW YORK TIMES BESTSELLING SERIES

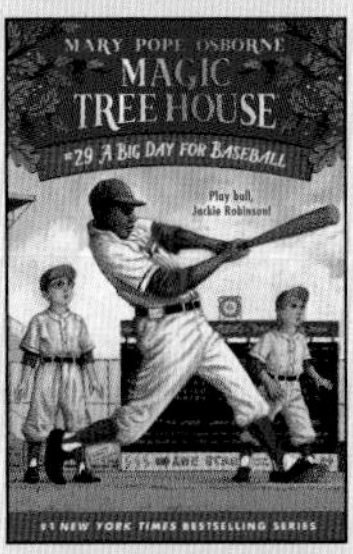
MARY POPE OSBORNE
MAGIC TREE HOUSE
#29 A BIG DAY FOR BASEBALL
Play ball, Jackie Robinson!
#1 NEW YORK TIMES BESTSELLING SERIES

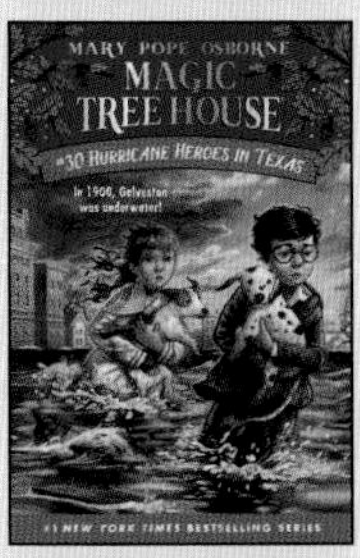
MARY POPE OSBORNE
MAGIC TREE HOUSE
#30 HURRICANE HEROES IN TEXAS
In 1900, Galveston was underwater!
#1 NEW YORK TIMES BESTSELLING SERIES

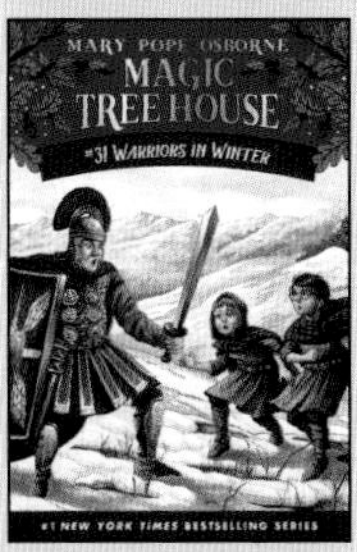
MARY POPE OSBORNE
MAGIC TREE HOUSE
#31 WARRIORS IN WINTER
#1 NEW YORK TIMES BESTSELLING SERIES

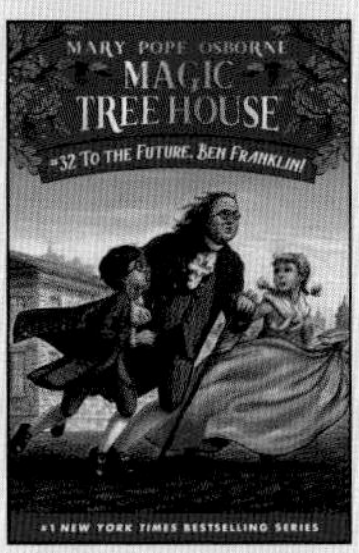
MARY POPE OSBORNE
MAGIC TREE HOUSE
#32 TO THE FUTURE, BEN FRANKLIN!
#1 NEW YORK TIMES BESTSELLING SERIES

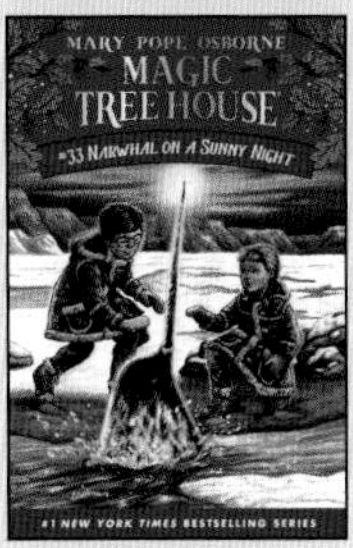
MARY POPE OSBORNE
MAGIC TREE HOUSE
#33 NARWHAL ON A SUNNY NIGHT
#1 NEW YORK TIMES BESTSELLING SERIES

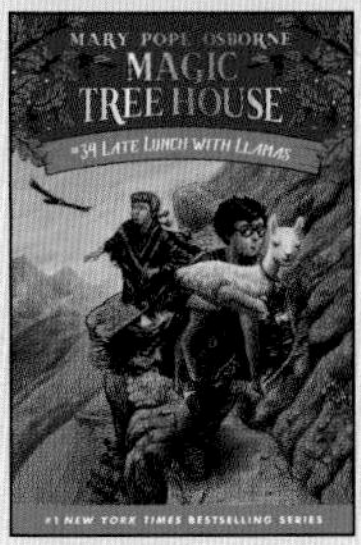
MARY POPE OSBORNE
MAGIC TREE HOUSE
#34 LATE LUNCH WITH LLAMAS
#1 NEW YORK TIMES BESTSELLING SERIES

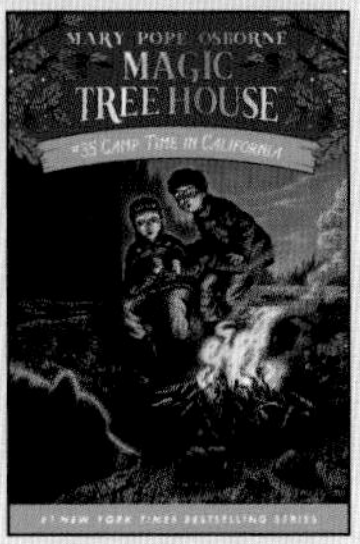
MARY POPE OSBORNE
MAGIC TREE HOUSE
#35 CAMP TIME IN CALIFORNIA
#1 NEW YORK TIMES BESTSELLING SERIES

Read all the novels in the #1 bestselling chapter book series of all time!

TRACK THE FACTS WITH JACK & ANNIE!

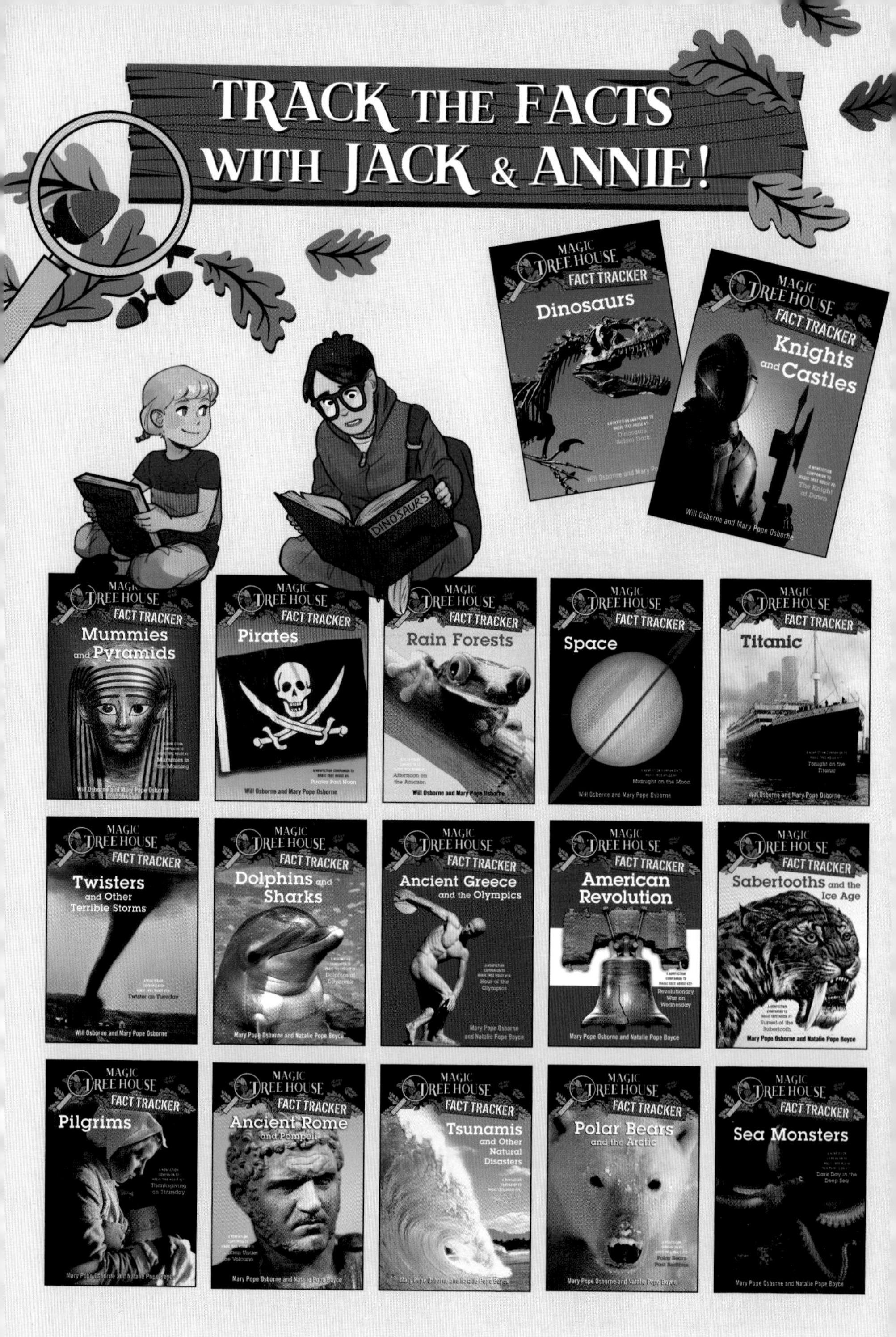
MAGIC TREE HOUSE FACT TRACKER
Dinosaurs
Will Osborne and Mary Pope Osborne
MAGIC TREE HOUSE FACT TRACKER
Knights and Castles
Will Osborne and Mary Pope Osborne
DINOSAURS
MAGIC TREE HOUSE FACT TRACKER
Mummies and Pyramids
Will Osborne and Mary Pope Osborne
MAGIC TREE HOUSE FACT TRACKER
Pirates
Will Osborne and Mary Pope Osborne
MAGIC TREE HOUSE FACT TRACKER
Rain Forests
Will Osborne and Mary Pope Osborne
MAGIC TREE HOUSE FACT TRACKER
Space
Will Osborne and Mary Pope Osborne
MAGIC TREE HOUSE FACT TRACKER
Titanic
Will Osborne and Mary Pope Osborne
MAGIC TREE HOUSE FACT TRACKER
Twisters and Other Terrible Storms
Will Osborne and Mary Pope Osborne
MAGIC TREE HOUSE FACT TRACKER
Dolphins and Sharks
Mary Pope Osborne and Natalie Pope Boyce
MAGIC TREE HOUSE FACT TRACKER
Ancient Greece and the Olympics
Mary Pope Osborne and Natalie Pope Boyce
MAGIC TREE HOUSE FACT TRACKER
American Revolution
Mary Pope Osborne and Natalie Pope Boyce
MAGIC TREE HOUSE FACT TRACKER
Sabertooths and the Ice Age
Mary Pope Osborne and Natalie Pope Boyce
MAGIC TREE HOUSE FACT TRACKER
Pilgrims
Mary Pope Osborne and Natalie Pope Boyce
MAGIC TREE HOUSE FACT TRACKER
Ancient Rome and Pompeii
Mary Pope Osborne and Natalie Pope Boyce
MAGIC TREE HOUSE FACT TRACKER
Tsunamis and Other Natural Disasters
Mary Pope Osborne and Natalie Pope Boyce
MAGIC TREE HOUSE FACT TRACKER
Polar Bears and the Arctic
Mary Pope Osborne and Natalie Pope Boyce
MAGIC TREE HOUSE FACT TRACKER
Sea Monsters
Mary Pope Osborne and Natalie Pope Boyce

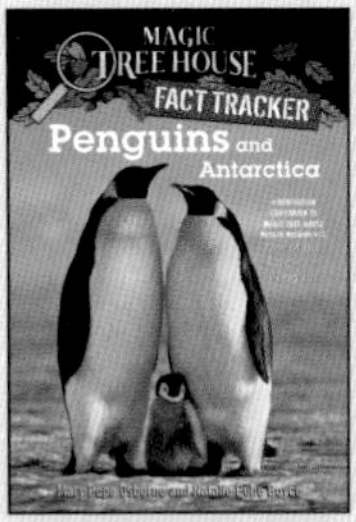
MAGIC TREE HOUSE
FACT TRACKER
Penguins and Antarctica
Mary Pope Osborne and Natalie Pope Boyce
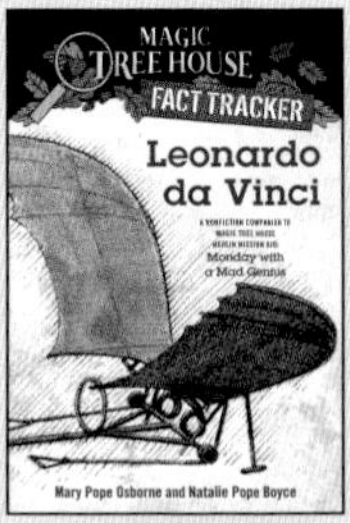
MAGIC TREE HOUSE
FACT TRACKER
Leonardo da Vinci
Monday with a Mad Genius
Mary Pope Osborne and Natalie Pope Boyce
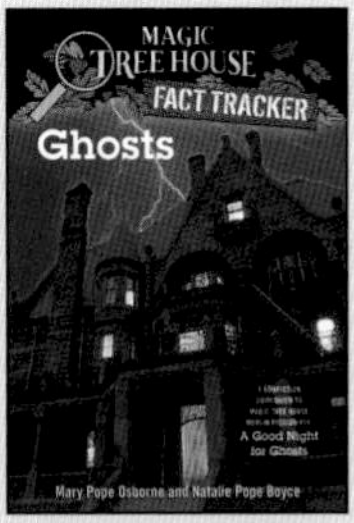
MAGIC TREE HOUSE
FACT TRACKER
Ghosts
A Good Night for Ghosts
Mary Pope Osborne and Natalie Pope Boyce
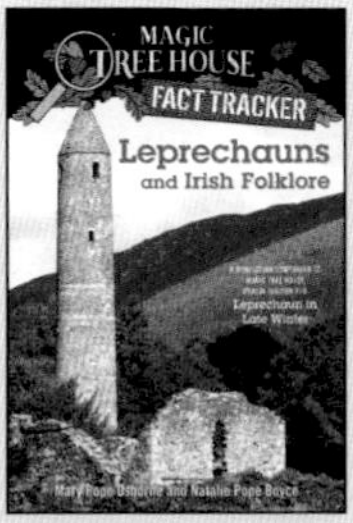
MAGIC TREE HOUSE
FACT TRACKER
Leprechauns and Irish Folklore
Leprechaun in Late Winter
Mary Pope Osborne and Natalie Pope Boyce
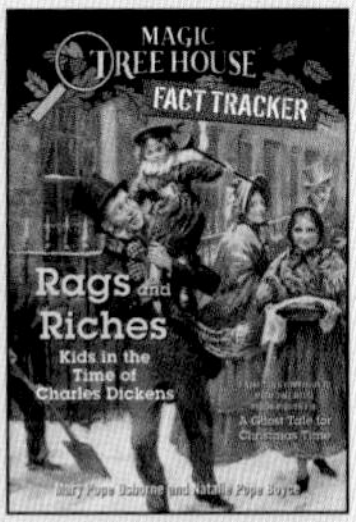
MAGIC TREE HOUSE
FACT TRACKER
Rags and Riches
Kids in the Time of Charles Dickens
A Ghost Tale for Christmas Time
Mary Pope Osborne and Natalie Pope Boyce
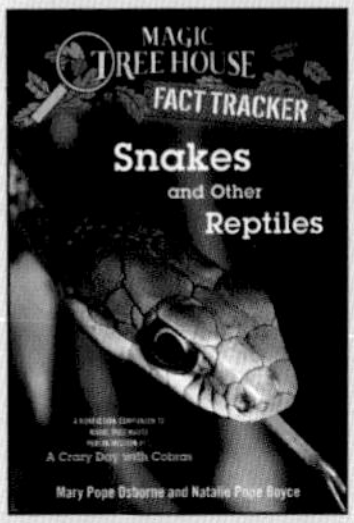
MAGIC TREE HOUSE
FACT TRACKER
Snakes and Other Reptiles
A Crazy Day with Cobras
Mary Pope Osborne and Natalie Pope Boyce
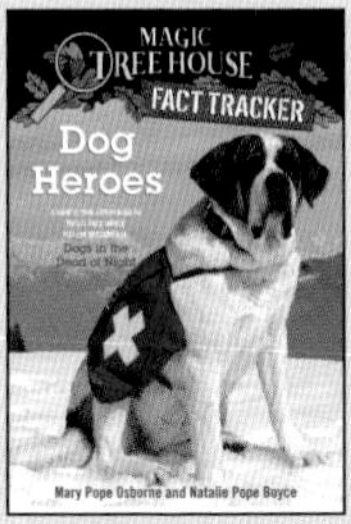
MAGIC TREE HOUSE
FACT TRACKER
Dog Heroes
Dogs in the Dead of Night
Mary Pope Osborne and Natalie Pope Boyce
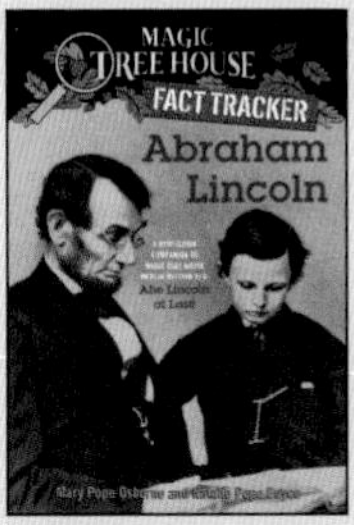
MAGIC TREE HOUSE
FACT TRACKER
Abraham Lincoln
Abe Lincoln at Last!
Mary Pope Osborne and Natalie Pope Boyce
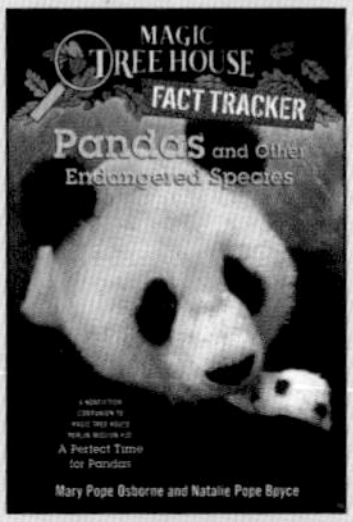
MAGIC TREE HOUSE
FACT TRACKER
Pandas and Other Endangered Species
A Perfect Time for Pandas
Mary Pope Osborne and Natalie Pope Boyce
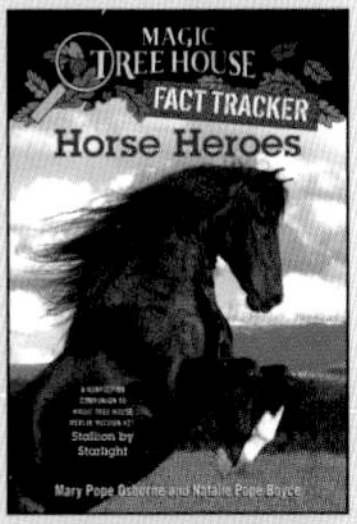
MAGIC TREE HOUSE
FACT TRACKER
Horse Heroes
Stallion by Starlight
Mary Pope Osborne and Natalie Pope Boyce
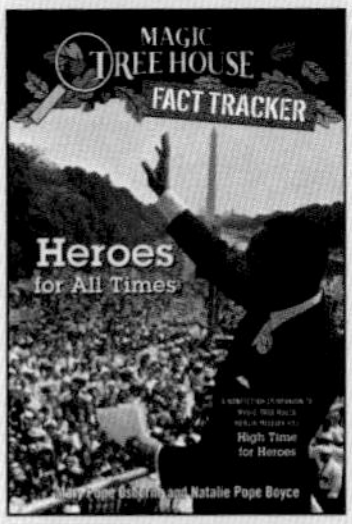
MAGIC TREE HOUSE
FACT TRACKER
Heroes for All Times
High Time for Heroes
Mary Pope Osborne and Natalie Pope Boyce
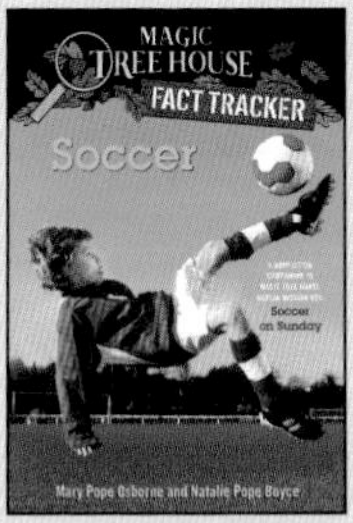
MAGIC TREE HOUSE
FACT TRACKER
Soccer
Soccer on Sunday
Mary Pope Osborne and Natalie Pope Boyce
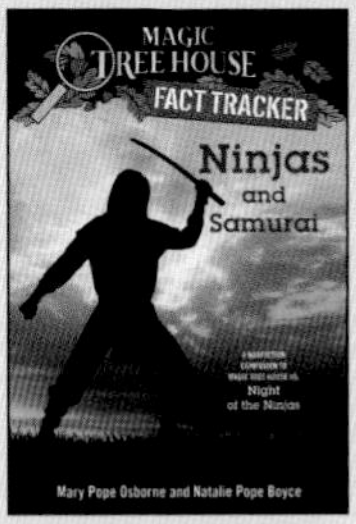
MAGIC TREE HOUSE
FACT TRACKER
Ninjas and Samurai
Night of the Ninjas
Mary Pope Osborne and Natalie Pope Boyce
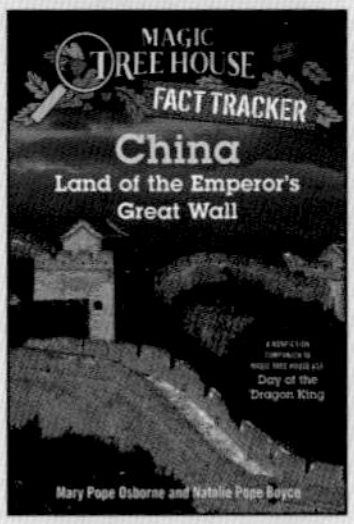
MAGIC TREE HOUSE
FACT TRACKER
China
Land of the Emperor's Great Wall
Day of the Dragon King
Mary Pope Osborne and Natalie Pope Boyce
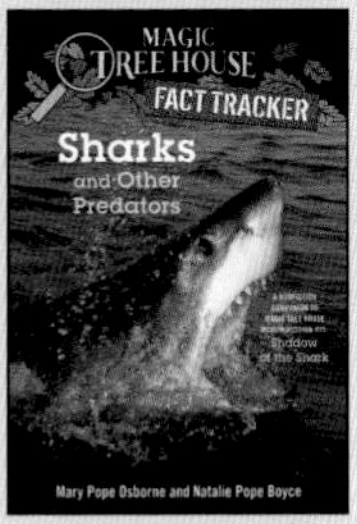
MAGIC TREE HOUSE
FACT TRACKER
Sharks and Other Predators
Shadow of the Shark
Mary Pope Osborne and Natalie Pope Boyce
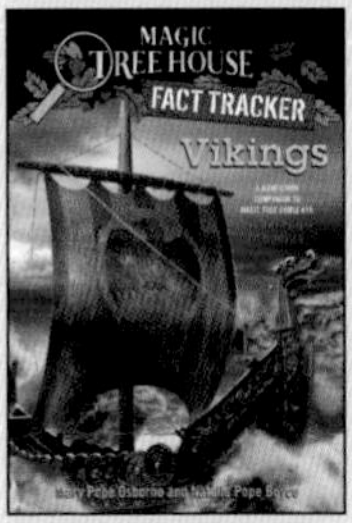
MAGIC TREE HOUSE
FACT TRACKER
Vikings
Mary Pope Osborne and Natalie Pope Boyce
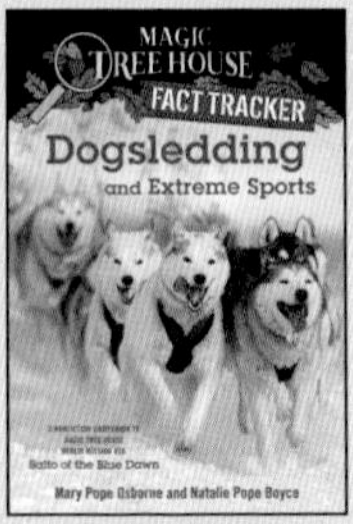
MAGIC TREE HOUSE
FACT TRACKER
Dogsledding and Extreme Sports
Balto of the Blue Dawn
Mary Pope Osborne and Natalie Pope Boyce
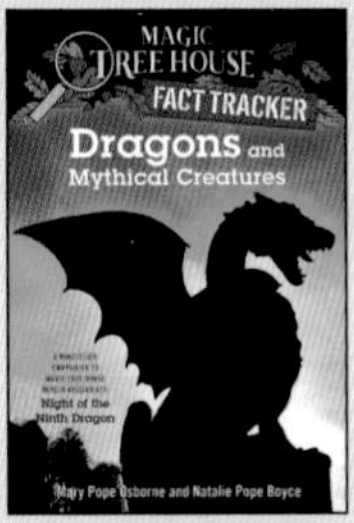
MAGIC TREE HOUSE
FACT TRACKER
Dragons and Mythical Creatures
Night of the Ninth Dragon
Mary Pope Osborne and Natalie Pope Boyce
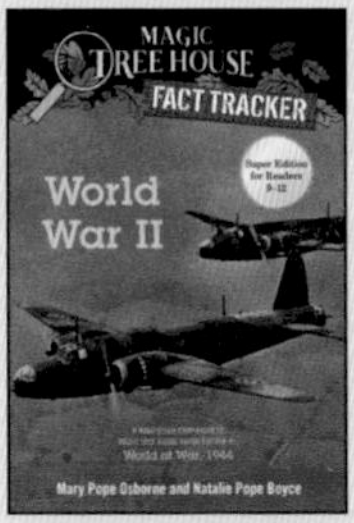
MAGIC TREE HOUSE
FACT TRACKER
World War II
World at War, 1944
Mary Pope Osborne and Natalie Pope Boyce
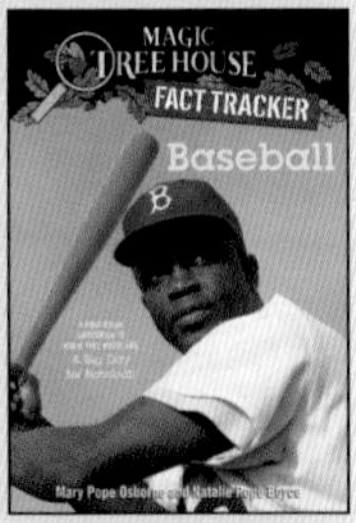
MAGIC TREE HOUSE
FACT TRACKER
Baseball
A Big Day for Baseball
Mary Pope Osborne and Natalie Pope Boyce
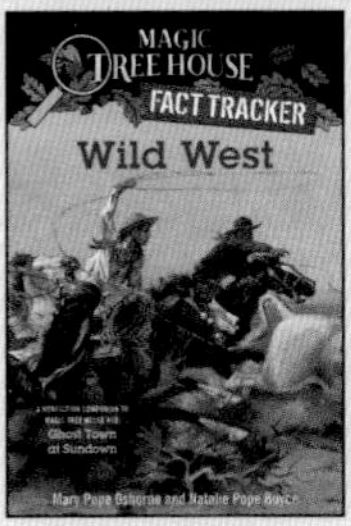
MAGIC TREE HOUSE
FACT TRACKER
Wild West
Ghost Town at Sundown
Mary Pope Osborne and Natalie Pope Boyce
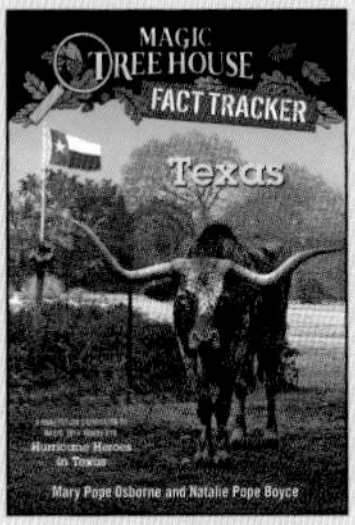
MAGIC TREE HOUSE
FACT TRACKER
Texas
Hurricane Heroes in Texas
Mary Pope Osborne and Natalie Pope Boyce
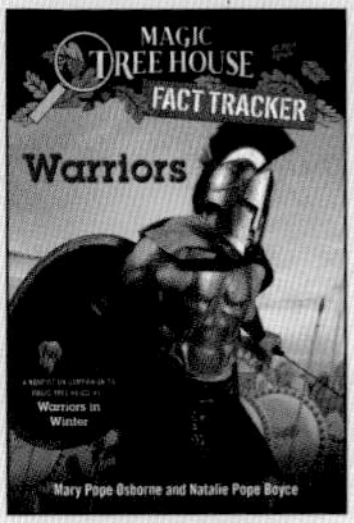
MAGIC TREE HOUSE
FACT TRACKER
Warriors
Warriors in Winter
Mary Pope Osborne and Natalie Pope Boyce
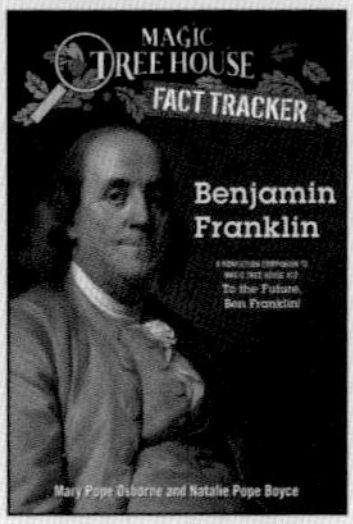
MAGIC TREE HOUSE
FACT TRACKER
Benjamin Franklin
To the Future, Ben Franklin!
Mary Pope Osborne and Natalie Pope Boyce
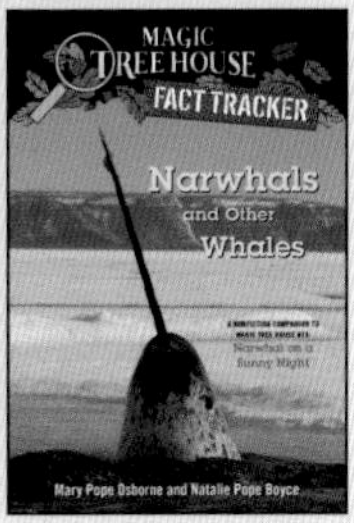
MAGIC TREE HOUSE
FACT TRACKER
Narwhals and Other Whales
Narwhal on a Sunny Night
Mary Pope Osborne and Natalie Pope Boyce

MARY POPE OSBORNE is the author of many novels, picture books, story collections, and nonfiction books. Her #1 *New York Times* bestselling Magic Tree House® series has been translated into numerous languages around the world. Highly recommended by parents and educators everywhere, the series introduces young readers to different cultures and times, as well as to the world's legacy of ancient myth and storytelling.

JENNY LAIRD is an award-winning playwright. She collaborates with Will Osborne and Randy Courts on creating musical theater adaptations of the Magic Tree House® series for both national and international audiences. Their work also includes shows for young performers, available through Music Theatre International's Broadway Junior® Collection. Currently the team is working on a Magic Tree House® animated television series.

KELLY & NICHOLE MATTHEWS are twin sisters and a comic-art team. They get to do their dream job every day, drawing comics for a living. They've worked with Boom Studios!, Archaia, the Jim Henson Company, Hiveworks, and now Random House!